Returning Home

A Novel

by

Mark MacMillin

Narration Publishers
Anaheim

Narration Publishers

2400 East Katella Avenue
Suite 1200
Anaheim, CA
92806
narrationpublishers.com

Narration Publishers Edition, January 2017

ISBN-10:0-692-83353-6
ISBN-13:978-0-692-83353-7

Acknowledgements

I want to thank all the brave people who have allowed me the privilege of joining them on their journey in psychotherapy with me. I have learned much from them about the desire for revenge and forgiveness, as well as the costs and benefits of both.

I also want to thank Dr. David Pickens for his invaluable feedback on earlier versions of this story. His creativity, insight, and tireless willingness to assist me with this novel have been invaluable. His profound understanding of human story continues to impact me greatly. I also treasure his friendship.

I thank Bia for her support and assistance in creating the cover. Her eye for style and design surpasses my own.

Lastly, I appreciate my kids, Justin, Maddie and Lexie, continuing to inspire me to keep writing.

Returning Home

A Novel

One

There lived a boy who had a dream. He lived in more ways than the usual. His dream occupied much of his thoughts, but he didn't share it with others. It was too precious to share, as others may not believe. Many of those about didn't allow themselves to dream, believing dreaming to be dangerous. Belief can give power to dream, while unbelief can sap its precious energy.

The boy often lay awake at night in his bed, pondering what might be. Exciting pictures raced through his mind. Sometimes he even imagined they might come to be. Other times he dared not belief such madness. At times his dreaming seemed real, and he would wake with a start, unsure if he were dreaming now or before. Whenever he dreamt for long, the vision appeared real. Sometimes distracting thoughts interrupted his dreams, telling him they were too fantastic to be true, and that only fools thought such things, and that dreaming only brought disappointment and heartache. At times this seemed to be true.

One day a knock came at his door. He looked through the window as his parents had taught him to do. An old woman stood on the stoop. She appeared kindly, but you can never count on appearances too much. The boy asked from the window, "What do you want?"

"I merely wish to speak to you, young lad."

"What do you wish to speak to me about?" Asked the boy.

"It can only be spoken face to face and eye to eye."

"How can this be true?" Asked the boy.

"For the most important stories must be told face to face, or their meaning diminishes in the telling. I know this must sound strange to you, but you must trust me in this."

The boy said, "I must think on this for a moment. If I'm to trust you, you must be patient with me."

"I will surely wait. I shall be sitting upon the old log in front of your house. I will remain there until the sun sets. If you don't appear to me before the sun leaves me, I will know you have decided to not trust me, and I will leave, never to return."

The boy nodded, and began to pace the floor. Not only was her appearance strange, but there was something in her voice. This something was difficult to put into words. He went to the window, and sure enough, the old woman sat on the log with her back to the boy. Surely this is an unusual woman, and an unusual invitation she offers. How will I know if it's wise to go out and hear her, he wondered silently? And then the answer came to him, "You must ask the teacher."

The teacher is the smartest being in the forest. Everyone knows he is wise and to be trusted. So the boy decided to seek the owl's counsel. The owl lived upon the oldest and largest tree in the wood behind his house. This tree spreads so far that it's difficult to tell where that tree ends and another starts. At times the boy thought that all trees connected to one another. In some lights the trees did appear endlessly interconnected.

The boy hoped the owl would be home, for you never knew when he'd be in. Owls cannot be pinned down to times and places. For everyone knows that such animals move about in unexpected ways. And yet, the boy had learned that the owl usually showed up whenever he needed him.

The boy climbed out the window in his bedroom. He peered around the house to catch a glimpse of the old woman. She sat patiently on the log. The boy ran off to find the owl's tree. He knew the way. He'd been there many times.

The boy ran over the hill, through the creek and into the huge meadow at the far end of the forest. He reached the clearing in the forest and found the huge oak tree that stood in the middle. He did not see the owl. The boy knew you cannot always trust your eyesight, so he called out, "Teacher, are you home. I need your counsel."

The wind rustling through the leaves was the only response. The boy thought of turning back to his home. He shrugged his shoulders and starting walking away, but something caused him to stop. The boy remembered the owl told him that he'd always be there for him when he needed him. The boy turned back and tried again, "Teacher, I need your help. Are you there?"

"Yes, my young lad. I'm here. How can I help?"

"Why didn't you answer the first time that I called?" Asked the boy.

The owl chuckled, "I did answer, but you did not hear."

The boy scratched his head and then asked his question, "An old woman knocked on my door and asked to speak to me. She asked me to trust her and come outside to speak with her face to face. I don't know if I can trust her. Help me to decide if I can."

"You are afraid," said the owl.

"Well, I do wonder if she's dangerous."

"So tell me lad, how will you know if you can trust her?" Asked the Teacher.

"I don't know. That's why I came to ask you. How can I know?"

"Come now lad, we've had this conversation before. You can only know by listening to her smell. And as you know, I don't mean the smell that comes through your nose."

"Yes I remember, you mean by the smell in my heart," said the boy.

"Now that's my lad. So how is the old woman's air?"

The boy crinkled his nose up as he scratched his head. Then he said, "Well that's just the strange thing. She smells fair to my heart, yet she looks strange to my eyes."

"How does she look strange?"

"It's really just one thing. All the women of this land wear hats upon their heads, but the old woman wears none. And there's something different about her," said the boy.

The owl laughed. "I see. It's the strange smell of your eyes that deceives you. You believe that trustworthy women only wear hats and seem common."

"Well, isn't that true?" Asked the boy.

"Of course not, lad. You can't trust your eyes alone any more than you can trust your nose alone. The only trustworthy sense comes through your heart. Trust in this alone."

"So I ought to speak with her?"

"Now set aside the appearance of your senses, lad. What does the smell of your heart tell you?" Asked the Teacher.

"My heart tells me that she smells fair."

"Then you have your answer," said the Teacher.

"Wait, but there's something else. There's something strange about her voice."

"And why does that concern you? Does her voice smell foul?" Asked the owl.

The boy laughed, "No, of course not. There's nothing foul about her voice, it's just that she speaks in a raspy whisper. I've never heard another speak that way."

The owl said, "Is it merely the sound of her voice? As you know, sounds can be as deceiving as sight. Remember to only trust the smell of your heart. There is only one true question: does she smell foul?"

The boy thought for a moment, and then said, "There is no foulness to her smell. I wondered if there was some trickery in her strange voice."

"You place too much importance on both the scent of the eyes and the sight of the ears. Only the smell of the heart matters."

"Yes, you have taught me this before. In fact, you've reminded me of this many times. Thank you for helping to trust my heart, once again."

The owl laughed and said, "We all need reminding now and again. You're quite welcome. Now go, and take the adventure that is sent you."

"What adventure?"

"Now you shall have to show up and see what comes. It wouldn't be much of an adventure if you knew the experience before the experience, now would it?" Asked the owl.

The boy laughed and smiled. He knew he'd received what he'd come for. He waved to the owl and started his trek home. With his hands in his pockets and his eyes on the ground he walked. This way of walking helped him to think, and think well. The boy kept wondering what the old woman wanted. He hoped it was nothing bad or frightening. In spite of his fears, he determined to trust his smell and trust his teacher.

He crested the ridge and looked down on the meadow. He loved this meadow. It had been his home his whole life. Something seemed different about his home. And then it came to him. The chimney smoked. That's strange, there was no fire burning when I left, he thought. After another moment's pondering he said aloud, "Well, there's nothing more to be done than to descend unto my home and see what adventure awaits me. I trust it will be good."

The old woman sat patiently upon the log, just as the boy had left her. The boy approached her cautiously. He paused and listened to the smell of his heart. All seemed well. So he sat down on the log next to her. She slowly turned her head towards him and smiled.

"I see that you've decided to trust me," she said.

"Yes."

"I suspect you're wondering what I have to say to you," said the old woman.

"Yes, of course I'm curious about your message."

"Who said anything about a message?" Said the old woman.

"Oh, well I just assumed you must have some message for me, if you wanted to talk to me."

"I suppose I do have a message, but not the kind that you might expect. My message comes in a story," said the old woman.

"A story? You mean you came all this way just to tell me a story?"

"Just a story? You speak as though stories have little meaning," said the old woman.

"Stories entertain, but for what else are they good?"

"Stories are good for conveying truth, that's all," she said with a smile. "Story are the horses upon which truth rides. What truth comes without its own story? All meaning come from stories, although not all stories have meaning," said the old woman.

"Well, I'm a little confused, but please do tell me your story."

"Ah, so you figure that this is my story. We shall see whose story it is," said the old woman. The boy gave the old woman a curious glance, and then waited.

The old woman began her tale.

Two

Long ago there lived two brothers. Their names were Shane and Tim. Shane was a year older than his brother. They worked the fields of their family farm. Times were difficult, so the brothers worked long days. They arose just as the sun pinked the sky, and except for supper, didn't stop their work until the sun grayed the sky. Their farm was divided into four parcels. The two most fruitful parcels were upon the rich soils on either side of the house. The third parcel lie in the wet lands below the house, and the fourth parcel lie upon the rocky hillside above the house. Today the brothers worked one of the rich parcels along the house.

A wealthy king ruled the land. His name was Lord Teagle. Lord Teagle sent his men to extract taxes from the farmers in amounts beyond their ability to pay. Farmers all over the area struggled to keep up with Teagle's tax demands. The king was ruthless in extracting his sums, having little sympathy for the farmers' pleas that they'd paid all they could. The farmers surely would have revolted, yet Lord Teagle always quickly sent his soldiers whenever any resistance arose.

Tim rested long enough to wipe his brow, when he noticed travelers in the distance. Tim nudged his brother and pointed.

Shane looked up and nodded. A grim look emerged on his face. "Let's listen from behind the barn," said Shane. The brothers waited behind the barn for the travelers to arrive. Father didn't like anyone else in the family being with him when he talked with Teagle's men. The travelers dismounted from their horses. One horse was uniquely black and white, while the other was an unremarkable brown. Father stood on the porch with his sheathed sword at his side. Father rested a hand on the hilt.

"You're a week early," said father.

"There's a storm brewing, so we came before the storm. It would be foolish to travel during a storm," said the taller of the travelers.

"It's foolish to ask for more than we can pay," said father.

The tall traveler laughed and said, "You'll pay whatever Lord Teagle demands."

"I haven't got the money yet," said father.

"Then you best go and find it, Dawkins," said the tall traveler with a grin. He continued, "Now hurry and fetch the taxes, we don't want this to become... unpleasant." The shorter tax collector slipped his hand down on the hilt of his own sword as he moved closer to father.

Father glanced at the short collector. "You can threaten me all you like. There's no tax money to find. You know very well that I won't have it until after market day," said father. As father said this little Amanda came outside to play, holding her doll by one of its legs. When Amanda saw her father she ran up and hugged one of his legs.

Father glanced down at Amanda, and then looked nervously at the front door of the house. Mother filled the doorframe and appeared worried. "Now Amanda, go back inside the house! This is no time to play. Go to your mother!"

"Now there's no need for that, Dawkins. Perhaps your precious little daughter can help us conclude our business," said the tall tax collector.

Father pushed Amanda off his leg, but she was nervous and clung all the tighter to her father. He pushed harder and said, "Go to mother, now!" Amanda began to cry. She wasn't used to father being so rough with her.

"I believe little Amanda has provided us with a solution. I don't think you're properly motivated to find that tax money. So here's what we'll do. We'll hold onto Amanda, so you aren't distracted with your fatherly duties, and then you'll be freed up to find that tax money," said the tall collector.

"No, you can't take her!" Screamed mother. She quickly covered her mouth when she saw the look the tax collector gave her.

As the tall collector said these words the shorter one took Amanda by the arm and pulled her away to the horses. Amanda cried and reached out for father, who tried to regain his grip on her. But the short collector was strong and father didn't want to risk hurting Amanda. The short collector succeeded in putting Amanda in front of him on his horse. The tall tax collector said as he mounted his horse, "We'll be back tomorrow, Dawkins. And if you don't want Amanda to disappear, you'll find that money."

Mother ran out of the door after the horses, crying for them to bring Amanda back. The collectors ignored her impassioned pleas.

"Why didn't you keep Amanda in the house, like I asked you?" Demanded Father. Mother responded only by crying. Father sighed and slowly walked up to his wife and engulfed her in his arms. She sobbed on his shoulder. Father guided her back into the house, offering promises to get Amanda back.

Tim turned towards Shane with wide eyes. "We have to do something," pleaded Tim. Shane nodded solemnly and rubbed his jaw, yet remained silent.

"Well, aren't you going to say something? We have to get Amanda back. We can't let her disappear like the others! You know people keep going missing around here, and are never seen again," said Tim.

"Of course I know, but how do we stop it?" Asked Shane.

"You're the older brother, you figure out a plan."

Shane paced the ground behind the barn. He scratched the back of his head. "I don't know! I'm working on it," said Shane.

"Well, work on it faster!" Pleaded Tim.

"For now, we better follow the tax collectors and see where they take her," said Shane.

"But if we ride after them they'll see us following."

"They won't see us if we're not on the road. Let's go!" Said Shane.

"But how can we follow them if..."

Shane wasn't listening. He'd already taken off at a run for the house. Tim hurried after his brother. Shane stopped at the door to the house and wheeled towards Tim. "Tim, run to the top of the rocky field and see which way they went." Shane ran into the house and found father and mother inside.

"Tim and I are going after them."

Mother cried, "No!"

Father put a hand on his wife's shoulder. "Yes go, but don't be seen. Just find out where they've taken Amanda, and then come back. Don't confront them! You are merely to watch," said Father.

Shane nodded and ran out of the house. By the time Shane crested the rocky ground above their farmhouse he found Tim crouched behind bushes. Shielding their eyes against the sun, the brothers searched for signs of retreating horses. There were two roads leading away from the farm. One ran West to East, and the other curved North towards the city. The brothers peered down the West road, but could not detect any movement. Off along the North road they could see a dust cloud following small, retreating figures.

Without bothering to confer, the brothers set off North. They ran down the hillside and crossed the West-East road, and angled Northwest. Shane led them across uncultivated land. They began to breathe heavily, and had to slow their pace. When they reached the top of Dunhamton Hill they paused to rest. Although they searched the North road, they could find no further signs of the tax collectors. Once feeling restored, the brothers raced down the backside of the hill.

The North road angled Northwest in order to circle around a deep canyon. Due to this curve in the road the brothers cut off many miles of road by heading Northwest from the start. Before nightfall they approached the town of Hanover. All they could see were the lamp lit windows of a cluster of small buildings. The brothers cautiously approached the first building. They peered through a curtained window. Inside they found a woman, a man and three small children sitting down to their supper.

"We'll be at it all night if we search every home in town," said Tim.

"I don't think we'll have to search through the whole town. Look across the street," said Shane. A smile came across Tim's face. Tied to the front of the tavern stood two horses. They were the only horses in front of the tavern, and one of them was a distinctive black and white horse.

Shane grabbed Tim's arm as he began to run across the road. "Wait a minute, we can't just walk into the tavern and look for Amanda," said Shane.

"And why not?"

"Because she'll give us away the moment she sees us," explained Shane. Tim nodded. "We'll have to see if we can find her without her seeing us," continued Shane.

The brothers crossed the road and walked all the way around the tavern. There were no windows on the ground floor. The only windows were on the second floor. They stopped behind the tavern. "Now what do we do?" Asked Tim.

"Let's ask at the back door," said Shane. They waited at the back door until a man opened the door. Shane approached the door and said, "Excuse me sir…"

The man interrupted Shane, "I don't have no extra food for you, boy. We don't give no handouts."

Shane said, "No sir, I'm not asking for charity. Have you seen a young girl come into your tavern?"

"A young girl? And who wants to know?"

Shane glanced at his brother, and then answered, "We're trying to find our sister, sir."

The tavern owner looked from one boy to the next, and then said, "I haven't seen no girl tonight." And then he slammed the door closed.

The brothers slowly retreated to the clump of trees behind the tavern. Shane said, "Do you think he's being straight with us?"

"No, I don't. I didn't trust him for a minute," said Tim.

"I didn't either."

"So now what do we do?" Wondered Tim.

"We figure out another way to see if Amanda's in the tavern."

"Let's just go in there and find Amanda," said Tim.

"No, we must be patient and find a way to see her without being seen," said Shane.

Shane surveyed the grounds, and found what he wanted. He ran over to the huge tree behind the tavern and began to climb. Tim didn't need to be told to follow him up the tree. From the upper branches they could see into the four second story windows. In the first one they saw an older couple. The man shined his boots with polish and an old rag. The woman sat in the rocker mending a garment.

The second window was dark, and didn't appear to be occupied. The third window was open, and a man blew smoke out the window. The brothers recognized the tall collector immediately. They craned their necks left and right, trying to find an unobstructed view of the room. But they couldn't see anyone else. The brothers listened, but the men weren't talking. They slowly climbed down the tree and took up position behind the bushes on the far side of the tree.

"We have to get into that room. I know Amanda's in there," said Tim.

"Now hold on, little brother. Let's not be hasty. I need to think of a plan," said Shane.

"What kind of plan do we need? Let's just go in there, knocks some heads and get our sister back," said Tim.

"Don't you remember what father said? He said to follow them and see where they take Amanda, but to not engage."

"I know, but we can't just let them keep her tied up in there," said Tim.

"I don't like it either, but they're grown men that are armed," said Shane.

"We're as strong as they are," said Tim rising to his full height.

"Even if we are as strong, they're armed with swords, and we don't have any weapons," said Shane.

"I'm so angry, I don't need any weapons."

"That's exactly the attitude that worries me. You're just as likely to get hurt, or get Amanda hurt rushing in half cocked," said Shane.

"You worry too much, big brother. We'll catch 'em by surprise before they even know what hit 'em."

"No, we leave 'em be. We watch and see where they take Amanda, and then report back to father."

Tim started to retort, but then changed his mind and nodded. "Well, I figure we'll need a place to bed down for the night then."

"We'll find where the horses are being stabled for the night and bed down there. That way they can't leave without us knowing about it," said Shane.

It wasn't difficult to find the collectors' horses. The tavern used the stable across the road. The brothers found a comfortable spot in the hayloft above, and settled in for the night. Then Shane got up and tested the stable door, and as he hoped, it squeaked loudly when opened. Satisfied with their reconnaissance, the brothers turned in for the night. After the long run they'd endured that day, both brothers fell asleep quickly. The relatively clean hay made a comfortable bed. Tim noticed his stomach growling in hunger, but there was nothing to be done about it. He would find something to eat tomorrow.

Shane woke with a bright light in his eyes. He blinked several times and put his hand in front of his face. A moment later he realized that the light was the morning sun. He'd slept so heavy, that he hadn't stirred all night. He sat up and said, "Hey Tim, you awake?" When Shane received no answer he looked to his right to find Tim's bed unoccupied. Frightening thoughts flashed through his mind, and he raced down the stairs of the hayloft.

Shane found both of the horses still in their stalls, and felt relief well up in him. Shane walked across the street as quickly as he dared, not wanting to draw any attention to himself. He crouched behind the same bushes in back of the tavern. There was no sign of Tim. He pondered his options, not being sure what to do.

Loud shouts emerged from the far upstairs bedroom. Then Shane heard a crashing sound, just before the window was thrown open. As he looked up at the window, out came a careening Tim. Fortunately Tim landed in a pile of garbage, softening his fall. The tall collector stuck his head out the window and said, "And don't even think about following us, boy! Not if you want your dear sister back in one piece." And then the window slammed shut.

Shane scampered over to Tim. "Hey little brother, you okay?"

"Yeah, I'm alright," said Tim. Tim sported a black eye, and a thin line of blood trailed down from the corner of his mouth. Shane pulled him out of the garbage and into the safety of the bushes.

"What is God's name happened?" Shane demanded.

Tim rubbed his sore eye and explained, "I didn't want them to leave before we woke. So I got up early, before the sun rose. And I waited behind these bushes until the tavern owner unlatched the door. Then I went upstairs to get Amanda from those animals...except the last part didn't go so well."

18

"That was damn foolish of you to try!" Said Shane.

"They were already up when I broke into the room...the two of 'em manhandled me pretty good and...well, you saw the last part."

"Damn Tim, you could have ended up hurt bad, or worse. Not to mention the fact that you took a chance with Amanda's life! Did you think of that? They warned us about hurting Amanda."

"Yeah, I know, but I can't just stand by with my finger in my ear and watch those animals keep hold of Amanda!"

"I know Tim, but..."

Tim interrupted his brother, "But I heard them talking before I burst into the room. The tall one's going back to get the money from father, while the fat one stays with Amanda. With only one of 'em guarding her, we can overpower him and get Amanda back!"

Shane stood and paced back and forth, and then said, "Maybe, but they'll be watching for us after the stunt you just pulled."

"So what? With the two of us we can take him, even if he is armed," said Tim.

"But what if he...wait a minute, there goes the tall one to the stables," said Shane.

The brothers watched as the tall collector emerged from the stables leading his horse. He tightened the saddle strap, mounted and rode off back South. "See what I told you? He's going back to get the tax money from father."

"Yes, probably so."

"I'm going to get Amanda before..."

Shane cut Tim off, "No damn it! Stay here so we can figure out a plan. No more going off without thinking. Look what good that did not thirty minutes ago."

"But that was because there was two of 'em, and now there's only one," said Tim.

"No, you run back to father and tell him that we know where Amanda is, and that she's safe. And I'll stay here and keep an eye on her."

"No, I want to stay here and watch Amanda, and look for a chance to get her back," said Tim.

"Damn it Tim, I'll stay. I can't trust you to just keep her in sight."

"I won't do nothing this time, unless I get a real good chance..."

"No Tim! Do as I say, and get back to father before the tax man does. Hurry and tell father what we know. You have to get to father first," said Shane.

"Wait a minute, you run faster than I do. You run back! You have a better chance of racing back before the collector gets there."

Shane started to protest, but stopped. He realized that Tim had a good point. Tim was bigger and stronger, but Shane was slimmer, faster and had better wind. Shane knew he'd get back home faster than Tim. "Okay Tim, I'll run back home. But you have to promise me that you won't do anything stupid...again."

"Okay, I promise," said Tim with an eager nod.

"Now I'm serious!"

"I know!" Said Tim.

With that Shane took off at a dead run back towards home. The collector had a head start on him, and Shane knew he'd have to push himself in order to beat the collector to their farm. Shane wanted father to know that Amanda was safe, so he wouldn't do anything foolish. He figured he'd run as hard as he could muster until he came to the well at Simonton's farm. He'd take in as much water as he dared, before making the final run for the farm.

Tim glanced up at the second story window, but could see no activity. He reevaluated his position, and noted that he could see both the back door as well as the stables where the other horse was kept. A number of thoughts raced through his head. Should I rush the room again? I did promise Shane I wouldn't do anything like that. But if I catch that fat collector by surprise, I know I can overpower him. Maybe if I find a good sized rock that I can whop him upside the head with, and send him to dreamland. But how would I explain it to Shane and father if something went wrong.

The front door banged open and the fat collector crossed the road, pulling Amanda by the hair. It angered Tim to see his sister treated this way, and he almost broke cover that moment, but fortunately he controlled himself, remembering his promise to his brother. The collector certainly would have heard him coming and been prepared in time. Tim stayed put. Moments later the collector emerged from the stables with Amanda crying in the saddle. He mounted the horse and headed up the road North.

Tim waited until they were just out of sight and then followed. He stayed in the brush off the road, not wanting the collector to look behind him and see that he had a tail. The low brush scratched Tim's ankles and arms as he went, but Tim didn't care. He had more important things on his mind.

As the day wore on Tim's energy flagged. He had to intermittently run and walk to keep up with the horse that carried his sister. Late in the day the collector turned his horse off the main North road to the West. Tim wondered where this led. He'd never been up that road. It wound sharply to the left. Tim hurried to keep up with the collector. Every time the collector and Amanda rounded a bend in the road, Tim lost sight of them.

Tim came around yet another curve in the road. When Tim came to the next straightaway, he didn't see them. He wondered if he'd slowed down too much and had fallen behind. Tim ran faster all the way beyond the next bend in the road. Still he caught no sight of them. Did I miss a turn off the road? Where did they go? He thought. Tim bent down and studied the tracks. The ground was so firm that it yielded no discernible tracks. He hurried ahead and found softer dirt. When he bent down he found what he wanted. Fresh tracks. Tim continued ahead more slowly now, being confident that he followed the right tracks. Suddenly they disappeared. Tim ran up the trail, but found nothing that resembled the collector's horse tracks. Tim came back to where the tracks ended. He bent down lower. The ground to the right was grass. Some of it had been trampled down. The trample marks led into dense woods. Tim took his time and followed the faint tracks.

Several miles later Tim crested a low hill and spied a ranch below him. He took cover behind a stand of trees and surveyed the ranch. The road dead-ended at a large house with a wraparound porch. To the left stood a well, with a long barn-like building behind it. The door to the barn was closed and it had only one window high in the loft. Off to the right were stables. The collector dismounted and helped Amanda down. He took care that she didn't fall to the ground. The collector handed the reins to a boy about Tim's age, and then turned and led Amanda to the house.

Tim remained in his hidden position until after dark. Then he descended the hill and circled around to the back of the ranch. From behind a couple of empty barrels Tim surveyed the house. The window on the right side was lit and he heard muffled voices. The windows on the left side were dark.

Tim decided to risk a closer look. He ran to the house and flattened himself against it. He waited and listened for sounds. Men's voices carried through the window, but Tim couldn't discern any words. He slid along the back of the house until he stood next to the window. Tim slowly inched his head to the lower left corner of the glass. He raised his head and peered inside.

To the right smoldered a fire with a pot suspended above it. A man stood at the pot with his back to Tim. He ladled food into his bowl. In the middle of the room sat five men at the table. One of them was the fat collector. They talked in low voices as they shoveled food into their mouths. Right in front of Tim was the kitchen. Tim realized he looked at the men from the window behind the kitchen basin. Dirty dishes filled the basin. There was no sign of Amanda.

Fearing discovery, Tim retreated to the safety of the barrels behind the house. What do I do now? And where do they have Amanda? There doesn't seem to be much else I can do tonight. So maybe I'll just find a place to hunker down for the night, he thought.

Tim retraced his steps back to the stand of trees on the hill in front of the house. Fortunately he'd found some old discarded bread along the way, which he ate for a less than satisfying meal. Shane had given him the water skins that he'd brought, so Tim had enough water for now. After the weariness of the day, Tim fell asleep before he knew it.

Tim felt a dull ache in his side. He wondered if he was dreaming. Then he heard a rough voice call out to him impatiently. He opened his eyes to see two men standing over him. It was dark, but Tim could see them dimly. One held an arrow on his string, pointed at Tim. He didn't recognize this man, but he knew the other one immediately. The fat collector kicked him again and said, "Well well, look what we have here. This young lad must have gotten lost on his way home, though we clearly told him to not follow us. Well now, if you're so eager to find your sister, I think we can accommodate him. What do you think, Smitty?" Smitty grinned and laughed and said, "I think we can help 'em out, Fats."

"On your feet, lad. And it's much too late to go home now. So if you try running, you'll find your back fitted with an arrow roughly in the middle."

Tim slowly got to his feet. Fats pushed him towards the house. Tim turned and gave Fats a nasty look, and then shuffled down to the house.

When Tim reached the base of the hill he headed towards the front door of the house. Fats laughed and said, "Now rat, you won't be going in there now. We've a better place in mind for you." Smitty laughed. "This will be your home," said Fats as he pointed with his long knife. Tim searched Fats' face, and saw that he was enjoying this. Tim shrugged and entered the barn.

The door slammed shut behind him. Tim heard a latch fall into place. He checked the door, and found it locked. Darkness filled the room. Tim waited for his eyes to adjust. A long corridor ran between rows of bunk beds. They seemed to go on forever, as Tim couldn't see the far wall. He shuffled to the first bunk bed and paused. A voice said, "This one's taken. Piss off!" Tim nodded and began his slow march down the row of beds. He stood still until his eyes fully adjusted to the dark. He stopped at each one to check if it was occupied. It was too dark to see anything more than a mound under a blanket.

Tim found an empty bed almost at the end of the line. The upper bunk contained a skinny lump, but the bottom bed remained vacant. He sat down. The wooden frame creaked under his weight. Tim glanced at the occupied bed in front of him, but the occupant didn't move. Now that his eyes had fully adjusted to the dark, he surveyed his new surroundings. A faint silver light lit the corridor. Tim searched for the source, and found a sliver of moon shining through the small window high on the far wall. There appeared to be nothing in the room but beds and their occupants. There didn't seem to be much else to see. Tim pulled off his boots, set them under his bed, and lay down. Under a thin blanket lay a well worn mattress of hay stuffing. The bed was hard, as the hay was thin. Tim pulled the blanket up to his chin and attempted to sleep. There didn't seem any point in holding a night vigil. However, sleep eluded Tim at first. He wondered where he was, and what would happen tomorrow. And why were all these men here? Were they all tax prisoners? Well, he figured he wouldn't know anything until the morning, and even then he may not.

Three

A loud clanging bell filled the morning air. Tim reflexively covered his ears with his hands. Blanket-covered mounds began to stir around the barracks. Mercifully the ringing bell ceased. Tim uncovered his ears and sat up. A rough, bearded man walked through the barracks wearing a long sword at his side. Behind him Fats walked and said, "Alright you rats, time to begin another day in paradise. Get your lazy arses up and get out to the fields." All the occupants sat up and put on their boots. Tim surveyed those nearby. All were men, a few were young boys and fewer were old men. Most wore blank faces, demonstrating little emotion. Whatever happens today, it's not good, thought Tim.

Tim stood and looked up and down the aisle, but could not find Amanda. He realized that she must be kept somewhere else, since there were no girls inside. The occupants began to shuffle out of the barracks. When Tim reached the door Fats grabbed him by the shoulder and pulled him roughly aside. "Well, it's our new worker rat, isn't it now. Where shall we put him, huh? Shall we give him the easy work?" Fats said this as he grinned at the bearded man at his side, who stood with arms folded. The man merely smirked.

Fats said, "I know, we'll put him in the just cleared field with the blue team. Johnson, be so kind as to show our new rat where to show up for duty, will you?"

Johnson nodded and pushed Tim to move. Tim thought about hitting Johnson in the face, but glanced at his sword and changed his mind. Johnson understood and said, "You want to take at shot at me, boy? I'd be eager to accommodate you, if so. Come on, I'll let you have the first blow." Tim glared at Johnson, but remained still. He realized it would be stupid to try anything now.

"I didn't think so. We got ourselves another yellow-bellied coward here. This way, rat," said Johnson as he pointed up the dirt path.

Tim marched up the path indicated. He noticed the other men breaking into groups as they headed out to the fields. Tim noticed women coming out of another door in the same barn that Tim had slept in. A few were children, perhaps as young as ten years of age. A young girl cried as a woman helped her tie the laces of her boots. Similarly, the women settled into groups of six or eight as they moved to their assignments. But still Tim could catch no sight of Amanda.

Above the path ran a low ridge. All along the ridge were men armed with bow and arrows. The archers spaced themselves every fifty yards and watched the worker rats. Tim passed a number of fields in differing stages of cultivation. The first fields Tim passed bore mature plants that seemed to be near ready for picking. The further Tim walked the smaller the plants became.

Then Tim came to a field that had no plants. It was merely dirt, but it had been cleared of rocks and stumps. Tim glanced behind him, and Johnson grunted for Tim to keep on walking. Finally they came upon a field littered with tree stumps and rocks of various sizes. Five men already stood at the edge of the field talking. They were all strong, younger men like Tim. Each of their backs bore a blue circle of paint. Armed guards stood with their hands resting on sword hilts and bows slung over their backs. The guards surrounded the field.

"Blue team rats, I have fresh meat for you," said Johnson as he shoved Tim at them. Tim staggered, but was able to keep himself from falling. The five men regarded Tim sympathetically, and then went back to conferring. Tim stood amongst them and listened to the planning of the work day. While Tim listened he felt a wet pressure on his back. He turned to see a guard standing behind him, holding a paint brush with wet blue paint. He grinned and walked away. Tim took off his shirt to see a large blue circle of paint. One of the other rats said to Tim, "Be careful not to touch that. It's hard to get the paint off your hands with nothing but water." Tim nodded.

The man who warned Tim said, "You'll be working with me and Thaddeus. Follow me."

Tim offered his hand and said, "I'm Tim."

The man looked at Tim's hand, but didn't take it. He said, "I'm Cummings. Grab one of these and let's go." Cummings and Thaddeus picked up an axe, a shovel and a set of leather straps. Tim picked up a shovel and axe and walked behind them. The other three men similarly outfitted themselves with tools, and then headed off in the opposite direction.

Tim and his team reached the far side of the field, and set down their tools. Cummings spit into his hands and rubbed them together. Thaddeus reached down and pick up a handful of dirt, rubbing it between his hands. Tim stood and watched. Thaddeus pointed at the ground and said, "Rub some dirt. It keeps the blisters from getting too big." Tim reached down and did as Thaddeus had done with the dirt.

"We'll start with the rocks, and then get to the boulders. Spread out and clear all the rocks you can handle on your own," said Cummings.

Tim watched as the two men started at the top of the field and began to make their way, walking in rows. Thaddeus stopped and picked up a rock and carried it off the field and dropped it. Cummings regarded Tim and said, "You waiting for a special invitation? Let's get to it. I don't want our rations cut today." Tim walked to the top of the field and began to walk down a row as the other two men did. He picked up a small rock and deposited it as Thaddeus had. Then Tim walked past a large rock and continued on. Cummings barked, "Hey kid, don't expect me to get that for you. I said to pick up anything you can handle on your own."

Tim looked behind him at the rock and his eyes grew large. "Are you talking about that one?" He asked.

"Do you see another rock behind you?" Asked Cummings as he continued down his row.

Tim had walked past this rock because it appeared well beyond his ability to handle on his own. It was also sunk down into the dirt several inches. Tim scratched his head, and then went over to fetch his shovel. He dug around the base of the large rock until he had uncovered the edge all the way around. Tim dropped the shovel and attempted to lift the rock. It wouldn't budge. Tim crouched lower this time and lifted harder. The rock lifted off the ground about a foot in Tim's hands, before he dropped it on the toes of his foot. He hopped around cursing and grimacing in pain.

Tim felt a hand on his shoulder. "Let's get this one together," said Thaddeus. Tim nodded and the two of them struggled successfully to clear the rock. As they dropped the rock off the field Cummings yelled, "Don't baby him, Thaddeus. He has to carry his own load!"

"Don't pay no attention to Cummings. Just call me over if you can't get one on your own," said Thaddeus as he went back to his own row.

"Thanks," said Tim. Tim noticed the massive size of Thaddeus' arms and shoulders as he walked away. When he looked over at Cummings he noticed that they both were strong. Tim was well put together and used to physical labor, but he wasn't sure he'd be able to keep up with his partners on the blue team.

Three hours later Tim dropped another rock off the field, just as Thaddeus was doing the same. Tim wiped his brow and asked, "So when do we eat?"

"Not till midday, lad."

"We don't get breakfast?" Asked Tim.

Thaddeus laughed, "No, I don't think they know about breakfast. We get our first meal when the sun reaches its height in the sky. And the only other meal comes at the end of the work day."

"And when is the end of the work day?" Inquired Tim.

"When the sun sets."

"Damn, so we're out here from sun up until sun down," said Tim.

"You got it, lad."

"So who are these people? And why do they have us here?" Asked Tim.

Thaddeus got a strange look on his face as he said, "You don't want to know." And with that Thaddeus went back to his work.

Tim groaned as they both went back to their rows. He could feel his energy flagging, having been hard at work for several hours now, and with nothing to line his stomach. Tim wished he'd brought more with him last night, as all he ate was some old bread. He kept pondering Thaddeus' strange response. Who were these people? And what did they want from him? Were they merely slave labor, or was there more to it? And where was Amanda? Tim watched for her all day, but still hadn't caught sight of her.

Tim kept an eye on the sun, longing for it to reach its zenith. His stomach rumbled and his hunger pangs grew as the morning wore on. Finally a mule drawn cart stopped in front of their field. The same annoying bell that dragged them from bed clanged now. All six members of team blue dropped their tools and eagerly made their way down to the cart.

A large barrel of some kind of soup sat in the middle of the cart. Each man picked up a clay bowl and a wooden spoon. A woman sat on a stool in the cart and ladled a single scoop of soup into each man's bowl. Another woman handed them each a skin containing water. They were allowed to keep the skins until supper time.

The soup diminished Tim's hunger pangs, but barely began to fill his stomach. He asked Thaddeus if there was seconds, and received a laugh in response. The men returned their bowls and spoons and went back to work with the skins slung over their shoulders.

At sunset the men brought their tools back to the tool cart. They then received another bowl of the same soup, and were allowed to refill their water skins. Tim examined his hands while he ate. They'd become more painful as the day wore on. His fingers and finger nails were scraped and torn, having been worn down from clawing at rocks. Tim's shoulders, arms and back were sore. He wondered how many days he'd have to endure this strenuous work.

The guards ate while the worker rats did, but kept a good distance away. When the guards finished their bowls of soup, they were given seconds. Tim and the other members of blue team watched with envy as the guards inhaled their seconds. When the guards finished their meal, they herded the blue team back down the hill. Tim's muscles ached in protest as he marched back. He couldn't remember being this sore. Then again, he couldn't remember working this hard. Tim, his brother and their father worked the fields of their own farm, but took more breaks, worked at a more leisurely pace, and ate more satisfying meals.

As Tim approached the barracks he noticed that the men and women entered through different doors. So that must be why I couldn't find Amanda amongst the bunkbeds; the women are kept in a different room, thought Tim.

The guards forced them back into the barracks and locked them in. The other slaves immediately turned into their beds. Tim watched an older man help a young boy out of his boots and into his bed. He hoped a kindly woman did the same for his sister. Tim gratefully found his own bunk, and couldn't find a comfortable position. It seemed like all of his muscles hurt. However, he was so tired that he quickly submitted to sleep.

The next day turned out to be much like the first day, only Tim felt more painfully sore as he marched back to the sleeping barracks. Throughout the march he kept an eye out for Amanda. As he neared the barracks, women from another path merged onto the same path. Tim began scanning the crowd for Amanda. A young girl stepped directly in front of Tim. She looked familiar. "Amanda, is that you?" Said Tim.

The girl turned and his smiling sister embraced him. "Oh thank God you found me, Tim!" Answered Amanda.

"I'm so relieved that you're safe!" Said Tim as tears formed in his eyes.

"Move it along you two love birds," said a gruff guard as he pushed Tim in the back. Tim felt so grateful to have found Amanda that he didn't mind, and ignored the guard. Tim began walking alongside his sister.

"Are you being taken care of okay?" Asked Tim. Before she could answer one of the guards pushed Tim towards the men's barrack doors and away from Amanda. Tim glanced over his shoulder to see Amanda crying as she was herded into the women's barracks.

Shane went down on a knee to rest at the crest of the hill overlooking the crossroads. Beyond the crossroads stood the Dawkins' farm. Shane searched the road leading up to their farm, and didn't see any travelers. The farm remained too far away to see if the tall collector had arrived yet. Having regained his wind, Shane plunged down the hill.

He ran into the house and called out for father. Mother appeared with alarm on her face. She said, "Your father's in the barn! Did you find Amanda? Is she okay?"

"Amanda's safe for now," said Shane as he embraced his mother. Then he quickly ran for the barn. He found father working in the barn.

"Father, we found Amanda! She's safe. Tim stayed back to keep an eye on her. So don't do anything foolish when the collector gets here."

"Oh thank God! Good work, boys! Where do they have her?"

"They have her at the Inn in Hanover," said Shane.

"And you saw her with your own eyes?"

"Tim saw her with his own eyes," said Shane.

"So where are they taking her? Did you hear anything that will help us?"

"No. They just said the tall one's coming back for the money, and the fat one is keeping Amanda," explained Shane.

They were interrupted by the sound of a horse approaching. Shane followed his father outside. They waited while the tall collector walked his horse up to them. He remained in his saddle. "So you'll have the tax money for me then?"

"I've got half of it, Lachman," answered father. Father tossed a bag of coins to the collector. The collector weighed it in his hand.

The collector laughed and said, "That will be Mr. Lachman to you. Now don't be playing games with us, Dawkins."

"Games? You know damn well that's the best I can do before market day," countered father.

"Well now Dawkins, that just isn't good enough for Lord Teagle. And as you know, the Lord gets what he demands. So, we'll just hold onto precious little Amanda for safe keeping, until you muster the motivation to find the rest of the money.

"Market day isn't for two more days yet! I won't have it until then," said father.

"Well then, I guess we'd better enjoy the pleasure of Amanda's company until then. I'll be back in two days. And if you want to see your daughter in, well let's just say new condition, you'll have the rest of the tax money by then." And with that Lachman turned his horse and galloped away.

"I'll go back to the Inn and make sure Amanda's still safe," said Shane.

"No, you'll stay here. I need your help getting ready for market. I won't take any chances of not having the money," said father.

"But what about..."

Father cut him off, "Stop it! Just do as I say." Shane looked at mother, but decided to hold his tongue.

Two days later Shane and his parents came back from the town's market day with the rest of the tax money, and a little extra to live off. They grew most of the food they needed, and traded for the few things they didn't grow themselves. Every Friday the whole town gathered to trade and sell the products they didn't need to sustain their families.

Father stopped the cart in front of the barn. Father helped mother carry the remaining produce into the kitchen, while Shane unhitched the horse and fed and watered her. As Shane rubbed down their horse, he wondered how Amanda fared. He also wondered if Tim was okay, and hoped he still had Amanda in his sights.

Saturday morning arrived and the Dawkins waited for the tax collector to bring home Amanda. They fretted over her safety, and occupied themselves with chores to distract themselves. Finally Father spotted the dust cloud of an approaching horse. Father and Shane stepped out to the front porch to await the riders. Father wore a sword at his side.

The rider rounded the bend and came into sight. Shane's stomach fell as he saw Lachman riding alone. Father swore under his breath. Mother poked her head out the door and asked, "Is Amanda okay?"

"Stay inside until he leaves," barked father.

"He doesn't have Amanda with him! What do we do?" Asked Shane.

"Be still! We wait and hear him out."

The tall collector stopped in front of the porch, and remained mounted. "So Dawkins, I figure you got the rest of that tax money for me?"

"Where's my daughter?"

"You daughter will be safe as long as we get the money," replied the collector.

"I want to see her before I hand over the money, Lachman."

Lachman hit Father on the side of the head with the flat of his sword, knocking him to the ground. "I warned you to give me my due respect. And you won't see your precious daughter again until I see that money!" Father hesitated, glanced at Shane, and then tossed the money bag to the collector. He took a quick look inside, and then said, "You're daughter will be delivered safe and sound soon." And with that he galloped off.

"Wait a minute! When do I get Amanda back," yelled father. The collector didn't respond.

"That son of a bitch! Let me go after him, father," said Shane.

Father thought for a moment as he rubbed the back of his head. He peered into the house. Mother saw father look her way, and ran out the front door. "Where's Amanda? Didn't they bring her back?" Asked mother.

Father slowly shook his head. Mother collapsed into his arms, and he held her tight while she weeped. Then he looked intently into Shane's eyes, and nodded. Without waiting for any instructions, Shane ran off after the collector. He paced himself more carefully this time, remembering that he didn't have the wind to run all the way to Hanover. Shane cut through fields whenever he could.

After several hours of running Shane reached the Inn of Hanover, where the collectors had kept Amanda the first night they'd taken her. Shane circled around to the back of the Inn and listened. When he didn't hear anything for a long time he made a decision. He walked in the front door. Shane surveyed the tavern that occupied the first floor. Several men sat together at a table to the right, and a young couple ate and chatted on the other side of the tavern. However, there was no sign of Lachman.

Shane left the tavern and walked across the road to the stables. Several horses were stabled there, but Shane couldn't be sure if any of them belonged to the collector. Unfortunately, the short collector had ridden the distinctive black and white horse. He went back outside and peered across the road at the Inn. Could I have arrived here before the collector? No, being on horseback and with a head start he certainly would have gotten here before me. Maybe he kept going this time, and didn't stop at the Inn, Shane thought.

Shane decided to continue further up the road to the north. He walked until he reached the edge of Hanover and then started running. Shane ran several miles before stopping to catch his breath. He shielded his eyes from the westering sun and gazed as far up the road as he could see. Nothing. He hadn't seen a single traveler since leaving Hanover.

Shane heard of rustling of leaves and turned around quickly. There stood Lachman. He held a sword pointed at Shane's stomach. "I figure you might be looking for me, boy. I thought I'd make it real easy for you to find me," said the collector.

"Damn," was all Shane said.

"Yeah, damn. I guess you weren't supposed to let me see you. That right?" Shane held his tongue. "Well then, let me make it real clear, boy. If I catch sight of you again, it will be the last day for you and your precious little sister. Are we clear on that?"

"Where do you have her? And when are you bringing her back?"

"You just worry about staying out of my sight, and keeping your head where it is. Do we have an understanding?" Shane nodded slowly as he averted his eyes.

The collector remounted his horse and left. Shane watched carefully which direction the collector went. Shane thought about trailing him, but dared not follow, at least not right away. So now what do I do? If I follow, then... Shane sat down on a rock and pondered what to do. He wondered where Tim had gone. He wondered about trying to follow the collector at a safer distance. Shane thought about returning to his father and mother with the news of losing the collector's trail. He groaned at the thought. His parents would be so disappointed. Finally Shane stood and walked back home.

Four

The next few weeks continued on with the same routine for Tim and Amanda. They looked for each other on the path to and from work, and on some days found an opportunity to talk for a moment. Amanda hated being kept prisoner, but she seemed to be treated well enough. An older woman took enough notice of Amanda to see that she ate enough and had her basic needs provided for. Tim noted a dimness to Amanda's eyes, that angered him. He often thought of how he'd repay the men responsible. Not having access to a mirror, Tim didn't realize that his eyes looked much like his sister's.

Tim's muscles hardened, and most of the soreness went away. However, most mornings he woke to some stiffness in his body. His hands had developed calluses, and didn't bleed much anymore. Tim's frame had leaned. He burned far more calories than he ate.

The blue team continued to clear the field of large rocks and boulders. By now they'd removed all the smaller ones that could be handled by one man. At this point they worked in teams of three. Two of the men would carry off the boulder they'd just excavated, while the third man began to dig around the base of the next one.

Tim began to dig out the next small boulder. He looked up as he wiped his brow. Tim watched as Thaddeus and Cummings dropped the boulder the three of them had just excavated. Thaddeus walked to the far end of the rock pile near a stand of trees. He unbuttoned his trousers and made water. Just as Tim leaned into the spade he heard a surprised cry. Tim glanced over his shoulder and saw Thaddeus rolling on the ground with two wolves on top of him, and a third wolf snarling nearby.

Tim immediately ran towards Thaddeus. Thaddeus worked furiously to keep the wolves from his neck. He knew one bite to the neck would be the end of him. The nearest wolf held firmly to Thaddeus' shoulder.

Tim caught the first wolf by surprise, swinging the spade at the side of the closest wolf. The spade hit the wolf in the shoulder and it let out a yelp and ran away. Tim swung the spade back around at the second wolf, catching him in the head and knocking it unconscious. The third wolf proved too quick for Tim, and he lost the advantage of surprise.

Just as Tim readied himself to strike at the last wolf, it lunged at his arm. The wolf sank its sharp teeth into Tim's forearm, knocking Tim to the ground in the process. Tim rolled over onto his back and hit the wolf with his free fist. The wolf left go of his arm and lunged at Tim's neck. Tim reflexively put up his arm and was rewarded by yet another deep bite into his left arm. Tim cried out in pain and tried to knock the wolf off his arm again, but it swung around so quickly that Tim only succeeded in landing glancing blows that had little effect on the wolf. Fear surged through Tim's veins, as he feared for his life. Tim desperately reached for a nearby rock and just as he swung the rock towards the wolf's head, it released its grip on Tim's left arm and lunged at his neck. Tim was taken by surprise and lifted his arms in defense.

Tim feared this may be the end for him. A moment later he felt the full weight of the wolf on his chest. Tim was surprised to not feel the bite of the wolf's teeth again, and wondered why. He pushed the wolf off him and jumped to his feet. The wolf lay dead at his feet with an arrow through its chest. Before Tim had time to understand what he saw, he heard a voice.

"I want that man in my squad." Tim followed the voice and found a soldier sitting on horseback. He held a bow with an arrow loosely fitted onto the string. Next to him sat another man on horseback. This man had the look of authority to him. It was his voice Tim heard. The man spoke again, "Sergeant, you will arrange to have this man placed in my squad immediately."

"With all due respect Captain, this man is only a worker rat."

"I meet plenty of men that run from a fight. I don't find many men that run towards a fight," answered the captain. And with that the captain turned his horse and trotted away.

The sergeant barked an order and a horse appeared at his side. The sergeant said, "What is your name, rat?"

"Tim."

"Well then, Rat Tim, mount this horse and follow me." Tim did as he was told, although it took some time for him to pull himself up into the saddle with one serviceable arm. His left arm bled as he held it against his chest. The pain of moving his arm brought him to the brink of unconsciousness several times while he rode the horse.

The sergeant led Tim down the usual road back towards the barracks for the first mile. Then the sergeant turned off to the left, down a path that Tim had never even noticed. It looked more like a game trail than a path that anyone used. The path steered around to the right, over a small hill and then opened up to a medium sized meadow. Surrounding the meadow on every side were trees and foliage. Within the meadow stood two buildings. One building was similar to the barracks that Tim had been sleeping in, and the other building was a barn.

Tim dismounted in front of the buildings, as the sergeant had done. A soldier took their horses into the barn. The sergeant led Tim into the barracks. The first room on the left had a red cross painted on the door. The sergeant pushed Tim into this room and said, "Hey doc, see to this man's arm." And then the sergeant turned to two soldiers standing nearby. "You two will stand guard over this rat, and bring him to the captain when he's fixed up." The two soldiers came to attention on either side of the medic's office.

The doctor pointed at a three-legged stool in the corner without speaking. Tim took a seat. The doctor rolled up Tim's bloodied shirt. It took the doctor a long time to pull the shirt away from the bite wounds, as the blood had begun to dry and the shirt stuck to his arm. Tim winced as the doctor tore the shirt from each tooth mark. Tears began to form in Tim's eyes, and he looked away, not wanting the doctor to notice. The doctor studied the bite wounds. He shook his head back and forth, and without speaking cleaned and wrapped Tim's arm. Tim kept his head turned away while the doctor worked on his arm, grimacing in pain. But it wasn't just the pain, Tim hated the sight of blood. The doctor finished his work and pointed to the door. When Tim stepped out of the door the two guards escorted him to the captain.

The captain's office was on the second floor of the barracks. He pored over papers when Tim was pushed through the door. The room was small, but filled with well-made furniture of wood and leather. Above and behind the captain was a portrait of the king. The captain sat on a leather-covered wooden chair at a small, dark-wooded desk. He looked up when Tim entered. "Ah, there you are. And what is your name, soldier?"

"Uh, Tim."

"So tell me, Tim, why did you charge those wolves? Are you some kind of simpleton?" Tim shrugged. The captain waited, and then said, "Come now, I want an answer. What were you thinking?"

"I didn't think. Thaddeus needed help. I guess I just reacted without considering."

"You might be some kind of idiot. However, you're exactly the kind of idiot that I need in my squad. Men that not only do what I say, but respond as the situation demands. In battle there rarely is time to think. You think for long and you're dead...so tell me soldier, what is it you want?"

The question surprised Tim. Once he recovered he answered, "What do I want? I want to go home."

"Home? Oh yes, we all want to go home. If only that were possible."

"And why can't I go home? Why are we being held here?" Asked Tim.

"You're now in the service of Lord Teagle. You're in his army. And you won't go home until the campaign is over. None of us can go home until all is finished."

"What campaign?"

"Ah yes, I'm sure you have many questions. All will be answered in time. For now put any thoughts of going home out of your mind. For now you are to learn the art of war. Do you have any experience with weapons?"

"Well, my brother and I make our own sling shots."

"No, that won't work. Sling shots are for children, and are basically useless in battle," said the captain.

"And we do some hunting with bow and arrows with our father, but I've never used a sword, if that's what you're asking," said Tim.

"We can fix that soon enough. And I have need of archers. You will report to Sergeant Hinters for training. You're dismissed," said the captain.

"Wait a minute, sir. There's something else I want. I want to be with my sister, sir."

"What does your sister have to do with me?" Asked the captain.

"She's being held back at the rat's barracks, sir."

The captain paused to consider this. "You'll have to earn my trust before I even consider doing anything for your sister. And even at that, I'm not sure that I can do anything for her. Now be off to the weapon's training."

"Wait Captain, you mean you might actually..."

The captain cut him off, "Now just forget about your sister for now. You just go learn the skills of war."

The captain stepped out of his office and said to the guards at the door, "You will tell Hinters I want this man trained in the sword, and put into the archery team." The guards nodded, and led Tim down the stairs.

Lieutenant Hinters paced back and forth as he watched the soldiers train. About fifty soldiers trained in roped off practice grounds. Each soldier wore a thick leather belt that contained a long knife and a sword. The soldiers also carried wooden shields. Some were plain wood, and some were covered with leather. A few men shot arrows at targets on the far side. Most of the soldiers spared with knives or swords.

The two guards told Tim to wait as they approached Hinters. They quietly conferred while Tim waited. The lieutenant nodded with a scowl on his face. He called over a soldier. The soldier appeared to be overseeing the sparing session. Hinters gave him instructions that Tim couldn't hear. The soldier then approached Tim and said, "I'm Simpson, the training sergeant. You will come this way." Tim followed Simpson to the archery range.

"Pick out a bow and string it," instructed Simpson. Simpson watched as Tim quickly strung the bow and tested its weight in his hands. "Now shoot at the near target," said Simpson. Tim gazed at the range and saw a near target at about 25 paces, a midrange target at about 50 paces, and a far target that must have been nearly 100 paces. Tim picked out an arrow and hit the near target just outside the bull's-eye.

"Not bad soldier. You've shot a bow before," said Simpson.

"Aye sir," said Tim.

"Where did you learn the bow?"

"From my father. He taught me and my brother to hunt small game on our farm," said Tim.

"That right? Take a shot at the second target," ordered Simpson. Tim shot and hit the outer edge of the target. A couple of the archers snickered and mumbled something. Simpson said, "Keep working at the middle target. I want you to practice till you can hit the inner two rings regularly." And with that Simpson walked away.

Tim fired three more arrows at the midrange target, and each time hit well wide to the right. He picked up a forth arrow and took more careful aim, but still missed to the right. A voice behind Tim said, "You're overall technique is pretty good, but you're lining up your aim wrong." Tim turned to find an older soldier standing with his arms folded across his chest.

"And who are you?" Asked Tim.

"I'm Quirius, and the old timer on the archery team. They call me Ol' Time," he said with a smile.

"There's nothing wrong with my aim."

"Maybe not, young lad, but let's see if we can get you to hit the inner circles," said Quirius.

Tim paused before saying, "Well, I suppose I could always improve. So enlighten me, why am I missing right every time?" Quirius pulled the bow off his own back and fitted it with an arrow, and took aim. He fired an arrow into the center circle of the midrange target.

"Do that again." Quirius took aim and fired a second arrow that landed next to the first one. "Teach me to do that," asked Tim.

Quirius taught Tim his technique. Tim spent the rest of the afternoon practicing. By the time supper was called, Tim was able to hit the second ring consistently, as Simpson required.

Quirius mentored Tim throughout the week, refining his skill. Each day he improved, and at week's end he could hit the inner circle of the midrange target most of the time. Each day he spent half of his time with the blades sergeant, learning the knife and the sword. By the end of the week Hinters reported to the captain that Tim had accomplished more than sufficient archery mastery, as well as the basic skills with the sword and knife. Tim was surprised to find that he actually enjoyed learning weaponry. Archery was his favorite, but he also enjoyed learning the sword. Tim never took to knives.

Tim's body regained weight, as he now ate three meals per day with the soldiers. The soldiers were given as much stew and bread as they wanted, and even a pint of ale in the evening. In a short time, Tim regained all of the lost weight. In fact, he was in the best physical shape of his life.

Early the next morning Hinters woke Tim early. "Soldier rat, you have been assigned guard duty to the field workers. You will join Quirius' team now. Get dressed and meet them in front of the barn." Tim dressed quickly. Up until this day, Tim had only been permitted to train in the meadow.

As Tim approached the barn Hinters spoke with Quirius. Tim heard Hinters say, "So that means the rat is to be killed if he makes any attempt. Are we clear on that?"

"Wouldn't it be enough to wound him?" Inquired Quirius.

"Absolutely not! Our orders are plain enough. This comes from above me. Are we clear?"

"We're clear," said Quirius with little energy. Quirius mounted his horse and the team of five archers assembled behind him. He said, "We move out to stand guard at seeding field five. Let's go!"

Tim and the other archers ran to the seeding fields behind the mounted Quirius. When they arrived Tim realized it was the same field that he, Thaddeus and Cummings had cleared. In fact, it was now completely cleared of all but dirt. A group of women of all ages worked the field. They wore bags of seed over their shoulders, and most wore boots with holes in the soles. A few of the women worked barefoot. The women walked up and down the rows scattering seed along the way. Each woman or girl walked a row. They made a hole in the ground, dropped a few seeds into the hole, and covered the hole with dirt. Behind them came a woman with a watering jug.

Quirius dismounted and said to the archers, "You will surround the field. If any woman or child attempts to run, you know what to do. We are instructed to shoot to kill. That means you will aim for the left center of their chest. Any questions?"

The men spread out to take their positions. As Tim began to follow the others Quirius stopped him. "Tim, a word. I want you to know that I've been ordered to keep a close eye on you. And if you make any attempt to run, you too will be shot with the aim to kill. Now look here, I don't want to have to kill you, lad. In fact, I almost like you. So make it easy on both of us and do as you've been ordered. Now don't make me do something I don't want to do. Do we have an understanding?"

"Yeah, I guess so," said Tim.

"Look Tim, I'm serious. Don't make me have to put an arrow in your chest. You know that I can. You got me?"

"Yeah, I get it," said Tim.

"Good. You will take up position there," ordered Quirius. Tim's position was on the West end of the field, farthest from the barracks. The distance between Tim and the other archers seemed far, yet shooting someone with an arrow doesn't require close range to be effective.

The morning hours passed uneventfully, as Tim paced back and forth along the ground assigned to him, as he saw the other guards doing. At first Tim carefully searched each of the women in the field, but none were his sister. Having given up on finding Amanda for now, Tim resumed pacing back and forth. At first Tim was relieved to not be forced to manual labor as he'd done with the rock clearing, yet after a couple of hours he became bored.

Not only was the pacing tedious, but the women's work so routine there was nothing interesting to look at. And Tim felt compassion for the women working without hats in the hot sun. Most of their faces were sunburned, as well as many of their arms, as only a few wore long sleeved dresses or shirts.

Quirius walked his horse around the field. He spent most of his time near Tim. Quirius knew his own life would be in danger if he did not return to the barracks with Tim in his company, dead or alive.

The other benefit of guard duty came with the meals. At the midday meal Tim was offered a second helping of the stew. As he saw the hungry faces of the women, he remembered how hungry he'd been while on the work crew. Tim hadn't felt hunger pangs since he'd been added to the militia. He even received bread and coffee before reporting for duty this morning.

After eating the archers went back to their assigned positions. Tim settled into his position and his patrol pacing. Throughout the day the women ignored Tim and his fellow guards, as if they weren't there. A young woman walked the row nearest Tim. She glanced up at Tim warily. Tim didn't think much of it. On her way up the next row she looked right at Tim and smiled. Then she stared at Tim again. Tim smiled back. The woman approached Tim and asked if she could relieve herself in the trees behind Tim. Tim turned to look for Quirius, but he wasn't nearby. He nodded permission to the woman. She walked around the largest tree and pulled up her skirt. Tim looked away, wanting to allow the woman the dignity of privacy.

A moment later another guard shouted, "An escape, an escape!" Tim whipped around to see the same woman fleeing. He quickly fitted an arrow onto his bow and took aim at her upper back. He hesitated. In the time he hesitated the woman ran behind a tree that blocked Tim's view of her. He ran after her until he gained a clear shot at her from a low rise.

Tim aimed at her heart. I don't want to shoot this poor woman. I wish I were fleeing with her, Tim thought. Tim adjusted his aim and let loose the arrow. The woman fell in a heap. Quirius galloped after her. Tim followed and arrived at where she'd fallen, and Quirius already had her hands bound behind her. She still lay where she'd fallen, with an arrow sticking through her left thigh. She whimpered in pain.

"Were you not told to shoot to kill!" Shouted Quirius.

"Yes sir," said Tim as he averted his eyes.

"Then why is there an arrow in her leg?"

"I must have missed, sir."

"You missed? You missed, my ass," said Quirius. "Help me load her onto the horse." Tim broke off the arrow head and pulled the feather end out of her leg. He gently picked the wounded woman up and lay her across Quirius's horse. Tim pulled his scarf off and tied it around the wound in her upper thigh.

"Return to your position. And no more missing," said Quirius with a wink. He mounted his horse behind her and trotted off.

Tim watched the woman bouncing in front of the saddle, and he winced. Quirius rode with a hand on her back. Tim returned to his duty position. I hope they get her medical attention, Tim thought.

On the way back to the barracks at the end of the day, Tim took careful note of the guard positions. He etched into his mind the spots that were relatively unguarded. There weren't too many of these. The field rats were closely guarded, especially the men. The soldiers enjoyed more freedom. Tim wondered how many of them soldiered voluntarily, and how many were forced like Tim.

Tim followed the other soldiers into the barracks, and laid down on his bunk. Loud shouting from above interrupted his private thoughts. "I say he's ready, and I need another good archer for the assignment. I have to have another archer!" Tim recognized Lieutenant Hinters voice.

"And I tell you, he's still unproven. You're taking a huge chance by putting him on the assignment so soon," said a second voice. This voice sounded like Simpson.

"Maybe I am taking a chance, but that decision is mine to make, so..."

"Look lieutenant, I don't want this coming back to me. I don't mean no disrespect. Just come watch him one day and see for yourself. He let a woman go today," said Simpson.

"He shot her in the leg. She didn't get away...but I will observe him tomorrow," said Hinters.

"Thank you, sir. I can't take all the responsibility for this one, especially with what happened last time," said Simpson.

The next morning Tim marched out to the same field behind Quirius. Tim took up the same position as the previous day. Tim studied the women carefully. The woman he'd shot in the leg wasn't there. Of course she wouldn't be there, as Tim realized she wouldn't be able to walk for awhile yet.

Late in the afternoon a rider approached the field. The rider led another horse, and he reigned in next to Quirius' horse. Tim recognized that the rider was Hinters. The two men conferred in quiet voices that Tim could not make out. They pointed towards Tim several times. Hinters walked his horse to Tim's position. Hinters said, "Soldier rat, you will mount up and follow me." Tim nodded and mounted the horse without comment. Hinters held onto the reigns of Tim's horse and led him back to the practice field.

"You will fire three arrows at the near target," ordered Hinters. Tim looked at Hinters quizzically.

"What's the point of..."

Hinters said, "Don't ask no questions, rat. Do as you're told." Tim shrugged and strung an arrow. He hit the center ring of the near target. Tim put the next two arrows into the center ring as well. Tim glanced up at Hinters, who pointed towards the middle target. Tim took aim and hit the second ring. He strung another arrow and hit the second ring again. Tim shook his head in frustration. With the third arrow, he took more time to carefully aim, and loosed the arrow into the center ring.

Hinters grunted, and nodded towards the far target. Tim took his time with all three arrows, and placed the first one in the third ring, and the second and third into the second ring. "Not bad rat, that will do nicely. You will be awakened an hour before dawn to join me. We will be off to the assignment," said Hinters.

"What's the assignment?" Asked Tim.

Hinters laughed and said, "You'll find out soon enough, rat. You will keep at it until you put three more arrows into the first two rings of the far target. Then you will be dismissed to quarters." And turning to Simpson, Hinters said, "Is that clear, Simpson?"

"Clear, sir." Tim hadn't noticed Simpson, who must have joined them while Tim focused on the targets.

Tim waited until Hinters left and then turned to Simpson. "So what's with the assignment?" Tim asked.

"You don't want to know, lad," said Simpson with a chuckle.

"Why don't I want to know? Can you give me some idea what I'm getting myself into?"

"No lad. We aren't permitted to speak about the assignment. You'll just have to see for yourself when you get there."

The next morning Tim awoke to Hinters shaking him. Tim groaned groggily. It felt like the middle of the night. The window was dark, and sunrise appeared to be hours away. Tim sat up and rubbed his face. "You will ready yourself and be outside in five minutes, rat. Got it?" Ordered Hinters as he tossed him a piece of bread and a water skin.

"Yeah, I got it."

Amanda woke to the loud clanging. Although she'd been living in the barracks for many weeks now, she hadn't become used to being jolted awake. The kindly woman who occupied the bunk next to Amanda helped her to lace up her boots and pull her hair back off her face. The woman called herself Carla. Carla wiped away the tears from Amanda's eyes and said, "Now there dear, don't let them have the satisfaction of tears. It's just what they want." Amanda nodded, though she didn't understand.

Amanda and Carla filed out of the barracks with the rest of the women. They hiked a couple miles to their assigned field. At the field Amanda and the others were given sacks that were about half full of seed. Amanda didn't know nor care what kind of seeds they were. She mindlessly walked her rows and filled her holes with seed, as she'd been instructed.

Amanda fantasized about being back home with Father and Momma. She imagined Momma holding her on her knee, as she often did after the dishes were cleaned up. Amanda's favorite part was sitting on Momma's lap and having her hair combed before going to bed. Momma would sing softly while she combed, and often listen to Amanda tell her about the events of the day. Sometimes Amanda prayed that she'd see Momma and Father again. As each day passed, it seemed less likely.

Throughout the day she looked for Tim. She hadn't seen him in many days. Amanda feared that her brother had been taken away, or killed. She worried she wouldn't see any of her family again. When she asked when she could go home, the guards merely laughed and slapped each other on the back. Amanda couldn't figure out what was so funny about her question, but she understood it meant they had no intention of sending her home anytime soon.

Carla worked a different field than Amanda. Amanda looked for Carla as well as Tim every night on the way back. She liked the comfort of Carla's presence. Tonight she couldn't find her. Just before she arrived at the barracks a soldier grabbed Amanda by the hair and pulled her out of line. He held onto her hair and asked, "Now little missy, you're a bit young, but what can you do for us weary and friendly guards? Can you dance?" Amanda was confused, as his face didn't seem friendly. Amanda thought about this strange question. She had danced in town when the men played their fiddles, but she thought it best to not tell the smelly guard this. Amanda shook her head from side to side.

"Well then, you can sing. If you can't dance, you must be able to sing." Amanda wasn't sure if this was a question or an instruction. She considered this question, and was about to shake her head again when the soldier added, "Now listen here missy, you will either be able to dance or sing for us tonight. You decide which."

Amanda began to cry and looked about for Carla, but she was nowhere to be seen. The soldier said, "Now stop that crying little missy, cause it won't work on me. You'll either dance or sing. There's no other way about it. So what will it be tonight?"

"I guess I can sing a little," said Amanda almost inaudibly.

"What's that?"

"I can sing," she said a bit louder.

Amanda hoped the guard would let go of her hair, but he didn't. He pulled her into the other building next to the barracks. She had to half run to keep up with his long strides. She had never been in this building before now. The inside of the house reminded her of her family home, but it was much larger. A group of many soldiers lounged in the great room near a roaring fire. They drank funny smelling water that almost looked like water, but not quite.

"Well now lads, I found us a little bit of entertainment tonight," said the guard holding Amanda's hair. The other soldiers gave a roar of delight. One called out, "Ain't she a bit young? Couldn't you have found a one a bit more...developed?" The soldier shook his head and pulled Amanda to stand in front of the fire place. It was hot, so she moved a little further away from it. She glanced at the guard, but he hadn't seemed to notice. The guard poured more funny smelling water into his cup, and then sat down with the others. He raised his glass and said, "Alright little missy, let's hear that song you're itching to sing for us."

Amanda wasn't sure what to do. She stared at the men. At first they didn't seem to notice her. After a few minutes the soldiers began to quiet down and pay more attention to her. Amanda became nervous. The more the soldiers watched her, the more nervous she felt. After awhile the soldier who had pulled her hair barked at her, "Come now missy, don't keep the lads waiting no more. Sing something pretty for us!"

Amanda had hoped the soldiers would forget about her and let her go back to Carla. Now it was clear they weren't going to do that. Amanda tried to think of a song to sing. She didn't know many songs, and she couldn't think of any that she knew just now.

Amanda fidgeted with her hands. She stole a glance at the soldiers, hoping one might help her out. She searched for a kindly face, but wasn't able to find one. Sweat formed on her face and began to trickle down her forehead and face. Amanda wiped her eyes, as the sweat stung them. Amanda searched again for a song to sing, but her mind was blank. She couldn't think of any song, whether she knew the words or not.

The soldier yelled to her more impatiently, "Let's have it, missy! Don't keep the lads waiting any longer now."

Amanda searched for the door, and found it to her left. She wondered if she could make it out the door before the soldier caught her. Then one of the other soldiers called out, "Sing for us the one about the hero come home from war."

Amanda breathed a sigh of relief. She knew that one. Her mother sang it often while she worked. Amanda began to sing. At first her voice was very soft, and the men yelled at her. Somehow she mustered some courage and sang a bit louder. Tears ran down her face as she sang, yet she forced a smile. The men stopped yelling. An hour later Amanda lie in Carla's arms, back in her bunk in the barracks. Carla rocked her and pet Amanda's hair until she stopped crying and fell asleep.

Rat Tim finished putting on his boots, and stumbled out to the stables. It was still dark, with no hint of the gray of morning yet. Hinters led the horses out and handed Tim the reins of one of them. Tim saddled up without comment and followed Hinters. The first hour of their ride was dark, and Tim had little idea where they went. He gave his horse the reins and allowed himself to fall into a somewhat restful stupor.

Once the sun arose, Tim began to pay attention to his surroundings, being curious as to where they went. They were in country that he didn't recognize. At midday Hinters stopped at a creek and allowed the horses to drink. He tossed another lump of bread to Tim. "So where are we off to?" Asked Tim.

"Oh lad, you aren't in any hurry to get there," said Hinters with a grin. "Just be glad to know nothing about it for now."

Tim imagined what might await him. Based on Hinter's comments, it couldn't be anything good. Since the possibilities that came to mind distressed him, he dismissed the thoughts and contented himself to merely wait and see. "You might want to refill the water skin. I don't know that we'll see any more water for awhile. And you might want this," said Hinters as he pulled an old hat out of his saddle bag and threw it to Tim. Tim was grateful for the hat, as the midday sun brought the full strength of the day's heat onto his face. His face had already reddened from the field work, and any relief from the sun was appreciated.

Tim refilled his water skin, turned up his collar against the sun and remounted. He followed Hinters through the afternoon. The terrain had been desert-like since shortly after their midday stop. Late in the day the ground began to rise, and vegetation became more plentiful. They left the desert scape and entered hills with plenty of trees. They ascended the foothills in the waning sunlight of the late afternoon. Just as dusk faded, Hinters dismounted at a small pool of water. The pool seemed to be fed by an underground spring, as the water bubbled and stirred without any external influence. Hinters pulled the saddle from his horse, and threw the saddle blanket over his shoulder, and waved Tim to do likewise and follow. Hinters dropped his blanket and saddle at the opening of a small cave that provided some shelter. Hinters reclined on the blanket with the saddle as pillow for his head. Tim dropped his blanket and saddle as he asked, "What about supper?" In response Hinters tossed him a small bag of jerky, and then turned over to sleep.

Soon Hinters slept. Tim got up and walked down to the horses. He looked back at Hinters. Although he couldn't see him in the dark, Hinters showed no signs of concern that Tim might escape. Tim thought about jumping onto his horse and making a break for it. It soon came to him that he had nowhere to go. Tim had no idea neither where they were going nor where they were now. He chewed on jerky and sipped from his water skin. Tim walked down to the pool to refill his water skin. Again, Hinters paid no attention. Tim considered scouting about, to see if he might discover a road of some kind, through which he might escape. Then he realized that he wouldn't be able to see much in the dark, and he resigned himself to his blanket and saddle. Tim lay awake much of the night, wondering what misfortune awaited him. He dreaded wherever they were going, expecting more tedious slave labor. Whatever it might, he knew it wouldn't be anything he'd like. Well past midnight he finally drifted off to a light sleep.

The next morning they remounted and continued their journey. Tim no longer bothered to ask their destination, as Hinters seemed to enjoy a private joke each time he was asked. Tim wearily followed the horse in front of him, yet kept an eye on the surrounding country. Just in case he became separated from Hinters, whether accidentally or on purpose, he wanted some idea of where he might head.

Late that afternoon Tim followed Hinters up a steep hill. The barely discernible trail switched back and forth across the hill. When they crested the hill Tim caught his breath. Below him lay a castle. To call it a castle might be too generous, as it was really a large fortified village. At the top of the tower flew a many colored flag, that waved in the brisk wind. Below the flags chaos reigned. Dozens of men stood along the top of the town's wall, firing arrows into a horde of invaders, and dropping large rocks onto the heads of those who tried to scale the wall. The invaders sent blazing arrows into the town, sometimes hitting the men along the wall and sometimes catching fire inside the village. Inside the village smoked curled into the air from numerous sources. Fire burned from several places along the wall and inside the village. Outside the village massed uncountable soldiers. Only a few wore uniforms, most were on foot and the officers in charge were the only ones mounted on horseback.

After taking a long look at what lie below them, Tim glanced up at Hinters. "And there you have the assignment, lad. We have arrived. And you have good reason to be afraid," announced Hinters.

"You can't be serious! What are we to do there?" Asked Tim.

"We are to defend Lord Teagle's village. You are now an archer in his army."

"Wait a minute, who are we defending them against?" Asked Tim.

"Now lad, does it really matter? Today it's one enemy, and tomorrow it's another. Lord Teagle has many enemies. I don't bother to keep up with who we are fighting this time. I just do my job. We will camp here until dark, and then we will make our way into the village."

"Into the village? How will be get in without being killed?" Asked Tim.

"We may very well be killed."

"Then we shouldn't try. Let's slip back behind the front lines," suggested Tim.

"Then we are certain to be killed. Lord Teagle suffers no cowards. We will make our way into the village tonight. And lad, this won't be my first time slipping past an enemy after dark," said Hinters with a grin.

Hinters laid down on his blanket and began snoring right away. Tim wondered how he could sleep with what lay below them. Tim didn't know if he'd be able to sleep a wink, with what awaited him. He laid down along the ridge of the hill and peered into the scene before him. His eyes scanned the enemy lines, searching for a way past them. Tim shook his head, as he couldn't imagine how they'd get into the village alive. Down below three men began walking towards Tim and Hinters. All three wore torn, dirty uniforms of green and brown. He ducked down. When he looked back up they were still coming. The men began to climb the same hill upon which Tim and Hinters camped. The men weren't coming directly at their camp, but close enough to alarm Tim. Tim shook Hinters awake, "Soldiers are coming, three soldiers, we have to leave!"

Hinters sat up, rubbed his eyes, and followed Tim to the edge of the hill. Hinters peered down at the three men. They had stopped climbing, and were standing on a large boulder looking back at the village. Hinters shook his head and went back to his blanket and said, "They're just getting a view of the village from higher ground. It's no concern to us. Don't wake me again until it's dark." Tim stared back down at the men, who stood on the boulder. It was true that they were several hundred yards away from their camp, and didn't evidence any awareness of Tim and Hinters.

Tim felt like he was in an earthquake. His whole world seemed to be shaking. A moment later he opened his eyes to see Hinters nudging him awake. Tim sat up and rubbed his eyes. It was completely dark. Tim looked down at the village, which was lit up by fires. He could hear the shouts of battle. "It is time. Pack up. Take what you want from the saddle bags," said Hinters. Tim looked for the men on the boulder, but they were gone.

"Why? Aren't we riding the horses into the village?" Asked Tim.

Hinters laughed. "No lad, for then we will surely be killed. There's no sense announcing our arrival. We will go by boot and by belly. This will be our only chance to keep our heads where they are, and not on a spike in the village." Tim stared down at the battle scene, wondering which way they might slip past the invaders. He pulled his eyes away from the battle, and grabbed his water skin and the bag that contained the last few strips of jerky from the saddle. Hinters yanked the harnesses off the horses, and slapped them both on the hind quarters. They took off at a trot.

Hinters slipped his arrows over his shoulder, pulling one out that he held on the string of his bow with his left hand. He checked to be sure his sword was in position for ready use. Tim did likewise. They set off at a trot. Tim followed closely behind Hinters. Although he didn't trust Hinters, he didn't want to be left alone out here. And Tim had seen Hinters at the practice grounds, and Tim knew that Hinters was skilled beyond his own abilities in war.

They moved quickly at first. The sounds of battle grew louder as they neared the village. Suddenly a new sound caught Tim's attention, but he couldn't place it at first. It was an awful sound, almost unbearable to hear. It reminded Tim of dying animals, and yet not quite. As they moved forward they came across two men lying on the ground. They both were badly wounded, and cried out in pain. Now Tim knew the strange sound. He'd never before heard men making such terrible groaning. Then it came to Tim; they must be dying. It must be the worst sound I've ever heard, he thought. Tim covered his ears with his hands. And I don't ever want to hear it again, he thought.

Hinters looked over the dying men. At first Tim thought he was trying to check their wounds, to possibly treat them. Then he noticed that what he searched for was weapons, not wounds. Hinters took a knife off one man, and slipped it into his belt.

A loud sound of approaching hoofs rang out, and Hinters grabbed Tim's arm and pulled him behind some bushes. They crouched low while two men rode past with swords drawn. While sitting still, Tim noticed that he had his arms crossed, as if he were trying to hold himself. His body shook. My God, I'm losing it, thought Tim.

"Come lad, now we make our run for the back of the wall," said Hinters. He took off at a dead run for a stand of trees near the wall. At first Tim's legs wouldn't move, but through sheer will and fear he got himself to dash after Hinters. Tim had just made it to the trees when several men ran past, shouting out. Hinters and Tim breathed heavily as they hid behind the trees. Hinters stared at the wall, and seemed to be studying it. Then he said, "That must be it, lad. Follow me, now!"

They darted for the wall. Tim wondered what they'd do when they got to it. There were few invaders at this section of the wall, but there did not appear to be any kind of door either. Tim shouted, "I can't climb that thing!" Hinters ignored Tim and kept running. As they neared the wall, two invaders confronted them. Without breaking stride, Hinters pulled his sword and slashed the legs of both men, who fell in a heap. Tim tripped over one of the fallen men and fell to the ground. He looked back at the man, and froze as he saw the fallen invader reach for Tim's legs. Though wounded, this man was still very much alive. The man grabbed onto Tim's ankle before he could move, and began dragging Tim to him. Tim began kicking at the man, but he was too strong to be easily shaken off. The invader pulled out a knife, and readied himself to plunge it into Tim. Tim closed his eyes and braced for the blow, which never came. Then a strong arm pulled Tim to his feet. Tim pulled out his sword as he opened his eyes, only to be staring into Hinter's face. Tim turned back towards the invader, and saw that his arm was no longer attached to his shoulder. The detached hand still held the knife. Suppressing an urge to heave, Tim hurried after Hinters.

Just as they reached the wall, Tim wondered how they'd ever scale the tall wooden wall. A moment later Hinters pulled Tim behind a large boulder and into a hidden hole in the ground. Tim never would have seen the hole on his own, as it was well hidden by both boulder and brush, not to mention the dark of night. Hinters scrambled into the hole on all fours. Tim needed no prodding to follow, after his brush with death. They seemed to crawl in the dark for an hour, but it was probably only ten minutes.

Tim emerged out of the hole into a courtyard. At first Tim didn't know where they were. But when he saw the wall behind them, he figured they had crawled through a tunnel under the wall. Hinters shut a trap door which covered the tunnel. Tim scanned the scene before him. Many women ran with buckets of water, throwing them on the many fires that burned in the courtyard. Men lined the wall, firing arrows and engaging in hand to hand combat with swords. Tim was surprised at the number of men who lay on the ground, appearing dead or badly wounded. A few men shouted orders here and there. A flaming arrow pierced the ground, not two steps from where Tim and Hinters stood.

After dusting themselves off, Hinters marched them into the largest building. They entered a large room, with candles ensconced along the walls. Debris was strewn along the ground. A man lay on the wooden table in the room, with a man and a woman tending to his wounds. To the right a doorway opened to a smaller room. Inside three men stood over a map, conferring in loud voices. They seemed to be arguing. The man in the center wore a uniform, while the others didn't.

Hinters approached the man in the uniform and said, "Hinters reporting for duty, sir."

A flash of hope crossed the officer's face. He said, "How many did you bring?"

"Just myself and this boy," said Hinters pointing to Tim.

"Just two? You can't be serious! I asked for a hundred men! Where are the rest?"

"I don't know, sir. We were sent alone," said Hinters.

"Damn them! What do they expect me to do with two men? Make that one and a half," said the officer as he eyed Tim. The officer turned to the men and conferred with them. One shrugged his shoulders, while the other didn't respond. The three men went back to arguing over the map.

After several awkward minutes, Hinters interrupted and asked, "And what are our orders, sir?"

"It doesn't really matter, Hinters. Go and man the south wall."

Hinters nodded and pulled Tim out of the room. Once they were outside Hinters said, "We got ourselves into another hopeless situation. See if you can find as many arrows as possible."

"But from where?" Asked Tim.

"I don't know! Just look around the courtyard. Meet me back at the door to this building. I've got something else to find," said Hinters.

Tim trotted outside. He stopped and searched the chaos before him. He didn't see any barrels of arrows. He noticed that the archers all stood along the wall. So Tim went to the base of the wall and ran along the length of the wall. Finally he found a large barrel, which still contained some arrows. He pulled out all that remained and ran back to the door. Hinters wasn't there. Tim shaded his eyes with his hands and scanned for Hinters. It was difficult to make out anyone clearly in the panicked chaos and smoke of the courtyard. Tim was so nervous that he couldn't stand still. He busied himself with pulling arrows out of the dirt, wooden posts, or wherever he could find arrows in usable condition.

Finally Hinters appeared and waved Tim to follow him. On the far side of the building was a manger. Inside was a dark liquid. Hinters grabbed a bunch of arrows from Tim and plunged them into the liquid. "Soak the tips of all the arrows." Tim obeyed. Once the arrows were ready, Hinters and Tim jogged to the stairs. They climbed the stairs to the catwalk along the wall. They had to hop over dozens of fallen men. Hinters stopped when he reached a torch attached to the wall.

Just as they set down their arrow stash, and large man hopped over the wall and confronted them with his drawn sword. Hinters had his back turned to the man, and Tim shouted out a warning as he drew his own sword. Hinters swiveled as he pulled his sword in one motion and slashed at the invader. The invader stepped back in time to keep one of his legs whole, and cried out as he Hinters slashed the other one. However, this only slowed him down. With surprising speed he charged at Hinters, knocking him off the catwalk. Without thinking, Tim plunged his sword into the invaders' side, before he could fully turn back around. The invader screamed and fell off the catwalk.

Tim searched for Hinters. He was limping up the stairs when Tim spotted him. Hinters went straight to their supply of wet arrows, and said, "Do what I do, and be quick about it, lad. We don't want anymore unexpected company." Hinters poked the tip of his arrow into the torch, and it immediately caught fire. He peered over the wall, took aim, and loosed his flaming arrow. Tim noticed he was breathing like he'd been running, though he'd been crouching down for several minutes. Tim felt panicked and his head swam. He tried to calm himself. Hold it together...don't lose it now, he told himself.

Tim peered over the wall, watching Hinter's arrow fly into the chest of a man, who fell back to the ground aflame. Hinters yelled, "Damn it lad, light 'em up and let 'em fly! Now!"

Tim lit his first arrow, and then searched for a target. There were so many invaders to choose from, Tim didn't know which one to shoot. Then he looked down and spotted two men placing a ladder against the wall just below them. Tim took aim and fired at the nearest one. Tim's arrow buried into the man's shoulder, catching him on fire. Before Tim could load another arrow, Hinters shot the other man between the eyes. The ladder also caught fire, and quickly burned.

Feeling more confident after hitting his first target, Tim quickly loaded and fired several more arrows, hitting his target with all but one of the arrows. Then Tim noticed several men placing another ladder against the wall near them, and stood up to his full height to get the angle Tim needed to fire at the men. Tim loosed his arrow and stuck the near man in the middle of his back. Out of the corner of his eye, Tim noticed an invader aiming at him, and quickly ducked down. An arrow grazed his hair, and stuck in a wood post behind his head. "Damn, that was too close!" Said Tim.

Being more cautious, Tim peered over the tip of the wooden wall, not exposing himself any more than he had to in his search for another target. He spotted several men running at the front gates with a battering ram. Tim quickly lit an arrow and took aim at the lead men carrying the ram. As soon as he loosed the arrow he ducked down, not wanting to give the enemy more than a moment's opportunity at him. He peered over the tip of the wall, and saw the lead man on the ground with Tim's arrow in his back. Another man quickly took his place, and the battering ram was again on its way to the gates. Tim loaded another arrow and loosed it. When he looked back over the wall, he saw that his arrow stuck in the ram itself, having missed its carriers. The battering ram was on fire, and the men near the flaming arrow dropped the ram, and it thudded to the ground. Officers shouted instructions, and soon a bucket was brought to the ram, and the fire was doused.

"Damn it all," Tim breathed. The invaders picked the ram back up, and ran it into the gates. The gates shuddered, but held. By now Hinters saw what was happening at the gates, and fired at the battering ram himself. Between Tim and Hinters, in the next minute, several arrows struck the ram and the men carrying it. With the ram on fire again, it was difficult for Tim to see through the smoke. Tim pulled himself up so that his head and shoulders were above the wall.

Just as Tim began to reach down for another arrow, he felt a burning pain in his left shoulder. Tim fell to the catwalk, grabbing for his shoulder. An arrow pierced completely through his shoulder. He cried out in agony. Tim couldn't believe he'd been hit. The pain was unbearable, and Tim quickly lost consciousness.

Five

Tim awoke to the sun shinning on his face. He rolled onto his side to get up, and pain shot through his shoulder and he cried out. Tim eased himself back down. The sun shown through a window without curtains. He lay on the ground with a dirty-smelling pillow under his head. Several other men lay on the ground nearby. They all appeared to be bandaged. Then Tim remembered about his shoulder, and that he'd been shot. Tim gingerly explored his bandaged shoulder with his fingers. The arrow was gone, leaving behind a tender shoulder. Tim's shirt had been torn off his left arm. He didn't recognize the room. He was curious about where he was, and tried to sit up, but his head swooned in pain and he fell back again.

A sharp pain woke Tim the next morning. He reached for his shoulder, but was stopped by a firm hand. Tim looked up to see an old man staring kindly at Tim. The old man worked on Tim's shoulder. The old man said, "Leave the shoulder to me, boy. I must change the dressing to prevent infection. I know it hurts like the devil. I'll give you something for the pain."

Tim nodded and put his head back down on the pillow. The old man finished redressing Tim's shoulder and went over to the only table in the room. He mixed some powder into a glass of water, and returned. The old man put the cup to Tim's lips and said, "Drink this. It will give you some relief." Tim stared into the man's face for a moment, and then obeyed. The elixir tasted awful, but being desperate for some relief, Tim drank it down just the same. A few minutes later Tim became drowsy and slept.

When he came to the next day, two men picked him up. Tim cried out in pain, yet the men didn't seem to notice. They took him outside, and loaded him into a wagon. The jarring of his shoulder was worse as they lifted him over the edge of the wagon,and he cried out in pain. "Aww! That hurts!"

"Oh my, be careful with the little girl, lads," said a voice. Tim turned his head to see a large man with a smug smile on his face. His face had a large burn mark on the left side. Tim immediately hated his face, and turned away. Another man was dropped next to Tim, bumping his shoulder hard enough for Tim to cry out involuntarily. The man with the burned face laughed.

"We've got all the wounded loaded, Marvinian," said one of the men.

The man with the burned face said, "Then get us moving! We've a long road ahead. I want to be in my bed by tomorrow night." Tim looked at the burned face and thought, I'd better remember Marvinian's name.

Marvinian grew up in the shadow of Teagle Castle. It was the only home he'd ever known. Bjorn, his father, had been a soldier in Lord Teagle's military, as had his mother. Bjorn's grandfather and father served as soldiers to Lord Teagle's predecessor, and they expected that Bjorn would follow in the family business. From an early age Bjorn was taught the skills of warfare. He grew up quickly. While other children played together, Bjorn trained with his father and grandfather in the sword, bow and knife. Bjorn's father pushed him hard, often injuring Bjorn. Father believed it his job to toughen up Bjorn, giving him his best chance of survival in war. Bjorn's grandfather, while a battle hardened veteran, approached Bjorn's training with a lighter touch. Grandfather pushed Bjorn to strengthen his skills, yet took care to not hurt Bjorn more than a bruise. He wanted Bjorn tough, but not afraid of being injured. Grandfather believed that a fearful warrior was a vulnerable warrior. He wanted Bjorn to be a confident warrior.

Marvinian's mother, Logertha, was raised a shield maiden from an early age. Being desperate for more troops, Lord Teagle created a shield maiden development program just after Logertha was born. She was amongst the first class of shield maidens, as her training began as soon as she was strong enough to lift a shield. Lord Teagle's captains examined all young girls, and selected the toughest and strongest. Her parents feared for Logertha, and begged the captain to relieve her of training, but he wouldn't hear of it. Logertha and nineteen others made up the first class of Teagle's shield maidens, and all of them were placed in a special unit of their own. They trained to fight side by side, using one another in a teamwork fashion.

Marvinian's parents met during Bjorn's first battle experience. Soon after the shield maidens officially joined Teagle army, they were sent out to protect Scerlandian from invading northmen. During the first day of battle Teagle's left wing was overrun by northmen, wiping out half of them. The next day the twenty shield maidens were sent to reinforce the remaining left wing. On the second day of the battle, the left wing was again heavily engaged. During the battle Bjorn became separated from his comrades, and found himself engaged by three northmen at once. Bjorn foresaw his coming death, but determined to go down fighting. He slashed at the first attacker's legs, disabling him. This gave Bjorn confidence in his chances, but not for long. The second attacker swung his sword at Bjorn, who just turned in time to save his arm from being severed, yet not in time to avoid a deep wound to his upper arm. Reduced to fighting two enemy with one good arm, Bjorn had little chance. Fortunately, his remaining good arm was his sword arm. He dropped his shield, no longer being able to raise it. He fought off the attackers' next advance by parrying one sword, and spinning out of the second's thrust, and was able to slash at his arm. Unfortunately, the wound he inflicted to the second attacker was not deep enough to slow him down.

Bjorn could feel his energy flagging, as blood drained out of his arm. He knew he wouldn't be able to stand much longer, not to mention fight. The two northmen came at him, and Bjorn blocked the first blow, yet he knew he could no longer move quick enough to dodge both attackers' blows. As Bjorn blocked the first northman's blow, time slowed down as he awaited the second blow. But it never came. The second attacker suddenly grabbed his gut and slumped to his knees. Bjorn turned back to the first attacker, noticed his surprise, and took the opportunity to thrust at his chest with his sword. The northman easily stepped out of the way of Bjorn's weak thrust, yet fell to the ground. Both of the northman's legs were severed. Bjorn looked up into the dark eyes of Logertha. Her presence and freshly bloodied sword explained the mystery of the two northmen's sudden death.

Bjorn stared at her, not knowing what to say. He'd never seen a shield maiden in action before, and the sight was more than he could take in. Not to mention that she'd just saved his life from certain death. Before Bjorn could manage any words, Logertha disappeared back into the battle.

After the battle Bjorn waited patiently while the medic tended to his wounds. He was told to lie down and rest, as he'd lost much blood. However, before he could rest, Bjorn had a mission to accomplish. He went in search of the shield maidens' camp. Bjorn quickly wearied, and was about to give up when he found them. Most of the shield maidens sat about the fire eating their supper. At first Bjorn couldn't find Logertha. Not knowing her name, Bjorn didn't know how to ask for her. They all dressed alike. While he stood there surveying the camp, a shield maiden approached him. "We don't allow men in our camp. You must leave."

"I'm looking for the maiden who saved...wait, it's you! You saved my life."

"And what of it? I did what any warrior would have done," said Logertha without expression.

"I came to express my gratitude. Yesterday was just my second day of battle, and I've never faced certain death before."

Logertha softened and said with a smile, "It's good to see you in one piece. I wouldn't want my efforts wasted." Bjorn felt light-headed and slumped to one knee. He awoke to the birds singing in the new morning. Bjorn looked about disoriented, until he saw Logertha sleeping nearby. They were married the next Spring, once the war ended.

Marcus Marvinian came into the world ten months later. His parents often went away to war, and young Marvinian and his even younger brother remained behind, cared for by the castle servants. Bjorn and Logertha had no one else with which to leave their son. Bjorn's father still fought in Teagle's army, and his mother had passed on to the next life. Logertha's parents were killed in a home fire.

Once Marvinian reached double digits in age, he no longer felt content to be left with the castle servants. They tried to watch over him, but he quickly eluded them. Marvinian preferred to be with the palace guard. After days of pestering the guards, they finally allowed Marvinian to train with them. The captain of the guard figured that Marvinian would quickly tire of being bested by grown men, but he would be mistaken in this. Marvinian's defeats by the guardsmen only fueled his resolve to master the trade of weaponry. He quickly became proficient in all forms of palace weapons, his father and grandfather already having begun his training.

The palace guards tolerated his presence, but they were not kind to him. The guards wearied of Marvinian's constant presence, and treated him harshly, hoping he would go away and leave them to their work. In spite of their treatment, Marvinian continued to follow them around like a mangy dog, even when his parents were home. Logertha often had to come to the guard training grounds to drag young Marvinian home.

Each Spring the guard held their tournament. The winner carried with him the title of palace champion till the next Spring. Most all guardsmen coveted this title, and found more energy for their training before each tournament. By the time that Marvinian turned sixteen years of age, he convinced the guard to allow him to compete in their annual tournament. The categories were the sword, the bow, and the knife. Marvinian entered the sword competition. He had limited skill with the bow and knife, but was quite confident in the sword. The guards snickered behind his back, dismissing him as merely a lad. Most of them thought the captain of the guard was merely humoring Marvinian by allowing him to compete. None took him seriously. Most of the guard hoped for the opportunity to humiliate Marvinian publicly, and wanted to be drawn to fight him first. They hoped this sound beating would once and for all rid themselves of his annoying presence. The tournament being single elimination, all expected Marvinian to only be in one fight. And they expected that one fight to be short.

Chester drew Marvinian in the first round. Being a big man, Chester was amongst the strongest in the guard, but his girth and advancing age made him amongst the slowest as well. As the fight began, Chester smiled and danced about the arena, hoping to elicit laughter from his fellow guardsmen. He expected this to be a comedic show, before finally dispatching young Marvinian in the end. Marvinian lunged at Chester, who easily side-stepped him and knocked Marvinian to the ground. However, Marvinian learned quickly, and found a way to get in a few blows. This got Chester's attention, who grew to soon treat Marvinian as a genuine match. In the end Marvinian surprised all as he prevailed over Chester. Chester was humiliated, and his fellow guardsmen were angry with the young Marvinian. When Longstreet drew Marvinian in the second round, he approached the fight with seriousness from the beginning. Longstreet had seen the Chester fight. Being younger and quicker than Chester, Longstreet gave the youngster a terrible beating. In fact, Marvinian's wounds were so severe, many expected him to not recover, but to die in his bed.

Marvinian lay in bed for a month unconscious, and a total of three months before being back on his feet. He remembered clearly the vengeful beating that he'd received, and privately vowed revenge, but was careful to not say anything to any of the guard. Marvinian took his time, and carefully planned the death of Longstreet. He watched Longstreet long enough to learn his habits. Marvinian quickly noticed that Longstreet always went to the tavern on the day he received his wages, and that he normally staggered home well intoxicated to his badgering wife. Marvinian laid in wait for Longstreet on one such evening, and struck him down from behind with his sword. No one ever learned the truth of Longstreet's cowardly murder, but some suspected Marvinian.

When Marvinian came of age, he requested to be admitted to the guard. However, the captain still held his suspicions about Longstreet's death, and refused. Marvinian begged his parents to go to the captain on his behalf. Logertha refused, although Bjorn reluctantly consented. The captain spoke plainly with Bjorn, saying he would admit no cowardly murderer to his ranks. At first Bjorn thought of challenging this charge, but in his heart of hearts he knew it was likely true. Bjorn couldn't put a finger on it, but he sensed something dark about his son.

In fact, Bjorn had spoken with Logertha about their son's nature, and both expressed concern. However, neither parent was skilled in the way of the heart and mind, and knew not how to speak to their son effectively. Bjorn tried on a couple of occasions, but both father and son quickly became confused during these conversations about the boy's nature. Bjorn didn't clearly know what he wanted to say, and his son had no interest in hearing it.

Only the captain granted permission to join the guard, with the exception of the king. But the king rarely interfered with the guard, and would certainly not intervene on Marvinian's behalf. With the captain being still of middle age and in good health, Marvinian figured he'd have a long wait before getting another opportunity to join the guard. He refused to wait years to join the guard, and he would have no other occupation. With the rumors of Longstreet's death being what they were, Marvinian knew that the captain must appear to die of a natural death.

Having little else to occupy his time, Marvinian volunteered to apprentice with the palace physician. As few others wanted this position, the old man delighted to have any apprentice. The long walks into the forrest to secure his needed supplies wearied him. The physician immediately taught Marvinian how to recognize and find the roots and leaves that he required for his medicines. The young apprentice was a quick study, and soon the physician trusted him to find the plants on his own.

Once he sensed he'd gained the physician's trust, Marvinian began asking to stay late after the physician left. At first the physician balked at his apprentice's desire to stay later, being a bit suspicious. The physician didn't believe Marvinian merely wanted to finish his chores. I mean, what boy stays late merely to work more? It took the apprentice changing his story before the physician was convinced. Marvinian cleverly admitted to wanting to stay late to study the physician's books on his own. He told the physician he desired to become palace physician when the old man retired. This pleased the old physician greatly, and then he readily agreed. The physician went so far as to leave out specific books to get his apprentice started out properly. On the first occasion of staying late, Marvinian made a show of gratitude, and sat down to study the physician's book with trumped up zest. After several minutes of this ruse, Marvinian went to the window to be sure the old man was truly gone. Satisfied that he was, Marvinian went to his true interest for staying late.

He climbed up on the stool and pulled down two texts that he'd been eyeing for weeks. One was named, *Poisons and Their Purpose*, and the other called, *Inedible Plants*. The young apprentice applied himself to these books all evening, finally awakening past midnight to a burned out candle and his head on a book.

The next morning Marvinian stumbled into the physician's ward bleary eyed and tired. A chipper physician met him there. "So my boy, tell me what you learned last night. I want to hear all about it."

Marvinian looked at him blankly, not knowing what to say. After a minute he managed to mumble, "I don't know...there was so much information, that..."

"Oh yes, my boy, I didn't mean to overwhelm you with too much to study. I will leave you with merely one lesson per night, and you will report to me the next morning with your learning and questions."

"Uh, yes sir..." Mumbled Marvinian.

So the young apprentice devised a new plan. He started each evening with the physician's lesson, and learned just enough to have a question or two to ask. And then Marvinian studied the books that truly interested him. This went on for several months, until Marvinian had learned enough. He'd come across a plant who's leaves were poisonous, that he could also readily find out in the forest. And if used in the correct dosages, could slowly kill a man.

The physician regularly mixed an elixir for the captain of the guard, who had trouble sleeping at night. Marvinian delivered these daily elixirs to the captain, who wanted them brought at the end of each day. The captain would go home and drink the elixir after he'd eaten his supper. That way the captain typically fell right to sleep. Marvinian began mixing small dosages of the poisonous leaves into the captain's elixirs. The trace amount was so slight as to be unnoticeable. At first the captain detected nothing amiss. However, after a couple of weeks he began to feel more tired. He dismissed it to his advancing age.

Once Marvinian felt confident that his additions were having the desired effect, he decided to make his move. Marvinian went to the guard's practice grounds, and demanded an audience with the captain. The guardsmen laughed and went to inform the captain. "What do you want now, young apprentice? I don't want my elixir till day's end?"

"I'm not here on the physician's business, but my own," said Marvinian.

"What business can you have with me that would interest me? I don't have time for games. Go back to your work and leave me to mine."

"I insist on being admitted to the guard! You know that I have the needed skills. In fact, I'll wager that I have skills beyond any of your men," demanded Marvinian.

The captain laughed. "No young apprentice, you will never be admitted to the guard, as long as I live."

"Then have it your way. I expected your cowardice. I challenge you to man to man combat with the sword! And if I win, you will admit me to the guard," said Marvinian.

Many of the guard had gathered around by now, and laughed when they heard the foolish challenge. For all knew that the captain was amongst the most skilled guardsmen. "Go home to your physician, and leave me be. I have no time for foolish challenges." The captain turned to go.

"As a matter of honor, I challenge you to the death! You cannot refuse, as your code demands," insisted Marvinian. He knew that when a guardsmen was challenged to the death, he could not refuse without suffering the loss of his dignity and honor.

The captain turned on Marvinian with wide eyes. "Foolish lad, you leave me no choice. You shall have your combat. It will be a sad day for your parents."

74

Marvinian had continued his training with his parents, and his skills were as sharp as ever. With the captain at his full strength, he knew he had little hope. But with the captain compromised, he felt confident of his chances.

The captain remembered Marvinian's humiliation of Chester, and took this challenge seriously. This would be no comedy. The captain planned to dispatch Marvinian swiftly. It appeared that he would, as the captain dominated the early going of the combat. Marvinian suffered cuts to both arms and to one of his legs. None of them were mortal wounds, but he was bleeding and losing energy. However, the captain tired quickly, thanks to the poison. The poison probably would have killed the captain months down the road, but Marvinian was impatient to get his commission in the guard.

Marvinian found his chance when he parried the captain's next blow, and quickly countered with his own blow to the captain's back. With the captain's spine severed, the fight was over. Marvinian gave the captain a swift and merciful death, for he held no grudge against him personally. It was merely a means to an end.

Two of the guardsmen immediately drew their swords, and charged Marvinian. He would have died then and there, had it not been for the lieutenant. Lieutenant Geiger drew his sword as he stepped in front of young Marvinian and said, "This ends here! You all know the code. When a man is killed in clean combat, we take no revenge. I will tolerate no breaking of our honor code. This man has earned his place in the guard, and you do not have to like it, but you will tolerate it!" And with this the guardsmen reluctantly stepped away. For they recognized that Geiger was now the captain, and there would be no bucking his authority without severe consequence.

The next day Marvinian showed up for his first day of guardsmen duty. Only Captain Geiger would speak with him. Marvinian made no effort to speak with the other guardsmen, as he had expected a cool reception, and hoped the other guardsmen would accept him in time. He had waited this long to become a guard, he could wait longer for the acceptance he desired. Marvinian kept his head down and worked hard at his assigned duties. And no one worked harder at his weaponry skills than him. The problem came at sparing time. None of the other guard were willing to spare with Marvianian. Captain Geiger thought about assigning someone the task, but decided that the damage to morale too great a cost, and instead chose to spare with Marvinian himself.

Now that he'd won his place in the guard, which he felt entitled to, Marvinian was content to slowly but steadily work his way up the ranks of seniority. He started out as a private, like all new initiates, but was promoted up the next year. As the years went by, Marvinian's ill history was forgotten by most, and overlooked by the rest. By the time that Marvinian made captain of the guard, those few who still remembered, acted as though they did not. All of the guard knew Marvinian to be a hard man, short on mercy and long on vengeance. The few foolish enough to oppose him tended to disappear, and never be heard from again.

Six

After a long dusty day of bouncing in the back of a cart, Tim groaned a sigh of relief when the cart finally came to rest. He faded in and out of consciousness throughout the journey, sometimes fatigue getting the better of him, other times fainting due to the pain.

Tim gently pulled himself up to a sitting position. He'd learned to move slowly. Tim rubbed his eyes and surveyed his surroundings. There were a half dozen carts, similarly loaded with wounded men. Several of the men stirred and looked about with apprehensive gazes, while other men remained still. Tim wondered if they were asleep, or worse. A soldier pulled Tim out of the cart, with no care for his wounded shoulder. Once on the ground, the soldier pulled Tim by the hair over to a tree. Tim stumbled along as best he could. Two men turned to look at Tim. One of the men had a burn mark on his face. Tim groaned.

"Tie him to the tree," said Marvinian as he pointed.

Strong arms pulled Tim against the tree, and bound him hand and foot. "Now rat, let's have a little man to man. My lieutenants told me to leave all of you to die, which I seriously considered. But then I remembered that there's something I need from you worthless, wounded slaves. You see, I have a need for certain information. And I'm guessing you have a need to keep your body in...let's say, fair working condition," Marvinian said with a smirk. "I will ask the questions, and you will answer. Do we understand each other?"

Tim feared what this monster might have in mind. Did he mean to kill him? Or to just make him suffer? And who is God's name is this man? Tim wondered. Tim nodded. "Good, then we can skip all the unpleasantness and get right to it. Tell me which way the invaders went."

What is he asking about? The enemy attacking the village? "Who exactly are you...?" Asked Tim.

"I thought we might avoid the unpleasantness, but alas, if we must," said Marvinian. He nodded to one of his henchmen, who pulled off Tim's boots and socks. Marvinian continued, "Now rat, I hope you won't require me to cut off all ten of your toes. We can still do this without it costing you any blood."

"Wait, don't cut anything! I'll tell you what you want to know! But you have to let me know who you're asking about."

Marvinian chuckled and shook his head. "Listen rat, I'm trying to be patient with you. We both know good and well that I speak of the invaders attacking the village. Of course, they're on their way to another of Lord Teagle's villages, but I must know which one," said Marvinian with a laugh.

Tim shook his head and groaned. He said, "You're probably not going to believe me, but I have no knowledge of where they went. I fell unconscious right when I was shot."

Marvinian rubbed his beard and said, "Well, have it your way, rat." Marvinian took a knife from his belt and knelt at Tim's feet. Without ceremony he cut off his little toe. Tim screamed in pain and bewilderment. He couldn't believe the monster had actually done it! He'd hoped it was only a threat, and that he wouldn't go through with it once he knew that Tim didn't know anything.

Marvinian stood and said, "Williams, bring me the iron." Williams handed him a red hot iron bar that he pulled from the fire.

Tim's eyes grew wide. "My God, what are you doing with that?" Without comment, Marvinian cauterized Tim's bleeding foot. Of course, it wouldn't do to have the boy bleed out before he could tell him anything. Tim screamed.

"Now then, rat, I'd rather not take any more of your toes, not to mention your fingers. They're of no use to me. You can stop all this nastiness by simple telling me about the regiment."

"But I don't know! But wait, I'll tell you what I do know!"

"Now we're getting somewhere. So out with it!" Said Marvinian.

Tim rushed to say, "I was captured by two tax collectors, and they took me to a slave labor camp. They made me clear fields for planting, my sister and I. When they learned that I knew the bow, they put me in their military, or maybe their guards. And then five days ago, Hinters and I were ordered to come help defend the village."

Marvinian rubbed the side of his beard while he considered Tim's words. "So rat, you're telling me that the entire regiment that was sent was two men?"

"Yes, that's it! I don't know about any other regiment, but Hinters and me were sent alone."

Marvinian laughed. "You really expect me to believe that they would send just two men, and one merely a boy? They might have not even bothered to send anyone. Perhaps I can jog your memory by performing a bit more surgery, rat."

"No! I'm telling you the truth." Marvinian bent down to Tim's feet. And then Tim remembered something else. "Wait a minute, there's something else."

Marvinian stood and waited, knife in hand. Tim continued, "The officer in the village was also surprised when just the two of us arrived. Hinters quietly pulled the officer aside and handed him some kind of a letter. I don't think he knew I was watching. The officer opened it, and his eyes grew wide when he read the contents. And then I slipped away from the door. I didn't want them to see me watching. And that's all I know! You've got to believe me!"

Marvinian considered this new revelation as he unconsciously rubbed his burn mark. And then he said, "Perhaps just two were sent because the mission was delivery of information, not village defense. But just the same, I have to be sure you don't know anything else." Marvinian bent and quickly cut off Tim's other little toe.

Tim cried out, but not as loudly. Through tears he said, "That's really all I know. You can cut off all my toes, but there's nothing else for me to tell you about the invading regiment!"

Marvinian nodded and cauterized his toe, and said, "Put this rat back in the cart."

Tim landed with a thud in the cart. He winced and held his shoulder until the pain subsided, but remained conscious this time. Something landed in Tim's lap, and he reached down and picked up a water skin. He sat against the side of the cart and drank eagerly. A voice next to him said, "So you're still alive, then." Tim recognized the voice instantly, and was both surprised and pleased to see Hinters sitting next to him.

"Hinters, you survived! I thought you were dead. I looked for you, and when I couldn't find you, I assumed the worse."

"I'm not sure that still being alive isn't the worst."

"What do you mean? It would be better to be dead?" Asked Tim.

Hinters wiped his brow and took another swig of the water that Tim handed him. "We're slaves of Lord Teagle, lad. And worse than that, we're under the authority of Marvinian. Do you know what kind of man he is?"

"I'm beginning to get a pretty clear idea," groaned Tim.

"We don't know what awaits us. I expect we're to be made slaves, which depending, might be worse than death."

Tim hadn't considered what awaited him. Horrible images of torture and dungeons flooded his mind. "Do you know where we're headed?" Asked Tim.

"I don't, but I expect we're going to Teagle Castle. It's the primary residence of Lord Teagle, although he lives in many places during a given year."

"And who is this Marvinian?" Asked TIm.

"You're better off not knowing," said Hinters.

By the afternoon of the next day, the slaves reached their destination. Tim had never seen anything so grand. Before him sprawled a gray castle that seemed to go on without end. Many smaller buildings surrounded the castle and people milled about the streets that wove through the city. Some of the streets were even lined with cobble stones, a luxury Tim had never seen before. A tall white wall wound its way around the entire metropolis, with men walking back and forth atop it.

Hinters waved towards the castle city and said, "that hell hole be your new home, lad."

"Is that Castle Teagle?" asked Tim.

"The proper name be Teagle Castle, but I've heard the men call it Hell's Holiday," laughed Hinters.

"What do they call it that?"

"I didn't hear them say, but I expect that we'll know enough soon," said Hinters with a grin.

"And what will I do there?"

"We'll do whatever Lord Teagle tells us to do." And with that Hinter lay his head down to rest.

The carts entered the Castle's sprawling village beneath huge wooden gates. Tim could have walked beneath them with Shane on his shoulders, and Amanda on his. Four heavily armed men guarded the gates, and watched without interest as the caravan entered. The carts stopped in front of the stables. One of Marvinian's lieutenants gave instructions to the stable boys for the care of the horses and carts. The wounded prisoners were led around behind the stables to a door in the side of the castle. Tim's stomach growled with hunger pangs. He hadn't eaten since being wounded. The lieutenant said with a smile, "Go into the kitchen and eat whatever scraps the cook has left on the floor. Eat up, rats."

Tim followed Hinters into the kitchen. Hinters helped himself to bread that was cooling on a table, and tossed a leftover crust to Tim, who eagerly ate. "Wait here," said Hinters. Hinters cautiously looked about, and then attempted to leave the kitchen. He was quickly stopped by guards. The guards bound Hinters and took him away. Tim remained next to the bread table. He wasn't sure what to do, without Hinters as a guide. As he looked around, he noticed that only a few other men had joined him in the kitchen. He wondered if the rest were dead. The men grabbed up all the available bread scraps and munched away.

Tim surveyed the kitchen. It was easily as large as his family's entire house. Two boys and four girls worked at various jobs around the kitchen. Nobody seemed to be in charge. Then a full-figured woman appeared and looked Tim up and down. "Well at least this one appears strong enough for the work. The recent new help looked half dead. I have no use for the dead. The last slave they sent me was almost no use to me. Well, don't just stand there, boy. Wash your hands and peel those potatoes in that barrel. And make sure you wash the dirt off first. And the rest of you, be gone! I have no use for you scarecrows."

"And what do I call you?" Asked Tim.

"You'll call me Madame Cook, boy."

Tim nodded and washed his hands in a basin. "So how do I peel these?"

"Oh for the love of the Queen!" Said Madame Cook. "They sent me another idiot! Where did they find you, boy? Why can't they find me boys that have seen a kitchen before?" She picked up the peeler and demonstrated the technique. "There you go, now you finish the rest."

Tim imitated Madame Cook's method and peeled the rest of the barrel. By the time he'd finished, only one kitchen girl remained. He asked her, "What do I do now?" She merely shrugged and went back to her work.

"Do you have a name?" Asked Tim.

"We aren't supposed to talk," said the girl without looking at him. Tim waited for more, but the girl returned to being mute. Tim wandered about the kitchen, not sure what to do with himself. Once he'd been over the entire kitchen, he noticed that the guards were gone. He wandered out the door. Tim found himself in a large room with fireplaces on both ends. Modest fires blazed in both hearths. The fires warmed Tim's cold heart ever so slightly, and he crouched in front of the large stone hearth. He warmed his hands.

A loud voice brought Tim out of sleep. "What in God's name are you doing, slave!" It took Tim a moment to realize who it was that addressed him. She yelled, "Why in God's name is a slave sleeping during work hours!" The volume of her voice immediately jarred Tim fully awake, and he quickly stood and faced the voice. A tall, thin woman in elegant clothing bore down on him. She stood with her hands on her hips and her face red with fire.

"Come with me and face the queen, slave!" Said the woman as she seized Tim's arm with her talons. Tim obeyed. They marched through several hallways and up a flight of stairs. The woman turned left and led him through an open door until they stood in a large den. Two armed guards were stationed outside the door. An older woman sat on a couch. She was dressed in even finer clothing than the first woman, and bore a pleasing face. She looked up in surprise, while her face briefly evidenced warmth before hardening. The woman created something out of yarn and fabric, though Tim didn't know quite what it was.

His captor addressed the older woman, "Your majesty, I've just discovered this lazy slave sleeping by the fireplace in the middle of the afternoon. I brought him to you immediately for proper justice."

"Thank you, Grace. You may leave his justice to me. I will see to him personally," said the queen.

"But your majesty, I am ordered to…"

"That will be all, Grace. You have faithfully discharged your duty. Rest in this knowledge," said the queen pleasantly and firmly. Grace bowed and left the room. The two guards stood aside and allowed Grace to leave. The queen set down her work and waved Tim to a chair. "Be seated, young man." Tim did as he was told. The queen examined Tim's face, noticing a strange mix. He appeared physically healthy, bright of mind, and ill of spirit. The queen wondered about the causes of his facial messages, and the true nature of his spirit.

"And what is your name?" Asked the queen.

"Tim."

"And what brings you to Teagle Castle, Tim?"

"I uh, I don't know, your majesty. I was wounded in battle…"

The queen smiled, "Ah yes, you have been brought without explanation. And were told of the horrors that awaited you here."

"But how do you…" began Tim.

The queen laughed. "How do I know? I know because I am not a complete fool, whatever you may have been told about the king and me." Tim nodded. "And what horrors do you fear await you?"

"I don't rightly…I suppose I fear something worse than the back-breaking boulder moving I was doing," said Tim.

"And you were right in suspecting as much," laughed the queen. "However, I shall give you a choice. You may accept the something far worse that awaits you in the king's service. Or you may serve me."

"But how may I serve you, your majesty?"

"I make no promises in advance what your specific duties might include. You would do whatever I commanded. However, you would join the servants that tend to me personally."

Tim made a face as though he'd caught wind of a bad smell. "I don't want to perform women's work."

84

"Women's work? What exactly do you picture that you would be doing for me?" Asked the queen.

"That you'd have me arranging flowers or something."

The queen laughed heartily. "Oh my precious lad, you've given me a most humorous moment. I have a mind to make you my court jester. However, because you have balked at my generous offer, you shall spend one month working for the king. At the end of that time I shall send for you. At that point you may be given one chance to reconsider your decision. And if you are half as wise as I believe, you shall have long since reconsidered before the end of the month."

And with that, the queen rang a bell. Grace immediately reappeared. "Take this servant to Grimwald. Tell him to place this servant in the refurbishment duty."

"As you wish, your majesty," said Grace. She glanced at Tim with delight upon her face.

Tim stood gawking at the queen, and regretted his hasty comment. But there was nothing to be done now except to take his medicine, and follow Grace to his fate. Tim tried to imagine what the refurbishment duty might include. He didn't know, but he was sure he wouldn't like it. Grace interrupted his reverie by saying, "What are you waiting for, slave? You will do as her majesty said and follow me immediately." Tim exhaled deeply, and followed Grace out of the den.

Grace led Tim back down the corridors and out through a rear door that he hadn't seen before. They walked along a dirt path behind the castle. Tim noticed a terrible smell, but couldn't place it. They entered a small wooden building. The building only contained a single room, with an older man sitting behind a rough, unpainted table. The man pored over papers that were scattered across his desk. He wore spectacles and looked up when Grace and Tim entered the room. Grace placed her kerchief over her nose and said, "Grimwald, I have a new slave for you. The queen commands that he is to be put into the refurbishment duty." With that said, Grace bowed stiffly, turned and left.

Grimwald smiled as he pushed back from his desk. "Of course you will be in the refurbishment business. That's the only business that I have," said Grimwald with a toothless smile. "Oh, you're going to enjoy the refurbishment duty, my young lad." He walked over to a barrel and pulled out a rag. The rag appeared to have been clothing at one time, but now looked like something with which to clean up messes. "Tie this over your nose, young lad," said Grimwald.

"Why would I want to do that? It stinks like pigs have been wrapped in it."

"Oh, I'm sure you'll find you want it quite presently, young lad. There are things worse than pigs," said Grimwald with a laugh. Grimwald waved Tim to follow him.

Tim stepped out through a back door, and turned and retched onto his boots. The smell was overpowering. It was the strongest, and most offensive smell he'd ever known. Tim eagerly tied the rag around his face, being sure to fully cover his nose, holding the rag in place with his hand. The smell remained awful, but Tim was able to prevent himself from retching again, at least for the moment.

"Like I said, you'll be wanting that rag. You'll find it will be your best friend," said Grimwald.

Tim followed Grimwald down stairs to the wall of the castle. Then they followed a fence that first ran perpendicular to the castle, and then turned at a right angle to run parallel to the castle. Along the fence were numerous chamber pots. About half of them were nicely painted ceramic pots, and the other half were plain brown pots. All the pots stunk to high heaven. The prevailing wind blew the smell away from the castle, which was how this location was selected.

Three boys were working with the chamber pots. Grimwald marched Tim up to the three workers and said, "I've good news for you lucky lads. I bring you fresh meat. You will teach this young lad here to master this most honorable trade." And with that Grimwald grinned, and turned to leave.

All three boys had rags around their noses. When Tim looked more closely, he noticed that they all had two or three rags. Tim immediately understood the purpose of multiple rags. The oldest boy appeared to be a year or two older than Tim. He said, "I'm Samuel. And who are you?"

"I'm Tim."

"Ok Tim, we take the brown pots and use them in the compost mix. And we take the picture pots and dump them into these large barrels," said Samuel.

"What are the picture pots?"

"They're the fancy ones painted with pictures," explained Samuel. "Come with me. You'll be paired with me today."

The other two boys were handling the brown pots. Tim quickly figured out that these were the pots that contained the constitutional excrement. The picture pots contained urine. "We have picture duty today. They have brown duty. No one wants brown duty, but we all must take our turn and do our duty," said Samuel.

The picture pots were light enough for one boy to handle them. Tim and Samuel took turns picking up the picture pots and dumping them into a large oak barrel. After a few minutes, Tim turned his head and retched again. "Next time you have to do that, take it over to those bushes. The smell's bad enough without you adding to it. And here, this will help some," said Samuel as he handed Tim another rag. Tim nodded and eagerly tied it to his face.

Four more times throughout the afternoon Tim had to run to the bushes to retch. He had to run since he didn't have much warning. The smell was so bad, that Tim always felt on the edge of heaving. The other two boys chuckled each time Tim retched. Samuel looked away.

Towards sunset Tim and Samuel had emptied all the lovely picture pots. Tim turned to Samuel and asked, "Now what?"

"Now we take the barrel to the tanner," said Samuel.

"What for?"

"You'll see soon enough," said Samuel.

Tim shrugged. Samuel put the lid on the barrel, and then Tim helped Samuel load the oak barrel onto a cart. Samuel tied the barrel in place, so that it wouldn't slide around and spill. Then Samuel took one handle, and gestured to Tim to take hold of the other handle. In unison they lifted the front end of the handcart, and began marching down the road. The going was slow and arduous, as the cart was heavy. "Wouldn't this be easier with a horse or donkey?" Asked Tim.

"Aye lad, it would indeed. If you've got an extra horse tied up somewhere, I'm sure if would be easier." Samuel turned to the right once they reached the main road through the village. They passed shop after shop. Even though pushing the cart would be less physically demanding, Tim felt relieved to have the lovely smell behind him, as he and Samuel pulled the cart.

The tannery was the last shop on the road, and there were no buildings nearby. No one wanted to set up shop next to the tannery. The smell was unbearable at the castle wall, and almost as bad at the tannery. Samuel guided the cart to the back of the tannery. They set the cart legs down and Samuel went inside to find the tanner. As the tanner stepped outside to where Tim waited, he waved to Samuel. Samuel said to Tim, "Bring back the barrel and cart when you're done."

"Wait, won't you wait and help me?" Asked Tim.

"Oh no, the new guy gets to help the tanner unload the piss. I wouldn't want to take any of the fun away from you," said Samuel with a grim face as he walked back towards the castle, untying his rags as he walked.

"Alright then, laddie, grab the other end of that barrel. We'll be taking it over to that pit," said the tanner as he pointed.

Tim and the tanner poured the piss into the pit. Inside the pit were dozens of folded cow skins. As soon as the barrel was empty, Tim turned and ran over to a nearby field and retched. The tanner laughed and said, "Ay lad, the new ones always do that. But it'll pass. It's not so bad once you get used to it."

"I don't want to get used to it," countered Tim. The tanner laughed. "And how is it that you don't wear a rag?" Asked Tim.

"Oh I did every day the first years of my work in the trade, but I haven't needed it for years now. See what you have to look forward to?" Said the man with a grin.

Tim rolled his eyes and loaded the empty barrel back on the cart and returned to the castle. When he arrived the sun had already set, and the yard was dark. No one was there. Tim left the cart there and went back to Grimwald's office. He wasn't there. Tim looked around, and couldn't find anyone. He went back inside the castle. The temperature had dropped below freezing by sunset, and Tim found his way back to the fireplace. It was the same place he'd warmed himself this morning.

Within ten minutes Grace found him. "What are you doing, slave? Didn't I make it clear that no slaves be allowed to warm themselves here? Where do you belong?"

"I don't know, Madame," said Tim.

"You will call me Madame Grace. And you belong in the slave's quarters." Grace took Tim by the collar and walked him through the kitchen and out behind the castle. There stood a long wooden building. Grace walked Tim to the door and said, "Find yourself an empty bed. And here's your supper." She handed Tim a burnt piece of bread. "There's a water barrel in the corner."

Tim found the water barrel and gulped down several cupfuls of water. He needed much water to choke down the burnt bread. His body also needed rehydrating. He'd lost much of his water to the retching. Once he'd finished with his meal, he surveyed his new home. The building resembled the barracks he'd lived in a short time ago, except that the bunk beds were built into the walls like a prison, and the door wasn't locked. Tim found an unoccupied bunk in the corner and lay down. He was without energy. Tim's loss of energy was partly the result of a long day's work, but partly due to his heart becoming heavier and heavier. How does a lad remain hopeful when nothing good comes his way? He fell asleep before he knew it.

The next morning he was awakened by Samuel shaking him. "Get up, Tim. Time for us to begin duty." Tim stared at Samuel blankly, and then remembered his afternoon the previous day. Tim groaned. He followed Samuel into the castle and up to the sleeping floor. He walked along the corridor and picked up the picture pots. They carried two each, leaving the brown pots to the other boys. Tim and Samuel carried the pots down to the castle wall. By the time they had all the picture pots at the wall, it was time for their meal. It was slightly better than the fine fare of last night. He gulped down dried bread, gruel and water. He was so hungry that it was difficult to think of anything else.

By the end of the second day on refurbishment duty, Tim thought about his mistake in judgment. Why was I so stupid to not take the queen's offer? I don't know if I can make it till the end of the month...I suppose I'll have to, though.

The days to follow came in two varieties. The good days were picture pot days. The bad days were brown pot days. By the end of the first week Tim was able to work the picture pots without retching. He never adjusted to the brown pots. Every brown pot day was retching day for Tim. By the end of the month Tim had lost weight. It wasn't from his diet that he lost weight, since he was given plenty of bread and even meat every other day. It was the retching that cost him precious pounds. Tim counted the days until the queen should send for him, if she did. Tim prayed she wouldn't forget.

The thirtieth day finally arrived. Tim had counted each day on a scrap of paper that he'd taken from the floor of Grimwald's office.

Tim found more energy this day. He kept watching for Madame Grace. Every twenty or thirty minutes he looked around for her. When the day finished he waited at the barracks' door. The sun set without Tim seeing her. Long after the other servants slept, Tim finally gave up waiting and turned into his bunk. The next day Tim kept an eye out for Grace. He again regularly looked up in the hope of seeing her. However, another disappointing day ended with no sign of her. Finally, two days after the thirty days had ended, Grace appeared at the barracks. She came just as Tim finished eating his bread and piece of meat. She didn't say anything, but merely waved him to follow her. Tim eagerly set down the last bit of bread and followed.

The queen sat in her den, as she had when Tim first met her. This time she held a small dog in her lap. The queen stroked the dog's head. The dog lay in her lap with his head on his front paws.

Grace said as they entered, "The slave that you requested, your majesty." The queen looked up at Tim, and waved him to a chair. She gazed at Tim leisurely as she cocked her head to one side. She noticed that the light in his eyes seemed dimmer than their first meeting. "I see that refurbishment duty has not suited you. You're bone thin. And your poor eyes have lost some light."

"Yes, your majesty. I was a fool not to take your offer," said Tim.

"Of course you were a fool. Yet perhaps you had to find out for yourself that the women's work I offer you is a privilege."

"I'm sure it is, your majesty," said Tim.

"So I now give you one final offer to work for me. And if you..."

"Yes, your majesty, I'll take it!" Said Tim as he interrupted the queen.

"Now don't you want to hear what the work shall be?"

"No, your majesty, I'll take any work that you offer," said Tim.

"Well, I see that refurbishment duty has refurbished your attitude, young lad."

"Yes, your majesty," said Tim.

"You shall report to Philippe. But first you shall be fitted for a decent set of working clothes. I won't have you working in or around the castle wearing those rags. And they stink to high heaven." The queen rang a bell, and Grace entered presently.

"Grace, you will take Tim to the tailor, to be fitted for proper working clothes. He shall be Philippe's apprentice. And once he wears proper clothing, you shall burn the clothes that he now wears. And see to it that he bathes," said the queen. Grace bowed, and gestured for Tim to follow.

"Thank you, your majesty. I thank you for your mercy," said Tim.

"Yes, now be off with you," said the queen.

The following morning Tim reported to Philippe as instructed. His shop connected to the castle, but on the opposite side from the waste refurbishment work, thank God. Tim asked for directions from a fellow servant, and found his way to Philippe. The shop had a strong smell of leather. Pieces of leather in various shapes and sizes adorned the shop. Two of the shop walls each sported a window. The windows were small, yet yielded some light.

A young man sat behind a counter, sitting on a stool and bent over a piece of leather in his lap. The leather was attached to something that resembled a boot. Philippe was the royal cobbler. He wore a vest, along with a waist apron. His shirt sleeves were rolled up to the elbow. In front of him was a low table, which held a number of tools. Philippe surprised Tim, in that he was only a handful of years older than Tim.

Philippe looked up when Tim entered. Curiosity quickly turned to amusement. Philippe offered his hand to shake as he said with a twinkle in his eye, "I'd stand, but I don't want to lose my soul. That would be terribly expensive." Tim stared at Philippe in confusion. Philippe responded, "You know, my soul, like the soul of the boot in my lap." Tim smiled politely and shook his hand,

and sat at the stool that Philippe offered. Normally Tim would enjoy such humor, but today he was too nervous to find much of anything humorous. "So, Grace tells me that you are to be my apprentice."

"Yes, that's what the queen told me," said Tim.

"Well then, we shall have fun together," said Philippe.

"Fun?"

"Oh yes, we shall have fun. And we shall work as well. The king and queen and their court expect their shoes to be mended," said Philippe as he waved at a long line of shoes and boots sitting against the wall. "And you shall learn to repair shoes as well as I."

"What sort of fun shall we have?" Asked Tim.

"You shall see in good time," said Philippe without looking up from the boots in his lap. "Perhaps even soon."

Another boy emerged from the back room. He carried a pile of boots and shoes of various sizes and shapes. The boy twirled around as though dancing, and spilled many of the shoes onto Tim and Philippe. The boy laughed and sang, as though he were at play. The boy stopped with his performance when he noticed Tim, and took Tim's hand and shook it warmly. "Hello my friend, I'm Andrew. I suppose we'll be work mates." Tim nodded and sat back down.

When Tim looked into Andrew's face, it seemed that something was missing. Tim couldn't quite put a finger on what it was, but Andrew seemed different. Perhaps it was merely that Andrew seemed a happy lad, though he must be about the same age as Tim. Or perhaps Andrew was simple-minded. Andrew returned to his singing and dancing about, as he placed the boots and shoes along the wall with the other shoes to be mended.

Tim looked over at Philippe, expecting some signs of annoyance and reprimand. Yet Philippe grinned and continued with his own work without the slightest sign of being perturbed. Tim thought that he must be amongst fools and idiots. Maybe any old fool can repair a shoe. No one else in the castle acts like this.

Tim sat and waited during what seemed an awkward silence. He expected Philippe to give him some instruction on whatever humiliating work awaited him. Tim decided to get it over with and asked, "So what duty would you have me do?"

"Ah yes, I forget myself. I sometimes get so caught up in my work that I forget about such matters as duty. So, I will teach you to make a basic repair. But first, you must wait while I finish the king's boot. For now, you may wander around the shop and acquaint yourself with its contents."

"Just wander about? That's all?" Asked Tim.

"Yes, my good man, that is all," replied Philippe.

"You don't have any trash to haul. Or any waste to remove? Or other such disgusting work that beacons?"

"Heavens no! You expect to be treated like a worthless slave," said Philippe with a hearty laugh.

"Well yes, I suppose I do. Isn't that what we are?" Asked Tim.

"No no, my good man, we are valued servants of the queen. You shall see in good time."

Tim's head seemed to spin. He sat back down to steady himself. This must be some trick...in a moment he'll show me the real work, and then laugh while I heave in the bushes like the last job. Perhaps someone is watching what a good trick I'm falling under. Well, I won't be fooled. I won't let my guard down and play the fool. We shall see what humiliating and degrading work awaits me, he thought.

When his head stopped spinning and he felt steadier, Tim stood and wandered about the shop, as he'd been instructed. After touring the shop several times, Tim became bored with its contents. All that it seemed to contain were leather, wood and various tools, and some thread. Tim sat back down next to Philippe and watched. Tim sat amazed at how quickly Philippe's hands moved, as though they required no instructions, but worked automatically.

When Philippe finished the boot, he set it aside and selected a simple boot from the collection along the wall. He sat back down next to Tim.

"Now you shall learn a simple repair." Tim nodded. "Do you see how the soul has become detached from the body of the shoe?" Tim nodded again. "You take a threaded needle and reattach it like this...It's just like people. They need to be reattached to their souls." Tim watched as the master quickly repaired the right boot. Philippe picked up a pair of boots and set them in Tim's lap. "Now you will do as I did with these," said Philippe.

Philippe watched as Tim began to work the needle and thread through the leather. Once Tim had the first two loops complete, Philippe stood and said, "And there you have it. Finish with that one and show me your work when you're done." And with that Philippe went back to his work.

An hour later Tim presented his completed work to Philippe. It was done, but Tim felt embarrassed. His work looked like a child's work next to Philippe's. "Well done! It's a good start. And now you are ready for another," said Philippe as he pointed to another simple pair of boots.

"But you must fix them. We can't give these boots back to the king! They look terrible!" Said Tim.

Philippe burst out laughing. "Of course we can't give them back to the king. They belong to one of the king's servants. You don't think I would have given you one of the king's personal boots on your first day, do you? Now, do as many of the boots along that wall as you can. They all belong to servants." Tim completed the same task again and again all day. And he continued to do so throughout the first week of his apprenticeship.

The next week Tim sat down in the cobbler shop to continue with the same simple work. Philippe put a hand on his shoulder and said, "Today I have something else for you. Together we will mend a pair of the queen's boots. Philippe set the boots down on the table in front of Tim. They were essentially the same as the other two dozen he'd worked on all last week, yet they were clearly of higher quality. "I don't know if I'm ready..."

"That's precisely why I shall assist you on these," said Philippe.

Philippe began the stitching with precision, completing the first three stitches. He said, "Now, do you see what I'm doing?"

"I guess so, but I don't think I can do that," answered Tim.

"Yes you can. So go and show me."

Tim examined Philippe's stitches, and then slowly attempted to replicate his work. Each stitch required Tim ten times longer than Philippe, yet they looked almost the same. "You see, you can do it! And once you have more experience, you will do it as quickly as I can," said Philippe with a slap on Tim's back.

Tim spent much of the rest of the day finishing the queen's boots. He finished by mid afternoon. Philippe handed Tim a rag and said, "Go over to the chimney and bring back a bit of the blacking."

"Why do you want that?"

"Just get it, and I'll show you," said Philippe.

Tim did as he was told, and returned with the fire blacking. Philippe took the rag and carefully spread it across the queen's boots. Then he took a clean rag and rubbed the boots until they shone. They looked as if new. "There we have it. Now take these to the queen," instructed Philippe.

Tim got lost trying to find the queen's apartments, having only been there twice, and being quite nervous both times. Before he could find anyone to ask for help, Grace found him. Grace seemed always to be watching the castle, as though she had no other duties.

At first Grace eyed Tim suspiciously, but relented when she saw the boots in his hands. Grace showed Tim to the queen once she understood his errand. Grace stepped into the drawing room first, and then announced Tim.

"Yes yes, show him in. I've been expecting him," said the queen.

Grace bowed and waved Tim in. Tim entered and immediately bowed. The queen pet a cat in her lap. When Tim entered the cat jumped off her lap and scampered out of sight. Tim waited for her to speak.

"Well hello, young lad. And why have you come to see me?"

"I return your mended boots, your majesty," said Tim.

The queen looked at Tim with surprise. "They're done already?"

"Yes, your majesty."

"Well then, let's have a look at them," said the queen. She examined them carefully, before saying, "And this is your work?"

"Not entirely, as Philippe helped me."

"You're learning your new craft quickly. Well done!"

"Well done?" Said Tim aloud. He wasn't sure he'd heard the queen properly.

The queen smiled and put on the repaired boots. She walked around the room in them, and being satisfied, she took them off. "You shall continue working under Philippe's teaching. And you shall personally deliver all the repaired boots to me. Do we understand one another?"

"Yes, your majesty," said Tim with surprise and more energy.

"Tell me of your home."

"You mean, my home before all this?" Asked Tim.

"Yes of course, I certainly don't mean the army barracks that you now live in. What other home do you have?"

"It's just been so long since I've been home; although I think of it every day...I live with my father and mother very far from here. We're farmers. Father taught Shane and I to work the land. Amanda, my sister, works inside the house with mother. She also milks the cow and helps with all the meals. We've lived on the farm all my life. In fact, it's the only home my father has known, and it was his father's land before him... but Amanda's no longer there."

"Whatever do you mean?" Asked the queen.

"The tax collectors took Amanda when my father couldn't pay his taxes. But it wasn't fair since the collectors came early. My brother and I followed the tax collectors to see where they'd take Amanda. Shane returned home, and I was captured. They took me to...well, I don't know what to call it."

"It was a slave farm in which you and other captured slaves worked the land under guard," finished the queen for Tim.

"Yes, that's right. I don't know how long I was there. When they found I could shoot a bow and arrow, they put me into the guard. Soon thereafter they sent me and Hinters to battle. We tried to protect a village under siege. But we didn't succeed. The village was overrun and I was wounded and left for dead. My captors, Marvinian's men that is, brought me to your castle. Wait, how did you know?"

"I know almost all of the king's doings," said the queen.

The queen stood at the window with her back to Tim. She pulled a handkerchief from her pocket and wiped at her face. Tim wondered why. He figured that it couldn't be that she was moved by anything about his story. The queen turned to him and regarded him.

"You've had a difficult time. We shall see what we can do about that," said the queen.

"But what, whatever can you mean? What can you do?" Asked Tim.

"I don't know yet. I must think on it," said the queen.

"Do you mean that you shall let me go?"

"Oh no, that isn't possible," answered the queen.

"Why isn't it?"

"You may return to your duties."

"But why isn't..."

"Return to you duties," said the queen more forcefully.

Tim returned to the cobbler shop. He sat back down and resumed his work mending boots. His mind continued to ponder the queen's comments. Why isn't it possible to free me? Is everyone here a slave? And why have they brought me here? None of this makes any sense, thought Tim.

"What's on your mind, mate?" Asked Philippe.

"Oh, nothing much."

"That don't look like nothing to me. Come on, out with it," persisted Philippe.

"Is everyone here a slave? Are you a slave?"

"Of course not," said Philippe with a smile. "I am the queen's nephew."

"You are? So you do this work willingly?"

"Why yes, I love my work. In fact, it is the work that I chose for myself," said Philippe.

"And Andrew, is he a slave?"

"No, he's been a friend these last years. He is my willing apprentice," said Philippe.

"Then no one else is a slave but me?"

"Oh no, there are many slaves in the castle, as well as the surrounding town. All of the men in the refurbishment shop are slaves. All of the men in the tannery are slaves, except for the tanner himself. Most of the servants in the castle are slaves, except for Grace," answered Philippe.

"Why not Grace?"

"She is a special case. The queen rescued her," said Philippe.

"Rescued her from what?"

"She and her husband worked as kitchen servants. And then her husband got moved to soldier, and he was killed in the war. They say he was some kind of hero. And then the queen took Grace for her head of household," said Philippe.

"What kind of hero was he?"

"It is said that he saved the king's life," said Philippe.

"How did he do that?"

"Enough questions for now. That is a story for another time. Back to work with you," said Philippe with a smile.

As Tim finished up the last boot of the day, he pushed back his stool and wiped his brow. He looked out the window, and saw that the sun had already set. He rubbed the fingers on his right hand. They were sore at the end of every day. Philippe emerged from the back room with a broad smile on his face. He said, "You all done, mate?"

"Yes, I just finished."

"Great, then you will join Andrew and me for a pint of ale at the tavern," said Philippe.

"Is this allowed for me?"

"It is allowed if I say it is," said Philippe. "Grab your coat and we're off."

Tim followed Philippe and Andrew out of the shop. They turned to the right, and wound their way through many streets. As they entered the tavern Tim saw that it already contained quite a crowd. Almost every seat was taken. The floor was covered with sawdust, upon which sat wooden tables with backless stools around them. A full-figured woman with graying red hair stood behind the bar preparing drinks and food. Two girls and a boy ran through the tavern serving the tables. Philippe spied what he looked for and waved Tim and Andrew to follow.

The three young men sat down at a table in the corner. Two others already sat at the table, and were arguing over something that Tim couldn't make out. As soon as they sat down, the other boys gave Philippe and Andrew a hearty welcome. Philippe waved at one of the serving girls, who smiled and raised a finger in response. She appeared at the table a moment later, and kissed Philippe on the cheek.

"Sonia! How is my favorite and most beautiful barmaid?" Asked Philippe.

"Oh, now stop with the flattery. Someone might believe you," said Sonia.

"You know I am quite sincere in my praise of you," said Philippe.

"What will it be now? I've got a tavern full of thirsty men."

"Three pints," said Philippe as he patted her backside. Sonia gleamed and hurried off.

An hour later they had finished their pints. Sonia appeared at their table, as if on cue. "Would you lads like another round?"

"Not for me, mates, but you stay and have another," said Philippe. He pulled several coins from his pocket and handed them to Sonia and said, "That's for a second round for my two mates, and keep the rest for yourself." Philippe slapped Tim on the back, winked at Andrew, and kissed Sonia on the check as he left.

Tim and Andrew chatted away while they enjoyed their second pints. Their laughter became louder and louder, as the alcohol took its effect. Tim rarely drank ale, and it had been a long time since his last pint. It was only on Saturday nights that father allowed Tim and Shane a pit with him after supper. Father said it was reward for a good week's work.

Andrew told Tim the story of how he met Philippe. Andrew became animated in the telling and sloshed ale on the man sitting behind him.

"What in the devil's name!" Bellowed the now wet man. He pushed back his chair and turned Andrew around. "Watch where you're tossing your ale! And you be a damn fool to waste it anyways. Oh, it's the cobbler's brat. I might have known."

Andrew laughed at the man whose hair was wet on the right side and dry on the left side. Tim winced when he saw the man's size. And then Tim froze. The man had a burn mark on the left side of his face.

"I'm really quite...I'm so..." but Andrew couldn't get an apology out in between laughing spasms.

"So you find this humorous, do you? I have a mind to give you something else to laugh about, you damn fool," yelled Marvinian.

"I'm…I'm so…" stammered Andrew. He tried again to spit out an apology, but couldn't get it out in between laughing fits. Marvinian grabbed Andrew by the collar and dragged him towards the door. Tim followed, but was delayed as the tavern was so crowded. The patrons parted for the angry man, but paid no attention to Tim's pleadings to make way. By the time Tim made his way out of the tavern door, Marvinian kicked at a sprawling Andrew. Blood spewed from Andrew's mouth.

Tim charged Marvinian and knocked him to the ground. Marvinian picked himself up slowly and awkwardly, as you might expect for a man who'd been drinking, and barked, "So you want a piece of this too? Ah, so it's the rat that's missing a couple of toes. I hope you feet healed up real nice," he said facetiously.

"No, I don't want to fight. Just leave my friend be, and we won't bother you anymore. He's most sorry for spilling ale on you," said Tim.

"No lad, it be too late for that. I'm already hot and bothered by the two of you." He came at Tim and threw a wild punch, which Tim easily dodged. The man sputtered out his frustration and whirled and threw another punch at Tim. Tim raised his arm to protect himself, and was knocked to the dirt. If Marvinian were sober, Tim and Andrew would be ready for a doctor by now. However, thanks to his inebriated state, Tim and Andrew still maintained their consciousness.

By this time a crowd had gathered. The tavern had emptied to watch the spectacle. Marvinian took stock of his audience. He seemed to make a decision, and moved towards the two boys.

This man's too strong for me. I have to get us out of here before he kills us. My only chance is to catch him by surprise, thought Tim. Tim feigned as if to run away, and quickly reversed his path and charged Marvinian again. This time he caught him off balance and knocked him into the side of the tavern. The man hit his head, and was temporarily confused. Tim ran to Andrew, picked him up and threw him over his shoulder and began to run as fast as he could, which wasn't very fast. Tim looked over his shoulder and saw that the man lumbered after them. Tim swore under his breath and tried to run faster, which was difficult with a boy almost his own size draped over his shoulder.

The offended Marvinian quickly caught them and sent them both sprawling to the ground like bowling pens. Tim rolled over and watched for the next blow. Fortunately, the man was picking himself up from the ground. Tim grabbed a piece of wood laying next to him and ran at the man, catching him on the side of the head as he was just standing up. Marvinian hadn't seen the blow coming and was knocked senseless back to the ground.

Tim didn't wait to see if he were out cold. Tim picked up his charge and hurried back to the cobbler shop. When he finally arrived he was exhausted. He set Andrew down and checked the doors. They were locked fast. In a state of panic Tim desperately searched for a way in. He considered breaking a window, but found an unlocked window that he was able to crawl through.

This was not Andrew's first experience with being pushed around. He grew up with his family in Teagle Village, the village surrounding Lord Teagle's castle. Andrew lived with his father and older brother, Jonathan. His mother died during his childbirth. His father slipped into a depression when his wife died, and never fully came out of it. She had been father's best and only friend. For a month he didn't do much of anything, except to stare out of the window. His brother and sister in law cared for the young boys until he came out of his stupor. Finally his brother pulled him out of it, reminding him that his Jonathan and Andrew needed him. Father nodded and resumed his work. His brother and sister in law lived with them for the first year after mother's death. Once Andrew reached a year of age, father was able to care for him on his own, with a little help from Jonathan.

Andrew and Jonathan worked with their father as carpenters. Jonathan took to carpentry right away, being sturdily built and having an eye for it. Andrew often found himself making mistakes. He would measure incorrectly, or he would cut outside the lines, and his work often resulted in Jonathan or father taking extra time to fix Andrew's work. Father and Jonathan often boxed Andrew's ears when he made a mistake. Father thought Andrew wasn't trying hard enough. Jonathan knew that his little brother didn't have the aptitude for the work, and hated him for it. Jonathan thought that Andrew was letting down the family, and especially father. When Andrew made mistakes, Jonathan would check to see if father was watching, and if not, he would knock Andrew to the ground. Father didn't tolerate Jonathan bullying his brother to that extent, and Jonathan quickly learned to make sure father didn't see it. Andrew took the abuse from his brother without protest. He felt like he deserved it. He merely picked himself up and went about his day.

Andrew loved to draw on paper. Whenever he found the opportunity, Andrew would draw charcoal drawings of anything and everything. At first Andrew would show them to his father, until he learned that father thought them a waste of time. Father wanted Andrew to spend more time working with wood, and less with charcoal. Jonathan saw that his younger brother had a talent, but could see no practical value in drawing. No one paid Andrew for his drawings, yet people did pay for the carpentry work. Jonathan called Andrew's drawing idle women's work.

For many years father tried to teach Andrew his trade. He kept thinking that with enough instruction and enough ear boxing, Andrew would finally catch on. Yet Andrew never did develop much skill with wood. Finally, at the prodding of Jonathan, father relented in trying to teach Andrew the trade. Father relegated Andrew to being the shop gopher. Andrew would go pick up needed supplies, and deliver the finished products to customers. He would sweep the floor and prepare the simple meals.

One day a young man came into their shop, and placed an order for a large wood table. Once it was completed, Andrew delivered the table to the cobbler's shop. Philippe immediately recognized Andrew.

"Hey mate, we used to play down by river, when we were just laddies," said Philippe.

At first Andrew's face remained blank, and then a dawning awareness emerged. He said, "Oh that's right, you were the one who always caught the fish that we'd cook for lunch."

"That's right, mate," said Philippe.

Philippe and his assistant helped Andrew carry the table into the shop. Philippe already had a table, but it was no longer large enough for his growing business. The new table was twice the size of the old one. Andrew was mesmerized with what he saw. With large eyes he gazed about the cobbler's shop, asking many questions. After answering more questions than he'd ever previously been asked, Philippe offered Andrew a job working for him. Andrew immediately became excited and agreed. However, he wasn't sure what father would say.

Philippe told Andrew to report for work the next morning. When Andrew hesitated, Philippe asked him what was the problem. Andrew said he wasn't sure his father would allow him to work in the cobbler shop. Philippe quickly understood and decided to address Andrew's father himself.

Philippe went back to the carpentry shop with Andrew, and discussed the prospect with Andrew's father. At first Father was reluctant, and wondered who would pick up supplies and make deliveries. Father was angry that Andrew was trying to get out of the family business, and considered it an insult. However, once Philippe mentioned how much he'd pay Andrew, it was settled. Andrew went to work for Philippe the next day.

Seven

Tim ran down the middle of the village. He kept looking over his shoulder at the ravenous wolves chasing him. Each time he looked back they seemed closer. He willed himself to run faster, but his legs tired. He glanced over his shoulder to see a wolf with a huge mouth lunging for him. Tim felt himself shaking. He figured the wolves had caught him. He was startled out of a deep sleep. Tim rubbed his eyes and looked up to find a confused Andrew. "How in God's name did we end up here? Were we so drunk we couldn't make it home?" Asked Andrew.

"Oh my God, it was only a dream!" Tim took a moment to rub his face and gather his cob-webbed thoughts. "No, you were knocked out cold, and I didn't know where else to go."

Andrew screwed up his face, and said, "How was I knocked out?"

"You don't remember spilling ale on that huge man, do you?"

Andrew rubbed the back of his head. "No. I remember drinking a pint with you and Philippe at the tavern, and the next thing I knew I woke up on the ground here." Tim recounted the details of last night's excitement. He was still attempting to jog his memory when Philippe came in.

"Wait a minute, now I remember," said Andrew. "I spilled ale on Marvinian! Oh my God, he'll kill me."

"Are you sure it was Marvinian? You might be confused," suggested Philippe.

"No, I'm sure it was him. Oh dear God, we have to run," said Andrew as he got up to leave.

"But Marvinian wasn't even at the tavern last night," said Philippe.

"He was there all right. He must have come in after you left. Come on, we have to leave now!" Said Andrew.

"Now wait a minute, let's not panic. We'll figure this out," said Philippe.

"Yes, I'm sure it was this Marvinian. We've been previously acquainted," said Tim as he rubbed his feet without thinking.

"Oh my God, I'm a dead man," moaned Andrew.

"It isn't as bad as that. There are limits to his powers. I'll speak to the queen about this," said Philippe.

"He's the king's man. He's the captain of the king's guard, as well as the king's secret warriors. They're sent on missions that the king denies any knowledge of. We're done for," said Andrew.

"Now don't get into a panic and lose your head. We'll just have to figure out a plan. And the queen will help us. In fact, I'll go and speak to her now," said Philippe.

Philippe had only been gone a few minutes when a knock came on the front door. Andrew darted for the window. He ducked quickly, and crawled back to Tim behind the counter. "We have to run out the back door. It's Marvinian! Follow me," said Andrew. Tim followed Andrew as they scampered to the back door. Andrew peered out the window, and then slowly unlocked and opened the back door.

The knocking at the front door became more insistent. A voice bellowed, "Open up in the name of the king! If you don't open up before I count to three, I'll break the damn door in." Tim recognized the voice as Marvinian, as well as his sadistic laugh. Andrew opened the back door wide enough to squeeze out, and Tim followed him out at a dead run. They ran for the forest that was 100 paces away.

They made it halfway to the trees when Marvinian called out, "They're off for the forest. Don't let them make it to cover, damn it!" Tim glanced over his shoulder to see five armed and uniformed men sprinting after them. Tim's head still hurt from last night, but he tried to ignore the pain and will himself to run faster. Andrew made it to the trees first, and darted to the right. Tim turned right and followed a faint path that wound through trees and clumps of bushes. The path came to an abrupt end. Tim stopped. He looked to the left and right, but neither heard nor saw a sign of Andrew. A loud whispered voice called out, "I'm in here. Hurry and get out of sight."

Tim headed towards the voice, and a hand grabbed him and pulled him behind some bushes. Andrew said, "Be silent and still! They can't be far behind." Tim's breathing appeared to him to be as loud as snoring. He willed his breath to deepen and slow. Muffled voices emerged from the stillness of the forest, followed by faint footfalls. Tim pressed into the bushes a bit further and crouched lower. The footsteps passed them. A voice said, "The brats could be almost anywhere by now."

"No, they can't be far yet. They're hiding somewhere nearby. You will keep looking for them. Scour every tree and bush, rock and boulder. We don't leave until we have them," said Marvinian.

Tim put his mouth to Andrew's ear and whispered, "We have to get further away. They'll find us here." Andrew nodded, and crept away slowly. They climbed a low hill. A small clump of boulders guarded the crest of the hill. Andrew and Tim crouched amongst them. They breathed easier. Tim could no longer hear voices or footsteps. Andrew and Tim collapsed onto the ground with their backs against a boulder. "I think they left," said Andrew.

"I'm not so sure. If these men are who I think they are, they won't give up so easily," countered Tim.

"We should stay here for awhile before we go back to town," said Andrew.

"And where are we to go?" Asked Tim. "They know where we work, and can't they find out where we live?"

"They probably already know where we both live. Marvinian can find out anything," said Andrew.

"Then what are we to do?" Asked Tim.

"How should I know? I'm never been in a spot like this before! Do you have any brilliant ideas?"

"I have no ideas! I need time to think," said Tim.

"Our only hope is in Philippe. We'll have to trust him," said Andrew.

"Philippe can't help you now, you scrawny brats!" Andrew and Tim looked up to see the burly Marvinian standing before them with three of his armed men. "And I appreciate you both arguing loud enough to bring us right to you. But no matter, we would have found you anyways," said Marvinian with a chuckle. "Bind their hands behind their backs."

Marvinian's men led them back to the castle. It was a long, weary walk for the boys. They stumbled and fell several times, as the soldiers pushed them along, scuffing their knees and much of the rest of their bodies. When they reached the castle they were taken down a long hall. At the end of the hall was a locked door that Tim had never seen before. Marvinian unlocked the door and lit a torch. Before them was a winding flight of stone stairs leading down into the dark. A dank smell became stronger and the air more stifling the further down they went. At the bottom of the staircase they were thrown into a cell, and the door was slammed and locked behind them. Marvinian's men left. A dim candle ensconced on the wall provided the only light, which wasn't much. As their eyes adjusted to the dark, features slowly took shape.

They lie on a thin layer of damp straw, beneath which was hard and rough stone. Their cell contained only a lidded-bucket in the corner. Stone walls surrounded them on two walls, while metal bars occupied the remaining two walls. Their hands were still bound.

"I don't know if we'll ever get out of this dungeon. Few that come in here are ever seen or heard of again," said Andrew.

"Turn your back to me so we can untie our hands," said Tim. Andrew pushed with his legs until his back and arms bumped into Tim's. It took awhile, but they eventually untied each other's ropes. Both boys rubbed their wrists, as their hands had gone numb.

"So now what?" Asked Tim.

"Now we wait."

"Wait for what?" Asked Tim.

"Until they decide what to do with us...or at least give us water and bread."

Tim stood and took hold of the barred door to their cell. He shook it. It held fast. He did the same with the other barred wall, and found the same result. Tim sat with his back against the stone wall.

"But won't Philippe help us? He said he would speak to the queen on our behalf," said Tim.

"I wouldn't count on that too much. Marvinian's a powerful man with the king."

"But isn't the queen powerful too?" Asked Tim. Andrew responded with a stifled laugh.

Tim woke with a start. The dungeon warden clattered their water cups onto the floor of their cell, and then dropped two lumps of stale bread onto the straw. He turned and left without comment. Just as Tim reached for his lump of bread, a rat pounced on it. Normally Tim wouldn't consider touching a rat, but given how hungry he was, he knocked the rat to the wall without even thinking. Then Tim had a second thought, and eyed the temporarily stunned rat, wondering if he could choke it down. Before he decided, the rat recovered and scampered away. One piece of bread per day barely kept them alive. Both boys sat and consumed their sumptuous meal in silence. When they had swallowed the last bit of bread Tim looked at Andrew and said, "It's been two weeks now. I don't think they plan to let us out of here."

"That's what I told you! We've been left to rot here. You don't cross Marvinian and live to tell about it," said Andrew.

Tim thought for a moment, and then bent down to his knees and inspected the walls and floor. He moved his hand over each stone and mortar. "What are you doing?" Asked Andrew.

"Searching."

"Searching for what? A secret trap door that leads to the maiden's dressing chamber," said Andrew.

"That's very funny. It's time we figure a way out of here. I'm not waiting any longer for us to be let out. We have to find our own way out."

"Well, good luck with that," said Andrew as he lay down on his side. Tim continued with his search. He carefully examined each mortar seam between each pair of stones. Tim had already examined the cell a couple of days before while Andrew slept, and hadn't found anything. However, he couldn't tolerate merely sitting and waiting and hoping for someone to come. He no longer expected that anyone would come, and Tim felt like he was beginning to go crazy. He sometimes thought he saw things in the dark dungeon. At other times he imagined that he heard voices, or even footsteps on the cold stone. In order to ward off insanity, he continued to explore the cell with more care this time, hoping that he'd missed something before. Plus, he didn't have anything else to occupy his time. There are few things more dreary than being confined.

Tim reached the back corner of the cell, where stone wall met stone wall. For some reason he couldn't explain, he allowed an even more careful examination of the corner. He couldn't see well, as this was the dimmest part of the cell, and he relied on his fingers. As his fingers moved over the stone just above the floor, he noticed a slight depression in the mortar. He ran his fingers around the entire stone and found that the mortar was thin throughout the perimeter of the stone, and even missing in some spots. His heart rate increased. Tim used his finger nails to scrape off the remaining mortar. As he became more excited, he scraped more vigorously. Tim's fingers began to bleed, but he paid no attention.

Once he'd scraped away all of the mortar, Tim wedged his fingers into the crevice on both sides of the stone and pulled. Nothing happened. The stone's weight made moving it at all a challenge. He sat down and put his feet against the wall on both sides of the stone and pulled again. Nothing happened.

Tim shook Andrew. Andrew pushed his hand away and said, "Leave me in peace."

"I think I've found something. Come check it out," said Tim.

Andrew immediately sat up and said, "Where?" Tim waved him over to the corner.

"Run your fingers around the edge of this stone right here."

Andrew did as instructed. "So what, it's a stone?"

"The mortar is at best thin, and I think I've removed what mortar there was. I think we can pull it out."

"And then what? What good will that do us?" Asked Andrew.

"We might be able to find a way out through that loose stone," said an excited Tim.

Andrew reached down and pulled on the stone, but to no avail. "It won't move. It won't move any more than any other stone in this cursed dungeon."

"Not with our hands alone. We need some kind of tool. We have to find something we can use to pry it loose," said Tim.

"Oh yeah, and we have so many tools to choose from, I'm not sure which one to use," said Andrew.

"Cut the wise cracks and help me find something," said Tim.

"Knock yourself out," said Andrew as he lay back down.

Tim paced back and forth as he said aloud, "There must be something in this dungeon that I can use...but what?" Tim reached into his pockets, but didn't find anything. He sat down and looked over his boots, but didn't see anything he could use. Then it came to him.

Tim scurried over to the bucket. He covered his nose with one hand, while he examined the bucket with the other. The top of the bucket had a metal handle. Tim needed the use of both of his hands. He took off his shirt and tied it around his face and covered his nose. He bent down over the bucket and took the handle off the bucket. Tim went back to the corner stone and tried to wedge the end of the metal handle into the opening between the stone and its neighbor. It wouldn't fit. The end of the handle was bent into the shape of a hook and wouldn't fit into the opening.

Tim put the hook on the floor and placed his boot over it. Then he pulled on the handle until he unbent the hook, leaving the handle with a fairly straight piece of metal. He bent down over the stone, and this time was able to wedge the handle in between the stones. Tim used a sawing motion to break up what mortar remained between the stone and its neighbors. After several hours of work, the stone was now mortar free all the way through.

Tim wedged his fingers along the two sides of the stone and pulled with all he had. This time the stone moved slightly. Tim grabbed Andrew by the shoulder and said, "Hey, I got this stone to move a little! Come help me pull it out."

Andrew said, "If I help you, will you leave me in peace to sleep?"

"If you help me enough to free the stone from the wall, then you can sleep all you want. You can stay here and catch up on your sleep, while I get out of here," promised Tim.

The two boys placed their boots on the wall next to the stone. They wedged their fingers into the space between the stones as best they could. On the count of three they pulled in synchrony.

The stone moved an inch at the most. With renewed energy, Andrew and Tim pulled and pulled, but the stone wouldn't move any further. Then it came to Tim, "We're doing it all wrong. Let's push!"

Tim and Andrew crouched down and pushed with legs, backs and arms. The stone moved several inches in. With renewed hope, they redoubled their efforts, and the stone pushed all the way through until it banged on the ground on the other side.

Tim quickly swiveled his head to see if the warden was coming. After several anxious moments, neither the warden nor the guard appeared.

The boys crouched down and peered into the space the stone had left. All they could see was blackness. The lone candle threw so little light into the cell, that almost no light reached the far corner. Tim reached his arm into the opening. His hand quickly ran into dirt. However, with a little pushing, the dirt gave way to an open space.

"Hey Andrew, this hole goes somewhere," said Tim.

"Get out of the way, let me see for myself." Tim backed away and Andrew reached as far as he could into the hole. The opening extended further than he could reach. "I wonder where this leads to?" Andrew wondered aloud.

"There's only one way to find out!" Said Tim.

"Be quiet! You'll bring the warden," warned Andrew.

"I think the hole is big enough for me to squeeze through," said Tim.

"No it isn't. I'm smaller than you, let me give it a try," said Andrew.

"But if I'm keeping you from your sleeping, then I'd be glad to give it a try myself," said Tim.

"Get out of the way, so I can crawl in there," said Andrew.

Tim eyed Andrew's frame, and had to admit that Andrew's frame was slimmer than his own. Tim backed up out of the way and Andrew lay down on the straw. Andrew reached into the opening in the wall with both hands, and turned his shoulders on an angle to fit them in between the stones. Once his shoulders were through the opening the rest of his body followed easily enough. Andrew's entire body disappeared into the hole. Tim poked his head in, but couldn't see anything. "Hey Andrew, where does it go?"

"I don't know yet. Give me a minute," said Andrew.

Tim sat with his back against the wall and waited. He kept looking at the opening. Finally he lost his patience, and called out to Andrew again, "Hey Andrew, where the hell are you?"

Tim received no answer. After a minute of waiting, he squeezed himself into the hole. It took some pushing and pulling for Tim to get his shoulders clear of the opening, but he was well motivated. It helped that he'd lost weight. Tim couldn't push both shoulders clear of the opening. Then he had an inspiration, he pushed both hands and arms through first, and put his hands on the far side of the stone wall, and pulled himself through the opening. He ended up fairly scratched up, but Tim did get himself through.

The opening went straight at first, and then bent to the right. Tim called out to Andrew again, but still received no response but the strange sound of his voice underground. Tim glanced back into the dungeon. He reached down and picked up the stone. He thought it would take Marvinian longer to figure out how they escaped if he returned the stone to it's original spot. It turned out to be quite difficult to replace the stone without Andrew's help. Not only was it heavy, but Tim scrapped up his fingers even more as he fitted the stone back into it's well in the wall. Tim rubbed his sore hands on his pants, and turned to leave.

Tim crawled on all fours. He scraped the sides as he crawled, as there was barely enough room for him in the tunnel. After what seemed like hours of crawling, Tim paused. He tried to look behind him, but everything was black in any direction he looked.

Tim considered turning around, but quickly dismissed the thought since there was nothing but death to return to.

Tim resumed his slow crawl in the dark. He had lost any sense of his direction, and had become disoriented in the total darkness of the tunnel. His breathing began to increase. His heart thumped so loud that he wondered if he were on the verge of a heart attack. Sweat poured down his face. Tim stopped and wiped his brow with the back of his sleeve. "Come on Tim, get ahold of yourself. Don't crack on me now," he said aloud.

Tim paused his crawling and forced himself to slow his breathing down, and take longer and deeper breaths. He knew he risked panic if he allowed his breathing to become too rapid. In a few minutes he felt calmer, but not much. He resumed his crawling, praying that he would get somewhere before he went crazy. The tunnel seemed to be sloping upward, but Tim couldn't be sure, since he continued to feel disoriented and on the point of panic. Then Tim felt something brush against his cheek. He swatted at whatever it was. His mind imagined spiders creeping on him, and he redoubled his crawling speed. Spiders or something continued to brush against his face. Tim tilted his head down. He began to sweat more profusely.

Tim crawled faster, feeling desperate to get out of this underground mine. A moment later and he burst out on the tunnel and rolled over several times before coming to rest against a tree. He wiped at his face, but didn't feel any insects on him. His side hurt where he fell into the tree. After he calmed down a bit, he picked himself up and looked around in all directions. Tim stood in the forest, but he didn't recognize exactly where he was. The thick canopy made the lighting dim, and he couldn't see much. Tim brushed himself off. When he glanced down at himself, he looked like he'd been rolling around in the dirt. Well, in fact, he had been.

"What took you so long," came a voice out of the forest.

Tim started and turned around. "Andrew, why did you go off without me? I almost had a heart attack in there!" Said Tim.

"I figured out where we are. Come check it out," said Andrew as he turned to head uphill.

Tim followed Andrew, running a bit to catch up. He didn't want to be left behind again. Andrew led them through a winding trail that slowly, but steadily went up a gentle incline. Once they reached the top of a hill Andrew crouched behind some bushes. Tim knelt next to Andrew. Andrew pointed off in the distance, "You see that? There's the castle."

"You mean we crawled all that distance?" Said Tim.

"You crawled? Shortly after I got through the opening I figured out that I could stand up. It didn't take me that long to get here."

"There was room for you to stand up in there?" Asked Tim.

"Yeah, it was narrow, but plenty tall. I can't believe you crawled the whole way. No wonder why I had to wait hours for you to get here."

"Oh my God, what an idiot I am," said Tim.

"Well, you're out now."

"So what do we do now?" Asked Tim.

"I've been thinking about that. You gave me plenty of time to do some thinking. I think we have to find Philippe."

"And then what? What's Philippe going to do for us now? We're escaped prisoners," said Tim.

"I know, but there's no one else we can trust to help us. We have to trust Philippe. Marvinian's men are probably looking for us by now. In fact, I wouldn't be surprised if they're already nearby."

"Then let's get out of here," said Tim.

The boys skirted around the castle, giving it a wide berth. Andrew led them to the West. The terrain was not as thick with trees, so the boys had to travel farther in some spots to remain hidden under the cover of the trees. Tim noticed that they did not seem to be heading towards the town. "Hey Andrew, where are we going?" Asked Tim.

"You'll see soon enough. We have to find a safe place." A half hour later they stopped in a clump of bushes. Andrew whispered for Tim to be quiet. Tim nodded. The boys peered through the bushes at a simple home of logs. At first all seemed quiet there. Andrew stood and began to walk towards the home when Tim grabbed his belt and pulled him to the ground abruptly. Tim put his hand over Andrew's mouth, and then pointed. Andrew attempted to swat Tim's hand away, but he wasn't strong enough, and Tim was determined. Tim pointed in the direction of the log cabin. As the boys looked through the bushes, two men armed with swords at their sides were walking around the log cabin.

"Damn, those must be Marvinian's men. They already found my aunt's place. Damn they're thorough!" Said Andrew. "Now where do we go?" Tim merely shook his head.

Andrew pointed at the door of the cabin. Marvinian pounded on the door. A frightened woman opened the door, holding a crying child on her hip. The woman shook her head from side to side, and then she nodded up and down. Then Marvinian took hold of her hair and gave it a firm yank. She fell to the ground, yet shielded her child from harm. Andrew stood up and took a step towards the cabin, before Tim pulled him back to the ground. Andrew tried to slip out of Tim's hold, but Tim was stronger and sat on him.

Through muffled cries Andrew said, "Damn it, Tim, let me up!" Tim kept his hand on Andrew's mouth, as he knew they were well within hearing if they cried out. Once Marvinian left, Tim let Andrew up.

"I won't let that son of a bitch hurt my aunt," said Andrew.

"Andrew, you can't react like that. There were at least three of them, and they're armed. All we have is our wits, and that won't be enough against three grown men with swords. Andrew kicked at the dirt, but stayed put. Though Marvinian left, the two armed men continued to patrol the property.

"I hate feeling so damned helpless! There's nothing we can do. I can't even hide at my own aunt's cabin. There's nowhere else to go! Now what do we do?" Said Andrew.

Tim shook his head slowly and stared off into the distance. "I so hate feeling afraid and helpless!" Suddenly it came to him, "I got it! We aren't without options. We won't let ourselves be helpless."

"What in God's name are you talking about?" Asked Andrew.

"We go on the offensive," said Tim.

"The offensive? What kind of nonsense is that?"

"We will follow Marvinian, and see what he's up to," said Tim.

For a moment Andrew looked at Tim as though he had lost his marbles. "But that would be suicide."

"It might be, but not if we don't let him see us. I won't run scared any longer," countered Tim.

Then a mischievous grin emerged on Andrew's face. "Well, I suppose you might be right, but just the same, I still think you're crazy."

"At least we will know where they are," said Tim. Andrew noticed a change in Tim. His face brightened a bit, more than it had in weeks.

The boys took off at a trot, knowing they had ground to make up if they were going to follow Marvinian. Every hundred yards they stopped and listened. The last thing they wanted to do was surprise Marvinian by running right into him. The first several times they stopped they didn't hear anything. Tim wondered if he and Andrew were heading in the wrong direction. Then the boys stopped at the crest of a low hill. Right away they heard low voices. They dropped to the ground immediately. They slowly lifted their heads enough so that they could see over the edge of the hill. Beneath them ran a narrow creek. The water chattered quietly and pleasantly.

Six men drank and refilled water skins. One of the men washed his face and neck. It was a warm day. Marvinian consulted with another man, who was pointing down creek. Then Marvinian pointed up creek. The other man nodded. He took two of the men with him and headed up creek. Marvinian waved the other two men to follow him. One of them carried a bow and arrows over his shoulder. All three carried a sword at their side. They walked casually and the other two men chatted as they walked. Marvinian led the way and kept his own counsel.

The boys followed Marvinian downstream. They kept a safe distance behind. They'd learned their lesson about being careless with Marvinian. After waiting until Marvinian and his men curved around to the right along with the creek bed, the boys trotted down the slope. They kept at a slow run until they spotted the backs of the men up ahead. Suddenly the men stopped and turned around. Both boys dropped to the ground without thinking. Tim lifted his head slowly up. Marvinian stared in their direction. Tim dropped his head back down.

"Don't make sudden movements. At a distance, the eye catches movement quicker than form," said Tim. Andrew nodded. Marvinian swept his head from side to side, and then back again. He resumed his march downstream.

The boys waited longer this time, not wanting any more close calls. Andrew picked himself off the ground and knelt on the ground. He waved Tim to follow. The boys trotted ahead, keeping a watchful eye out for Marvinian. They kept at their pace for better than a mile, and wondered if they'd lost them. Then the creek bed opened up into a wide opening. More than twenty men stood talking. Two men stood with hawks sitting on leather strapped forearms. Marvinian stood with another man in the middle. The other man was dressed in fine, yet comfortable clothing. Marvinian spoke, while the other man listened with his arms folded across his chest.

"That's the king," whispered Andrew.

"The man that Marvinian is talking with?" Asked Tim.

"No, I mean the man with torn clothing and a bare head that is carrying the king's stool." Tim punched Andrew in the shoulder. Andrew pushed him back.

"Let's try to get closer and hear what they're saying," suggested Tim.

"Do you know what happens if they catch us?"

"I'm sure it won't be good, but we have to hear what's going on. Maybe we'll hear something about their plans for us," countered Tim.

"You go right ahead. I'll stay right here and keep my neck in its current condition."

Tim shrugged and made his way closer. He hugged the dense foliage along the edge of the clearing. He paused every few paces. The hair on Tim's neck stood up straight. His stomach felt queasy. When he was within a hundred paces he went down on all fours. He crawled forward, making sure to move slowly enough to not make a sound. Tim kept his eyes glued to the men below. One of the hawkers turned and stared in his direction. Tim froze. The hawker went back to talking with another man. Tim exhaled and resumed his hands and knees crawl.

Tim finally reached the thick trunked tree that he'd been aiming for. He lay flat on the ground, and poked his head around one side of the trunk. Marvinian listened to the king. Tim couldn't make out what the king said, as the king's back was to Tim. Marvinian waited patiently for the king to finish, and then said, "But your majesty, I understand that you need me to find the woman. I humbly pledge to find her before the night is out. I beg your majesty for the rest of daylight to find the men that humiliated me." Then the king responded.

Marvinian said, "Yes, your majesty, I will have her before you awake tomorrow morning." The king extended his ringed hand, which Marvinian kissed as he bowed.

Marvinian signaled to his two men. He approached a third man and said something to him. Then the four men walked towards town. Tim stood up and was about to return to Andrew when he heard rustling nearby. Tim dropped back to the ground and waited. Tim heard approaching footsteps, yet couldn't see anyone yet. He dared not move. A man walked passed Tim and set down a bow and quiver of arrows on a rock, and then took a few more steps away.

Tim discerned that the man made ready to make water. Tim crouched down and slowly approached. He took care where to place his feet, not wanting to give away his presence. Just as the man was finishing his business, Tim took the final few steps to the rock and snatched the bow and arrows. He scampered silently away and hid behind a large tree.

The man said, "What the...I could have sworn I put the damn thing right here. Where the hell is it? Did I leave it behind? Maybe I had more ale than I thought I did." Tim peered out from behind the tree and watched the man trot back to the group with the king. Tim took the opportunity to hurry back to where he'd left Andrew.

"Where did you find that?" Asked Andrew.

"One of the men was kind enough to offer it to me."

"Yeah, I'm sure he did. How did you get it from him?" Asked Andrew.

"I stole it while he made water."

"My God, you're taking too many chances. Just think what would have happened if he'd seen you," said Andrew.

"We needed a weapon. I won't stay in hiding forever. It's time for us to hit back."

"Did you hear anything that was said?" Asked Andrew.

"Marvinian promised the king that he'd have some woman for him before morning, and that he wanted permission to go after the men who humiliated him."

"I guess that would be us...but who is the woman?"

"I was hoping you would know," said Tim.

Andrew thought for a moment, and then said, "I have no idea."

"Then we'll find out," said Tim.

Tim headed off in the direction that he'd seen Marvinian leave, and Andrew followed. They quickly found Marvinian, as they were moving slowly. Marvinian stopped at a building just behind the tavern in which the trouble began. He gave his three men instructions, and they marched off to take up positions surrounding the building. Marvinian knocked at the front door. The boys couldn't see the door from where they hid, but they could see that he was talking to someone. Marvinian laughed in response to something, and a moment later a woman burst out the rear door. The men waiting for her subdued her, and tied her hands behind her back.

The woman wore a simple dress, plain in style and color. Her hair was tied behind her neck. Marvinian leisurely approached the woman. He smiled broadly, taking pleasure in her plight. The woman hurled curses at him, which evoked further laughter from Marvinian. He grabbed the woman by the hair and kissed her roughly. Marvinian released her, and she spat in his face. He slapped her with open hand. He barked orders to two of his men, who responded by each taking her by the arm and leading her away. The men led the woman past Tim and Andrew. In spite of her tear stained face, Tim was immediately struck by her beauty. And even beyond beauty, something else about her face impacted Tim, but he couldn't put his finger on it.

Marvinian waved another man to follow him into her home. The two men disappeared through the rear door.

"Wait a minute, I remember that I saw that woman at the tavern last night," said Tim.

"She sat with Marvinian! I didn't remember until I just saw her up close," said Andrew.

"Who is she?"

"I don't really know, but I think her name is Marjorie. I've seen her at the tavern many times, but I've never talked to her," said Andrew.

"Maybe she's the one that the king said he wanted."

"She must have something they want. The only reason to go back in there would be to search for something."

"Or to search for someone. Let's go see," suggested Tim.

"Don't get too close! We won't get out of the dungeon next time."

Tim already approached the building, and didn't pay attention to Andrew. Tim paused below a window, and slowly raised his head up to take a look inside. Tim saw a simple cottage with a stove in the center of the room, a bed in the corner, and a bunch of bags against another wall. Tim was puzzled when he didn't see the men. Then movement caught his eye. He darted his eyes towards the blur and saw the other man coming down stairs just to the right of Tim. Tim ducked to the ground.

Tim scrambled back to the trees where Andrew waited, breathing deeply to catch his breath. He peered out from behind the tree, but there was no sign of the men. "Did they see you?" Asked a frantic Andrew. "Should we run?"

"I don't think so, but..."

"But what?" Asked an exasperated Andrew.

"But I think we'd know by now if they'd seen me. They'd be out running after us."

Both boys peered back at the building. Marvinian and the other man stood just outside the rear door. Marvinian held a book in his hand, and turned several pages. He smiled with satisfaction and nodded his head. Marvinian put the book under his arm, turned and walked past where the boys hid. He said, "Now that I've got the wench and the book, we can be off to find them damn brats. I've got something for them."

"Yeah captain, I'll bet you do, maybe a stay in the dungeon," the other man said with a laugh.

"Something like that," said Marvinian.

The boys watched the direction he headed. Then they huddled together to discuss their plans. "So now what? Do we go and hide somewhere?" Asked Andrew.

"No, we follow him. I'm done hiding. We track him and see what he's up to. He can't surprise us if we know where he is."

"I don't know, that still seems risky to me. What if he sees us? Haven't we taken enough chances," said Andrew.

"If he sees us, he sees us. We'll just have to deal with it. I won't live in fear, running the rest of my life. It's time to take our fate into our own hands. We follow him, and respond as seems best at the time. Let's go." Tim didn't wait for Andrew's response, but merely turned and headed out in the direction they'd seen the men go. Tim led them through the cover of the trees that surrounded the town. They quickly found Marvinian. He was easy to find as he walked through the middle of town. Before long it was clear where Marvinian was going. He went in search of Philippe.

Marvinian and his men entered Philippe's shop without knocking or announcing himself. Tim and Andrew ran around to watch from behind the shop. Marvinian found Philippe sitting at his stool attending to his work. He looked up at his guest and said, "So will it be a repair or a new pair of boots that you'll be wanting?"

"We'll see how long you play the court jester. Where are they?" Demanded Marvinian.

"And which boots do you inquire after?"

"Cut the comedy, cobbler. You know who I'm after."

"I have no idea where my apprentices are," said Philippe with a bored sigh.

"Then you'll have no objection to me tearing your stop apart looking for them?"

"Do you really think they'd be stupid enough to hide in the first place you'd look for them?" Said Philippe.

"No amount of stupidity would surprise me. And they can't expect to hide for long. Nobody can stay hidden from me, and they better know that. My reputation ought to be clear enough."

"Yes, everyone in town knows you're a saint," said Philippe.

Marvinian laughed, and then he and his men began searching the shop. Philippe continued with his work. The men made a mess of his shop, yet Philippe ignored them as though they weren't there. "Hey boss, why ain't the cobbler scared of you? Everybody else in town is," asked Thompson.

"Never you mind. Just look for those brats," said Marvinian.

"But the cobbler acts like you're nobody. Everybody knows you're the king's man," persisted Thompson. Marvinian ignored him, and continued his search of the shop in the back room.

Thompson remained in the front room with Philippe. He watched Philippe. "So cobbler, why ain't you scared of Marvinian?" Asked Thompson.

"Oh, he's not so intimidating once you get to know him. He's actually quite a softy. A real nice guy," said Philippe with a grin.

"What are you talking about? Do you have any idea how many men, and women Marvinian's killed?"

"I suppose it would be well north of a hundred," said Philippe.

"He's planted well over two hundred! You must be soft in the brain if you think he's a nice guy." Philippe merely continued his work without looking up. "Marvinian doesn't take too kindly to men that don't respect him. In fact, I've got a mind to teach you a little respect," said Thompson. Philippe continued his work with the boot in his hands.

Thompson unsheathed the knife in his belt, and approached Philippe with his knife raised. Marvinian appeared in the doorway and said, "Thompson, I told you to leave the cobbler be. He's a protected man. Our work's done here. The boys aren't here." Marvinian walked through the front of the shop and left through the front door.

Thompson persisted, "So you're a protected man, huh? Do you warm the king's bed for him? Is that it?" Philippe didn't respond, not even bothering to look up.

"You ignoring me, cobbler? Well, protected or not, I think it's about time somebody taught you a little respect. Nobody ignores me when I talk to them." Philippe watched Thompson in the mirror on the wall, seeing that he swung at him with the hilt of his knife, and didn't bother to protect himself. Thompson's knife handle slammed into Philippe, knocking him senseless to the ground. Thompson laughed heartily, kicked Philippe in the back, and left after Marvinian.

Once they were sure Marvinian had left, Tim and Andrew entered the shop through the back door. Philippe lay unconscious on the ground. Andrew ran to get a wet towel. Tim checked Philippe's head for blood, but found only a bump. Tim found something that would serve as a pillow to put under Philippe's head. Andrew returned with a damp towel and gently wiped Philippe's head.

Andrew said, "Philippe, can you hear me? Philippe, wake up. Come on, wake up for me." Philippe's eyes fluttered, and then they focused on Andrew, and then Tim. "What happened to you?" Asked Andrew.

"I'm confident that we know what happened. Either Marvinian or one of his goons knocked him in the head," said Tim.

"That's right. It was one of his men. Marvinian wouldn't touch me. He knows," said Philippe with a groan.

"He knows what?" Asked Andrew.

"We have to figure out what to do with you two," said Philippe.

"And you too. Now you're involved," said Tim.

"No, I'll be alright. Marvinian won't come after me," said Philippe.

"How can you know that? You should hide with us," said Andrew.

"I'm not hiding anymore," said Tim.

"We have to figure out a plan, a good plan. I think I know where to go," said Philippe.

"Where?" Asked Andrew.

"You'll see soon enough," said Philippe.

Philippe locked up the shop, and led the boys out the rear door. They trotted up into the forest that stood a short distance behind the shop. Philippe stopped a little ways into the forest and watched. "What are we doing?" Asked Andrew. Philippe signaled for him to be quiet and wait. The boys crouched and watched. Once Philippe was satisfied that they weren't watched, they headed out.

They jogged along an unmarked trail for several miles through the forest. Tim figured that Philippe must have been wherever they were going many times, as he didn't hesitate at any point. Philippe led them over the crest of a hill, and they began to descend the far side.

He stopped at the creek at the bottom of the hill, and pulled three water skins off his shoulders. He tossed one to Tim and the other to Andrew. The boys drank and filled their skins, and then resumed their trek. Philippe led them up a gentle grade.

Suddenly Philippe stopped behind a clump of bushes and watched. Tim and Andrew understood to remain quiet. After several minutes of watching, Philippe stepped out of the bushes and walked a short distance to a tower. The tower stood so well hidden that Andrew and Tim didn't see it until they stood on its doorstep. The tower was made of stone, and stood a good forty feet or more in height. The stone tower was not only hidden by trees, but covered almost completely with various vines. Only patches of stone could be seen here and there.

Philippe pulled a key out of his trousers and unlocked a large padlock. The hinges of a great wooden door groaned as Philippe pulled it open. He signaled for the boys to enter. Philippe shut the door, and reengaged the lock on the other side of the door. Philippe checked to make sure it held fast. He fumbled in the dark for something. Then Philippe struck a match and lit a candle.

The candle illuminated the dusty, stone tower that was almost perfectly round. The tower extended straight up with several wooden landings built into the stone wall. Wooden steps traced upwards along the stone wall, forming a staircase that wound all the way up to the top of the tower. Every twelve or fifteen feet stood a landing. Tim couldn't see what was on the landings. Wooden boards made up the floor of the tower. Upon these boards swords, spears, shields, bows and arrows were stacked. They were dusty and some of them were covered in cobwebs, as though they hadn't been used in ages. "What is this place?" Asked Andrew.

"It's a watchtower. It used to be one of many towers that were manned with guards to protect the castle, but they fell out of use. The king's father rebuilt the guard towers into the castle itself, and these towers were abandoned to spiders and rats. I hope you like it, for this will be your new home...at least for the time being," explained Philippe.

Tim pulled a candle from a sconce, and lit it from Philippe's candle. Tim climbed up the stairs to the first landing. It contained much of the same as the ground floor, more weapons. Tim mounted the stairs up to the second landing. Bunk beds were pushed up against the walls, many still containing straw and blankets. The third landing contained more bunk beds. When Tim climbed to the highest landing, he bumped his head on something. When he shined the candle higher up, he saw that his head had hit a trap door in the ceiling. He pushed with his free hand, and the trap door immediately lifted up. Tim gave it a last hard push, and it fell open. A bunch of dust regaled his head, leaving him coughing and spitting. Tim wiped his face on his sleeve, which didn't help much, since his sleeve hadn't been washed since he'd been thrown in the dungeon.

Tim stepped up onto the landing. The top landing opened up to the elements. Stone battlements provided protection against arrows and spying eyes, while the spaces in between yielded an amazing view. Tim could see for miles in every direction. Behind him stood the castle in the bottom of the valley, and to the right of it lie the town with its streets of cobble, stone and dirt. Tim could see that only the main street was lined with cobble stones, and that the other streets were strictly dirt. To his left and before him spread a vast forest. Tree after tree extended as far as he could see.

Tim turned around as he heard footsteps, and Andrew and Philippe appeared at his side. "Wow, this place is amazing. I've never been this high up before. It's a bit frightening," said Andrew.

"If you keep a sharp watch out, no one will be able to surprise you here. Anyone approaching in daylight will be plainly seen, and no one will be able to find you in darkness. The one danger is to maintain the cover of darkness. You must make sure to extinguish all candles by sundown; otherwise you will give away your position. Marvinian must not know that you're here. If he sees any lights up here, he will be suspicious enough to investigate," said Philippe. Tim nodded.

"How long will we have to stay here?" Asked Andrew.

"Until it's safe to leave," said Philippe.

"What will we do all day?" Asked Andrew.

"We'll train," said Tim.

"Train to do what?" Asked Andrew.

"We have all the weapons we need to train us to defend ourselves," said Tim.

"And I shall show you how to do so. Tomorrow I'll be back with food and more water. Then the training will begin," said Philippe.

"Wait a minute, you're not leaving us here alone, are you?" Asked Andrew.

"I'll be back at first light," said Philippe. "And I have an errand to dispatch." And with that he descended the stairs. Tim remained where he was, while Andrew followed Philippe down. Andrew begged Philippe not to leave them. Once Philippe left and locked the tower, Andrew fell onto the floor in a heap of tears.

Tim leaned against the battlements of the tower and gazed at the castle in the distance. Thoughts of Marjorie came to mind. There was something about that woman that seemed familiar. But he couldn't place her. Tim felt confident that he'd seen her before the night in the tavern, but when? Then it came to him. Philippe had brought Tim to the castle one night for a dinner. The queen had invited Philippe and told him to bring Tim. After desert had been served a beautiful woman had sung for them. Tim remembered being struck by her voice of gold. He'd never heard anyone sing like that before, and sat mesmerized throughout her performance. It wasn't just her voice or her beauty, there had been something else about the woman that struck Tim. He'd wanted to meet her to discover what that something was, but had found no occasion. "Yes, Marjorie was the name she gave when she was introduced, now I remember," said Tim aloud.

Tim stared at the castle, looking for the dungeon. He wondered if Marjorie sat locked in the dungeon right now. That must be where they'd taken her, thought Tim. And he knew then that he had an errand to dispatch as well. He couldn't leave her there.

Eight

Marvinian always was the first to arrive at the guardhouse. As captain of the guard, he wanted time to think through the day, before the others arrived. By mid morning Thompson hadn't reported for duty. Marvinian looked at the position of the sun, judging the hour of the morning, and then exhaled loudly. Marvinian felt sure he knew what had become of Thompson, but he went to his quarters to see for himself. He hated to lose another man. It's not that Marvinian would miss Thompson personally, it's just a bother to expend the time and energy to train a new man. And he never ceased to be impatient with the stupidity of men who didn't listen. By now all in the guard should be well aware that the cobbler remained untouchable.

Marvinian walked down the corridor to Thompson's quarters. The door to Thompson's room remained shut, as it had been all night long, except for about one minute. Marvinian opened the door. The room was dim, only lit by sunlight streaming in from a small window in the stone wall. Thompson lay on his bunk, turned towards the wall. A cup lay on the stone floor. For a moment Marvinian hoped that Thompson might have had too much alcohol and overslept, yet that hope didn't last for long. Marivinian turned him onto his back. Thompson's eyes stared blankly at the bunk above him, and his shirt bore a large blood stain on the left side of his chest. Marvinian tore his shirt away and inspected the wound. A single knife wound to the heart. Just as I expected, Marvinian thought. He exhaled deeply and said aloud, "I knew the damned fool wouldn't heed my warning about the cobbler. The problem is, he just don't seem dangerous with that school-boy grin." Marvinian sighed, and left the door open to the room.

Tim looked to the west and glanced at the western sun. It was just above the tips of the trees, and it would be dusk soon. He turned around and stared at the castle. He could make out the four towers of the castle. Tim noticed a flicker of light in one of them, and thought that the guard in that tower must be smoking. Tim realized that he must extinguish his candle, as the guard would be able to see his candle, if Tim could see his light. Tim squeezed the candle wick between his fingers and descended to the floor of the castle.

"We're locked in," called Andrew to the back of the door. Philippe had locked the tower door from the outside when he left, effectively locking Tim and Andrew inside. Andrew waited, but no answer came. He called out again, "Philippe, you've locked us in!"

"Shut up, someone will hear you," warned Tim.

"But I want someone to hear me. Maybe Philippe doesn't realize…"

"He knows perfectly well that he's locked us in. He has to, or it might draw attention to someone passing by, if they found the tower disturbed and unlocked. They would know someone has been here. Any attention we receive here would not be good attention," said Tim.

"I don't like being locked up. What if we had to get out?" Said Andrew.

"I can only think of one reason we'd have to leave before morning."

"You mean if someone walks nearby?"

"No, if there's a fire. The only danger to us is fire. So we'll keep just one candle lit long enough to get settled into the bunks, and then we go dark until the morning," said Tim.

"But what if I have to make water?"

Tim laughed, "Then make it over the wall."

"But what if Philippe doesn't come back?"

"He'll be back," said Tim.

"But what if..."

"Stop being afraid! It isn't helping you, and I don't want to go there. I'm going to bed. Let it go, and go to bed yourself," said Tim.

"But I can't stop fretting, what if..." Tim turned on his side and put a pillow over his exposed ear.

The next morning Tim awoke to the sound of metal on metal. He sat up and looked around the dim room. At first he didn't recognize where he was. Then Philippe's friendly and familiar voice reminded him, "I'm back! Are you sluggards awake yet?"

Tim rubbed his face and climbed down the ladder. When he reached the floor Tim found Philippe nudging Andrew. Andrew had slept next to the tower door, with some kind of burlap sack under his head. Andrew woke, and quickly gave Philippe a hug. "I told you I'd be back. Let go of me so that I can give you breakfast," said Philippe with a grin.

"So what did you bring us? I hope you brought us something good to eat," said Andrew. Philippe opened his rucksack and brought out a loaf of bread, a jar of olives, a hunk of cheese and fresh water skins. The boys' eyes grew wide and they fell to the provisions with eagerness. They hadn't eaten since yesterday midday. Philippe joined them in their meal, as he'd left before first light, and hadn't taken the time to eat yet himself.

As they finished their humble meal, Tim turned to Philippe and said. "I won't hide for long. This is no life, living to avoid others. I will take matters into my own hands, and I hope you both will help me. I want to train to go on the offensive."

"That's the spirit! You have found a way out of fear, good for you! We will begin training at once," said Philippe.

"What kind of training?" Asked Andrew.

Tim walked over and picked up a sword, a shield, a bow and a quiver. "This is the kind of training that we will do."

"But I've never even held a sword before. I don't know how to use that," said Andrew.

"And you shall learn," said Philippe.

"But what if we get hurt?" Asked Andrew.

"You might. But you will pay close attention to my training, so that you're less likely to be wounded," said Philippe.

They each picked up a sword, a shield, and a bow and a spear. Philippe showed them how to put on a sword belt and scabbard properly, and how to sling the shield over their shoulder so that it rests on their backs. Philippe relocked the tower and led them away from the castle.

"Where are we going?" Asked Andrew.

"I don't want to train close to the tower. We must keep your whereabouts secret," said Philippe.

"But how far..."

"You'll see," said Philippe as he cut Andrew off. Philippe grew weary of Andrew's almost constant questions, but tried to keep his frustration to a minimum. He knew Andrew was afraid. In fact, Philippe was afraid for him. Andrew was not only young, but had no experience in taking care of himself. He was more of a playful child, and seemed far from manhood. Philippe eyed Tim momentarily. Philippe breathed a prayer of thanks that Tim seemed different. Although he didn't expect that Tim had any experience with weaponry, he seemed almost a man. Tim displayed some of the toughness that he wished Andrew had.

They reached a small clearing in the forest. The boys set down their weapons. Philippe stepped off twenty-five paces and stopped. He turned and faced the others and said, "We will start with the bow and arrow. No matter how large or how skilled your opponent may be, mastery with the bow and arrow will level any playing field."

Philippe set up a target against a tree. He showed Andrew and Tim how to string a bow, and fire an arrow. Andrew shot first. He missed the target with his first two attempts, and caught the edge of the target on his third try. Philippe helped Andrew correct his technique, and then Andrew hit the outer portion of the target about half of the time, with an occasional wide shot that wasn't even close.

Tim hit the target with his first shot, drawing surprise and relief from Philippe. As Tim accustomed himself to his new equipment, his shots became more and more accurate. Philippe asked him, "Where did you learn the bow and arrow?"

"My father taught me the basics, and then the soldiers helped me develop my skill. In fact, I have been in battle. I expected that they brought me to the castle to fight in some kind of war."

"We may find that being nearer the truth than you now know," said Philippe.

Looking eagerly at Philippe, Andrew said, "Teach me to shoot like that."

"Perhaps Tim can teach you. I fear that he's a better shot than I," said Philippe.

Tim helped Andrew refine his skill until he was able to hit the target somewhere, almost every time. It took several hours to accomplish, yet Andrew's eagerness to learn, combined with Tim's patience kept them at it until Andrew achieved the basics of archery. The boys spent the rest of the day exhausting themselves as they trained with the sword and spear. Andrew learned each of the weapons from scratch, with this being his first exposure to weapons of any kind. Tim already knew the bow and arrow along with the sword, but had never wielded a spear before. Philippe knew the essential skills with all three weapons.

When the sun began to fade into the western sky, the boys headed back to the tower. Once locked safely inside, they consumed a meal of the same ingredients as the first two meals of the day.

Marvinian knew Andrew. He had apprenticed himself to Philippe several years ago. And the other boy looked familiar, but Marvinian couldn't place him. He figured that he'd interrogated him somewhere along the way. Marvinian had interrogated many, and had taken many toes, but didn't bother to pay close attention to their identities. He'd ask around. Marvinian had already been to Andrew's home and felt confident that Andrew hadn't been home since the incident. If there was one thing he knew, it was how to convince people to tell him what he wanted to know. Andrew's father begged Marvinian to not hurt them, or their boy. No, he knew they would have told him if they knew where their son or brother hid. None of Marvinian's usual informants knew much about the new kid. The only useful information he'd come across came from his contact at the refurbishment barn. Grimwald told him that a boy named Tim had worked there for one month, and then been reassigned to the cobbler. That was all that Marvinian had learned of Tim.

Marvinian presented himself to the king. Every morning Marvinian reported to the king for orders, unless he was away on a mission. Marvinian knocked on the door of the king's apartment. The butler opened the door, and allowed him to enter without a word exchanged. The butler nodded and went to announce the visitor. A moment later the butler waved him in to see the king.

The king stood on his balcony, gazing out at his kingdom. He smoked. Marvinian entered the balcony and said, "Orders for today, sire?"

"Does my dungeon hold the whore?" Asked the king.

"It does, sire."

"And I expect that you have what I sent you to find?"

"Of course, your majesty," said Marvinian as he handed the king the book. The king opened the book and glanced through it briefly. He shut the book abruptly and put it under his arm.

"And is the whore convinced there's no need to create another such book?" Asked the king.

"I'm not sure, sire."

"Then go and become sure! She shall not leave the dungeon until she is sure!" Said the king.

"I will personally see to it at once, sire… And may I ask you about another matter?" When the king remained silent, Marvinian continued. "There is a boy named Tim, who is recently apprenticed to the cobbler. Do I have your leave to do with him as I please?"

"What is that to me? You have my leave to do as you please with any apprentice. However, the cobbler himself remains the lone exception. Do I make myself clear?" Said the king.

"Yes your majesty, perfectly clear."

"Then go and make sure the whore is perfectly clear as well," said the king. Marvinian bowed, and took his leave.

Once Marvinian left, the king reopened Marjorie's book. It contained her journal entries. The first half of the book were accounts of her life before arriving at the palace. None of this interested the king. He flipped ahead until he found what he wanted. The entry for Marjorie's first encounter with the king didn't hold much interest for him. However, a number of entries thereafter did concern the king. He read through her recounting of the king requiring her to wear the green dress and the red wig. Marjorie also recorded having her face make-up done in a way to exactly imitate the king's late mother. In fact, Marjorie was so detailed, she even recorded the royal make-up artist doing her face in front of a portrait of the late queen. I suppose there was no hiding what I wanted, laughed the king to himself. However, the most humiliating part came next. Marjorie faithfully wrote almost exactly the words that the king made her say, "My son, you are safe in my arms. My love will keep thine enemies from thy door. None will harm thee, for I am here."

The king closed his eyes and winced as he read these words. He felt both comforted and embarrassed at the same time; a strange combination of feelings. The king opened his eyes and read on. "The king commanded me to hold him in my arms, which proved almost impossible due to his immense girth, yet we found a way to make do. I then stroked his face as I kissed him, repeating the comforting words as though to a child. The king required me to keep the red wig and the green dress on throughout our love making. However, love had nothing to do with what the king and I did together. And once the king finished, he bade me to sing him a lullaby. The king fell asleep before I finished singing the song. I learned that the song was the same one his mother sang to him each night when she put him to bed."

The king slapped the book shut and tossed it into the flames of his fireplace. He stood there and watched until he was sure it was no longer readable. The king stroked his beard with both hands, as if washing away memories. He thought, I must not have made myself clear that the bitch was not to write ANYTHING down of her privileged encounters with my royal self. Well, she will be made to understand now.

The men led Marjorie into the dungeon, threw her in and slammed the door shut. The warden locked the door. He peered through the bars and said, "You won't be alone for long, Ms. Marjorie. You can take comfort in that." Marjorie remained on the stone floor where she'd landed, and wept. She expected that Marvinian had found what he wanted, so what did they want with her? Why didn't they let her go, if they'd found it? And how could they not find it? There weren't too many places to look in her simple home. My God, I never should have come! How young and foolish I was to agree to the offer. How could I not see through the simplicity of the deception? Why didn't I trust my instincts, and say no? And now I am to die in this God-forsaken castle. Marjorie wept anew.

The king had sent his most trusted man to search for the best singer in the whole land of Scerlandia. He didn't want any of the local girls, nor were any of them talented enough to entertain the king and his guests. They were either untalented or too nervous to perform for the king. The king didn't concern himself with reasons, merely results. Marvinian traveled all across Scerlandia, from village to village, hearing all the female singers the land had to offer.

After eight months of travel, Marvinian came to the village of Randley. Marvinian and his men arrived in Randley hot and thirsty, and sought the tavern. As they enjoyed their pints of ale, Marvinian inquired about the singing talent in the village. He learned that the theatre held a performance each Saturday night, and that the best singers performed there. As the next night was Saturday, they made arrangements to be seated in the front row of the theatre that night.

The theatre show opened with children singing and dancing. In fact, the first seven acts were all children, along with a clown who played along with them. After the fifth act, Thompson leaned over to Marvinian and said, "Captain, we're wasting our time. Let's go have a pint or two, and move on tomorrow."

Marvinian almost agreed, but decided to make an inquiry first. He said to Thompson, "Wait here." Marvinian went to the back of the theatre and asked for the theatre's manager. Marvinian asked him, "Are there any ladies that sing? Or am I wasting my time watching a children's show?"

"Oh no, the pride of Randley will sing. Ms. Marjorie sings every Saturday night, and she always sings last. You must be patient if you want to hear her."

"Is the wench Marjorie anything to look at?" Asked Marvinian.

"She's no wench. Ms. Marjorie is a complete lady, as you may judge for yourself." And with that the theatre manager excused himself and returned to his duties. Marvinian thought about demanding that Ms. Marjorie sing immediately, but thought better of it. He didn't want to cause a scene, or at least not yet.

Marvinian went outside and relaxed himself with a smoke. He'd instructed Thompson to fetch him if Ms. Marjorie appeared. After two smokes Marvinian returned to his seat. Two young ladies sang a lovely duet. They were both pretty, although young. "I hope neither of these is Ms. Marjorie," said Marvinian under his breath. They would simply not do, as they were not quite what he searched for. He knew the king would not be happy with anyone who appeared to be a child. The king wanted a woman with a woman's body.

After two more acts that were unmemorable, the moment he waited for arrived. The theatre manager appeared on stage and announced Ms. Marjorie, and the audience responded as though to royalty. When the curtains parted, Ms. Marjorie sat on a stool with her back to the audience. As soon as she sang, energy shot through Marvinian. And the moment she turned to face the audience, Marvinian knew his search had ended. Ms. Marjorie's beauty struck him dumb. When Thompson leaned over to comment on her, he had to repeat himself and nudge Marvinian in the shoulder before he responded.

After the performance, Marvinian made arrangements with the manager to have a private audience with Ms. Marjorie. He presented her with the king's offer. Of course she thrilled to be invited to sing for the king. And the chance to live in the king's castle as his personal singer took her beyond her dreams. Marjorie eagerly agreed at once.

The next morning Marvinian waited at his room above the tavern for Ms. Marjorie to prepare for the journey to the castle. A knock came at the door to his room. "Thompson, get the door,"

141

said Marvinian. He stayed in his chair, blowing smoke out the window with his boots on the window cell. Thompson handed him a note. "What's this? And where's Ms. Marjorie?"

"I don't know, Captain. A man handed me this note from her," said Thompson.

Marvinian read the note. He crumpled it up and threw it out the window. "This bloody wench can't say no to the king. She thinks she's given a choice," said Marvinian.

"I'll go fetch her and drag her back over here by the hair," suggested Thompson.

"No no, we can't do it that way," said Marvinian, exhaling his frustration. "He did not want us to bring back a prisoner. The king was quite clear about his instructions.
I'll go and speak with her. We have to convince her to come of her own accord...or at least the appearance of her own accord."

"We brought the last one back a prisoner to the king," protested Thompson.

"And how well did it work out?" Said Marvinian.

"Well, it could have gone better, I suppose."

"The king doesn't want another one by force. He was quite clear that we're to find a way to get a singer to come voluntarily," said Marvinian.

The next day Marvinian packed Ms. Marjorie's box onto a wagon. He'd hoped to not have to offer much to convince her to come, but she'd been surprisingly stubborn. Ms. Marjorie thought she could create a nice career without the king's help. It usually went better when the singer thought the king her only chance to make it. However, the king empowered Marvinian to offer whatever it took to bring him the best talent in Scerlandia.

Marvinian mounted his horse, and waved Thompson to get them moving. Two men hugged Ms. Marjorie. One of them wiped tears from his eyes. The other one held his face in a stoic and immovable gesture. The tearful one whispered something urgently into her ear. She smiled and nodded in assent. Marvinian nudged his horse over to them. At his urging she mounted the wagon, and they moved out. The stoic one called to Marvinian, "Might I have a word?" Marvinian nodded for him to speak.

"If any harm comes to Marjorie, you're the first person I come looking for, Mr. Marvinian."

"Is that a threat?" Asked Marvinian.

"You can take that any way you like," said the stoic man. Then he turned and went back inside.

Marvinian trotted his horse alongside the wagon where Ms. Marjorie rode. "Ms. Marjorie, who's the man I just had a word with?"

"That's Matthew. He's my brother. Why, did he ask you to make him a promise?"

"Something like that," said Marvinian.

Upon arriving at Lord Teagle's castle, Grace led Marjorie to her room. The room was spacious with a generous window, providing her with a nice view from high above the grounds. Marjorie had an adjoining room for her to attend to her toilette. Marjorie had lived in a lovely room back in Randley, but nothing as beautiful as this. Grace gave her a couple of hours to settle in, and said she'd be back to fetch her for an audience with the king. Grace instructed Marjorie to wear the green dress that Grace left for her. Once Grace left the room, Marjorie danced about and shrieked with joy. She'd finally made it. All those hours practicing singing had finally paid off. What could be better than singing for the king? She would be the most famous singer in all Scerlandia. Marjorie pranced around her new room, exploring all that it contained. Grace surprised her when she came in to see if Marjorie was almost ready. Marjorie couldn't believe that it had already been almost two hours. "You must be ready for the king on time," said Grace.

"Oh the king won't mind waiting a few extra minutes for me. Surely he understands that I've just arrived, and must be allowed time to adjust to my new arrangements."

"You will come to know the king soon enough, and will discover that he allows no such indulgences. He will expect you to be ready in a timely fashion, and wearing the dress that he indicated. You must hurry!" Said Grace. Marjorie began to wash and dress.

Two hours after her arrival, Grace led Marjorie to the king's apartments. Grace left her in the anteroom, and went in to speak to the king. Grace indicated a chair for her to sit upon, yet Marjorie preferred to walk about the ornate room. Upon a table sat an elegant tea pot and set. The room was hung with large, framed paintings that covered much of the wall. One of the walls was draped in a large tapestry of many colors. Marjorie wandered over to the window, and looked down upon a bright green lawn of grand scale. A stone wall surrounded the lawn, and armed men walked along the thick wall.

Marjorie glanced back at the door through which Grace disappeared, yet it remained empty. It seemed like hours since Grace had left her. Marjorie wondered why the king kept her waiting this long. She'd rarely been kept waiting, yet she'd never before had an audience with a king. She sighed, and continued her inspection of the room. After what seemed like another hour, Marjorie walked over to the doorway through which Grace disappeared. Marjorie peeked into the room, yet dared not enter. The curtains were drawn, leaving the room in semi-darkness. Upon the far wall was a closed door. On either side of the door were portraits. The left portrait was of a regal looking man, while the right portrait contained a haughty looking woman, with eyes that dared her audience to not look at her. At first Marjorie didn't pay too much attention to the portraits, and her eyes began to wander to other objects in the room, yet something about the woman in the portrait caught her eye. Marjorie initially couldn't put her finger on it, and then it came to her. The woman wore a green dress, that made her red hair appear to almost be aflame. She put her hand to her mouth as she took in her breath quickly. At the same time Grace opened the door in between the portraits, and strode quickly to Marjorie.

"Do I alarm you, young lady?" Said Grace.

"Oh no, I was just..."

"You were just trying to find out where I'd disappeared to for so long," finished Grace.

"Well, I was looking at the portraits beside the door. Who are those people?"

"Those people are the father and mother of the king, the former king and queen. The king will see you now," said Grace. Grace pointed towards the door she'd left open, and then she left the room.

Marjorie took several deep breaths. She had not anticipated being this nervous, though she'd never met any kind of royalty before. Marjorie exhaled loudly, and then marched into the inner room. The room was twice the size of the room in which Marjorie had waited. The decorations rivaled those in the anteroom. While she still took in her new surroundings, a booming voice said, "You will sit there."

Marjorie oriented herself to the location of the voice, and saw a large man sitting at a larger desk. The king wore his hunting suit and tall boots. He held a feathered pen in his hand, and impatiently waved her to the chair again.

"Oh yes, your sire, uh majesty, uh kingship," stumbled Marjorie.

"Your majesty will do nicely. Now, before you sit, let me get a good look at you. Do a complete turn." Marjorie quickly turned in a circle. "No no, do it again. And this time more slowly. I want to get the size of you."

"My size, your majesty?" Asked Marjorie.

"Never mind about that, just turn in a slow circle." She turned in a complete circle, this time intentionally slowing herself down.

When she had completed her turn, she faced the king and searched his face. He waved her to the chair, and returned to writing something with the feathered pen. Marjorie felt her feminine confidence return to her, and she batted her eyes as she completed three more turns, this time as though she were on stage. However, the king's eyes stared at the document on his desk, and he missed her performance.

Marjorie said, "Your majesty, allow me to provide you with a proper turn."

The king glanced up and said, "Yes yes, you may sit. I've already had a good look at you." He returned his eyes to the papers before him.

Marjorie sat with her knees together and her hands on her knees. The king continued to study his document. Marjorie took the opportunity to adjust her hair and dress while she waited. The king noticed her movements and looked up at her. He grinned, and made a final marking upon the papers.

"I have guests arriving shortly. I must know if you can sing. You shall sing for me now," said the king.

"But what am I to sing?"

"I don't care, sing anything you know," said the king.

"But I know dozens of songs. How shall I choose?"

"Pick any song you like, but do so quickly before I lose my patience with you," said the king.

Marjorie stood and straightened her dress, and moved over to stand in front of the fireplace. After all, it wouldn't do to damage the king's ears with her powerful voice. She fiddled with her hair, cleared her voice, and voiced a quick scale of notes. Then she belted out one of the songs that had made her a celebrity in her home town of Randley.

The king pushed back his chair and folded his hands across his lap. A grin slowly appeared upon his face. When Marjorie finished he stood and walked over to her. He put his hand on his chin as he gazed at her. "Your voice will do, but we must do something about this," said the king as he touched her hair. Then the king walk to the door and rang a bell. Grace appeared immediately. The king said, "This woman shall sing tonight for my guests. Prepare her and the music for the event. She shall sing the same song she just sang for me. And you will fix up her hair. It just won't do as it is." The king left the room.

Grace said, "Come along miss, we've much to do to make ready for tonight."

"But, did the king like me?"

"Of course he liked you. You wouldn't be allowed to sing tonight if he didn't. Now follow me," said Grace as she led the way out of the room.

Grace arrived at Marjorie's room to fetch her. Marjorie had made all her preparations to perform. "Now sit at the dressing table," said Grace. Grace placed her hands on Marjorie's hair and proceeded to pin it up.

"But whatever are you doing? I always perform with my hair down. It shows off my face better," said Marjorie.

"You will be wearing this wig," said Grace as she placed it on the dressing table. Then Grace finished pinning up Marjorie's hair.

"But why am I to wear this red wig?"

"No questions, just wear whatever I place on your head," said a stern Grace. Marjorie sighed and submitted to the wig. When Grace finished she pulled Marjorie up out of her chair. "Now stand there and let me have a look at you. Yes, that will do. And don't mess with that wig. The king requires it."

Marjorie followed Grace into the dining room. The king sat at the head of a large table along with the queen and his guests. They all sat at a long, single wooden table. The table glowed in beauty, with a recently oiled finish and exquisitely carved legs. To the left of the table was a low stage. Upon the stage stood a large harpsichord, and a man sitting behind it on a stool. Grace introduced Marjorie to Godwin, her accompanist. Godwin stood

and bowed slightly. "Do you know the music I'll be singing?"
Asked Marjorie.

"Yes my lady, I've been informed of your selections."

"Splendid...so when am I to perform? Do I sing now?" Asked
Marjorie.

"No, my lady, you must await the king's signal."

"But perhaps I shall surprise the king and his guests and begin
singing now," suggested Marjorie.

"That would be ill advised, my lady. The king takes no surprises
well. It would be best to wait."

"Yet the king has yet to be surprised by me. He might take
kindly to such a surprise," said Marjorie.

"Yes my lady, if you fancy the dungeon, then this would surely
be the best course."

Marjorie laughed nervously and stared Godwin in the eye.
Then she said, "Well, if you put it that way, then perhaps I shall
wait. You are a strange man with no humor." Godwin stared back
with a grim expression.

Marjorie didn't know what to do with herself while she waited.
She pulled the other stool nearer the harpsichord and sat. Godwin
stood and went behind the door. He returned a moment later
with two cups. He offered one to Marjorie and said, "Take some
mead, my lady, it may calm your nerves."

"I need no calming. I'm a professional and have sung for
thousands of people, young and old. I will be fine just as I am,"
said Marjorie.

"As you wish, my lady."

When the king and his guests finished eating, the servants
came and removed the food and plates. The servants refilled their
goblets. The king signaled to Godwin to begin. All the guests
turned their chairs so that they might look directly at Marjorie.

"It is time, my lady," said Godwin. And Godwin began to play.
Marjorie began to sing. At first her voice projected little, and the
king and his guests leaned forward to hear. Realizing her mistake,

148

Marjorie suddenly increased her volume. The king and his guests leaned away, being startled by her abrupt loudness. Marjorie noted their reactions, and put her hand to her throat. Her voice cracked, and she stumbled over the words of her song. The king quickly waved over his servant, and fervently whispered in his ear. The servant immediately approached Marjorie. He said, "The king demands to know what is the meaning of this? You will pull yourself together and sing as you did in his chambers. You shall not embarrass him before his guests!" The king slammed his hand down on the table. His scowl quickly turned to a forced smile. Marjorie jumped. The servant returned to his post. Marjorie nervously looked at the king. His eyes bore into her.

Marjorie fiddled with her dress. She turned to Godwin, hoping for some inspiration. "I don't know if I can sing well tonight. It's as though I've lost control of my voice. This has never happened to me before. What am I to do?"

Godwin already held one of the cups of mead. As soon as the king called his servant, Godwin knew what needed to be done. He offered the cup to Marjorie, "Drink, my lady, this will calm your nerves."

"But I've never drank before singing. I don't know what will happen," said Marjorie.

"What will happen is this mead will keep you from spending the night in the dungeon. Drink, my lady." Marjorie took the cup and gulped it down in one draught. She sputtered, and wiped her mouth with her handkerchief.

"Are you ready, my lady? It's best to not keep the king waiting." Marjorie nodded and she returned the cup to Godwin. Already she felt a little better. She turned away from the king and his guests and softly sang a scale to test her voice. She nodded to Godwin, who began to play. This time her voice started out softly, yet clear. As her confidence returned, she slowly increased her volume until she sang as she did in the theatre a few days ago. As she sang, Marjorie watched the king's face. His features relaxed their scowl. And a few minutes later the king's face formed into a slight grin. He surveyed his guests, who appeared to enjoy the renewed performance.

After Marjorie sang her first two songs, the queen led the ladies out of the room for tea and dessert. The king lit his pipe, and his male guests followed his lead. Godwin had changed the order of the songs, and waved Marjorie over to look at the music before him. She shook her head, and turned the music to the song she wanted to sing. Godwin began to object, but her insistence stilled him.

Marjorie now had summoned full command of herself, and approached the table as she sang. She flirted with each guest, touching them as she sang seductively to each of them. Marjorie then sat in the king's lap, and winked as she followed the outline of his jaw with her hand. The king grinned, yet didn't otherwise respond.

After two more songs, the king called for his man in waiting. The king whispered in his ear. The man nodded and left the room. The king and his guests stood and left the room. The man in waiting approached Marjorie and said, "You will come with me."

"But where are we going?" Asked Marjorie. However, the man merely waved her to follow. The man led Marjorie back to the room in which she had met the king. He pointed her to the same chair and simply said, "You are to await the king here."

"But whatever for?" Asked Marjorie. The man turned on his heels and left the room.

Marjorie sat down. She fiddled with her dress and hair, and nervously watched the door. She grew weary of waiting and wandered about the room. She found herself staring at the woman in the green dress. The woman's eyes bore into Marjorie, as though the woman were alive. Then Marjorie noted the woman's hair. It was the same as the wig.

"So you've found the old girl," laughed the king as he entered.

"Who is she?" Asked Marjorie.

"My mother, of course. You don't recognize the old queen?" Said the king. Then the king's countenance changed, and he growled, "Who gave you leave to leave the chair?"

"I didn't realize I was shackled to it, your majesty."

"The instructions given you were clear. You were to remain in the chair until I came for you," said the king. Marjorie opened her mouth to respond, but something in the king's face warned her to silence.

"You will follow me into my bed chamber." Although this surprised her, Marjorie followed the king. He shut the door behind her. He removed his outer robe, and turned to her. "You will remove your clothing," said the king.

"What? I don't quite..."

"There's nothing to understand. Simply remove your dress, as well as anything else you're adorned in," said the king.

"But I, but I'm an honorable woman, your majesty. I thought I am to be your singer."

"You are to be whatever I tell you to be. Now remove your clothing, before I have them removed by my manservant," said the king. Marjorie closed her mouth, and did her best to gather her wits. She considered her options. Although she desperately wanted to keep her clothes on, she didn't seem to have any other good alternative. Marjorie walked to a chair near the window, and with her back to the king, began to slowly remove her garments. The king sat in a chair and watched.

Once naked, Marjorie turned to face the king. She reached up and began to remove the pins that held her red wig in place. "No! The red hairs stays," shouted the king.

She replaced the pin that she'd taken from her hair, and then held her arms so as to cover her breasts, while her hands covered her privates. The king regarded her for a moment, grinned and then asked her to come closer. Marjorie hesitated, and then slowly approached. The king said, "You will put your hands behind your back."

"But your majesty…"

"But nothing! You will do as I order. I am the king. You won't tell me what to do, mother!," Said the king.

"Mother?"

"I said MARJORIE. Don't be ridiculous," said the king.

Marjorie choked back the retort on the tip of her tongue, and remained silent. Marjorie looked at the king. The intensity of his gaze frightened her. She clasped her hands behind her back. A moment later her shame got the best of her and she returned her hands to cover herself. The king smiled, and walked to his bed. He removed a chord from a drawer and approached Marjorie. He pushed her onto his bed, face first. The king leaned into her and bound her hands behind her. "There, now you shall have no trouble keeping your hands where I wish them to be. I won't have another woman disobey me," said the king. He pulled her back into a standing position and turned her to face him.

The king sat back down in his chair and regarded her naked form. He rubbed his jaw. Marjorie glanced at the king's face, and turned her eyes to the ground. Then she made a decision. Marjorie looked the king in the eye and said, "Your majesty, you will make your intentions plain to me. I won't be treated like a common whore."

"You will be treated however I wish to treat you. However, I like your spirit, and so I will grant your request. Tonight you shall be granted the rare opportunity to share the king's bed. Your form pleases me, and your singing seduced me."

"So I am to be amongst your courtesans?"

"You may call yourself whatever you like," said the king.

"But your majesty, I am an honorable woman. Please don't treat me otherwise. I am to be your court singer. Don't treat me as a whore."

"I don't trouble myself with titles. You have my leave you call yourself the royal singer if you like. However, whatever you call yourself, you shall warm my bed tonight," said the king. And with that, the king picked Marjorie up and deposited her onto his bed. Marjorie stared at the king with wide eyes. She considered protesting further, yet again something in the king's countenance gave her pause. She decided it might go better for her if she remained silent for now, and allow the king to do with her what he will.

Nine

Shane and his parents worried when Tim didn't come home the next day. By the end of the week they knew that something had gone wrong. Mother barely slept, waiting up for hours staring out the front windows, watching the road. She couldn't rest until her babies were safely home. Most nights Father carried her into bed sometime after midnight. He tried to get her to go to bed with him at their usual time, but Mother refused. Father slept some, but kept having dreams of something missing that he couldn't find, nor even remember what he sought. Other nights Father dreamt of feeling helpless, unable to accomplish his mission. He woke troubled. Neither of them slept well. Shane's room felt empty to him, with Tim's bunk empty. Shane found himself often looking for Tim, searching his bunk regularly, as though he would magically appear. Shane often woke with a start, as if he must act immediately, but there was nothing to do. By the eighth morning, they all felt it time to decide what to do.

After breakfast they quickly cleaned up and then sat back down at the table. Father began, "Okay, we decided to give Tim a week, and today's the eighth day. We can't wait forever for them."

"But they said if you paid the taxes in full, then they would return Amanda," said Mother.

"You know as well as I that we can't wait on Lachman. He isn't an honorable man," countered Father.

"We can't just accept his answer. They can't keep Amanda forever," said Shane.

"They can do whatever they like," said Father.

"But we won't stand for that. We have to do something. I have to find Amanda. I have to know that she's okay," said Mother.

"What are we to do? We don't even know where Amanda is. And we have no idea where Tim is. Probably they have him too," said Shane.

"I think we have to assume that they have Amanda as well as Tim. At least I hope they have Tim. The alternative is worse," said Father.

"What alternative? What do you think happened to Tim?" Asked Mother.

"The best we can do is hope that Amanda and Tim are safe, and together somewhere under their watch," said Father.

"Then we have to find them, and rescue them," suggested Shane.

"Yes! We have to get them back," said Mother.

"We must find out where they're being held. Shane and I will go to Hanover and see what we can learn of their whereabouts," said Father.

"You can't leave me home alone. I'll come with you," pleaded Mother.

"But someone has to stay home and care for the land and the animals," said Shane.

"I'll go alone. Shane you stay home with Mother and keep the farm going. We can't afford to let it go to hell," said Father.

"But I want to come too! I have a right to know where my babies are," said Mother.

"This isn't about rights. Our rights have been violated time and again. This is about us doing what we can for our own. I need you to stay here and help Shane care for the farm. We can't get any further behind with our taxes," said Father.

Mother looked away and folded her arms across her chest. Shane put his arm around her shoulder and pulled her tight. Mother's eyes filled with tears. Father said, "We'll get them back, Mother. Don't you fret." Father's eyes teared, and he paused to wipe his eyes with his rolled up sleeve. Then he continued with resolve, "Damn it, if it's the last thing I do, we'll find a way to get them back. I'll leave for Hanover at first light. And I won't come home until I know something." Shane nodded. Mother cried with her head in her hands. Father sat next to her and put his arms around her until her sobs ebbed.

"Shane, I'd like a word with you outside," Father whispered when Mother had left the table. Shane followed Father out to the barn.

Father said, "Shane, I don't know how long I'll be away. I need you to take care of Mother. You know how she gets. Don't let her sit by the window all day and all night. You must keep her working. This is for her own good, but she won't see it that way. You'll have to insist. Can I count on you in this?" Asked Father. Shane nodded as he looked down. He kicked at the straw and dirt floor.

"But how long will I have to keep this up on my own?" Asked Shane.

Father rubbed his brow before answering, "I wish I knew, son. I sure wish I knew. I suppose however long it takes for me to learn something, anything about the whereabouts of your brother and sister. I don't know how hard it'll be to find out. Son, I need you to be the man, at least while I'm away." Shane nodded soberly.

Father walked into Hanover at midday the next day. He scanned the only road in town, which contained a blacksmith stall, a tannery, a cobbler shop, a stable and a tavern that doubled as a hotel. He walked into the tavern and ordered ale and a loaf of bread and butter. He slowly ate for a time, and then began talking of the weather and other trivialities with the tavern owner. Once

156

the owner began to warm to Father, he readied himself to address his business. "Do tax-collectors frequent your tavern?"

The tavern owner started and looked to the door, and replied quickly, "No never, but I must return to my duties." The owner went back behind the bar and began washing mugs and plates. Father tried to catch his eye, yet the tavern owner kept his eyes on his work. When Father finished his meal, he approached the tavern owner cautiously, not wanting to scare him off. "My good man, I merely seek information. I'm looking for a collector named Lachman. Do you know of him?" Asked Father.

"Like I said, I know nothing of tax-collectors. They mind their business and I mind my own. Now, if there be nothing else, I'd be obliged if you'd be on your way. I don't want no trouble here."

"I seek no trouble, my good man. I merely seek my daughter and my son, who are missing these past ten days. I'd be grateful if you could tell me anything that could help me," said Father.

"You've finished your meal, now be on your way." The tavern owner walked to the door, opened it, and held it open for Father to leave. Father sighed, gathered himself and his pack, and left. Once Father had left, the tavern owner scanned the road in both directions, and then closed the door with a bang.

Father crossed the road and paused. He turned and looked back at the tavern. When he saw the door closed he turned away. A man on horseback rode up to a nearby stable and dismounted. He handed the reins to a boy, and crossed the road and went into the tavern. Father had a spark of hope, and went inside the stable. The stable boy verified that all guests of the tavern kept their horses with him. The boy knew nothing of Lachman, or any other tax-collectors for that matter. Father described Lachman to the stable boy, who merely shrugged his shoulders. "I don't pay no attention to the people, just the horses they bring in."

Father left the stable discouraged. What else could he do? Where else could he ask after Amanda or Tim? The sound of the blacksmith swinging his hammer caught Father's attention. He approached the smithy. "I'm taking no more work for today. Come back tomorrow," said the smithy.

"No, I'm not here to hire you. I'm looking for information." The smithy eyed him suspiciously. Father saw no benefit in holding his cards to his vest. "My daughter and son are missing these past ten days. They were last seen at the tavern across the street...I'm hoping you might have seen something. They were with, well at least my daughter was with Lachman, the tax collector. Have you seen anything?"

As soon as Father mentioned Lachman, the smithy became tense, and quickly looked up and down the road. "No, I ain't seen nothing. Now be on your way."

"Is everyone afraid of the tax collectors? No one will talk to me! Please tell me something," pressed Father.

"I've learned to keep my mouth shut. And everyone else here in this town that has a brain has learned the same thing. You won't learn anything here. Now be on your way."

He had no idea where to turn. Father wandered around the town, looking for anything helpful. However, he didn't even know what would be helpful, short of catching sight of Amanda, Tim or the tax-collectors. And especially now that the smithy and tavern keeper had been clear that no one would tell him anything. Discouraged and unsure what else he could do, Father left Hanover and headed for home.

Father walked with his head down, lost in his thoughts. He tried to imagine where his son and daughter might be. He wondered in what condition they might now be. Father cursed the tax-collectors at the thought that his children might be mistreated. Suddenly two riders passed him along the road. Being lost in thought, Father hadn't heard their approach. Father turned to catch sight of them. He didn't recognize one rider, but he was almost sure that the other one was Lachman.

Father ran after them. By the time Father reentered Hanover, the town was quiet. He went back into the tavern, but Lachman wasn't there. Father ran across the street to the barn, but the stable boy said there had been no new arrivals. Father ran to the far edge of town and strained his eyes to look down the trail. Yet he could see nothing of the retreating riders. Father kicked at the ground and cursed. He walked through town, carefully examining every building, yet found nothing of the riders. Father resumed his slow walk home. Although he'd promised to not come home without some information about his missing children, he had no idea where else to look.

After a full week of training, the boys sat together in an awkward silence. They had all been thinking about the future. It was time to consider the next move for Tim and Andrew. They knew they couldn't hide in the tower forever. Eventually someone would discover their presence, as it was just too uncomfortably close to the castle. By now Tim felt confident with all three weapons, while Andrew felt he knew the mere basics. He didn't have the natural knack for them, like Tim did. This might give them a fighting chance, if it came to that. Although, not much of a chance against battle hardened men. Philippe started by saying, "My friends, even though I'm careful, I'm afraid someone will eventually follow me out here to the tower. I know I'm being watched. Every day I see men keeping an eye on me. We have to come up with a more permanent plan."

"I agree, we can't stay here much longer," said Tim.

"Maybe we can go back and apologize to Marvinian," suggested Andrew.

Phillipe and Tim laughed and shook their heads. Philippe said, "You might as well just hang yourself, lad. That way you would steal the pleasure from Marvinian."

"What if I somehow made it up to him?" Suggested Andrew.

"Nothing short of your death will satisfy him now. You and Tim have humiliated him by evading capture this long," concluded Philippe.

"Even if I offer to be his personal slave?" Pressed Andrew.

"No way! I won't offer to be anything to that monster, except for the man who takes his life," said Tim.

"I suppose there's a chance he would accept you as his personal slave, but he just as easily might hang you. You'd be taking a terrible risk," said Philippe.

"Enough talk of turning ourselves in! I won't hear of it. What other options do we have?" Asked Tim.

"I've been considering that ever since I brought you to the tower. The only idea I can see is for you both to go on the run," said Philippe.

"You mean run away?" Asked Tim. "I'm done running scared."

"No, I don't mean running scared. I mean for you to find another place to live...permanently," suggested Philippe.

"The only place I'll go permanently to is my family home," said Tim.

"No, you cannot! That is the first place they will look for you. The king's tax collectors know where you live. Marvinian is surely already keeping an eye on your family farm," said Philippe.

"Maybe we can sneak back into my parent's home, if we did it in the middle of the night," said Andrew.

"And then what?" Countered Tim. "This is the first place that they will look for you."

"We have to assume they are watching both of your family homes. These are both out of the question," said Philippe firmly.

"Then where can we go," cried Andrew as he began to weep. "I miss my Papa. I miss my home. I want to go home!"

Philippe put his arm around Andrew's shoulders, and turned his face towards him. Philippe said gently, but firmly, "Listen to me, Andrew. I know you want to go home. I understand that you miss your family. But you can never go home. You must accept this. The day you go home is the day you are a dead man. Do you understand me? I need you to understand the seriousness of your situation." Andrew wept harder, and buried his face in Philippe's shoulder.

"Philippe's right, we have to leave Scerlandia. We'll never be safe here. At least not for many years...not until Marvinian is dead," said Tim evenly.

Philippe nodded slowly, and said, "It's best that you accept this right now. There is no other option."

"So where do we go?" Asked Tim.

"To the north. In the north live peaceful peoples, who will take you in. You can make a good life there," said Philippe.

"I don't want a good life out of Scerlandia! It's my home, and I don't want to leave it," said Andrew through his tears.

Philippe slapped Andrew in the face, and then tilted his face up to his. "You have to let that go. It's a hard blow, but you have to accept that your youth is over! Now you must be a man! I need you to grow up," said Philippe. Andrew stared into Philippe's eyes. Andrew was stunned, as Philippe had never been that tough on him before.

Tim nodded and said, "To the north it is. But first I have something to do."

"There's no time to waste, you must leave at once," said Philippe.

"There's one errand I must accomplish first," insisted Tim.

"Then at least let me help you," said Philippe. Tim thought for a moment, and then nodded his assent.

Andrew stayed back at the tower and prepared supplies for their journey. Tim suggested this, but the truth is that Tim didn't want Andrew on this errand. Philippe he trusted. Andrew recently lived in fear, and Tim didn't want fear along on the mission.

Tim and Philippe hid in the bushes and waited. Below them lie the opening to the tunnel that Tim and Andrew had used to escape from the dungeon. "Are you sure you want to do this? You're taking a terrible chance," said Philippe.

"I can't leave her there," said Tim.

"How do you know she's in there?"

"I don't know for sure...but I can feel it. I know this sounds strange. I won't leave her to that bastard's mercy," said Tim.

"Well alright then, if you're determined, then let's do this. I will keep guard here," said Philippe as he reached for the hilt of his sword.

Tim took one last look left and right, and then scampered down the slope and slipped into the tunnel. He slowly stood up, expecting to hit his head any moment. Once he stood at his full height, he reached up with his hands, and found the roof of the tunnel just a couple of inches above his head. Tim crouched slightly, and began his fast walk to the dungeon. He kept his hands on both sides of the tunnel, as it was pitch black once he moved much beyond the entrance.

After walking almost a mile, Tim wondered if he had missed the dungeon. Maybe he had gone past it already. He went down to a crouch, brushing the left side of the tunnel wall all the way down. It was still all dirt. Tim continued his march, but more slowly, feeling the left wall as he went. Finally Tim felt stone with his left hand. He knelt down and examined the stone with both hands. The stone wall extended all the way from floor to ceiling. This must be the dungeon wall, thought TIm. He slowly ran his fingers along the lower two feet of the wall. At first all he could find were solid, unmovable stones. Maybe I'm in the wrong place, Tim wondered. However, he had felt no other stone along the way thus far, and he didn't know where else to look, so he kept at it. Finally his fingers found a stone with no mortar along the edges. This must be it! Tim slide his fingers as far into the slight opening along the edges as he could. He braced his legs against the surrounding wall and pulled.

At first it didn't budge. Tim repositioned himself to get the full strength of his legs and back into it, and this time pushed for all he had. This time the stone moved an inch. Encouraged, Tim pushed again and again until the stone fell into the dungeon. He cursed under his breath. He heard a small voice make a muffled cry. Tim considered offering her some kind of assurance, but thought better of it. After all, it may not even be Marjorie in this cell. He sure hoped the occupant was Marjorie. It would be an awkward moment if the cell did contain her, since they had never before met. Although it would be a dangerous encounter if it was someone else. Regardless of who it was, Tim didn't want to frighten them further. He got onto his knees, and squeezed into the dungeon cell. Once he'd fallen fully into the cell he went up on his hands and knees and looked around. There didn't appear to be anyone in the cell. Did I get it wrong? Did I imagine hearing a voice? Maybe Marjorie isn't in here, thought Tim.

As Tim turned to the left, someone bowled him over onto the ground, face first. Fists hammered his head and back. At first Tim covered up to protect himself, and then it came to him. These blows are not hurting me much. Tim twisted around and pushed his assailant off of him, and jumped on top of them and quickly pinned them down. Though her face looked crazed, Tim recognized Marjorie in the dim candle light. Tim held her arms with one hand and put his other hand over he mouth. "Stop yelling! You're going to bring the jailers on us!" Tim whispered urgently. She bit his hand. "Ouch! Damn it, that hurt!" He cried out. Tim pinned her arms down with his knees, and covered Marjorie's mouth with his hands, careful not to give her another opportunity to bite him. Although Tim covered her mouth fairly well, muffled cries leaked out.

Tim quickly regained his presence of mind. He searched the entrance to the dungeon, and was relieved to see no one coming. At least not yet. "Marjorie, I'm here to help you! Stop crying out.

You'll bring the guards!" Tim said in a whispered shout. He removed his hands to allow her to respond.

"I won't let you trick me, you scoundrel! And I won't let you rape me without a fight," said Marjorie.

"What? I'm not here to rape you. I'm here to help you escape. We have a common enemy."

This gave Marjorie pause. She stopped struggling and stared Tim in the eye. "What common enemy?"

"Marvinian. He has wronged me too. That is why I'm here. I won't stand by and let him ruin someone's life, and he has mine," said Tim.

"Get off of me! And tell me what he's done to you," said Marjorie.

Tim released her arms and got off of her. "I'll tell you everything, but not here. We aren't safe in here. Come with me and escape."

"Where would you take me?" Asked Marjorie with suspicion.

"Andrew and I are going to the north people, to find refuge."

"How do I know this isn't a trick to lure me somewhere?" Asked Marjorie.

"You're in a dungeon, and you worry that I'm taking you somewhere bad?" Said Tim with a laugh.

"How dare you laugh at me! Lately I've learned to not trust anyone. So tell me where you'd take me, or get out and leave me to my fate."

"Philippe has a plan for where we can go and be safe. To the northern lands," said Tim.

"Philippe is with you? You mean Philippe, the cobbler?"

"Yes, you know him?"

"Of course I know him. Everyone knows the queen's nephew. I've sung for him." Marjorie stood and paced the cell. Then she made a decision, "Let me gather my coat, and then I will come."

Tim went through the opening in the stone wall first, and then he helped Marjorie slip through. Tim put the stone back in place, rubbing dirt along the edges before he slid it in place. Maybe Marvinian wouldn't notice that stone right away. Then he stood and felt for Marjorie's hand. Tim put his other hand along the tunnel wall, and began to walk slowly. Marjorie stumbled several times, being afraid in the dark, and the ground was uneven. Finally they emerged into the dim light of the early evening.

It took Tim a minute to reorient himself to his surroundings. Tim had entered the tunnel in the afternoon sunlight, but it was now dusk. The fading sunlight filtered through the trees, and Tim rubbed his eyes as they adjusted to being out of the pitch black tunnel. He spotted Philippe waving them over, and pulled Marjorie towards Philippe and his hiding place. "So Tim was telling the truth. You are helping him," Marjorie said to Philippe.

"Helping Tim? Oh no, I've never met him before," said Philippe.

"What? Then what are you doing here?"

Tim and Philippe laughed in unison. Philippe put his arm around Tim's shoulders and said, "No, in all seriousness, I know him well. We are trying to get him out of danger. And Tim insisted on bringing you with him, although I counseled against it. He took a terrible risk in attempting to rescue you." Marjorie regarded Tim with new respect, and the suspicion began to fade within her. "Now, we must get back to the tower. We have dawdled here too long. Marvinian likely already knows of your disappearance," said Philippe.

Philippe unlocked the tower door, and had only taken one or two steps inside when Andrew flew into his arms. "Where have you been so long? I thought you were captured and never coming back! Did you get attacked?" Asked Andrew.

Philippe pushed Andrew off of him, and held him at arms distance. "All went as planned, and there was no trouble. Stop your fretting. All is well." Andrew breathed a sigh of relief. And then he saw her, "Oh my God, it's the woman from the tavern. I saw you the night we ran into trouble with Marvinian," said Andrew.

"Yes, I wish I'd never seen that tavern, nor this God forsaken village! Nor that God forsaken king or his thug Marvinian!" Said Marjorie.

"We're sorry for your trouble. Andrew and I saw Marvinian lead you away from the tavern the other day," said Tim.

"You were there?"

"We were shadowing Marvinian, and we followed him to the tavern. I saw him kiss you. And I silently cheered when you spat in his face," said Tim.

"That was the only satisfying moment...but the scoundrel took his revenge on me," said Marjorie in a softer voice as she looked away.

"What do you mean?" Asked Philippe.

"I don't want to speak of it. It's too terrible to think about," Marjorie said as a tear formed in her eye.

Philippe nodded and changed the subject, "So Andrew, what grub do you have for supper?" Andrew eagerly pulled out bread, a hunk of cheese, and four small sausages. They all fell to their meal with eagerness. Only Andrew had eaten since breakfast, and the rest were famished.

Once they were all sated they reclined on the floor of the tower. Tim rubbed his short beard and said, "We must make a plan for tomorrow. Now that Marjorie is with us, we dare not delay our leaving."

"Absolutely, they will certainly know of Marjorie's escape by morning, if they don't already. They will be scouring the area, knowing that she can't go far without a horse," said Philippe.

"I'm still afraid to leave Scerlandia! It's the only place I've ever known. Isn't there another way?" Said Andrew.

"Andrew, we've already had this conversation. You must leave, and leave at once. There's no more time for fear and fretting. You must act the man, even if you don't feel it. If not, go climb back into the dungeon," said Philippe sternly. Andrew wiped his eyes and slowly nodded.

"Can you make us a map to these northern peoples?" Tim asked Philippe. Philippe pulled out a leather scroll from within his tunic. He untied it and lay it flat on the ground. Tim and Philippe bent over it, and Philippe explained the course they must take. After asking several questions, Tim was content that he knew their route, or at least the beginning. He rolled the leather map back up, and slipped it into his pack.

The next morning all three travelers packed up. Before he unlocked the tower, Philippe took a look around, making sure they had no unwanted company. Satisfied that they were alone, Philippe came back into the tower. "So my friends, now is the moment of truth. Are you all prepared to leave?" Philippe looked at Andrew, and saw words forming in his mind, and with a glance warned Andrew off. Marjorie shrugged her shoulders. Tim nodded.

Philippe led them all out of the tower and to the north. Tim and Andrew each carried a sword, bow and full quiver of arrows. Marjorie carried a dagger. She had rummaged around the tower and found some old soldier's clothes that were a bit big on her, but fit well enough with a belt. The torn dress she'd worn in the dungeon wouldn't do for travel. Not to mention that it carried certain terrible memories for her.

Philippe led the party throughout the day. They stopped to refill their water skins twice, and once for dinner around midday. While the others ate, Philippe slipped off to higher ground. He crouched down to survey the valley below him. To the West lie a barren land, with little life. Behind him to the East lie mountains and a dense forrest. After scanning the valley for an hour, Philippe was content that there was no evidence of anyone shadowing them.

By the end of the day, Philippe took off his pack and stopped under the shelter of a large tree. "Why are we stopping?" Asked Andrew.

"This is the edge of Scerlandia. Look across the meadow below us. Do you see the trees just beyond the meadow?" Andrew nodded. "That is the northern boundary of Scerlandia. This is as far as I go."

"What? You aren't going with us to the northern people?" Asked Andrew.

"Now Andrew, you've known all along that I would not be joining you on this adventure. I am not being sought, and it would be suspicious if I were to disappear for more than a few days. As it is, I'm sure I'll be questioned for being gone these past three days, especially given my association with you two criminals."

"We're not criminals! All we did was..."

Philippe cut him off as he slapped Andrew on the shoulder, "Of course not! I'm merely playing with you. And as I was saying, in the morning you all will go on, and I must return to my shop." Andrew knew to not protest further, and ran his sleeve across his eyes while he nodded.

Tim awoke to his arm shaking. He looked up into Philippe's face. "Tim, I need to have a word with you," said Philippe in a whisper. Tim rubbed his eyes with both hands, and glanced around the camp site. Andrew and Marjorie both slept. Philippe urgently waved Tim over to a spot out of ear shot of the sleepers. Tim gathered himself and met Philippe. "I must be off soon, and I think it better to leave before Andrew awakens. He will struggle to let me go, and I believe it will go better for him to find me gone when he arises...and better for me as well," Philippe added with a smile.

Tim nodded slowly. "Maybe, but Andrew might feel betrayed if you leave without saying goodbye."

"Yes, that could be. Please tell him that my thoughts will be with him, and that I trust all will be well. I want to get back before sunset, so I'm off," said Philippe. Tim embraced his friend and said, "I'm grateful for your kindness to me. And for treating me almost like an equal."

"You are an equal," countered Philippe. Tim smiled and waved, and Philippe headed off on his trek home. Tim felt a heaviness in his heart as Philippe slipped out of sight. Tim stood long after he was gone, staring after him. Tim turned as he noticed a hand on his shoulder. Marjorie said, "What are you doing up so early? And what are you looking at?"

"I've just said my farewells to Philippe...he's gone," Tim said with a low voice.

"It's just as well for Andrew. He will cry when he discovers his best friend is gone, but less than if Philippe were still here," said Marjorie.

Tim nodded, and said, "I am sad as well. He has been the truest friend I've had. None other than my family has done anything for me, until Philippe."

"I'm sorry for you, and for all of us. I didn't know Philippe well, but I knew him to be a man of honor. It would have been a comfort to have him with us on this journey," said Marjorie.

Tim and Marjorie walked back to the camp. Tim bent down and lit the fire, and put on the coffee pot. Marjorie and Tim folded up their beddings. Andrew awakened to the morning sounds. He smiled and rubbed his eyes pleasantly. Then he made the upsetting discovery. "Where's Philippe? Is he off scouting?"

Tim looked at Marjorie, hoping for some help. She shrugged and went back to her packing. Tim said, "Philippe's already headed for home."

"What?"

"He said to tell you that all will be well, and that his thoughts will be with us," said Tim.

"He left without saying his farewells to me? I can't believe he'd do that to me!"

"If the truth be told, he did you a kindness," interjected Marjorie. "Philippe knew you would cry and lose your sense of manhood, if he said his farewells to you in person."

"I wouldn't lose my manhood if he..." Andrew's protests were interrupted by Tim and Marjorie's laughter.

"Stop it! Stop laughing! You both think I'm a baby," said Andrew. Tim and Marjorie stopped laughing for a moment, glanced at each other, and resumed laughing even more vigorously. Andrew began to tear, and then he stopped himself and laughed with them.

When they stopped laughing, Tim put a hand and Andrew's shoulder and said, "I'm proud of you. You did well to stop yourself. I understand you missing Philippe, and truth be told, I shall miss him as well. However, we must accept our situation and get ourselves to safety. Well done!" Andrew beamed.

"I hate to interrupt your congratulating one another, but breakfast is ready and getting cold," said Marjorie. All three fell to the coffee and food with eagerness. They ate mostly in silence, as they contemplated what lie before them. None had ever been outside the boundary of Scerlandia. They tried to imagine what might await them, each with their own hopes and dreads. Andrew imagined dangerous criminals and fire-breathing dragons trying to kill them, and shuddered. Tim pictured grand adventures mixed with dangerous situations, and Marvinian hot on their trail. Tim didn't think Marvinian would ever give up on tracking them down. Tim also hoped for a reunion with his family. Marjorie dismissed thoughts about what awaited them, although she had a dim image of a difficult life ahead.

Once they were all packed up, the three travelers shouldered their packs and descended down into the meadow. They crossed it and stopped as they reached the tree line. Tim said, "Here we go. We leave Scerlandia...maybe forever. I don't know what new adventures await us, but I shall take them, whatever they be. While I anticipate that danger awaits, I intend to face it without fear. Or at least as little fear as I can muster."

Marjorie smiled and said, "We probably go to our deaths." Tim and Marjorie crossed into the tree line. Andrew paused and look back over his shoulder and longed for his dear friend Philippe. Then he apprehensively searched ahead to their new path. Suddenly Andrew realized he could no longer see the other two, and he hurried ahead to catch them. "Wait for me! I'm coming!"

Ten

Philippe arrived back at the castle just after the sun set. He decided to go see the queen directly. The guards stepped aside when he reached the queen's apartments, as everyone in the castle knew Philippe. As always, Grace remained on guard within the outer rooms of the queen.

Philippe said, "Hello Grace, please announce me to the queen."

"The queen has retired for the day. You must come back another time," countered Grace.

"Come now, Grace, there's no need for us to have a competition of wills. Please make my presence known to the queen, and if she doesn't wish to see me now, I shall willingly come back another time."

Grace sighed deeply and then said, "Very well, but in the future you shall visit the queen during the day, just like every other resident of this castle."

Philippe grinned, and decided not to say anything further. He knew that Grace must have her sense of power and control, even if illusory. Philippe sat down in a chair and waited.

The queen appeared presently, saying, "My darling Philippe, so good to see you. Please do come in." Philippe stood and followed the queen into her inner rooms. Grace glared at him as he walked past her. Philippe paused and kissed Grace on the cheek. Grace's face flushed and she averted her gaze until Philippe was safely inside the inner rooms.

The queen spoke as she sat down, "I'm truly sorry for the difficult time that Grace continues to give you, Philippe. I've spoken to her about this many a time, but I'm reluctant to be too heavy handed with her. For she does mean well."

"Don't give it another thought, auntie. Poor Grace does no harm. She's merely afraid."

"I fear you are far too kind with her," said the queen with a sigh. "So you appear to have something on your mind."

"Yes, I've just seen Tim and two friends off to Fois...Each time I do so I miss the old country something terrible."

"Oh dear God, I do too. I often fantasize about returning there myself, but...the cost would be too high at this time," said the queen.

"Our work here is essential...but I am aware of the great sense of loss for me to remain here. At times I consider returning. My life in Fois has been the best of times for me...It does me some good to send three souls off to Fois. I saw the look in their faces, they have no idea what blessings await them, in fact I'm sure they are afraid."

"What a gift you give them! I imagine so much good coming to them...as once came to me. I will be forever grateful. And I can never thank you enough for sending me there once upon a time. I had no hope that such a place existed. And don't you dare go back home and leave me alone here," said the queen.

"I make no such promises. One day I may not be able to resist the pull to return. And I hope that these three will be as helped there as you and I," said Philippe.

"Do you have any concern that Marvinian will catch them?"

"No, the Fois won't allow him to do so. I sent word ahead. They will make it," said Philippe.

"How far did your map provide directions to them? Are you sure they will be able to find it?" Asked the queen.

"I have no confidence that these travelers will find Fois, but every confidence that Fois will find them."

"I will pray for their safe arrival," said the queen.

"Well, I must be off to my quarters, as I'm about to fall asleep in this chair," said Philippe.

"Then be off with you," said the queen as she embraced him.

Late the next day the three travelers tired. The sun had been hot, yet was cooling in the late afternoon. Tim blazed the trail, with Marjorie behind him and Andrew bringing up the tail. Tim wiped his forehead with his sleeve. He looked behind to see the other two trudging after him. Tim returned his gaze to the ground ahead, trying to keep to what appeared to be an established trail. Then Andrew cried out, "Wait Tim, she disappeared!"

"What are you talking about?" Asked Tim as he turned to face Andrew.

"She just, I mean, Marjorie is gone!"

Tim scanned the trail, and could find no sight of Marjorie. "How can she have just disappeared? Wasn't she right in front of you?"

"Yes, but one moment she was just in front of me, and the next she was gone," explained Andrew.

"How can that be? Where would she go?" Tim walked back towards Andrew, and almost fell into a hole. "Wow, where did that come from?" Said Tim. Once he'd regained his footing, he peered over the edge of the hole in the ground. The hole was about eight feet deep, and at the bottom lay Marjorie. She lie in a heap face down. "Marjorie! Are you okay?" She didn't answer.

"She's unconscious," said Andrew, who now stooped next to Tim.

"Yes, I have to get down to her," said Tim. He went to his pack and pulled out a rope. He tied it around the trunk of a tree. Tim pulled on the rope several times, and it held. He wrapped the rope around his waist, and lowered himself down to the bottom where Marjorie lay. Tim let go of the rope and knelt next to Marjorie. She didn't stir. Tim put his hand on her back and called her name. She didn't respond, but at least she was breathing. He brushed her hair back. He gently rubbed the back of her head, and then turned her over so that he looked into her face. Tim could see she'd injured her forehead, as it was bruised and slightly bloody. While she bled a little, her injury didn't appear to be serious, except that she was unconscious. There wasn't much room to maneuver about, as the bottom of the hole was only three or four feet wide.

"I'm not sure how we'll get her out of here," Tim called up to Andrew. Andrew shrugged. "Maybe I can push her up the side and you can pull her up the rest of the way," suggested Tim.

Andrew looked down doubtfully. "I don't know if I'm strong enough to pull her up when she's unconscious. I mean, she'll be dead weight."

"What other option do we have? I won't leave her down here."

"I don't know," said Andrew.

"I'll push her up as high as I can, and you'll have to at least hold her there until I can climb out and help you pull her up." Andrew nodded without enthusiasm. Tim gently pulled Marjorie up into a standing position against the side of the hole. She groaned, but remained unconscious. "Ok, are you ready?" Tim asked.

"I guess so."

"Andrew, you have to be ready to hold her in position. You can't let her drop. Are you ready?" Asked Tim.

"Yeah, okay, I'm ready."

While Tim held her against the dirt wall, he picked Marjorie up just below her waist. Fortunately she was fairly light. As he kept her in contact with the dirt wall, Tim slowly hoisted her up the wall. "Ok, can you reach her?" Asked Tim.

Andrew laid on his stomach and reached down with his arms. He was able to reach the top of her shoulders, but couldn't grab onto her. "I can't get a hold on her. Push her up higher."

Tim adjusted his grip a little lower, down around her upper legs, and then pushed. He kept his head against her stomach, so that she wouldn't fall forward. Andrew reached down and hooked his hands under her armpits. "Have you got her?" Asked Tim.

"I think so," said Andrew through clenched teeth.

"Are you sure? I don't want to let go unless you can hang onto her."

Andrew looked behind him and noticed a nearby small boulder. He wedged his left foot between the boulder and the ground, and then edged another couple of inches down into the hole. Andrew could now hold onto Marjorie by hooking her armpits on top of the inside of his elbows. "Ok, I think I've got a pretty good hold now. Hurry up and come help me."

Tim let go of Marjorie, and waited to see if Andrew could hold her full weight. Then Tim quickly grabbed onto the rope and climbed out of the hole. He scrambled over next to Andrew. Together they pulled Marjorie the rest of the way up the dirt wall, and out of the hole. Once she was safely lying on the ground, both boys lay back and rested, breathing hard.

Tim pulled his blanket out of his pack, and put it over Marjorie. He took off his coat and put it under her head. Her eyes fluttered for a moment, and then closed again. Tim poured some water from his canteen onto the tail of his shirt, and wiped the blood off of her forehead. Marjorie gasped and opened her eyes. She looked from Tim to Andrew, and then said, "What happened to me? Why am I lying on the ground? And what are you wiping my face for?"

"You fell into a hole. You were hurt, and unconscious. We just pulled you out a few minutes ago," said Tim.

"Really? I don't remember that...the last thing I remember is following you, and then I tripped."

"You tripped all right. You tripped into about an eight foot hole. It's probably a trap set by hunters," said Tim.

Marjorie lifted up on her elbows and stared at the hole. She grimaced and laid back down."What idiots would dig a hole right in the middle of a trail? Why don't they hunt somewhere else?"

Tim smiled. "Do you want some water?" Marjorie nodded, and Tim supported the back of her neck while she drank. After she'd had her fill of water, Marjorie fell asleep. Andrew and Tim made camp, deciding not to try to move Marjorie until tomorrow.

The next morning Tim awoke first. He rekindled the fire and made coffee. He warmed his hands, as the morning was cool. The smell of coffee woke the other two, who joined Tim for a cup. "So how are you feeling?" Tim asked Marjorie.

"Much better, I think," said Marjorie as she sipped her coffee.

"Do you think you can hike today?"

"I think so. My head still hurts, but not as much," said Marjorie as she put her hand to her head.

After eating their breakfast, they broke camp. As soon as Marjorie stood, she cried out. "Oh my God!"

"What is it?" Asked Andrew.

"It's my ankle. It hurts," said Marjorie as she rubbed her right ankle.

"Can you put weight on it?" Asked Tim.

Marjorie accepted Tim's arm in holding her up. She favored her right foot. She put one arm around Tim's waist as she attempted to take a few steps. Marjorie's first step was painful, yet her ankle loosened up a bit as she walked around. "I can walk, but I'm afraid I'll walk at a turtle's pace."

"Here, sit down. Maybe it would help if I wrap it up, and give it some support." Tim took an old bandana out of his pack, and tied it around her ankle. When Marjorie stood to try it out, Andrew produced a stick.

"I found you a walking stick. Maybe this will help too," said Andrew. Marjorie accepted the stick and took several steps without Tim's assistance.

"This is better. I won't be as fast as yesterday, but I can travel like this," said Marjorie.

"Great, so let's be off," said Andrew. Tim shouldered both his pack as well as Marjorie's. Tim nodded to the other two and headed out on the trail.

Marjorie protested, "I can carry my own pack! Don't treat me like an invalid."

"I'm not," said Tim.

"Yes you are, by carrying my pack, as if I'm a helpless woman."

"I'm treating you like a lady," countered Tim.

"Well, then on that account, I accept," said Marjorie with a smile. "Wait a minute so I can catch up," said Marjorie. Tim turned and waited until she walked abreast of him. The two began walking shoulder to shoulder. They walked in silence at first. Then Marjorie said, "I want to thank you for pulling me out of that hell hole."

Tim smiled and patted her on the back. "You got it, Marjorie."

"Call me Maggie."

"Maggie?"

"It's what my friends call me," said Maggie.

"Ok, Maggie it is. So we are now friends," said Tim. Maggie looked away and wiped at her eyes. "What is it?" Asked Tim.

"I'm not, I'm just not used to people doing much for me...everything I've got, I've had to get for myself." Tim put his hand on her shoulder.

Maggie wiped at her eyes again. "I haven't had many that I'd call friend...it's strange to feel...to open up to someone new."

Tim smiled, "I'm honored that you are trusting me."

Maggie smiled, and then looked away as her smiled turned to sadness. Tim noticed, yet decided to let her be, and didn't say anything. After a few minutes Maggie turned back to Tim and said, "Well, we'll just see how this goes." Tim nodded.

Maggie grew up in Randley, and had never been beyond the surrounding country of the village until Marvinian presented her with the king's offer. Maggie had been the apple of her parents' eye for the first four years of her life. When she wasn't with her mother helping with household chores, she shadowed her father at his blacksmith shop. Her favorite thing to do was put more wood in the fire. She would gather several logs and patiently stand by the furnace until Papa said to put it in. Papa was careful to not let her get too close, but this was unnecessary. Maggie could feel the great heat, and had no intention of getting anywhere near enough to get burned.

Mother preferred to keep her daughter home with her, but Maggie was strong willed, and insisted on following Papa out front to the smithy. The walk didn't take long, as they lived right behind the blacksmith stall. Maggie like to hold Papa's hand as they walked out to the shop. Mother often came out to check on her, and sometimes Maggie would follow Mother back inside to help out with cooking. The first thing Mother would do is wipe the soot off Maggie's face.

Mother and Papa thought Maggie would be their only little angel, as they thought Mother could no longer have children, due to the complications of Maggie's birth. The doctor said to expect no more children. However, soon after Maggie turned four, a younger sister was born. At first Maggie thrilled to care for Lilly, her little sister. Maggie thought of her as a doll. Maggie often spent hours dressing and undressing Lilly. Lilly might wear five or six different outfits in a given day. When little Lilly would cry, Maggie begged to hold her. As long as she was seated, Mother would allow it.

However, the party soon came to a crashing end. Little Lilly was never right, and once she was six months old, Mother and Papa realized she was different. Lily was slow to achieve developmental milestones, and didn't learn as quickly as Maggie had at the same stages. Mother and Papa fawned over Lilly, and spent money they didn't have, begging the town doctor to make her right. Maggie understood that something was wrong with her sister, but didn't understand why Mother and Papa didn't pay her as much attention. Mother no longer wanted Maggie to help her with household chores, as almost all of her attention went to the home and to Lily. Papa continued to allow Maggie to accompany him to the shop, but he seemed a bit distracted. At bedtime each night, Mother and Papa fervently prayed that Lily would become like a normal child. This went on for 20-30 minutes each bedtime.

At first Maggie thought that she'd done something wrong. She prayed to God to make her a better little girl. On one occasion, she promised Mother that she'd be a better girl. Mother said, "Oh dear, whatever are you talking about?" Maggie was confused by Mother's response, but continued in her efforts to make herself better.

When Maggie was six years old, Lily became ill. Not only did she now have her developmental delays, but she had the gripe. Mother and Papa fretted over her health, and feared that they would lose her. Papa kept up with his blacksmithing work, as he still had to put food on the table. Although every minute he could spare was with Lily and Mother. However, Mother neglected their home, except for what was essential to keep the family going. The home became dirty, their clothes unwashed, and only the simplest meals prepared.

Maggie received even less attention. She felt that she wasn't wanted anymore. So Maggie started saving up bits of bread. She found an old water skin that Papa had discarded, and put it in her stash. Maggie decided that Mother and Papa no longer wanted her, and that she must do something about it. She even wondered if they were her real parents. And she decided to run away and search for her true parents.

The next morning Maggie awoke before the sun. She had packed her few possessions, water skin and bread scraps the night before. She quietly put on her boots, and slipped out of their home. She walked across the dirt path to the trees behind their home and stopped. Maggie turned back and looked at the sleeping home. Smoke gently rose from the chimney, but all else was still. She secretly hoped that either Mother or Papa would notice that she was not in bed, and come out and search for her. No one came. Sadly, she turned and walked away.

By the end of the day Maggie had walked as far as she could for one day. She stopped by a creek and filled her water skin. She drank and ate some of the crusty bread in her pack. Once she finished her humble meal, she laid back on the grass. Maggie thought she'd just rest for a moment. The next she knew the morning sun shinning in her face woke her.

At first she didn't know where she was. Maggie searched about her camp site, and then remembered leaving home. She wondered if anyone looked for her. She doubted it, but secretly hoped they were. Maggie thought about her real parents. Where might they be? Did they live in another village? Or were they nearby? And were they searching for her? Maggie didn't know where to look. She began to cry. Maggie's soft cries eventually grew loud enough that she was overheard. A man hurried through the brush and came upon her camp site.

"Maggie, my God, what are you doing out here!" Cried Papa with tears in his eyes. He picked up Maggie and hugged her a little too hard. Maggie put her arms around Papa's neck and cried anew.

Papa set her down and searched her face, and asked again, "Maggie dear, why are you out here, miles from home? I've searched for you all night!" Papa looked exhausted.

Maggie wiped her eyes and said, "I'm looking for my real parents."

"Whomever do you mean? We are your real parents! What gave you the crazy idea that we're not?" Maggie looked away and shrugged. She didn't know how to tell Papa how she knew. Papa searched Maggie's face, and then had an inspiration. "Oh my God, we've been neglecting you, child. With your poor sister being ill, we haven't given two thoughts to you. I'm so sorry, my dear

Maggie." Papa picked her up again and held her tight. He gathered her few possessions and took her home.

Mother held onto Maggie even more than Papa, once they arrived home. Neither parent had slept, staying up all night looking for Maggie. Mother was angry with Maggie for leaving, but was even more grateful to have her back. Mother questioned her about why she left, not being satisfied with what Maggie had told Papa. However, Maggie didn't know what else to tell her. Maggie thrilled with all the attention.

Maggie had new hope that all would be as it was before Lily was born. This hope didn't last long. While Mother and Papa gave Maggie renewed attention for a week or two, then the new energy faded, and things reverted to how they'd been. One day Maggie asked Papa if she'd done anything wrong, and he dismissed her question as silly. Maggie slowly slipped into being sullen. She relied more and more on herself, not expecting much from anyone else. She still helped Papa in the smithy shop, but without the excitement she'd once had. Maggie helped Papa since there was nothing else for her to do. In time Lily healed. Maggie's parents were now less distracted, but the change was subtle. Maggie felt like a bother to them both.

A few years later she sat in church with her parents. The family hadn't gone to church until the girls were old enough to keep quiet during the service. Sometimes Mother had to take Lily out of church, as she didn't know to keep quiet during the service. Maggie had not wanted to go to church. Her friends had told her it was boring. And they were right. At first she played with a doll she'd brought with her, while some man talked about boring stuff. Then a voice began to sing. A thrill went through her body. Maggie looked up to search for the voice. It was the most beautiful sound she'd ever heard. The voice belonged to a woman of about her parents' age, but with a warm and inviting smile.

Maggie felt a stirring in her soul, although she didn't know what it was.

After service Maggie sought out the singer. She introduced herself as Evangeline. Maggie pleaded with her to teach her to sing. Evangeline was delighted to be asked, and readily agreed to teach her, assuming her parents consented. Mother and Papa agreed, and were happy to see Maggie interested in anything. The lessons began that very week. Maggie walked over to Evangeline's home each day after morning chores. Evangeline was married to the pastor of the church, and they lived in the rooms above the back of the church.

Maggie took to singing straight away, and soon was on her way to developing a nice voice. She also enjoyed her time with Evangeline, who gave her plenty of attention. Evangeline couldn't have her own children, and was pleased to have the opportunity to be a parent of sorts to Maggie. As time went on Maggie become more interested in being with Evangeline than her own parents. They didn't seem to notice that Maggie spent more and more time at the church. Mother and Papa continued to be focused on Lily, who had never outgrown her developmental delays, although she did fully recover from the gripe. It appeared that she'd never be quite right.

Soon Maggie sang in church alongside Evangeline. Maggie loved wearing the special red robe that Evangeline had sown for Maggie herself. It matched Evangeline's robe. Mother and Papa were proud of Maggie's talent, and never missed when Maggie sang in church.

Two years after Maggie had begun singing with Evangeline, tragedy struck. At first Evangeline appeared to merely be more tired, and thought she was aging and just needed more rest. However, soon she spent more and more time in bed, and before long, she didn't get out of bed. Maggie visited Evangeline every day, although the doctor only allowed short visits. Talking seemed to drain what little energy that she had.

Maggie privately wondered if Evangeline was merely tired of Maggie's company. On one occasion she even asked Evangeline. Although Evangeline reassured Maggie that her fatigue had nothing to do with her, Maggie was unconvinced. Evangeline died soon thereafter. Maggie attended the funeral, but refused to speak to anyone. She wore her red singing robe. At the end of the service, Maggie went up to the coffin and looked at Evangeline. She looked so peaceful, like she might be sleeping. Maggie touched her hand, which was cold, and Maggie quickly pulled her hand back. Maggie took off her robe and placed it under Evangeline's hands, and then went home.

Maggie retreated into herself. She stopped joining Papa in the shop, and only helped Mother with cooking when asked. Maggie spent most of her time either practicing her singing, or wandering about the forest near the house. Papa tried to invite Maggie to help him in the smithy, but she politely refused. Her only interest now was singing, and her quiet walks alone. For awhile she only sang alone. Maggie would wander out into the forest to sing. She was careful to go far enough, so that no one was likely to hear her.

A couple of years later, the people of Randley decided to build a theater. It seemed like an extravagant expense to many, but it actually didn't add up to that much, since most Randley citizens contributed whatever skills or materials they had. Papa did all the metal work. At first Maggie didn't take much interest in the theater, except to watch the progress of the construction. However, once it opened, the locals performed plays and musicals. Once Maggie heard the singing, she was intrigued. It didn't take much for the theater director to get Maggie to join the group of singers. With Evangeline gone there was no one to offer any kind of instruction, so Maggie taught herself to sing more and more songs. Evangeline had taught her to read music, so she could sing just about anything for which she had the range. Soon Maggie was a regular performer at the theater.

The other children invited Maggie to play with them after singing rehearsals, yet Maggie politely declined. She would enjoy them while at the theatre, but always refused anything outside of it. Many of the other children thought Maggie saw herself as too good for them. They were mistaken. Maggie would no longer take the chance of becoming attached to someone that might go away.

The town theater held a performance every Saturday night, and Maggie always participated. She often spent most of her time from Sunday to Saturday learning and practicing the new songs for next Saturday's performance. Maggie didn't have much interest in anything else. By the time the king's men came through Randley, Maggie had established herself as the town's favorite singer.

As the day wore on, Maggie's ankle loosened up more and more. By mid day she untied the bandana around her ankle, no longer feeling the need for the support. Although Maggie continued to use the walking stick. She walked alongside Tim throughout the day, chatting casually. Maggie had not been very talkative prior to her fall into the hole. Something about being rescued from her fall had changed her disposition, especially towards Tim. Maggie surprised herself as she found herself drawn to Tim. She normally kept herself from getting too attached to anyone, ever since Evangeline's death. However, she couldn't help herself, she talked with Tim throughout the day, allowing herself to become more and more engaged. While Maggie felt nervous letting herself reach out to Tim, she also noticed being energized by the interaction, which was enlivening.

Tim had been drawn to Maggie from the moment he saw her. The first day he and Philippe rescued her from the dungeon, Tim had tried to talk with her. However, Tim quickly noticed that Maggie didn't want to talk about herself much, and would politely answer Tim's questions with brief answers, not elaborating at all about herself. Sometimes she didn't even answer at all, acting as though she hadn't heard Tim. Maggie did politely listen to Tim's stories about himself, but asked few questions, and her mind seemed to be somewhere else. After an entire day of trying to get Maggie to warm up to him, Tim backed off and decided to let her be.

Now Maggie surprised Tim as she asked numerous questions, and told him many stories about her own life. At first Tim didn't know what to make of the new Maggie, but at some point he shrugged his shoulders, and merely decided to enjoy her. And he certainly did enjoy Maggie's newfound interest in him. In fact, he delighted in her interest, as well as her willingness to make herself know to Tim.

Andrew felt left out. He desperately missed his good friend Philippe, and hoped that Tim would at least partially fill the gap. At first he and Tim talked much, but all this changed after Maggie fell into the hole. Andrew tried to join into Maggie and Tim's conversations. As Tim and Maggie walked side by side, Andrew tried to walk alongside them as well. However, in many places the trail was too narrow, and Andrew fell back behind the other two. Then Andrew tried to talk with Maggie and Tim from behind them. At first they gave him polite attention, but then began ignoring many of his comments. The truth being, they were far more interested in their own conversation than what Andrew had to say. Eventually Andrew stopped trying to participate in their conversation, and fell to sulking behind them, walking with his head down.

Eleven

Several days later Tim, Maggie and Andrew climbed to the top of a rise. They stood on the crest of a hill, looking down at a dense forest. Tim gazed off in the distance, and then regarded the map in his hands. The map ended here, as this was the extent of Philippe's directions. Tim turned to Maggie and Andrew and said, "We're on our own from here. I don't see any trail to follow."

"No, I don't either," said Maggie.

"Didn't Philippe give you any directions from here?" Asked Andrew.

"He said to keep going the same direction, and to keep the setting sun directly to our left, so that we're always heading North from here on out," answered Tim.

"But I don't see any trail heading that way," said Maggie.

"I suppose we must blaze our own trail from here on out. And we must keep track of the setting sun, so we don't lose our way," said Tim.

"What land are we in?" Asked Andrew.

"I have no idea. Once we left Scerlandia, we left lands about which I know," said Tim.

"Papa told me that the ancient people live out here to the North," said Andrew.

"What ancient people?" Asked Maggie.

"The ancient ancestors. They were the first people to live in these lands, according to legends," explained Andrew.

"But who are they? Do they have a name?" Asked Maggie.

Andrew shrugged his shoulders and said, "The ancient ones is the only name I've heard."

"Have you ever heard of them?" Maggie asked Tim.

Tim shook his head, "No, my parents never spoke of them to me."

"Maybe they're just the stories of myth for children," suggested Maggie.

"We better find some real people soon. We're running out of supplies," said Tim.

"Then maybe we ought to start hunting," suggested Maggie.

"Yes, I guess we'd better," said Tim. He pulled his bow off his shoulder and said, "We best keep an eye out for game, or our meals are about to become thin. Off we go." Tim began to hike down the back side of the hill.

Late that same day Tim raised a hand to stop. He listened, turning his head from left to right. He pulled an arrow out of his quiver and put it to the string. Tim crept forward slowly, looking from side to side as he went. Maggie and Andrew followed, but neither carried a bow. A hundred yards up Tim caught a glimpse of what he sought. Off to the right stood a deer eating leaves. The deer turned to look in this direction, and Tim and the others ducked down. Satisfied for the moment, the deer went back to eating. Tim positioned himself for a clear shot, pulled back the arrow and loosed it into the shoulder of the deer. The animal started and took off running.

Tim yelled to the others, "Run after it! That's our supper running away."

All three of them took off after the deer. It was still fast, and they lost ground quickly. Tim realized he wouldn't be able to catch it until blood loss tired it, so he slowed himself, and began to follow the trail of blood droppings.

A mile later Maggie said, "Hey Tim, stop for a minute! Did you hear that?"

"No, hear what?"

"I hear something, and I don't mean the deer. I'm pretty sure there's someone else out here," said Maggie in a whisper.

They all turned to look back. And then they saw the first one. A soldier, dressed in something resembling Lord Teagle's army uniform could be seen walking through a small meadow about a half mile behind them.

"Oh my God, it's soldiers!" Yelled Andrew.

At the sound of Andrew's voice, the soldier looked up and pointed towards them. Another soldier came up to join the first one, and both of them peered ahead towards the hunters.

Tim, Maggie and Andrew ran through the forest, looking over their shoulders for signs of their pursuit. Tim worried that he'd trip, as the forest floor held vines, branches, rocks and low bushes that were difficult to see at a dead run until Tim was right on top of them. Tim tried to follow Andrew, who ran faster and was ahead of Tim. Maggie stayed right on Tim's heels. Thank God that her ankle no longer bothered her.

They ran down a gentle grade and then up a steep hill. Tim glanced up as Andrew neared the summit of the hill. Tim couldn't see over the top of the crest and what lie below. Tim quickly returned his eyes to his feet. Just as Tim neared the summit he heard Andrew cry out. Tim was startled and slowed his pace out of concern for what lie ahead. Just as Tim stopped, Marjorie plowed into the back of him, and both of them fell in a heap. They picked themselves up and looked down a cliff at the river below. Just five feet below Tim was a stone ledge, and holding onto the ledge were Andrew's hands. Andrew cried out for help. Tim glanced behind him and saw men running up the hill. Tim quickly surveyed the ledge. He'd have to jump down to get to Andrew, but stop himself quickly, or he'd end up in the river far below. "Tim, they are almost upon us! We have to get out of here!" Yelled Maggie.

Tim nodded and said, "Maggie, run into the forrest over there, and Andrew and I will find you when we can. I must pull him up."

"Tim, you must hurry! They're almost upon us! Maggie took one last look at the soldiers and hesitated, and then ran off to the right. Tim took two steps back, as he prepared to jump down to where Andrew held on for his life. Just as Tim prepared to jump, he took one last look over his shoulder. He saw in an instant that he had no chance to pull Andrew up before Marvinian's men got to him. Tim suddenly changed his mind and darted behind a nearby tree.

Tim peered around the tree at the approaching men. He felt certain of his discovery, as he stood only a handful of feet from the men. Just as Tim took a step back, he whispered under his breath, "Oh God, somebody help me!" Strong arms grabbed Tim from behind, and a hand covered his mouth so he couldn't cry out. Tim was pulled up into the trees and set on a high branch. His head was turned so that he peered into the face of his abductors. They were two young men. Their faces were painted black and green, making their features almost impossible to discern. One of them placed a finger over his mouth, and gently released Tim's mouth.

Tim whispered, "Who are you?" The man signaled for Tim to be quiet, and pointed to the men below. Marvinian's men looked over the cliff into the water below. They swept their heads from left to right, and then one of them pointed downstream and said, "There's one of the them!"

Marvinian walked up to the edge of the cliff and demanded, "So where are the rats?" One of the other three men pointed downstream to Andrew. "Well, the rat made it into the river alive." And then turning to two of his men, "And make sure that we have a welcoming party waiting for him when he leaves the river. You will stay with me," Marvinian said to the third man. The first two men ran back down the hill the way they'd come, discussing how they might intercept Andrew downstream.

190

Marvinian turned to his man and said, "Now, find the other two! They can't have gone far. We won't leave here without them."

"Maybe they went into the river also," suggested the man.

"No, don't be an idiot. It was plain as day that at least one of the rats ran off into the forest. We will search the forest, one tree at a time if we have to," said Marvinian. And with that they retraced their steps back down the hill, searching for signs of Tim and Maggie's trail.

When they were out of sight, Tim returned his gaze to his captors. They both seemed to be older than Tim, appearing to be in their twenties. They wore short beards and short hair, as well as robes that were charcoal gray. Their feet were clad in some kind of animal skins that were made into boots. Once Tim had scanned them, he returned to their faces. Their eyes were unusually bright. As Tim pondered what this might mean, one of them spoke, "Do not be afraid. We intend you no harm. We pulled you into the tree when you asked for help."

"How did I ask for help?"

One looked to the other and asked, "What exactly did he say, Alec?"

"I believe it was, 'Oh God, somebody help me.'"

"And you're God?" Asked Tim.

The two men laughed. "Of course not, but we gladly serve Him."

"Do you know who Marvinian's men are?" Asked Tim.

"We know all the peoples of Scerlandia."

"And who are you?" Inquired Tim.

"We are the people of Fois. My name is Alec, and this in Calum." Tim nodded and scratched his head. And then Alec said, "And do you have an audible name?"

"Oh sorry, I'm Tim."

Both Alec and Calum bowed their head in greeting. Tim smiled and said, "So why did you help me? I still don't understand."

Alec and Calum looked at each other and laughed. "You know, it's the most curious thing that people are often baffled at our willingness to help, especially when we've been asked. We never cease to be amazed at your surprise. This is simply our way."

Tim pondered this before asking, "What do you mean it's your way?"

Alec answered, "I don't believe I can explain it to you in words. But come and see for yourself." Alec and Calum hopped down from the tree quickly and easily and began walking. Tim hurried to catch them, as he needed much longer to make his way to the ground, and fell awkwardly the last six feet to the base of the tree.

"Where are you going?" Called out Tim as he caught his breath.

"Come and see," answered Calum without turning his head.

"Wait a minute! There is a young woman with me. We must find her before Marvinian does. He might already have captured her," said Tim.

"Oh she is in good hands," said Calum.

"What do you mean? Do your people have her?"

"Yes, of course. The other guardians pulled her up just before we got to you," said Alec.

"But how do you know this?"

"You mean you did not hear her cry out? I feared that Marvinian might hear her, but then I remembered how poorly you Scerlandian folk hear," said Calum.

"I can hear just fine!" Countered Tim. Calum and Alec looked at each other and laughed.

Tim walked behind them, listening to them chat casually. Every so often Calum and Alec would stop and listen briefly, and then resume their march. Tim concluded that they seemed to be listening to the sounds of the forest. For what forest sounds, he didn't know. After walking for several miles, Alec and Calum disappeared. Tim walked not far behind them, but didn't know where they'd gone. Tim walked on for another hundred feet. He paused and looked all around. Then he turned back to where he'd lost them. Suddenly Calum popped out of the rock wall and said, "This way, Tim."

Tim followed Calum through a slight opening in the rock wall that had to be less than eighteen inches wide. They stepped through the opening to a path along cliff walls. Tim lost his balance and began to fall. Just as he was sure he fell to his death, Alec pulled him back, and then said, "You Scerlandians are strangely unbalanced amongst both trees and rocks."

Once Tim regained his composure, he glanced down at a sheer drop of several hundred feet of rock wall. He shivered at the thought of what might have been his fate. Below the rock cliffs lay a valley that spread out for many miles. At the bottom of the valley ran a swift river, although Tim could only catch glimpses of it from the path. Tall Pine and Aspen trees filled the valley, with occasional open spaces of meadow. It was the most beautiful place Tim had ever seen. He only hoped he survived the climb down so that he could see it.

Alec and Calum had already started down the path that wound along the cliff walls. Tim began his trek after them, yet took his time. An hour later they entered the valley. Tim breathed more easily, now that he'd made it down the cliff. He looked back up, and was surprised to see how high it looked.

Every so often they walked past huts. Some were quiet with no activity. In front of other huts were people about their chores of splitting or gathering wood, cleaning clothes, preparing food, sweeping porches. Children played carefree without concern. Everyone wore robes similar to Alec and Calum's, yet they varied in colors.

They reached a large clearing near to the river. There stood a large hut, many times larger than any of the others that Tim had seen. Next to it was a smaller hut, built on top of a wood platform. Alec and Calum took Tim directly to it. "You must wait here," Alec said to Tim.

A moment later Calum emerged from the door, and waved Tim to follow him in. The room was modest in size, and warmly lit by one window and several candles. A fire burned in the hearth, adding to the light and warmth of the room. On a chair sat an old woman. Alec and Calum bowed their heads to her, and then left the hut. Tim watched them go, wondering where they went. Then he turned his gaze to the woman. Her eyes surprised Tim. They were as bright and vibrant as Alec and Calum's, and yet she appeared to be as old as the sun. Her face bore a timelessness that was difficult to place. She wore long, salt and pepper hair that was pulled back into a single braid. Her robe was black. She said, "Welcome home wanderer, I am Sileas."

Tim stared at her for a moment and then said, "And who are you?"

"The people of Fois have appointed me their sagart."

"What is a sagart?" Asked Tim.

"If you remain with us, you shall come to know."

"Wait, 'welcome home,' is that what you said?" Asked Tim.

"Yes lad, I did."

"But I've never been here before. This isn't my home. I live far away," said Tim.

"You speak of the home that you barely know and remember. I speak of the home that you intimately know but don't remember," explained Sileas.

Tim scratched his head and stared out the window, before saying, "I don't understand what you mean. I don't mean no disrespect, but that all sounds like gibberish to me."

"Yes, I'm sure it does for now. But give yourself time and see what you might remember. In any case, you are quite welcome here," said Sileas.

"What is it that you want from me? I hope you don't intend to put me on refurbishment duty," said Tim.

"Why would I want to do that?" She said with a laugh. "We have no such duty. We all tend to our own waste," said Sileas with a smile.

"You do?"

"Yes, of course. Here we all take responsibility for our needs, at least to the extent of each person's ability. We ask for help when we are in need."

"But what do your slaves do?"

"Slaves? We have no such person," said Sileas with a chuckle.

"You mean you don't have any slaves, or even any servants?" Asked Tim.

"We have no need for slaves, and wouldn't accept one. And yet we are all servants."

"How can you all be servants? Is there no king or queen?"

"No, we see no value in such titles," said Sileas with a laugh.

"How can that be? I thought all peoples had rulers. How can you rule a people without a ruler?"

"Not all people require ruling. The most evolved rule themselves...but I don't see how I can explain it to you in words. If you stay long enough, perhaps you shall see for yourself," said Sileas.

"You mean I am free to leave? I'm not a slave here? Or an indentured servant?"

"Did you not hear me, lad? Or perhaps you did not believe me. We have no such person here," said Sileas. Tim scratched his head, and glanced about the room.

"I see that I have confused you. You are welcome to stay as long as you like. And I do believe that you might evolve if you remain with us. We don't require you to stay, nor do we ask you to leave. And do not expect to understand much on your first day here. Yet all will become clear as you come to live it. The understanding of the head is greatly overrated," said Sileas.

"But what other kind of understanding would there be?"

"Why, lived understanding, of course," said Sileas.

"I don't know what that is."

"Which is a fine place to start. Do you wish to stay here for now? If not, I shall ask Calum and Alec to lead you back safely. However, my guess is that you would benefit from time here."

"Well yes, I will gladly stay. I have no other place to go. I am being hunted, and fear for my life."

"You will be quite safe here. None penetrate our boundaries unless we bring them in as guests. And I will send you back to Alec and Calum. They will show you where you shall live while you are amongst us. And I have someone to show you," said Sileas. She waved to someone standing nearby, and a moment later Maggie walked into the room. She ran over to Tim and embraced him. Maggie cried on his shoulder, and Tim had to hold himself back from crying himself, but was not entirely successful.

"Thank God you're safe! When I didn't see you, I feared that Marvinian had captured you," said TIm.

"I haven't seen Marvinian since I left the cliff. I began to run, and the next thing I knew I was hoisted up into a tree. At first I thought they were monkeys," said Maggie.

Tim laughed and said, "Yes, I was pulled into the trees as well. It was the strangest experience. I didn't know what was happening to me."

Tim returned his gaze to Sileas. He tried to stop his head from spinning, while he watched Calum and Alec quietly conferring with Sileas. They finished their conversation and Calum returned to Tim's side. Calum put a hand on Tim's shoulder, and nodded for he and Maggie to follow. Tim stared at Sileas for a moment. She held his gaze with kindness and warmth, yet a look suggesting that she needed nothing in return.

Tim followed Calum out of the hut. They all walked down to the river. Alec and Calum took off their outer garments and washed in the river. Alec suggested that Tim do likewise. Maggie went around a bend in the river to bath in private.

An hour later they stood on the porch of an empty hut. Alec

opened the door, and signaled for Tim and Maggie to enter. The single room was tidy and surprisingly clean. A fire burned in the hearth. On the right stood a hammock, tied to the far and near wall posts. Alec went over to a closet, and pulled out a second hammock. He hung it directly above the first. Notches had been cut into the wooden posts, onto which the hammock's ropes were placed. A basin filled with clean water sat on a table, along with freshly picked fruit and vegetables. "Is this where we are to live?" Asked Tim.

"Why yes, this shall be your home for as long as you wish," said Calum.

"How is it clean, with food and a fire burning, if it has been uninhabited?"

"Uninhabited does not mean unattended, for the Fois. We always keep a home prepared and waiting for guests. We simply built a fire and brought in fresh food and water," said Alec with a grin.

"This home is better than I had hoped for, or even imagined...But what shall I do while I live amongst you?"

"And what will I do here?" Asked Maggie.

"You shall both work and participate in the community," said Calum.

"Oh I knew this was coming. What disgusting work do you have for me?" Asked Tim.

Both men laughed, and Calum said, "You did not believe Sileas. We have no such work. However, perhaps we could invent some such work, if you would feel more at home."

"Oh no, that won't be...but what work would you have me do?" Asked Tim.

"I thought you might dig toilet pits for us," said Alec.

"See, I knew this was coming!" Said Tim. Alec and Calum laughed so hard that their sides hurt. "Wait, you're joking with me! There really is no grunt work?" Said Tim.

"Of course not! What purpose would that serve in our community?" Said Calum.

"To put people in their place by humiliating them," suggested Tim.

"Or take advantage of their good nature," added Maggie.

"We absolutely want to put people in their places, but not as you imagine. We find that most forget their true place, and need help being restored to it," said Calum.

"But what is my true place?" Asked Tim.

"And mine?" Asked Maggie.

"All will be known in time. Be patient with yourselves. For now it is enough to allow yourselves time to settle into our fellowship. We will help you find or create work that fits you and benefits the community. And the same for you, Maggie," said Alec.

"Benefits the community? Like what?" Asked Maggie.

"We don't know yet. We shall have to see what suits each of you and would make a contribution to us. At what are you skilled?" Said Alec.

Tim and Maggie glanced at each other and shrugged. "I have only known singing...and helping mother prepare food for us," said Maggie.

"Uh, well, all that I have known is farming. My brother and I help my father and mother farm our land," said Tim.

"Then we shall see how we can best apply each of your skills to our needs. But that can be figured out later. There is no need for you to begin work right away. For now, we'll give you time to settle in to your new surroundings, and relax into no longer being hunted. It must be a huge adjustment. We'll come and fetch you when supper is ready," said Calum.

Tim and Maggie watched them leave. Tim then turned his attention back to his new surroundings. Tim walked over to the door, and checked to see if it was locked. It wasn't. In fact, the door had no lock. Tim wondered if there was a way he could install a lock.

Maggie went over to the table. Above the wooden table were simple shelves built into the wall. A dozen books sat upon the shelves. Maggie examined the titles, but didn't recognize any of them. She hadn't done much reading, so she really didn't expect to know any of the books. Maggie quickly lost interest in the books, which seemed strange to her. She moved into the kitchen and began opening cupboards and drawers. The utensils, cups, bowls and plates seemed simple enough. Maggie began to close the cupboard, but something stopped her, and she decided to examine these items more closely. Although they were simple, something looked different about them. As she took a closer look at one of the cups, she noticed that it was exquisitely made. Unlike the cups she grew up with, these were perfectly round, with handles that seamlessly blended into the cup. They exhibited no cracks. Maggie picked up one of the bowls, which was as expertly designed as the cup. In fact, everything in the cupboard appeared to have been made by master craftsmen, except for a few items. Off to the side sat a set of four simple plates. They were far from round, and had been painted with simple pictures of suns, moons and stars. With the exceptions of the pictures on them, they resembled the plates that Maggie grew up with.

Tim wondered about the room, picking up items as they caught his eye. He sat down on the upper hammock. He swung his feet back and forth, and then laid down. The hammock was surprisingly comfortable for a rope bed, and included a nice feather pillow. The next thing Tim knew someone gently shook him. He opened his eyes to look up at Calum. "Wake up, little brother, it's time for supper. You fell asleep."

"I'm sorry, I didn't mean to fall asleep on the job...I just wanted to rest my eyes."

"No problem, there's no job to sleep on. You were tired, and now you've rested. All is as it should be," said Calum. Tim looked Calum in the face, searching for signs of deception. He didn't find any, though he expected to. Tim searched for Maggie and found her talking with a woman near the door. She looked refreshed and rested.

Calum continued, "Come with me, Tim. They wait for us to eat."

"Who's waiting for us?"

"Come and see," said Calum. He led Tim to the door and introduced him to his wife, Cilia.

Cilia surprised Tim with a warm embrace, without asking nor seeming to need permission. Her eyes radiated warmth and a smile. Her hair was long and wavy, and a bit unruly. She quickly released Tim, took Maggie by the arm and led her towards their hut. Tim walked alongside Calum.

Tim and Maggie followed Calum and Cilia through the trees and to an opening in which stood two huts. Out in front was a sturdy, but rough table. Upon it was a generous spread of food. Three children played about, while Alec and a woman readied the meal.

"Alec and I live here with our families. Alec is my brother. You and Maggie will eat with us whenever you like."

Tim and Maggie took the places offered at the table. All of the others sat down. Then everyone quieted as Alec blessed the meal. Tim kept his eyes open during the blessing, and grinned at one of the children who peeked at him. The child giggled and shut her eyes.

The food was simple, and yet surprisingly good. While the little girl show her mother a skinned knee, her older brother quickly stole her bread. He turned his head and took one bite, and then gave the rest to the dogs. When the girl turned her attention back to her plate, she cried out, "Hey, what happened to my bread?" Her brother feigned disinterest and looked intently at his own plate.

Alec said, "Ian, do you know anything of your sister's bread?"

"Uh, well, I think the dogs ate it," said Ian.

"And how did they come to have the bread? I didn't see any of the dogs jump up upon the table." Ian hesitated as he gazed down. Alec continued, "Ian, I want you to be honest with me. You know the importance I place on being truthful." Ian nodded slowly. "Then out with it boy."

"Yes, I took Gizzy's bread, and gave it to the dogs."

"That's better, lad. I appreciate you coming clean. Now, why do you think you took her bread?" Asked Alec.

"I was hungry, and wanted more bread."

"Aye lad, now let's return to the truth. You know as well as I, that if you request more from your mother or me, you can have it for the asking. You know that, right?" Ian nodded his head. "Then out with it, what prompted you to take your sister's bread?"

"I was mad," said Ian.

"Okay now, that's a good start. And what prompted your angry with Gizzy?" Asked Alec.

"I don't know..."

"Did something happen while you all were playing before supper?" Asked Alec. Ian nodded and looked away. "And what would that be?"

"I don't want to tell you...you might be mad," mumbled Ian.

"Well now, I might be mad. I might be mad for a short bit, but I rarely hold onto it for long. Now isn't that true?"

Ian nodded again, and said, "But I still get scared when you're mad."

"Well, that's fair enough then. And I'll be more likely to be angry if you don't come completely clean to me."

"Okay...I was mad because you played with Gizzy more than me today."

"Oh lad, is that so? Well, we'll just have to fix that after supper. Perhaps you and me can play some catch. Would you like that?" Asked Alec. Ian looked up and nodded vigorously. "Now that we've addressed your anger, how can you make things right with Gizzy?"

Ian averted his eyes and shrugged his shoulders as he said quietly, "I don't know."

"I have an idea, you can give your bread to Gizzy," instructed Alec.

"Oh Da, do I have to?"

"Yes lad, you have to. Unless you can produce another piece of bread from up your sleeve. I'm more than glad to be with you after supper, but we still have to make amends for your sister missing her bread. Gizzy can't very well retrieve her bread from inside the dogs now, can she? Do you think she can reach her arm down the dogs throat and grab her bread from his stomach?" Ian laughed and shook his head. Then he picked up his bread and set it down on Gizzy's plate. "There you go, lad, nice work," said Alec.

Tim felt a unique satisfaction after the meal, as though his stomach was not merely full, but his whole body energized. Tim noticed he felt lighter as the meal progressed, as though his muscles and bones no longer weighed as much. The parents seemed to take genuine joy in their children, laughing and telling stories with them. They all drank wine with the meal. The children's cups had been softened by water. Tim tried to think of how to describe these strange Fois, but the words eluded him. They were like no other people he'd met. Tim wondered if they were the strangest people he'd met, or perhaps they were insane. Or maybe they were the most sane that he'd met. Perhaps both. Tim glanced at Maggie, who winked at him. He wondered if she also thought these people were curiously odd.

Alec led them back to their hut, and Alec show Tim and Maggie where the fire wood was piled outside. Alec revived the fire before he wished them good night and left. Tim looked at the hammocks, and noticed they contained pillows, but no blankets. "Hey Maggie, have you seen any blankets around here?" Asked Tim. She shook her head as fell into the lower hammock.

"I'm so tired that I don't care. I didn't take an afternoon nap, like you," said Maggie with a grin. Tim found two blankets folded up on the bookshelf. He tossed one onto Maggie, and curled up in the other blanket on the top hammock. Tim was tired too, but the strangeness of this new place kept him awake.

"Is this the strangest place you've ever been?" Tim asked. When he received no reply he turned over and looked at Maggie below him. She snored without stirring.

The next morning Tim awoke. The sun pleasantly filtered in through the opaque curtains. He stretched and yawned. Tim felt different, but wasn't sure why. Then it came to him, that he hadn't slept that well in weeks. It was the first night in a long time that he didn't worry about Marvinian. He felt rested. Maggie still slept below him. Tim got up and refueled the fire, and washed himself in the basin. As he looked around for food, he found bread, fruit and vegetables left for them. As Tim cut up the food and put it into two bowls, Maggie awoke to the cutting sounds. "I hope you left me something. Did you already eat?"

"No, I'm just preparing our breakfast." They sat at the table and ate in silence.

As Maggie cleaned up their few dishes, she said, "It's so strange being here. I feel like I'm asleep in a dream, and keep expecting to wake up and find myself back in the forest...but it's a wonderful dream."

"These people are like none I've ever met. I keep wondering if they're tricking us," said Tim.

"I doubt they're tricking us. But I fear Marvinian showing up at any moment. I'm sure he hasn't given up on finding us."

"I worry about him too. And I fear that we are truly slaves, but they have yet to tell us. I dread the awful punishment they have in store for us," said Tim.

"Maybe these people work for Marvinian? Perhaps he's laughing at us right now?"

Calum knocked on his door. "Good morning! I am here to laugh at you on behalf of Marvinian," said Calum.

"What?" Said Tim and Maggie in unison.

"Yes, Marvinian waits for you," said Calum. A moment later a broad grin appeared on his face and he laughed from his belly. "You two live in such terrible fear! We know no Marvinian, except for briefly seeing him trailing you when we pulled you into the trees. He is not here, nor is he our friend. You don't trust that you are as safe as happy children."

Tim and Maggie looked at each other and shrugged. Tim felt foolish for Calum overhearing his fears of the Fois' evil intentions. "I'm an idiot. I should never have doubted you. I have insulted you," said Tim.

Calum laughed, and said, "How can I be insulted? I know that what you think has nothing to do with me. These thoughts come from your own fear."

"I feel like an idiot for being afraid."

"You treat yourself with so little mercy. You will continue to think such thoughts until you are ready to not," said Calum.

"Ready for what?"

"Ready to no longer be afraid," explained Calum.

"But how can I be ready to not be afraid?"

"Stay with us, and we will teach you."

"Can't you just tell me how to get rid of my fear? I am quite determined to not be afraid," said Tim.

Calum thought a moment. Then he said, "I don't think I can. It is only partly a matter of determination. You must come to know that you are safe."

"Safe? But how can I be safe as long as Marvinian seeks us?"

"You will come to see how little power he truly has. You have much more power over yourself than any other lad," said Calum. Tim scratched his head, and looked at Maggie.

She shrugged her shoulders, and said, "I'm not afraid."

"You will come to see that you are as afraid as Tim, but perhaps of different things. You will both be afraid until you are done being afraid. But come, it is time for us to discuss your work," said Calum. "Do you both wish to have an idle day, or do you want to begin your work?"

Tim and Maggie looked at each other and Maggie said, "I'm ready to work."

Tim said, "I don't want to sit in the hut by myself all day, so I'll work too. But what work am I to do? Am I to work in the fields of your farms?"

"Yes, that is what we thought would be good." Then Calum noticed the bow and arrows next to the door. "Wait a minute, is this your bow and arrows?" Asked Calum.

"Yes, I stole them from Marvinian's men."

"That's right, I saw them when we saved you. I had forgotten all about them. Are you skilled at the bow?" Asked Calum.

"I know the basic skills."

"Then perhaps you are better suited for guardian duty. We don't need another farmer at this time, yet we are stretched a bit thin at guardian.

"What does a guardian do here?" Inquired Tim.

"Protects the perimeter of the community."

"Do others attack you?"

"Some would if given the chance. Your job will be to prevent them from having the opportunity," explained Calum.

"Would I be watching out for Marvinian's men? I'm eager for a chance to kill them."

"No little brother, we do not kill, unless a man would have it no other way. Your job will be to prevent Marvinian and all outsiders from entering uninvited." Tim's face fell. "Don't be disappointed for long, for you shall learn another way with men like him," continued Calum.

"He deserves to die. What better way is there for men like him?"

"Remain with us, and you shall see. But for now, we must go. Guardian duty begins presently. You shall work alongside me. Come." Calum turned to Maggie, "And Cilia shall be along presently to take you to your work." Calum picked up a pair of skin boots that were on the ground next to the fireplace, and handed them to Tim. "Put these on."

"But why? My boots are still in good working order. I've recently repaired them," said Tim.

"They won't do. The boots of the Fois leave almost no impression. Once we leave the boundary we shall travel without leaving a trace." Tim waved goodbye to Maggie and followed Calum out.

Calum led Tim back along the path they had taken when he arrived yesterday. They walked past a stream. Several Fois washed clothes in the stream. They walked past fields, with many tending fruits, vegetables and grains of various types. Further along the path Tim watched others building huts. There was something strange at the way the Fois worked, yet Tim couldn't quite say what it was.

An hour later they slipped through the narrow opening in the rock. Calum said, "Now that we're beyond the boundary of the Fois, we shall only speak in whispers, for we are now on duty. This ridge of rock is the southern boundary of our people. We allow no one to enter without our leave. You will help me keep intruders from approaching this place."

As they walked away from the rocks Calum carried a small tree branch, which he used to erase their tracks. When they reached the area near where Alec and Calum had found Tim, Calum pointed for Tim to climb a large tree. After brushing away the last of their faint tracks, Calum followed Tim up the tree. They climbed high up into the canopy of the large trees. Tim glanced down at the ground, and swooned. He clutched the tree more tightly.

"You shall become more confident in trees," said Calum with a smile.

Calum appeared relaxed as he sat amongst the branches. He casually scanned the ground in all directions. Tim nervously clutched the trunk of the tree. Calum waved Tim to join him, a bit higher up. After glancing down, Tim slowly made his way to where Calum sat. Tim's sweat poured profusely out on his brow. Calum ruffled Tim's hair and said, "Don't worry, little brother, you shall come to feel quite at home up here. And the less you stare at the ground, the sooner you will become comfortable."

"I can't imagine ever feeling comfortable this high up. Can't we watch from lower down?" Asked Tim.

"No, we can see much better up her, and there's little chance of us being seen." For the first time Tim noticed that the robes that he and Calum wore had a hint of green to their gray shade.

"Is that why our robes are this gray-green color?" Asked Tim.

"Of course, so that we might blend in and remain unseen. We wouldn't be much good as guardians if we wore bright orange, and others could see us from five miles away. Now hold still." Calum spread some green paste on Tim's face. Tim made a face, as it had an odor.

"Do I have to wear this awful green paste?"

Calum laughed. "Of course, it completes our being invisible."

"Who is it that might see us?" Wondered Tim.

"Mostly it is the people of Scerlandia, but occasionally we see travelers from other lands. We find that most people are peaceful and want no trouble, yet many of the Scerlandians seek conflict."

"Yes, I've noticed, but why do they seek conflict?"

"I'm not entirely sure, but they must not be at peace with themselves...it's also possible," said Calum, and then he stopped himself in mid-sentence as he put a finger to his lips. Calum pointed to the place where he'd found Tim. Three men approached the place where Andrew went off the cliff into the river. They bent down and examined the ground. One of them pointed to the ground, and then shrugged his shoulders. The second man stood and turned towards Calum and Tim. It was Marvinian. Tim tensed as he saw him.

Marvinian said, "I understand the damned tracks disappear here. And I also understand that the boy cannot fly. So where did he go?"

"I don't know," said the tracker.

"Now listen here, I brought you all the way out here because you're the best damn tracker amongst the king's men. You will track the rat, and figure out where he went. We found the other rat, but I won't stand for either one of them getting away. Or that damned whore. Now find them!" Growled Marvinian. The tracker began walking towards Calum and Tim's tree.

Tim pulled his bow off his shoulder, and fitted an arrow in the string. "This is the chance I've been looking for to kill that bastard," Tim muttered.

As he began to take aim, Calum pushed his arrow down and shook his head. He whispered, "No, this is not our way."

"But it is my way," said Tim as he raised his arrow to his shoulder.

Calum pushed it down again and said, "Watch and do as I do."

Calum deftly fitted an arrow into his string and pulled it to his shoulder in one motion. He briefly aimed and loosed the arrow. The arrow took the hat off the tracker and stuck soundly into a tree. The tracker dropped to the ground. "Who the hell did that?" Asked Marvinian.

"Drop to the ground," shouted the tracker. "It is the ghost assassins."

"Ghost assassins, my ass. The ghost assassins are merely legend," scoffed Marvinian.

"The arrow sticking through my hat ain't legend. I have encountered them before, and they are not to be trifled with," said the tracker.

"Have you ever seen one?" Asked Marvinian.

"Of course not, they're invisible."

"Yeah right, they're invisible because they don't exist. Nobody's ever seen one. Keep going," said Marvinian. He stood and began walking towards the Fois boundary. He only made it ten steps before a second arrow took his own hat off. The third man ran off. Marvinian ducked behind a tree. He called out, "Show yourself, cowards! If you be of any courage, come out and fight like a real man."

Calum held his finger to his lips. Tim nodded.

"Don't push it, Marvinian! They're said to be crazy, and fear being seen. The ghost assassins believe a man can take their soul if they're seen," said the tracker.

"Oh that's hog's wash. That's all dim-witted wenches' tales. Get up and find that damned boy and his whore!" Shouted Marvinian.

"I have no wish to die. Go right ahead, if you don't value your life," said the tracker. Marvinian strode over to the crouching tracker, and pulled him up by his hair. Marvinian turned his head to face him and said, "You will resume your tracking, or I will take your life myself. Either way, you don't have to worry about no ghost assassins."

The tracker swallowed hard, and nodded. He returned to where Tim's tracks disappeared and resumed his search. He circled the tree nearby. He crouched and looked around with wide eyes. Then the tracker began moving towards the Fois boundary. After a few steps an arrow pierced completely through his left foot. He cried out and rolled on the ground in pain. "You see what I'm telling you. These people are real, and so are their arrows. We have to leave, now! I can't track no more anyways."

Marvinian sighed deeply. Then he called out, "Manson, get your arse over here, now!" Immediately Manson appeared from behind a nearby tree. Marvinian grabbed him by the collar and said, "If you ever run off without my leave again, I'll give you a permanent leave. You get my meaning?" Manson nodded his head and he stared at the ground. "Now get over there and pull the arrow out of his foot," ordered Marvinian.

The three men returned the way they came. Calum climbed around to the far side of the tree, to watch their retreat. Once satisfied, he returned to where Tim clutched the tree. "Why didn't you kill them? We had a perfect opportunity," said Tim.

"There was no need. Like I have said, little brother, we Fois do not take a life, unless they leave us no other way. We do not see it as our right to decide when another will leave this life for the next."

"Marvinian seems to have no reluctance to send a man into the next life. Why does he get to decide?" Countered Tim.

"That is not for me to say. And he must live with his own demons."

"What demons?"

"I don't see how a man can take another's life without suffering himself. These actions do not come without consequences to the soul," explained Calum.

"He doesn't look like he's suffering any consequences."

"I don't see how you can overlook it. Did you not notice anything of his countenance?" Asked Calum.

"Well, I suppose he seems angry all the time."

"Yes, and is not that a consequence?" Asked Calum.

"Anger doesn't seem like that much of a consequence to me."

"No? Would you like to live with constant anger and resentment?" Asked Calum. "I believe you might find it more consequence than you know."

"I'd still like to give him another consequence, a consequence with my arrow in it."

Calum laughed and ruffled Tim's hair. "Yes, I know you desire this. We shall see what comes of it," said Calum.

"But what is the point of shooting arrows through their hair?" Asked Tim.

"We have two aims. One is to prevent them from crossing into our boundary. And the second aim is to help men like Marvinian with their intentions to attack." Tim looked puzzled, and Calum continued. "Many men intend harm to others, but do not realize such intentions return to them."

"How is this possible? If I kill Marvinian, he can no longer kill me."

"Perhaps, but if you continue intending to kill him, such intentions will boomerang back to you. Such intentions do not merely go in one direction. All intentions, whether for good or evil, return to the sender."

"So how does it help Marvinian for you to shoot arrows into his hat?" Asked Tim.

"My hope is that my arrow may give him pause, that he may reconsider his ways."

"A man like that won't reconsider. He's bent on finding me and killing me, unless I can either evade him or kill him myself."

"You may be right. However, it is still my intention to give him the chance to reconsider, even if he doesn't take it. If I kill him, I take away any chance he has to change his intentions, and thus, the direction of his life. I pity Marvinian that he requires himself to live in a mind like that."

"I still think you're deluding yourself that you do him any good. He will never change."

"Well little brother, you may be right. We shall have to see," said Calum.

Tim couldn't have found the opening in the rock wall on his own, although he'd been through it twice before. Once inside the boundary again, Tim asked, "So do we have supper, now that guardian duty is over?"

"Guardian duty is never over, but we are off till morning. And yes, we shall eat and then the best part- dessert."

"What is for dessert?"

"Worship. We eat for the body and worship for the soul," answered Calum.

"You mean dessert is singing? That's all?"

Calum grinned and said, "You must never have truly sung. It is healing to the soul. It is like...no, I can't describe it with words. You must experience it for yourself."

"Maybe I'll skip the singing. No offense, it just ain't my thing," said Tim.

"No, you must come to worship. It is the heartbeat of the Fois. If you miss the worship you miss the Fois."

"Well, if you insist, I suppose I can sit through a few minutes of it."

"Good, then it's settled. Now let go and eat. I'm famished," said Calum.

Maggie and Cilia were already at the family huts when Calum and Tim arrived. Alec had just returned from Guardian duty as well. All of them helped prepare the food, which included fruit, vegetables, grain and cheese. There was a strange sense of anticipation during the meal, as though something sought after awaited. During the food preparation Maggie began to sing. Tim turned to Maggie and said, "My God, Maggie, you have the most beautiful voice I've ever heard!"

"Oh, thank you. I didn't even realize I was singing, until you said something."

"I must agree with Tim, you're voice is lovely. Have you found work with the singers? A large number of us dedicate themselves to singing," said Calum.

"Cilia mentioned them to me. I hope to meet them soon," said Maggie.

After supper with Alec and Calum's families, Tim and Maggie followed them back to the large clearing where Tim and Maggie had met Sileas. A large crow of Fois gathered. They all wore the now familiar robes. The children's robes were of brighter colors, while the adults wore subtle shades of gray, green, brown and black. The children ran around playing, while the adults conversed in small groups.

Someone rang a bell, and everyone knelt or sat in the grass around a fire pit. A man lit the fire. Near the fire were five chairs. Sileas occupied one of them. Two men and two women occupied the remaining four. One of the men stood and nodded towards the porch of the nearby building. Tim hadn't previously noticed, but several people sat on chairs on the porch, each holding an instrument. At the signal, they all began to play music. All of the Fois began to sing. At first the singing was low and like a chant. Tim rolled his eyes. This was going to be boring and a waste of time, just as he's suspected, he thought. He glanced at Maggie, who's eyes danced with anticipation. She loved all forms of music.

Then the chanting subsided, and the men began to sing. Their voices were clear and surprisingly beautiful. Tim felt a stirring within him. This surprised him, as he'd never felt anything for music before. And then the women all began to sing. Their collective voices were as angels, even more lovely than the men. Tim closed his eyes and focused on their voices, though he didn't understand the words they sang. His mind quieted and the singing seemed to be the only happening in the world. Beautiful colors appeared to his closed eyes. Many of the colors he'd never seen before. Warm liquid splashed the backs of his hands, which sat on his knees. Surprised, Tim realized they were his tears. These tears were not of sadness, yet he couldn't put a word to what brought them forth.

The singing stopped. It seemed like it had only lasted a few minutes. Tim wanted to cry out for them to continue. He opened his eyes, and was startled at the darkness. Only the fire provided light, as the sun had set during the singing. Tim felt a hand on his shoulder. He turned to look up at Calum, who said, "Was that the waste of time you had anticipated?" Tim had no words, and merely shook his head. Calum smiled.

Maggie jumped up and embraced Calum. "I've never heard music so beautiful!"

"Indeed! I never tire of our worship." After a brief silence Calum offered, "Do you want me to walk you and Maggie to your hut? It is dark, and you may not find it easily."

One of the female singers approached Maggie, and said, "I noticed your countenance during the singing. I could see that you are a lover of song."

"Yes, I do. I love to sing myself...but it has been some time since I last sang more than a passing mumbling," said Maggie.

"Then come and sing with us now. While most go to their homes, a group of us stay to further worship and practice our singing skill."

"Absolutely, I would love to!" Maggie turned to Tim and said, "I will see you tomorrow. I must stay with them." Tim nodded and smiled.

After Maggie left, Tim hesitated as he thought over Calum's offer. And then he asked, "Would it be alright if I stayed the night with your family?"

"Of course you may. However, the only space we have for you is the hay loft. You are welcome, if you think you'd enjoy sleeping with the animals."

"Yes, thank you. I do not want to be alone tonight," said Tim.

"Then come along," said Calum.

When they reached their hut, Calum first helped his wife to put the kids to bed. Then he carried a candle out to the barn, and showed Tim the stairs to the loft. When Calum left, Tim kept thinking about the worship. He had heard plenty of singing in his life, but nothing like that. This singing seemed to emanate from the soul, not the lips. It wasn't that the Fois were blessed with more gifted singing voices, but the songs were as though from another place.

Tim lay in the hay loft. "God, I don't know if you exist, in fact I doubt it. But if you do, help me." Where did that come from? Did I really just say that, wondered Tim? Above him two beings drifted slowly to him. They were beings of light. Tim wasn't sure if they were light or wore garments of light. The beings did not appear to bear wings. They lifted him from his bed, and bore him up. They did not seem to be taking him to another place, but rather another time. The light beings brought him to the tower in which he'd spent weeks. They drifted through the walls, as though nonexistent. Inside Tim saw himself sitting upon his bunk bed talking with Andrew. Tim remembered the conversation. They spoke of plans to kill Marvinian and his men. Andrew and Tim spent hour upon hour making such plans. Tim noticed his countenance, and the delight he took in contriving such plans. The look on his face both surprised and disturbed Tim.

Then the beings bore Tim away from the tower. They traveled across a mountain range and arrived at the fortified city, and Tim saw himself lying on the floor with the doctor tending his arrow wound. Tim shook his head as the doctor offered to stay and listen, if he wished to talk. Tim wondered why he's turned away the kind doctor, as he'd clearly missed out on something. They travelled over the forests and meadows for many miles. They alighted at the field where Tim had removed tree roots and rocks with team blue. Tim's gaze focused on his face, which was downturned and troubled. His face appeared without energy, as though he were alone and without a friend in the world. Tim watched Thaddeus reach out to him, putting an arm around his shoulders and inviting him to speak. Tim watched himself gently push Thaddeus away.

The next moment Tim flew away with the beings, if flying be the right word for the way in which they travelled. Tim saw himself walk into the tavern inn to find the tax collectors holding Amanda prisoner. With eyes blazing Tim charged them, muttering promises to end their miserable lives. A moment later Tim found himself floating off again. Tim recognized his family farm. The angels brought Tim to the kitchen where his mother worked with Amanda. Then Tim saw himself come into the back door from outside. His eyes were downcast and his shoulders slumped. His mother dried her hands on her apron and put her hand on Tim's arm, inviting him to talk with her. He shook his head and continued on to his room. His mother watched him go with concern.

Tim woke to a gentle shake. He opened his eyes to see Gizzy crouching beside him in the loft. The morning light backlit her face, as the sun shined through a window behind her. She smiled as she looked at him through a stray strand of hair. "Wake up, Mister Tim." At first Tim wondered if she was an angel, and then he recognized her.

"Okay, I'm awake."

"Uncle Calum says to come to our morning meditations," said Gizzy.

"Morning meditations? Are you sure that's what he said?"

"Uh huh, we do morning meditations every day," said Gizzy.

Gizzy led Tim back to the hut. Both families were gathered in Alec's hut. Alec glanced up at Tim and Gizzy. "Now then, we're all here. Let's begin."

Tim groaned inwardly as he found an empty chair and sat. Oh God, now we're going to have church. I hate church...But I must be gracious to these people, for they have been kind to me, he thought. Calum glanced at Tim, seeing if he was settled. Tim smiled and nodded. Calum began the meditation. Tim expected rituals to wade through, mechanical prayers to recite, and repetitive readings to enunciate. None of this happened. Calum led them through a guided meditation. Tim couldn't even describe exactly what it was. Yet he knew he was left with a pervasive sense of peace, a peace that words failed to fully express. Later he tried to tell of it, and merely fumbled with many words, until he gave up trying.

While Tim sat with his eyes closed, a golden light flickered before him. The flickering seemed almost like laughter. The light poured into him through his head. Peace and joy filled him. Tim's body seemed almost to float, as though being beyond the reach of gravity. And yet he still felt the chair beneath his legs and behind his back. He didn't want it to stop. Tim glanced down and saw black smoke leaving him through his feet. Where had this strange blackness come from. It couldn't have been inside him. Or could it have, wondered Tim. Tim pictured those he loved before him; his mother, father, Shane and Amanda. The golden light emerged out of Tim's mouth and swept into his loved ones. Strangely, Tim felt no less full of light, although much of it had left him for each of his family. Tim said to them, "I will see you again," though he did not use his mouth to tell them this.

Tim was startled out of his meditation by Alec's voice. He gently and briefly blessed all present. Then Alec said, "We have fed our souls, now we shall feed our bodies." Breakfast was served. Throughout the meal Tim kept thinking on his experience. He tried to understand what had occurred, but for the life of him, he couldn't figure it out.

Twelve

A week later Calum arrived at Tim's hut as he ate his breakfast. Maggie had an early breakfast, and was gone by the time Calum showed up. Maggie had found her work and rightful place amongst the singers of Fois. Tim offered Calum to sit and eat. Calum went to the fire, and poured himself a cup of tea. Calum held the tea in both hands, and sipped while he spoke with Tim. "So where have we been assigned guardian duty today?" Asked Tim.

"We have been relieved of duty today. I will bring you to Sileas."

"To Sileas? Whatever for? Am I in trouble?" Worried Tim.

"Oh no, I don't think so. You will be given an opportunity to expand yourself."

"What does that mean?"

"You have been with us two weeks, and still do not understand that we live to enjoy and expand ourselves," said Calum. "But come and see what Sileas has for you. You may be surprised."

"Then tell me what it is."

"Sileas will give you a great opportunity. This is all I will say," said Calum.

"Whatever is this great secret. Why not simply tell me what this is about?" Pleaded TIm.

Calum thought for a moment before saying, "There is no secret. I would gladly tell you more, if only I could think of how to say it. For this opportunity to make sense to you, I think you will need to experience it with Sileas."

"I don't understand why you Fois are such a mystery. Why don't you make yourselves plain?"

Sadness flashed across Calum's face, which faded to mirth, "I only wish it weren't so to you." In spite of Tim's efforts to pull more information out of Calum, he would say no more. Finally, Tim gave up and simply followed Calum to her hut. Calum waited outside while Tim went in alone.

Tim seated himself on the mat before Sileas. She appeared deep in thought, and Tim waited. Then Sileas turned her head and regarded Tim quietly for a moment. Then she smiled and said, "You shall be given a great chance to evolve, a chance beyond what many ever receive. But I'm getting ahead of myself. Let me ask you, what is your greatest desire?"

Tim breathed deeply and said, "I have two great desires, my lady. The first is to find my sister and take her home with me to my family. We have been apart too long. And the second is to kill Marvinian."

"Yes, you love your family," she said with a smile. Sileas' face darkened as she continued, "And you are consumed with hatred and fear. This takes great space in your mind."

"But you don't know what he has done to me, and what his people have done to my family! I hold him responsible for all that has been done to my family."

"Then tell me," said Sileas as she smiled. Tim went on to tell her of all that had occurred, starting with the tax collectors, through being tortured, and ending with Tim's escape from Marvinian's dungeon. Sileas listened patiently without interrupting, and was especially sympathetic for Amanda's plight.

After Tim finished Sileas thought for a moment. "Tim, I'm sorry for your troubles, and share your concern for your sister. And when the time is right, we shall see to her safety and release. But for now, my concern is for you."

"Wait, you will help me rescue Amanda?"

"Yes, of course. All will be done to bring your sister home," said Sileas.

"Thank you! But if you consider me to be full of hatred and fear, how is it that you will help me?"

"I know you to be afraid, but I perceive no hatred in your desire to bring Amanda home to your family. I honor this desire of yours."

"But..." began Tim.

Sileas interrupted Tim by saying, "For now I'm more concerned with you, than Amanda. I hear that much harm has been visited upon you, and Marvinian may have done you the greatest harm. And yet he also provides you an immense opportunity. This will probably sound crazy to you, yet he can also be your teacher. In fact, he can become your greatest teacher to date. For Marvinian has given you a great opportunity to release yourself from hatred and guilt and find peace."

"You want me to let him off, after all he's done to me?"

"Why yes, of course," said Sileas.

"I will never forgive Marvinian!"

"Then I fear that peace will continue to elude you," said Sileas.

"For me? You ought to fear for Marvinian, for I shall end him. I would have my first week here, were it not for Calum preventing me."

"Calum did you a great service," said Sileas.

"I don't understand...but more to the point, Marvinian does not deserve forgiveness! What has he done to even begin to deserve this?

"This is not about Marvinian," said Sileas.

"Do you refer to the tax collectors? Yes, they must be dealt with as well."

"My concern is not for any of the three. There is another, someone you most need to forgive," said Sileas.

"What are you talking about? There is no one I hate more than Marvinian."

"Yes, in time you must forgive Marvinian. I've found that the hardest person to forgive is often quite a surprise."

Tim thought for a minute, and then said, "I have no one else to forgive, beyond Marvinian and the tax collectors. Yet Marvinian is the one with much blood on his hands!"

"I can see that we have much work to do. You must learn that it is not possible to hate another without hating yourself; for they are one and the same. The flaming arrows of hatred never fire in a single direction. You have blinded yourself to the arrows you fire towards yourself, and we must pull the scales from your eyes, that you may see," explained Sileas.

"This is utter madness. How can you be the priestess of the Fois, when you speak such foolishness?"

Sileas smiled warmly, and said, "In time you may come to know me and can judge for yourself. But for now, your work begins."

"Are you not going to explain your simple-minded statement?"

"No, I don't believe it would help. Although you are right about the idea being simple, and yet most have the most difficult time grasping this great truth."

"You make utterly no sense to me," said Tim.

Sileas stood and opened the door and called Calum in to join them. "Calum, you will escort Tim to the safety cell. You must keep Tim from furthering his own destruction."

"Yes Sileas, I know my task. And yet I may need your counsel in this case. It won't be easy," said Calum.

"I know, my son, and my door shall remain open to you to come as you find the need," answered Sileas.

Calum nodded to Sileas, and gestured for Tim to follow. Calum led him out of the hut and along a trail to the right that Tim had not yet seen. Tim puzzled over Calum walking more slowly than his usual brisk pace. After pondering this mystery, Tim asked, "Calum, why do you walk so?"

"I grieve for your suffering," said Calum.

"My suffering? My suffering will end as soon as Marvinian lies beneath the ground." Calum nodded sadly, but said no more.

After walking a mile or more, they came upon the hills. The hills were of dark rock and dirt, with bushes growing from the dirt spots in between rock. They rose a hundred feet or more. As they neared the rock hills, the sun emerged from behind dark clouds, and it suddenly became more light and bright. An opening in the rock appeared before them. Tim followed Calum into a cave. The inside was lit by torches. The walls were made of solid rock, and appeared to be well worn. Tim wondered if many had come this way. Along the right wall water slowly dripped to the dirt, and left a dark stain behind.

After walking through a narrow passage, the cave opened up into a more spacious room. This chamber was lined with many lit torches. The chamber contained two openings: the one through which Tim and Calum had just entered, and an opening on the far side. Fois guards stood at the opening to the other passageway. Calum took down one of the torches, and nodded to the guards. They stood aside for Calum and Tim to enter.

Tim followed Calum through the dark passageway. After walking fifty feet, they entered another larger chamber. Inside were three dungeon cells. The cell to the left was large and empty. To the right were two smaller cells. One was empty and the other contained a man. The man wore a military uniform with a sword belt, with no sword in the scabbard. His clothes were disheveled and torn, and his hair appeared to have been unwashed for weeks. Both his arms were newly bandaged. Blood seeped through the bandage on his left arm. At first Tim didn't recognize him, and then the man spoke.

"So you've brought the rat here to torture me," growled Marvinian. Tim was stunned to recognize his voice. Tim pulled his knife and lunged at the prisoner. Marvinian laughed after he stepped back from the bars. "You didn't think I'd make it that easy on you, did you rat?" Said Marvinian.

"Open the cell, so that I can kill him," pleaded Tim.

"No, I desire to assist you in your journey, and I won't help you bring further harm upon yourself," said Calum.

"You speak foolishness like Sileas, making no sense. Open the damned door that I may exact my due revenge."

"You know I won't allow that," Calum whispered as he pulled Tim back into the dark passageway out of Marvinian's hearing. "You are not here to kill him. You are here to make your peace with yourself first, and with Marvinian."

"I will never make peace with that monster, and…"

Calum cut him off, "You will give me your knife." Tim reluctantly handed Calum his knife. Not that he wanted to, but rather that he'd learned that Calum didn't say things he didn't mean. Calum slipped Tim's knife into his own belt, and invited Tim to return to the chamber. As they entered the dungeon, Calum whispered so that Marvinian couldn't hear, "You must learn that your knife will only bring you more destruction here, and less peace. A knife has many uses, but none of them present themselves here in the safely cells. I know that you intend to harm Marvinian, but you must realize that it is only yourself that you harm. Be kind to yourself, and begin to make your peace with both of you." Tim glanced at Calum as he rolled his eyes. Tim thought Calum simpleminded.

Tim approached the bars, while Calum stood several paces behind and to the side. Tim said, "Where is Andrew, and what have you done with him?"

Marvinian laughed, "The rat Andrew is where he should be, and has been done with as he deserved."

"Speak plainly! What have you done with my friend?"

"Your friend is it? I didn't know you two were so familiar. I figured you were merely a pair of common criminals. Andrew is now fertilizer for the king's field, where he belongs. His blood provides the ground the necessary nutrients to make the king's food supply strong."

"You son of a bitch! I may not be permitted to kill you now, but make no mistake, you will never leave here alive!" Promised Tim.

"Oh, you may be right, but it will take more than the likes of a scrawny rat to end my life, even with that knife." Marvinian turned to Calum and said, "Grant me a small favor and give the rat back his knife, that we may settle our business." Calum remained impassive.

Marvinian held onto the bars while he taunted Tim. Tim lunged at Marvinian and succeeded in putting his hands around Marvinian's neck. The stronger man laughed and easily pushed Tim's hands off him. "You've got courage, I have to give you that. And yet I wonder how much courage you'd have if your friend wasn't here to protect you. But even still, courage won't be enough to do away with the likes of me. You still be a wee lad, and have only the strength of a bairn."

"Open the door, Calum," begged Tim. "Give me back my knife and let me have a chance at him."

"Oh lad, that butter knife you've got won't ever be enough for the likes of you," mocked Marvinian.

Calum shook his head sadly, and said, "This be not what you're here for. You misunderstand Sileas' intentions in sending you here. Your lust for vengeance merely darkens your heart further."

"So be it. I'll gladly trade a darkened heart for a darkened life of that monster!"

"You don't know what you say, lad," said Calum as he turned away, waving Tim to follow.

Tim reluctantly followed Calum back out to the corridor and said, "I know you don't want me to kill him. And I understand that you think it will somehow do me ill, but what you fail to understand, is that I don't care. I just want that bastard dead, and I'll live with whatever consequences may come."

"You have no idea what you're saying. My hope is that in time you will come to know. I must be honest with you in saying that I don't share Sileas' optimism. She believes you will come to peace. But just the same, I will attend to my duty to give you every opportunity to expand yourself."

"I don't give a rat's ass for expanding myself. All I want is to expand my knife deep into that bastard's chest. And maybe you and Sileas are right, that I'm somehow damaging myself by killing him. Well, so be it!" Said Tim.

Calum signaled for Tim to follow, as he turned away to leave the dungeon. "We're done for today. We'll try again tomorrow. You will have until the morning to think on this."

"What difference will that make? I've made up my mind."

"I fear that you are right. And yet my hope is that you will remain open to changing your mind. You must choose your own path, but I do hope that you will consider what Sileas and I tell you. Also, I hope that you will hear what Marvinian truly says. I don't believe you hear what he says beneath his words. And I fear for you if you continue on your present course," said Calum.

"I hear what that monster says quite plainly."

"And what is that?" Asked Calum.

"That Andrew and I deserve death, and that he intends to kill me as well."

"Yes, that is the external content of what he says, but what do you hear beneath the words?" Pushed Calum.

"Beneath his words? What sort of nonsense is that? There is nothing beneath his words but hate, and I intent to return hate for hate."

"Then you shall suffer the fruit of hate, as Marvinian does...and this saddens me," said Calum.

Tim fumed and fussed, and attempted to engage Calum in a debate over the merits of killing a thug like Marvinian. Yet Calum remained resolute, refusing to spar with Tim. Calum merely shook his head slowly and said, "We will talk further another time...perhaps when you are in a different state of mind."

Tim returned to his hut. He sat in the chair and stared out the window. Images came to mind of taking Marvinian's head back to the castle, and displaying it on a pike for all to see. Tim fantasized about what he might write on the post below his head. *Here's what becomes those who take others' lives and happiness*, is what came to mind. Immediately Tim had the thought that he wanted to take Marvinian's happiness and life, which was doing the same thing that Marvinian had done to Tim and his family. For a moment Tim had a strange thought as he wondered if he was being as Marvinian. He did sound similar. Tim dismissed such thoughts before he had much time to think on them.

The fire burned low. Tim put more wood on the fire and put a tea pot on the hook over the fire. He watched as the fire consumed the wood, darkening it to blackness. Tim wondered if this was what Sileas and Calum meant about his own heart. Was he blackening it, as the fire did to the wood? Should he let the monster off the hook? The door on Tim's curiosity closed as quickly as it opened. It angered Tim to even entertain the thought for a moment. Tim shrugged his shoulders and pushed away such annoying thoughts, and attended to his daily chores about the hut.

The next day Calum appeared at his door. Calum nodded by way of greeting, and accepted a cup of tea. Calum spoke less than he normally did, about which Tim inquired.

"You're right, I'm not feeling too chatty today. I'm worried about you, Tim."

"You mean because of Marvinian?"

"No little brother, this isn't about him. This is about you, and your own mind," said Calum.

"Well, maybe it is...but I still want the same thing."

Calum nodded grimly. "That's what worries me."

"You shouldn't worry about me. I can take care of myself. All I need is to be given an opportunity to right a wrong that's long overdue."

"You hold to the illusion that revenge will benefit you."

"Yes I do," asserted Tim.

"This is madness and fantasy," countered Calum.

"Give me the opportunity to find out for myself," pleaded Tim.

"It may come to that, but I can't help you in your destruction. My task is to keep you from this opportunity, so that another opportunity may arise," said Calum softly.

"And why not, for God's sake?"

"My concern is not for God."

Tim rolled his eyes and said, "I know that your concern is for me, but I don't share your concern. Let me kill that animal and find out for myself if it harms me."

Calum shook his head slowly. "I fear you underestimate the damage this may cause you."

Tim shrugged his shoulders and said, "Perhaps."

When they arrived at the dungeon, a woman stood before the bars of the other cell. Alec was at her side. The prisoner hung his head and nodded as the woman spoke. She said, "I understand that you were hungry and only wanted a meal. Do you know that in killing my cow for a meal, you took away meals for me and my two children?"

The prisoner nodded. He said, "I am filled with shame for what I've done to your family. Is there a way that I can repay you?"

"My family is only myself and my two children."

"And what of your husband?" Asked the prisoner.

Tears formed in her eyes for a moment, and then she brushed them aside and said, "He has passed. The fever took him."

The prisoner looked surprised and grieved. He said, "I'm sorry for your loss. What can I do?"

"You can spare me your sympathy! I want none of it. And you can repay me by Alec breaking your arm," she said. And then quickly added, "No, that's not what I want. I mean, it is what I want, but I know that an eye for an eye solves nothing."

"Then what can I do? I desire to make this right," said the prisoner.

"You can bring me another cow," said the woman.

The prisoner shook his head slowly. "Madame, I have no money to buy a cow. I would gladly do this if it were only under my power to do so. Is there something else I can do for you?"

The woman thought for a moment. She pulled Alec out of the prisoner's earshot to confer with him, and then returned to the prisoner. "There is something else. As it is harvest time in my fields, you may repay me by working the harvest season to bring in the crop. It is difficult to accomplish since my husband has left us. And when it is in, you will leave this land."

The prisoner face brightened and he nodded his head and said, "Yes Madame, it is the least that I can do."

"Then it is settled. You shall be released to work for Abby, and will work under the watch of a sentry for the remainder of the harvest. This will be for Abby's safety and for yours," said Alec. Abby nodded. Alec turned the key and opened the cell door. The prisoner left with them.

Marvinian was once again the dungeon's sole occupant. He said, "Now don't be thinking that I'll plow your fields, rat, because that ain't happening."

Tim stood and watched Alec and the other two leave through the passageway. Tim looked at Marvinian, who scowled and said, "What are you looking at? There won't be no happy ending between you and me, rat."

Tim regarded Marvinian for a moment, and then turned to Calum and said, "I want to watch."

"Watch what?" Asked Calum.

"I want to watch Abby and the thief. I want to see how she is with him."

Calum smiled and said, "Then you shall. Let's go."

"Wait! Don't you have any empty threats for me today?" Taunted Marvinian. Tim turned to regard him, and opened his mouth to speak. Then he thought better of it and turned to follow Calum.

Calum led the way to the Abby's farm. She lived near Calum and Alec. Along the way, Calum explained the thief's story. Alec had caught the man eating Abby's cow. His name is Kavan, and he is Fois. Kavan fought with his siblings over how the family land should be divided. The Fois way is that all offspring inherit an equal part of the land, once both parents have passed. When his parents passed, Kavan thought that he and his brother should divide the land in two. Since his sister was married, and her husband had his own share of land, Kavan argued that she ought to forfeit her share. When his brother and sister disagreed, they argued for many weeks. Finally despairing of a satisfying solution, Kavan chose to leave the Fois and seek his life elsewhere. Kavan could not bear the thought of Abby having both her land share as well as her husband's. The last day he lived amongst the Fois, he and his sister's husband fought. Kavan broke the man's arm. He recovered from a broken arm, and died of fever two years later. Kavan has been gone these past seven years, until yesterday. Kavan is Abby's brother.

They arrived at Abby's field. Kavan conferred briefly with Abby, and then nodded and headed out to the barn. He emerged with a couple of tools in his hand and headed out to the fields. Abby went inside her hut and came out in her rougher work clothes. She walked slowly out to the fields, side by side with Alec. Alec walked with his hand on Abby's back. Tim and Calum watched them work the fields. Kavan worked hard, only stopping briefly for a drink of water throughout the day. Abby worked the same field as Kavan, yet kept her distance. She also kept an eye on him, always aware of his whereabouts.

After watching for an hour, Tim and Calum helped out in the fields as well. At the end of the work day, all four of them returned to the barn. After putting his tools away, Kavan said, "I don't expect you will be able to forgive me now, or maybe even anytime soon. But for your own peace of mind, I hope you will be able to find it in yourself to do so."

"I don't think I'll ever be able to fully forgive you, brother. I won't give you the satisfaction."

"It isn't for my satisfaction. I'll admit, I would like you to forgive me for my sake, but I'm more concerned about you doing it for your own benefit. I am most in need of another's forgiveness," said Kavan.

"Who else is there to forgive you? My husband is long dead, and our brother no longer concerns himself with your affairs."

"No, it is neither of them. I most need to forgive myself. I am greatly ashamed of myself, and feel no worth within me. I don't see what else I can do with my life, as it is. I have merely wandered about with no purpose or direction. I have come to see that I lack...something essential. Without some kind of change my life is all but over. I must find a way to reinvent myself," said Kavan.

"I don't care if you forgive yourself or not. Just help me bring in the harvest, and then I never care to see you again."

"It will be as you wish," said Kavan. He hung his head, and then looked up at Alec. "Where am I to sleep during the harvest?"

"You will be my guest. Come with me," said Alec.

"Do you not worry for your own safety?"

"I do not. I probably will sleep with one eye open, but you are welcome to sleep in my barn. You will be welcome, for as long as you treat us well." Kavan followed Alec home.

The next day Tim stood outside his hut when Calum arrived. Tim held two cups of tea, handed one to Calum and began marching towards the holding cells. Calum said, "So why the hurry?"

"Just come and see," said Tim. Calum took a long look at Tim, nodded and merely followed him to the safety cells, curious to see what his young friend had in mind.

Tim went straight to Marvinian, approaching the bars while remaining out of his reach. Tim said, "Marvinian, I have important questions for you. And I want..."

Marvinian interrupted Tim, "I have no answers for you, rat. Just get on with killing me. Or should I say, get on with trying to kill me."

"Yes, I would like to get on with putting you out of your misery, but first I want to know some things," said Tim. Marvinian took a step back and folded his arms. Tim continued, "The first thing I want to know about is Andrew. Why did you kill him?"

Marvinian rolled his eyes, "I think the answer to that be plain enough. You already know the answer."

"Yesterday I would have said that you killed Andrew merely out of nastiness and a murderous thirst for blood. But last night I realized that there may be more to it."

"I'm not interested in any kind of question and answer game, rat. Just get on with whatever torture you have for me."

"It's no game. I really want to know. Maybe there's more to why you killed an innocent young man," said Tim.

Marvinian chuckled, "Oh rat, that's precious. Nobody's as innocent as pure white snow. Everyone has a dark side."

"Then tell me of Andrew's dark side."

"You really don't know?" Began Marvinian, looking genuinely surprised. Tim shook his head. Marvinian continued, "You've been working with him all this time and you don't know how he makes a little extra? The rat you like to call Andrew, has been stealing boots from me and my men for some time now. I didn't have proof until recently."

"That's not possible! He wouldn't be so stupid to steal from you," said Tim.

Marivinian threw his head back and laughed, "Oh now rat, I think you be the innocent one. You really don't believe your friend be capable of evil."

"I know that you're capable of enough evil for all of us...so how do you know this?"

"I found a man in town wearing my boots. When I began to punish him for stealing my boots, he pleaded his innocence and swore that he bought them from the young cobbler. And when I didn't believe him, he swore he could take me to many others who could tell me the same thing. I decided to spare his life long enough to see that he lied, and told him that his death would be long and painful if he lied. The man surprised me with his resolve, so I allowed him to lead me to many other villagers. At first they feared to say anything, but in the end, they confirmed the man's story. It didn't take long to discover that the rat Andrew be the young cobbler who sold them boots at half price."

"I don't believe it!" Said Tim.

"I don't care much what you believe, rat. You asked for the truth and you got it. If you're too innocent a dove to recognize the truth when you hear it, then God help you," smirked Marvinian.

"I can't believe Andrew...wait a minute...there was the time I saw..."

"Saw what, rat?" Ask Marvinian.

"I did see Andrew out behind the store handing boots to a couple of men in whispers," said Tim.

"There you go, rat! Of course you saw him selling boots, and boots that were not his own."

"I figured he was just returning the finished boots to their owners, but he must have been..."

"He must have been selling stolen boots," said Marvinian.

"So...is that why you killed him?"

"I don't allow men who steal from me to live. Do you think I'd kill a mere boy for simply spilling a pint on me? Come now, I've killed many a man, and I must say that I usually enjoy it, but it takes more than spilt ale for me to do it," said Marvinian. Tim looked away thoughtfully.

After waiting several minutes, Calum put his hand on Tim's back and led him out of the holding cells. Tim remained silent while they walked back to Callum's hut. Tim sat down and stared out the window while Calum pulled together some fruit and nuts for a midday meal. When Calum sat down Tim glanced up and said, "I didn't expect that."

"What do you mean?"

"I didn't expect to feel that. I didn't think I'd have any understanding of Marvinian...other than thinking of him as evil. That was the only explanation that made sense to me...now I'm not so sure," said Tim.

"This be a great moment for you, Tim. You've taken a great step towards peace," said Calum with a satisfied smile.

"Oh I haven't forgiven him."

"No, but you've begun. Or at least you have a greater chance at peace."

"I don't know about that," said Tim.

Tim pondered this new revelation while he and Calum ate. Tim ate without conversing. By the end of the meal, he pushed back from the table and walked to the door. Tim stood in the door and stared outside. Calum patiently waited at the table. He filled the time by pulling out his pipe, packing it, and smoking with one leg up on the stool. Tim kicked at the dirt. And then he turned to Calum.

Tim nodded towards Calum, and headed out the door. Calum followed, puffing on his pipe. Tim approached Marvinian slowly, still trying to work something out in his mind. Tim said, "I have another question for you." Marvinian sat in the back of the cell, leaning against the stone wall. He remained silent. "I want to know why you have been tracking me down to kill me."

Marvinian regarded Tim silently before saying, "I would think it be quite plain, rat. I kill all involved in stealing from me."

"You think I had something to do with stealing your boots?"

Marvinian chuckled to himself, "I don't trouble myself with asking too many questions. You being involved with the rat Andrew be enough for me."

"This has nothing to do with the night that Andrew spilt ale on you?"

Marvinian laughed, "Oh rat, I may be a cold-blooded murderer, but I don't kill people for being fool enough to spray a bit of ale on me. Or even for helping out a drunken mate."

"You mean that you'd let that go?" Asked Tim.

"Oh I didn't say that I'd let it go now. I had every intention of getting back to both of you for that night."

"What do you mean?" Asked Tim.

"Oh I would have enjoyed giving both of you lads a good hiding for that little incident at the tavern. You see rat, it was the next morning that I came across the man that gave me proof of Andrew's little side business."

"Let me get this straight, you're not hunting me down because of the tavern, but due to me being friends with Andrew?"

"You got it, rat," said Marvinian.

"So just because I work with Andrew makes me guilty?"

Marvinian smirked. And then he said, "I suppose you could look at it that way."

"How else can I look at that?" Asked Tim.

"I don't give a rats' arse how you think of it."

"No, I really want to understand. Do you think I had something to do with stealing your boots?"

Marvinian rubbed his beard for a moment before responding, "You know, rat, I don't bother myself with details. When I catch somebody stealing from me, I kill everyone involved."

"But that just isn't fair! I had nothing to do with your boots! At least I had nothing to do with stealing them."

Marvinian shrugged. "That may be, but by killing all I leave no man unpunished."

"But that's unjust. I didn't even know Andrew was stealing from you."

"And if you had known, what would you have done?" Challenged Marvinian.

"I don't know...I suppose I'd have to think..."

"That's right, rat. You'd protect your friend, even when he's stealing from me," interrupted Marvinian.

"I didn't say I'd protect him."

"Yes you did, lad. You're not being honest with yourself. We both know that you'd look the other way," countered Marvinian.

Tim scratched his head as he looked down. He shook his head slowly. "You might be right."

Marvinian smirked. "We both know that I'm right," Marvinian said slowly.

"I might have confronted him," said Tim.

"That's all? A little slap on his wrist?"

"Well..."

"You see rat, that's where you and me be different. I won't be satisfied with merely talking to someone. That's what weak-minded fools do. You commit a crime and you pay the price, that's the way it is with me," said Marvinian.

Tim looked away and pondered Marvinian's comment. He had to admit that he was probably right. Tim didn't think he would have done anything more than merely ask Andrew about the boots being sold in secret. Perhaps my idea of justice isn't entirely justice. I suppose I do let people off fairly easy...at least people that are on my side, mused Tim. He stood and paced the dungeon.

"So I got you to think, rat. Is that it? You liked to see me as some evil, blood-thirsty thug. Which is pretty much true. But the problem is that you see yourself and your friends as innocent doves, white as the driven snow," said Marvinian. Tim opened his mouth to respond, and realized that Marvinian was probably right. Calum could see that Tim needed to do some thinking, and nudged him towards the doorway.

Calum led Tim back to his own hut for dinner. Tim was kind with his hosts, but didn't say much throughout the meal. When the children asked Tim to play, he agreed. But his mind was somewhere else. The children quickly tired of Tim's energy-less participation, and moved on to other play. After the meal was cleaned up, Calum pulled Tim aside. "So what's stirring in your mind? You've been quiet ever since we left the cell."

"It's just not what I expected...I expected Marvinian to have no reasons for what he does...I suppose I expected him to be pure evil, and to kill for the pleasure of killing, like some animal. But the monster actually has a code of ethics. A twisted code of ethics, but a code just the same. I'm just not sure what to do with that. I've been mulling it over all afternoon, and I'm not sure how to think about him...and how to think about myself. I'm not sure that I'm as completely different from him as I'd thought."

Calum smiled, "This is good, my young friend, very good. This bodes well for you. Stay with your journey." Calum clapped him on the back, and went to put his children to bed. Tim turned towards home, yet found himself wandering aimlessly.

At first he walked familiar paths on which Calum and Alec had taken him. Without realizing it, Tim found himself in an area he'd never seen. As dusk had came, Tim decided to find his way towards his new home. While distracted with thoughts of Marvinian, he didn't watch the trail well. Tim glanced down just in time to grab the branch of a nearby tree as he slipped and lost his footing. He scrambled to get his feet under him, as loose soil prevented him from finding secure footing. Tim's feet fell down to a ledge. He looked over his shoulder to find a drop down a cliff wall. Tim grabbed for a better grip of the tree branch, but instead lost hold of it completely. He started to slide down the cliff. Frantically he reached out for anything, and found a tree root sticking out of the soil. Tim latched on with both hands, and thank God it held. Otherwise he'd be lying at the bottom of the gorge by now. Tim carefully pulled himself back up onto the top of the cliff, and fell gratefully to the ground. After regaining his breath, he crept back to the cliff edge for a better look. Boulders, loose rocks and trees lined the steep slide down to a creek. Tim backed away on all fours, before risking standing. He decided he'd had enough fun for the night, and determined to make it back to his hut as quickly as possible.

After darkness had enveloped the valley, Tim made it home to his hut. He sat in his favorite chair and pondered his troubling thoughts. His mind kept working over his recent conversations with Marvinian. Tim tried to reach some kind of conclusion, yet didn't seem able to. When Tim tried to imagine forgiving Marvinian, he just couldn't picture it. A picture of the monster with a grin of triumph came to mind. In other moments Tim thought he might be able to actually give up his thirst to kill the monster. Yet he didn't think he could bring himself to fully walk away from revenge. The best that he could imagine was putting off his taking of revenge. None of the possibilities seemed entirely satisfying. Tim missed Maggie, and wanted to discuss Marvinian with her. However, Maggie had been staying with some of the women who sing, and Tim rarely saw her the last several days.

The next Tim knew he startled awake. He glanced around the hut and the gray of morning came through the window. At first he was disoriented, and then realized he'd fallen asleep in his reading chair. He stared at his cut and bruised hands in surprise, and then remembered his encounter with the cliff. Tim washed his face and changed his shirt. He'd made up his mind. He quickly grabbed something to eat, scribbled a note for Calum and left.

An hour later Calum knocked on Tim's door. When Tim didn't answer repeated knocks, Calum let himself in. He found Tim's note on the table. It said,

Calum,

I went to the cell early. I want to talk to Marvinian alone. There's no need

for you to come.

Tim

Calum dropped the note and ran out the door, leaving it wide open. The moment he read the note he sensed trouble. He ran full speed to the holding cells. This didn't last long, as he wasn't able to sprint the entire way to the cells, even though he was in excellent condition, and had to settle for a fast jog most of the two miles to the cells.

Calum didn't bother to greet the guards, rushing past them. Calum feared what he'd find in the holding cells. When he rounded the corner Calum found Tim slumped onto the floor, leaning against the stone wall. Tim sat with a bow and a single arrow in his lap. Calum shouted, "Tim! Are you alright?" When Tim didn't respond, Calum shook him, "Be you okay, Tim?"

Tim slowly raised his head, and regarded Calum with dull eyes. Calum quickly searched Tim's body for wounds, but found none. Then Calum looked for Marvinian. At first he didn't see him, as his eyes still adjusted to the darkened prison. Then he spotted Marvinian lying on the stone floor near the rear of the cell. Calum approached the cell and peered through the bars to get a better look at him. An arrow stuck out of his hand. A second arrow protruded from his shoulder, and a third arrow stuck in his chest. "My God, Tim, you've killed him! Do you know what you've done?" Tim merely nodded, without lifting his head from staring at his feet.

Once Calum was convinced Marvinian wasn't moving, he slumped down next to Tim. He gathered his thoughts, giving Tim a moment with his own. "What were you thinking, Tim?" Tim shrugged his shoulders without looking up. He turned to face Calum, and showed him the tears in his eyes.

Calum's anger melted away, and he exhaled deeply. Calum asked, "So what happened?"

"I don't know...I suppose, I guess I lost it," began Tim.

"Lost it?"

"I don't know, it's like I lost my mind...I went crazy. What Marvinian was saying so enraged me that I couldn't stop myself...or I didn't stop myself, or I don't know what happened. One moment we were talking, and then I lost it and started shooting him."

"Your note sounded like you came here to kill Marvinian. Was not your intention to kill him?" Said Calum.

"Yes, and no, I'm not sure."

"You brought your bow with you. You haven't done that before. You must have thought you might kill him," said Calum.

"Yes, you're right, I did think I would kill him. Or at least shoot him. I wanted him to suffer. And then I went crazy with rage, and I couldn't stop myself. It's like I turned into this person I don't even know. The way he taunted me, I just couldn't...I can't believe I did that. I mean I can believe it, but I can't understand how I turned into a monster like that. How could I actually go through with..."

"Oh lad, you met a version of you that you don't recognize," said Calum.

"Yes! How can I be like that? And now I can't take it back. I've killed him. I allowed myself to be taunted to the point that..."

"And now the killing is done," said Calum.

Tim merely shook his head, slowly from side to side. Then he offered, "I didn't expect it to be like this...I thought it would feel

239

done...I mean, somehow better...but not like this. I mean I felt victorious at first, but it didn't last..."

"You thought killing him would help you feel better," said Calum.

Tim nodded. "You said it wouldn't do me any good, but I didn't believe you...I thought it would bring me peace, a sense of closure or something, sending that monster to his peace."

Calum gently nodded, "It doesn't work like that. Another man can't give you peace. You must find it within."

"I can find no peace within me. In fact, I feel worse!"

"I know, my friend," said Calum sadly.

"When I finally killed him, I felt a moment of triumph. But the good feeling only lasted a few seconds, perhaps a minute...and then the bad feelings came, worse than before, and they remain," said Tim. Calum put his arm around Tim's shoulders. "I thought you and Sileas were just trying to spare the monster's life. I didn't believe you were truly concerned for me...I figured it was just a trick to keep me from killing him." Calum shook his head from side to side. "Yes, I can now see that it wasn't," said Tim.

Calum said, "I'm deeply sorry for you that you found out this way. You've chosen the more painful path." At this Tim began sobbing. Calum pulled his head onto his chest and held him.

When Tim finally stopped sobbing he looked into Calum's eyes and said, "Can you ever forgive me?"

Calum smile and said, "I have already done it. That is the easy part. The great challenge will be for you to forgive yourself. It will be more difficult now."

"You mean you're not angry that I've killed the monster?"

"At first I was angry, but that was soon replaced with concern for your suffering...which I now imagine to be much greater."

"I feel indescribably terrible about myself...I'm now a monster!" Cried Tim.

"I'm so sorry that you've done this to yourself," said Calum.

When Calum judged it had been long enough, he pulled Tim to his feet. Tim was like dead weight, neither resisting nor helping. Calum led him to the first place in Fois that Tim had been. After a brief wait, they were led into Sileas' chamber. Sileas said, "And what brings you to me?" Tim kept his eyes on the ground. Sileas continued, "I can see that your state of mind has worsened. What has happened?" Tim didn't respond.

After a moment Calum said, "Marvinian is dead...Tim took his life."

Tears came to Sileas' eyes. She said, "It saddens me that you have brought more suffering to yourself." Tim glanced up at her briefly, and then returned his eyes to the ground.

"Now our task will be more great, much greater, and I hope not impossible. We will still help you to find peace," said Sileas.

Tim shook his head and looked at her with unfocused eyes. "There is no peace for me. I've become the monster now. I'm as bad as Marvinian. I've done the same as him."

"It's true that you've made your journey a steeper climb. And I understand your guilt. AND peace is yet attainable. However, peace is only possible if you allow us to help you with your journey. You can't do this alone," said Sileas.

"What can you do? I've brought this on myself. There is nothing you can do for me. I must leave and see if I can find my sister. I might be able to accomplish something if I can find a way to free her. There is nothing else for me. I don't know if I can bring myself to go home. I don't know if I can face my father. I can't bear the thought of looking into his eyes, with this terrible guilt upon me."

"No Tim, stay with us and we will help you to face this shame, and guilt. I fear it will go harder for you alone, and likely will end badly. Go home with Calum, be with him and Alec, come to me as often as you like. And for your own sake, let us help you to do the work you must do," pleaded Sileas. Tim nodded dutifully, without looking her in the face.

"Tim, look at me," began Sileas. Tim slowly looked up. "This is a time of great danger. You must allow us in. The danger is that you might shut us out, leaving yourself without help or hope. You must not do this!" Tim averted his eyes and nodded. Calum bowed slightly to Sileas and turned to go. Tim allowed Calum to lead him to their home.

When they arrived at Calum and Alec's homes, Tim sat on a stump outside. Calum pulled Alec aside to spoke with him in lowered voices. Several times Alec glanced over at Tim, while he listened intently to Calum. When they finished talking, Alec approached Tim. He placed his hand on Tim's shoulder and regarded him silently. Then Alec said, "I'm sorry for your suffering, brother. I will do whatever I can for you. Feel free to come to me as much as you like. I open my door to you." Tim looked up at Alec and nodded. Then he looked away without speaking. Alec went inside to help the others prepare the midday meal.

Once Alec went inside the hut, Tim was alone outside. Tim hung his head and wondered what to do. He scanned the homestead to be sure he was unobserved. He'd made a decision. Tim quickly stood and wandered into the forest. He took the most direct path to his own hut. Tim went inside and quickly packed his things into a sack. He stepped outside the door, and then turned around. Tim went back inside and grabbed whatever food he could quickly find, as well as a water skin. Then he left.

When the meal was prepared, Alec went outside to invite Tim in to eat. Not seeing him, he wandered into Calum's hut. "Calum, the meal be prepared. Come and bring Tim," said Alec.

"He's right outside on the great stump," said Calum.

"Not any longer. I don't see him anywhere outside. I figured he went inside with you," said Alec.

"No, where could he be? Oh my God, he must have fled. I will run to his hut. He must not leave on his own!" Calum ran the mile and a half to Tim's hut, and rushed inside. There was no Tim. Calum saw that all Tim's belonging were gone, including his bow and arrows. Calum ran back to tell his brother.

Thirteen

Tim had not hiked more than a few miles up the trail to the cliff. He now stopped every few minutes to listen. He knew they would come after him. Tim didn't want to be found. Another mile up the trail he saw that he could see the entryway through the cliff wall. Tim found a large tree to stop behind. He looked and listened until he was satisfied that no one drew near. He pulled off the top of the water skin and took a long draught. He replaced the water skin over his shoulder and resumed his trek.

Once Tim was through the cliff wall and out of the Fois territory, he drew a sigh of relief. It would be difficult for them to find him now, or so he thought. As quickly as he felt relief, a sadness came over him. Tears formed in his eyes. He wiped them away. For a moment he considered going back and begging for help, but he quickly dismissed it and turned to go.

Tim quickly departed from the familiar path that he, Calum and Alec had traveled many times. Tim found a switch and did what he could to disguise the point at which he left the main path. He'd learned to disguise his path from the Fois. In fact, Tim took the time to erase his tracks well beyond the point where he departed the path.

Once Tim had traveled well beyond the Fois territory, he felt comfortable stopping for a rest and refreshment. He found a tree that provided nice shade and sat against it. He pulled fruit and nuts out of his pack, and leisurely ate. Tim didn't think they would bother to track him this far from their lands, and he allowed himself to sleep briefly.

Tim awoke refreshed, and stood and stretched. He studied the sun, and judged that he still had an hour or two before sunset, and resumed his trek. Tim took his time, no longer fearing being found. He meandered amongst tall trees, often stepping over large roots amidst a forest floor covered in fallen leaves and pine straw.

Now that Tim was safely out of Fois, troublesome thoughts came to mind. What do I do now, Tim wondered? I suppose I could go free Amanda...but I don't think I can pull it off without help. Although I can't go home without Amanda. There's no way I could face Mama and Father without bringing her back. So then what will I do? How could I get help to free her? Do I ask Father and Shane to help me? Maybe I could ask Philippe to assist me? But I can't go back to the town of Teagle Castle, for they will be looking for me there. At this point Tim pushed these painful thoughts from his mind. He'd figure it out tomorrow, or the next day.

Once the sun began to approach the horizon, Tim searched for a suitable place to spend the night. Just before dusk he discovered a huge fallen tree, that had hollowed out over time. It was large enough for Tim to slide into and sleep. After the emotion and exhaustion of the day, he slipped into slumber almost immediately.

He awoke to two familiar faces staring down at him. "We've found you at last, my dear little laddie," said Alec. Calum smiled and nodded. Tim rubbed sleep from his eyes, as he thought he might be dreaming.

"How did you find me this far from Fois?" Asked Tim as he climbed out of the fallen tree.

"You are not as difficult to track as you might imagine," returned Calum.

"It was as easy as following my baby girl," added Alec.

"How can that be? I took my time and erased my tracks well beyond the path."

"You know lad, it was almost as if you left a painted sign pointing the directions," said Alec with a laugh.

"I didn't think you'd bother coming this far south of Fois," said Tim.

"You underestimate us, and the bond of our friendship," said Calum.

Tim's pleasure and surprise turned to a frown. He said, "But I can't go back with you."

"Of course you can," said Alec.

"No, it's not possible," said Tim.

"And why would that be?" Asked Calum.

"I can no longer face neither you nor Maggie...or Sileas. I have become a common criminal, no better than Marvinian."

"Is any man better or worse than another?" Countered Alec.

"You know what I mean. I'm now a murderer."

"And you imagine that Calum and I are saints?" Asked Alec.

"Why yes! At least compared to me."

"Alec here just may very well be a saint, but I certainly am not," said Calum.

Alec playfully punched Calum in the shoulder as he said, "Said like a true sinner."

"You both can make fun of me all you want, but I know the truth about myself," said Tim.

"Tim, come with us back home, and we will help you come to know more of the truth about yourself. We will help restore you to wholeness. You can't leave yourself like this. You may never get past it on your own," said Calum.

Tim gazed off with a grim face before answering, "I so wish all that you said were possible. No, I don't think I can ever forgive myself...not now."

246

"This is exactly why it is critical for you to come back with us. You must let us help you. This is too great a task for any one person," said Alec.

"I can't face being with you all, especially Maggie and Sileas. They will hate me."

"Come now lad, you underestimate them, and overestimate yourself. Come back to my home, and you will see them when you are ready," said Alec.

"I don't know when I'd ever be able to face them again," said Tim.

"So be it, then you shall never see them," said Calum.

"You mean I wouldn't have to?"

Calum and Alec looked at each other. Calum said, "Absolutely not. Did you think we would try to force you?"

"I know it's not how you both have been with me, but yes, I suppose I did expect you to pressure me into something."

Alec picked up Tim's rucksack and said, "Come now, let's go back to our home for now, and start with that. No pressure for anything else."

"But what will I do there? I don't know if I can face even you two every day. I can't stand to look you in the face now."

Calum turned Tim's face to look directly at him. "You must get past your shame and guilt. It will only destroy you if you leave it be."

Tim pulled away from Calum and began to weep. He walked a short distance away and crouched down as the tears flowed. Calum crouched down next to him and put an arm around his shoulder. Tim allowed this and sobbed even harder. After a time Tim's sobs faded, and a strange calm came over him.

Alec said, "Come, we must start back for home, so that we will make it back before dark." Tim nodded and started back on the trail to Fois. Calum put his hand on Tim's shoulder as they started their trek home. Tim walked with his head down, looking at his feet.

When the trio reached the rock wall that made the southern boundary of Fois, Tim stopped before entering. A moment later Calum came back through the break in the wall. "Having second thoughts?'

Tim nodded. "I don't know if I can do this."

"Don't think about it further. Come home with us and consider your future from there. There's too much danger in you making this ponderous decision alone," said Calum. Tim sighed and followed Calum through the opening. He couldn't think of anything else to do. For that matter, he didn't even know where he was heading when Alec and Calum found him. Tim couldn't imagine facing his parents and brother without Amanda. He had considered trying to rescue Amanda on his own, but that fantasy quickly faded, as he remembered how well guarded the slaves were. He'd have no chance. So what else could he do, except follow Calum and Alec home. There was no where else to go.

At dusk they approached Alec and Calum's home. Maggie ran out the door and right up to Tim and embraced him. "Thank God you're alright! I had feared I'd never see you again."

Tim paused. It felt so good to see her again, and he was enormously relieved at her response to seeing him, but his shame got the better of him. Tim pushed her arms off of him, and held her at arms distance. "It might have been better had that been true."

"Forever why? Of course I want to see you! You've become dear to me," countered Maggie.

Tears formed in the corners of Tim's eyes, but he quickly brushed them away and said, "Yes, but now I've ruined all that."

"I'm both and angry and pleased that you've killed Marvinian. I'm angry because I wanted to do it myself," said Maggie.

"Oh Maggie, believe me, the fantasy is far better than the reality. I'm so ashamed of what I've done." Maggie put her arm around Tim's waist and walked him into the hut. It was all he could do to allow her arm to remain around him, but he somehow tolerated it. Tim kept his arms folded across his chest. He knew couldn't afford to alienate the few friends that he had, although it was tempting. Come to think of it, the only friends he had were the ones he was now with, save Philippe.

Tim washed up and insisted on helping his friends prepare the evening meal. The last thing he wanted was to sit idle and be with his thoughts. Every thought reminded him of his crime.

Everyone kept the conversation light, and far from Marvinian. His friends knew Tim's frame of mind fragile, and that he needed time to heal. At first Tim didn't say much, yet as the meal progressed, his tongue loosened. As they cleared the dishes from the table, Alec observed, "It's good to see you smile, my friend. I hadn't seen you smile all day until supper." Tim smiled and looked away.

The next morning Tim remained in Alec and Calum's hay loft well beyond sunrise. Maggie slept near him in the loft, but arose shortly after sunrise. She thought about waking Tim, but thought better of it. She knew he must be emotionally exhausted. By midmorning Calum sought Tim in the hay loft. He remained where he had been all night, yet sat with his back against the wall when Calum climbed the loft ladder. Tim's face was in his hands, with his elbows on his knees. He didn't look up when Calum sat down opposite him.

"Do you plan to stay here all day?" Asked Calum.

"I don't know...I have no idea what to do with myself...and I didn't want to see anyone right now."

"I imagine you've had a rough night," said Calum.

Tim nodded. "I tossed and turned all night...didn't sleep much. I kept having terrible nightmares that woke me again and again."

Calum rubbed his jaw with his hand and said, "Enough of nightmares, come down and be with your friends."

Tim hesitated before responding, "Just give me a few more minutes."

"I will if I must, but I think it wiser for you to come with me now. There's nothing but nightmares and bad feelings for you up here." Tim sighed deeply, and began to cry as he nodded.

Calum crouched next to Tim and put a hand on Tim's shoulder. "Come lad, there's nothing good for you up here." Tim wiped his eyes and followed Calum down the ladder.

When they arrived at Alec's hut, Tim startled to see Sileas sitting there with Alec. She smiled and waved Tim to sit with them. "Come and join us, Tim. You must have great need of us." Tim smiled weakly and sat. "So tell us where your journey has taken you," continued Sileas.

"I'm not sure what to tell you. I'm miserable. I awoke a dozen times last night, and each time with Marvinian's face before me...most times I relived the murder...other times I wondered why I went through with killing him. And every time I ask myself how I've become the very thing I hate."

Sileas said, "You torture yourself."

"But how can I not? I am worthy of nothing else."

"This dark belief about yourself will keep you in hell, where you now live," said Sileas.

"I am in hell, where I belong."

"This fantasy will keep you there as long as you believe it. Let us help you free yourself," said Sileas.

After pondering Sileas' words, Tim said, "I long to be free of this torment, but how can I free myself. I have no idea how to accomplish this."

"By forgiving yourself," said Sileas.

Tim laughed, and said, "You make it sound so easy."

"It is easy, once you are ready. The difficulty is becoming ready and willing," said Sileas.

Tears flowed from Tim's eyes, "Teach me to do this!"

"You have been the one in need of forgiveness all along. You only imagined it was Marvinian. Now that he's gone, the illusion has vanished with him. Even if he were still living, you would still be in need of your own forgiveness," explained Sileas.

"But that doesn't make any sense! What did I have to forgive...until I killed Marvinian?"

"Much more than you know. Nothing as dramatic as killing perhaps, but plenty for which you've carried guilt," said Sileas.

"Like what? I can't think of anything else."

"I don't know the specifics. I merely sense your guilt. You don't know because your guilt is out of awareness...except for Marvianian of course," said Sileas.

Tim sat with his head in his hands and searched his mind, but nothing came to him. He searched Sileas' face, and then Calum and Alec's, but didn't find what he searched for. "I don't know how to find this guilt you speak of. If it is truly unconscious as you say, then I am at a loss for how to find it."

"You must meditate, and ask for help to know your guilt. You cannot let it go before you know it," said Sileas.

"Meditate? You mean chanting with my eyes closed?"

Sileas laughed along with Alec and Calum. "I suppose that is one form of meditation, but perhaps not what you need. Calum and Alec will teach you to meditate, that you may come to know your mind more intimately."

Tim gazed at Calum, and then Alec. Alec nodded and said, "Yes, my friend, we will certainly teach you. We will begin at once." Turning to Calum, Alec said, "I will help him meditate now. And you can later."

"I will attend to the family's needs, while you help Tim," said Calum.

The first day of meditation proved strange and boring. Tim often found his mind wandering, and other times he nodded off to sleep. He tried to follow Alec's instructions, but couldn't focus for more than a few minutes at a time. After a time Tim grew frustrated, and barked at Alec to show him the point in all of this.

251

Alec decided to call it a day, patted Tim on the shoulder, and left the room.

Calum took meditation instruction duty the second day. Tim found himself able to concentrate for longer periods of time, which lifted his spirits. Yet Tim still found little value in the process, and he asked Calum what was supposed to happen, since nothing seemed to be happening. All Calum suggested was to be patient, and that it would come in time. And the most puzzling comment of all being that Calum said that maybe "nothing was something." Calum suggested taking time to be still, in addition to meditating. So Tim took regular walks in the forest.

By the end of the second week, Tim found he could meditate for longer periods of time, rarely falling asleep. His mind still wandered, but he learned to patiently bring it back again and again. Tim meditated with either Calum or Alec for an hour in the morning and an hour in the evening. As the evening meditation ended with Calum, Tim said, "I think something's starting to happen. I don't mean that I have down, but that I think it's helping me some."

"What do you notice?" Asked Calum.

"I think I feel a little more relaxed...and there are moments when I feel at peace, well, at least for a few moments. Though these moments don't last long, but they are so satisfying when I can get to them."

Calum smiled, "That's very good, my friend...very good."

"But when will I be get to my guilt? I don't see that any good has come of my guilt. In fact, I'm still not sure that I have any, beyond Marvinian."

"Be patient, all will come if you stay with it," said Calum.

"Has meditating helped you?"

"Absolutely! It has changed my life," said Calum.

"How has it done so?"

After considering Tim's question, Calum responded, "I don't know how to tell you. I'm at peace much of the time. And when I find myself troubled, I can usually regain my grounding fairly quick."

"What kind of peace? Do you mean that bad things don't happen to you?"

"No, not that kind of peace. I usually have peace on the inside. I mean that I'm at peace with myself, even when bad things happen on the outside," explained Calum.

"How can you be at peace when bad things happen?"

"Peace is an inside job. Sure, it's nice when things go well on the outside, but I don't need them to," said Calum.

"You don't care if bad things happen?"

"Of course I care if bad things happen...but I'm not attached to liking the way external events turn out," said Calum.

"But how can this be? Do you mean you pretend to not care, but you really do?"

Calum laughed and said, "No lad, I mean that I've tried to accept what happens in the outside world, and focus on what I can change."

"What can you change?"

"I can change my mind. I can choose how I perceive external events, or even internal events," said Calum.

"I don't see how that can be any more than just pretending. I either like what happens and I'm happy, or I don't like it and I'm upset. You must be putting a happy face on a load of shit."

Calum pondered Tim's comments before responding. "I don't know how else to explain it to you. I suppose internal peace may not be something that you yet desire, or may not even make sense to you yet. But I trust that it will if you stay with it." Tim frowned.

Alec stuck his head in the room and said, "Sileas called for you, Tim. I will walk with you to her."

Tim followed Alec into Sileas' hut and took a seat. Alec went into the back room to find her. Sileas came out and smiled as she sat down. "So Tim, tell me how your meditation sessions are progressing."

"Just fine, I guess. I think I've learned to meditate okay. At least I'm not falling asleep much anymore. In fact, I only fell asleep twice while meditating this week."

"Very well, and what do you notice while meditating?" Asked Sileas.

"Sometimes my thoughts quiet down and I feel more relaxed. Other times I get bored and nothing really happens. I'm not sure how this is supposed to help me with feeling so bad about myself."

"It's time you go beyond merely meditating. You will now meet with me each morning after your meditation session. I believe you are ready," said Sileas.

"Ready for what?"

"Come tomorrow morning after meditation and you shall see. But first, I want you to go home and meditate on forgiveness." Tim began to ask a question and Sileas put her hand up. "You will begin meditating as you always do, and then I want you to ask yourself who are the people that I have need to forgive. That is all for now, I will see you tomorrow." With that Sileas stood and went into the back room.

When Alec and Tim arrived at Alec's home, Tim said, "I want to go for a walk alone. Don't worry, I'm not running away again."

"You don't want company," said Alec.

"No, I want to be alone with my thoughts." Alec thought for a moment and then nodded.

At first Tim merely wandered aimlessly, without thinking about anything in particular. Then Tim did what Sileas had suggested. He stilled himself with a brief meditation and then asked himself who he had to forgive. Except for Marvinian, no one came to mind. Tim sat on a fallen tree with closed eyes. Who do I have to forgive? He said aloud. This time both Marvinian and himself came to his mind's eye. Tim wasn't too surprised, since he thought of himself as a murderer. Oh, what is the point of this exercise, Tim wondered. I already know that both Marvinian and myself are criminals. I really don't see the value in this.

Tim stood and began walking back to the huts, but something stopped him. He felt drawn to be still again and sat back down. He asked again, who do I need to forgive? Again, he only saw images of himself and Marvinian, but this time the image of himself came first. He wondered at this, but nothing more came to him.

The next morning he sat with Sileas, and told her about the results of his assignment. She nodded, and appeared to be in thought. "Why do you suppose that you came to your mind first?" Asked Sileas.

"I don't know...I suppose because I think of myself as being as evil as anyone, even Marvinian."

"Is that all that comes to mind? Do you believe this is only because you have killed Marvinian?" Asked Sileas.

"Well yes, why else would it be? I didn't feel bad about anything until I killed him."

"In this you are mistaken. You have carried guilt and fear since you were a young boy, but didn't know it. And you are not alone is this, as we all have been so afflicted. This is perhaps the great infirmity of mankind, that we laden ourselves with such a great burden, yet believe we are merely being honest with ourselves. This can begin with honestly, but must go beyond that to giving up an unmerciful sense of badness and fear," said Sileas.

Tim stared out the window as he thought about this. He considered that Sileas might be crazy, but quickly dismissed this possibility. Tim knew her well enough by now to know her to be quite sane. In fact, she was frighteningly sane. Yet he couldn't muster a memory of what she spoke. Tim was just about to protest, when a thought came to him. He remembered something about when Amanda joined the family. At first Tim thrilled to have a little sister. He'd always had a brother, and had often begged father and mother for a sister. When little Amanda was born, Tim thought his parents had granted his wish.

Tim spent as much time with his baby sister as possible, sometimes neglecting his chores in order to spend a few more minutes with her. He especially liked to rock her cradle as Amanda fussed herself to sleep some nights. Tim took great satisfaction in being able to help her find sleep.

This went on for many months, until Tim's energy about being with Amanda began to fade. He spent less and less time with her, and before long, refused to be with her at all. As usual, Mother would ask Tim to help with Amanda, but he would say, "I can't Mother, I must be about my chores."

At first Mother was satisfied with this, as she wanted her son to take his contribution to the family seriously. Yet after many refusals to help Amanda, Mother became concerned. She pulled Tim aside. "Son, I've noticed you no longer play with Amanda. What is wrong?"

Tim responded without taking time to think, "I'm ready to give her back." Mother laughed, but stopped herself when she saw that Tim was quite serious.

"But why do you wish to give her back?" Asked mother.

"I'm done playing with her. She's a brat who wants all of the attention, and I want her to leave now."

"Oh Tim, father and I must not be giving you enough attention," suggested mother.

"No, it isn't you or father, it's that baby. She's selfish." Mother put her arm around Tim's shoulder and pulled him close. She held Amanda in the other arm. Tim took one look at her and jumped up and ran out the door. Tim ran into the hills to be alone. He didn't come back till supper time.

Father and mother made several more attempts to talk with Tim about Amanda, but he just shook his head, refusing to say another word. After conferring together, mother and father came up with an idea, as they hoped to help reconcile Tim to his new sister. Of course there would be no giving her back.

Mother said, "Tim, I want you to go to the Simpsons and ask for two cups of sugar. I'm baking pie for supper and don't have enough."

"Ok Mother," said Tim as he prepared to leave for the Simpsons, who were their neighbors to the East, about two miles away.

"And take Amanda with you. She's fussy and won't go down for her afternoon nap."

"No, she will just slow me down," protested Tim.

"I can't prepare the food with her fussing all the time. Take her in the backpack, it won't slow you down much."

Tim opened his mouth to protest, but saw the firm look on Mother's face, and relented. Mother gently loaded Amanda into the backpack, and helped Tim into it. She walked him to the door and saw him away. Father walked up to Mother and put his arm around her waist as they watched them walk over the hill and out of sight.

At first Tim walked slowly, kicking at the dirt. Amanda fussed, but Tim ignored her. Eventually she went to sleep, being soothed by the gentle rocking of his strides. Tim resented having to take Amanda with him, and considered walking roughly to bounce Amanda about. The only reason he didn't do this being that he didn't want to wake her, and hear more of her fussing.

Tim crested the hill that separated the two family properties, and the Simpson farmhouse came into sight. And then it came to Tim. This errand provided Tim with just the needed opportunity to dispatch with his sister once and for all. A quarter mile short of the Simpson farmhouse was a pond. Actually it was the Simpson's water source. When Tim reached the pond he unloaded his backpack. He pondered whether to put Amanda in the pond in the backpack, or ought he to take her out of it first. He decided to leave her in the backpack, as he didn't want to wake her.

Tim held Amanda in his arms and looked into her sleeping face. He was old enough to understood that she would quickly drown in the water. Just as Tim readied to toss her into the water, Amanda opened her eyes. She smiled at Tim and cooed. Tim set her down on the ground and paced back and forth. He looked back at Amanda, who continued to gaze at Tim and smile.

At that moment Tim changed his mind. He couldn't go through with it. He lifted Amanda and the pack back off the ground. As he lifted the pack to his shoulders, Amanda began to cry. By the time he had her firmly set on his back, she screamed as loud as ever. At first Tim just tried to ignore her, but with her inches from his ears, he couldn't. Then he put his hands over his ears, but that only muffled the annoying sound. Amanda's crying seemed to be at the perfect pitch and volume to be maximally agitating. After a few minutes Tim couldn't take it any long. He ran back to the pond, took the pack off his shoulders and threw her in the pond. She sank instantly. A few seconds later Tim dove in and quickly pulled her out of the water. Amanda sputtered and choked for several minutes, and Tim feared she'd die. But after several minutes Amanda seemed okay. Miraculously, Amanda stopped crying. Tim took off his shirt and dried his sister off as best he could. He strapped her onto his back and approached the Simpson house.

Tim knocked on the door, and Mrs. Simpson answered, "Hello Tim, come in for a lemonade. Oh, and you brought your baby sister. How sweet! And oh dear, why are you both all wet?" Tim gladly complied and entered the house, as he'd worked up a thirst on the walk over. He took off the pack and set Amanda on the ground. Mrs. Simpson served Tim a lemonade and then picked up Amanda and played with her. When Tim finished with the lemonade he asked Mrs. Simpson for a pencil and paper. She provided him with the writing tools and went back to attending Amanda. While she bounced Amanda on her lap, Tim wrote a note.

When he'd finished the note, Tim packed up the sugar and Amanda, shouldered the pack and thanked Mrs. Simpson. He walk out the door and took and few steps and then stopped. He waited until Mrs. Simpson closed the door fully. Then he carried out his plan and made the trek home. When he arrived home, Mother was not in the house. Tim set the sugar on the kitchen table and then went out to the fields to do his work alongside Shane.

An hour later Mother found Tim out in the fields. "Tim, thank you for the sugar, but wherever is Amanda?"

"I gave her back," said Tim simply.

"Gave her back? Whatever do you mean? And I thought we already discussed this."

"I wrote God a note, that we don't want her anymore, and could her please give her to another family that wants a sister," explained Tim.

"Oh my God, where did you leave her! You must tell me where she is!"

"I don't know where she is, I'm sure that God has her somewhere safe," replied Tim.

"No, stop this gibberish about God. Where did you leave Amanda?"

"I gave her to another family that wants her," said Tim.

"Oh no! Father, come quick!" Shouted Mother as she ran for the barn. She ran all the way to the barn, and stopped short just as she rounded the corned of the barn. There in front of the barn was Father talking with Mr. Simpson. He sat on his horse, and was just handing a backpacked Amanda to Father. Amanda cried loudly, and Father took Amanda and gently rocked her. Mother swooped in and snatched Amanda from Father's hands. Father smiled.

"Where is God's name did you find her?" Mother asked Mr. Simpson.

"Mrs. Simpson heard a baby crying not thirty minutes ago. At first she couldn't figure where the crying came from. After looking all over the place, she finally opened the front door to find Amanda laying on the stoop in that there pack. She recognized Amanda right away, and here I am. Oh, and this note was underneath the baby," said Mr. Simpson.

Father unfolded the note which read, "Dear God, thank you for the baby sister. But I made a mistake when I asked for her. Kindly take her back and give her to a good family that wants a sister. Thanks, Tim."

Father laughed aloud, and handed Mother the note. She wasn't amused, and only frowned. "Now you go and talk to your son right away about this," said Mother. Father chuckled and headed off to find Tim.

Father found Tim right where Mother had left him. Father pulled Tim aside and said, "Tim, we need to talk about the note that you wrote to God."

Tim averted his gaze, and then looked at Father and nodded. Father continued, "Now Tim, I gather that you don't like..."

"I know, I know, it's all my fault," interrupted Tim.

"What do you mean, son?"

"It was me that asked for a baby sister. I shouldn't of asked for her. But I thought it might be okay with God if I gave her back. I figured there must be lots of families that want a baby sister, but not me."

"But son, why don't you want Amanda?" Asked Father.

"Because she's selfish. She wants all the attention. And you have to take care of her all the time."

Father laughed, and then said, "You must not remember when you were a baby. You were just like that too."

"No, that can't be. I wasn't that selfish."

"Son, we all are that selfish when we're babies. Not just you and Amanda," said Father.

Tim gazed at the ground as he pondered Father's words. "You mean I cried all the time and wanted to always be held too?"

Father nodded, "Yes son, but that isn't a bad thing. When we're little we need somebody to pay attention all the time. Or at least almost all of the time. You see, little babies can't do for themselves, so they need us bigger people to do for them."

Tim thought for a minute or two, before saying, "Okay, but can we still give her back?"

Father began to laugh, but noted the serious look on Tim's face, "No son, we're not giving her back. But you don't have to do for her as much. Mother and me can do for her just fine." Father put an arm around Tim's shoulders and pulled him close. Tim nodded, but didn't say anything further.

Tim looked up into Sileas' eyes, and tears came to his own. She smiled in understanding. "I see that you are remembering more than merely your encounter with Marvinian. This is good. You're healing has begun. Tell me what came back to you."

Tim told her about Amanda. When he finished he said, "I have to bring Amanda back home with me. I can't go home without her. I tried to give her away before...well, actually I tried killing her, more than once...and now I can't let somebody else take her away."

"We will tend to Amanda when the time comes. For now it's time to focus on Tim," said Sileas.

Tim said, "I remembered more than just about Amanda. Actually, I remembered much more. My God, there is so much I'm ashamed of, I don't know that I can stand to think of it all. I have such a Hall of Shame."

"You have reconnected with your guilt and shame, and this is good. As long as we don't leave you there. You see Tim, your Hall of Shame is both real and illusory. It must be faced as real, and then released as imaginary."

"I don't understand. How can it be both real and imaginary?" Asked Tim.

"This will be difficult to understand. You must trust me for now. For now it is enough to face what is real, and remember what you have done."

"The remembering is too much for me," said Tim.

"It is for now, but stay with your process, for it will not always be so."

"So what do I do now?"

"Continue to allow yourself to remember all that is true about you. This is enough for the time being," said Sileas.

"But how shall I bear it?"

"You will bear it by continuing to talk with me and your friends. There is no other way it will be possible. No mind alone can bear itself," said Sileas.

"I just remember and tell someone?"

"Yes, and allow the feelings and images that come with the memories," said Sileas.

"The feelings are the worst part."

"Yes. We will help you to bear your looking long and hard into the mirror," said Sileas. "Return tomorrow morning and tell me what else has come to mind."

On the way back to the huts, Tim kept thinking of Maggie. At first he wasn't sure why she came to mind. When he got back to the huts, Tim found Maggie. "Hello Maggie." Maggie glanced at Tim and nodded. "I know we haven't talked in days," said Tim.

"Days?"

"Has it been longer than that?" Asked Tim.

"It's been over a week!"

"Oh wow, has it really been that long?" Asked Tim. Maggie sighed and nodded. "Look, I uh...I didn't realize..." Maggie gave him a minimal smile, but didn't say anything.

"Can we go for a walk?" Asked Tim.

"You want to talk now? You have been avoiding me the past week. Why is it that you come to me now?" Asked Maggie.

"I'm sorry...I now realize that I've been pushing you away. I've..."

"Come, let's walk. You can tell me then," said Maggie with a sigh.

Tim looked at her with relief and followed her out the door. Maggie folded her arms and waited. She refused to make this easy on him. They walked in silence for several minutes. Tim started to speak several times, but each time stopped himself. He struggled to find the right words. Finally he said, "Maggie, I truly am sorry for holding you away. You are one of my only friends, and I...and I need you. Wow, it's hard for me to say that."

Maggie smiled and said, "And yet good for you to eat some humble pie and spit those words out. You aren't too good at letting yourself need others. Are you?"

"No, I'm definitely not good at that. I've always been so self-sufficient. I've never expected anyone to do much for me. Sileas just finished telling me that I'll need my friends to get through this...I know she's right."

Maggie took Tim's hand in hers and grinned. "Well, it's about time you were honest with me." Tim smiled and looked away. Her touch felt good. And he was relieved she forgave him so quickly. He feared she'd punish him before relenting, if at all. They walked in silence for several more minutes. Then Maggie said, "So out with it."

"What?" Said a surprised Tim.

"Come on, you know what I mean. Tell me what's been such a secret for you lately."

"I don't know about a secret," began Tim.

"Now cut the crap. You've turned over a new leaf and started to be honest. Now stay the course."

"Ouch! That's a little rough," said Tim.

"Rough? You just go back to being in denial, and then you'll see rough."

"Okay, I know I have to do this...I'm realizing that there's more to my shame than just killing Marvinian. He's just the tip of the iceberg. In truth, I've felt afraid and ashamed of myself for years, maybe for my whole life. And I'm just now allowing myself to remember all there is. Well, at least more of it. I've pushed away all the painful memories, and forgot all the bad stuff. I forgot all the bad stuff before they took Amanda prisoner. I had thought there were no bad memories before the tax collectors left with Amanda. Now I see there's so much more. And fear. I've acted as though the tax collectors and Marvinian were the only things I feared. But this is clearly not the case. I see now that I've been afraid all my life. My God, what a humbling realization that's been! I don't want to live in fear, not to mention shame and guilt any longer. Yes, I've successfully put it out of consciousness, but not out of mind. They've always been there. I've only had the illusion of these bad feelings going away. It's time to face them...Although I have to admit, it's really tempting not to. I sometimes think about running away and simply starting a whole new life. But I don't know if that would really fix anything. Anyways, with you're help, and the help of the kind Fois, maybe, just maybe I can do this without running away."

Maggie put her arms around Tim and embraced him. "Oh Tim, I'm so glad you're going through this too. I didn't know what you were dealing with, but I sensed it was something painful. I too have been meeting with Sileas, and have been on my own journey. I have much work to do. I thought Marvinian and his dreadful king had ruined my life, and that I'd allowed it, maybe even invited it. I'm now beginning to see that while my external life seemed good, my internal life has been mostly dead. And Tim, I can't live that way any more. I must find a way to live! I think I've deadened myself most of my life. It's really quite sad for me to think about. But I must think about it, as I have to finally face the truth about how I've lived. Sileas teaches me that nothing will be different until I face my deadness."

"I had no idea that you felt that way. You don't seem dead to me, but I'm not sure I know what you mean," said Tim.

"I know, I didn't seem dead to me either, until I met Sileas. By deadness I mean not allowing myself to fully experience life...to be open, that kind of aliveness."

"I suppose neither of us has known ourselves," said Tim.

"But we will now. And we will support each other in this journey to come more alive, and free ourselves of fear and guilt and deadness."

"I'm so grateful for your friendship, Maggie," said Tim.

"And you better not express your gratitude by pushing me away again." Tim grinned.

They walked arm in arm while Maggie brought Tim up to date on her story. While she spoke Tim noticed the difference in her while she spoke. He said, "You do seem different to me."

"Different in what way?"

"Uh, your face is more expressive. And I hear more energy in your voice. I feel more drawn to you now," said Tim.

"You didn't feel drawn to me before?"

"No, I did before too, but more so now. Do you understand?" Asked Tim.

"Yes, I get it. Before I bored you and seemed drab."

"No, that's not it at..." And then Maggie laughed.

"Even that kind of humor seems new to me," said Tim.

"Yes, I suppose it is. I haven't laughed often. It's long past time that I did."

The next morning Tim walked to meet Sileas on his own. Neither Alec nor Calum offered to escort him, so Tim figured he was no longer seen as an elopement risk. He smiled as he thought this. Tim noticed the trees as he walked. He realized that he normally didn't notice trees, or anything else in nature much. The colors of the trees seemed unusually vibrant to Tim. The swaying of the trees in the gentle wind caught his attention. The trees truly exude nobility and stability, Tim thought. He hadn't given much thought to trees before, except their value as firewood or shade. Somehow the trees seemed comforting to Tim.

When Tim arrived, a woman offered him to sit and handed him a cup of tea. He gladly accepted the tea, and sipped it slowly. The flavor of the tea struck him. Tim enjoyed the earthiness and simple goodness of the tea. He savored the warm smell.

Soon Sileas joined him. She smiled warmly and waited a moment. Then she said, "How does your work come?"

"What work? I haven't been on guardian duty since I was brought back."

"You were brought back? Did they carry you?" Asked Sileas.

"No, of course not. I walked behind Alec and Calum," said Tim with a chuckle. Then he added, "But you certainly know this. Why do you ask the obvious?"

"You don't take responsibility for yourself. This will hinder your journey," explained Sileas.

"But how am I not taking responsibility? I know what an evil murderer I am."

"That's vilifying yourself, not agency. That isn't what I mean. Condemning yourself has no value to it. Just as blaming Marvinian did you no good. By taking responsibility I mean owning who you are, and what you are, and who you want to be. This is deeper than merely naming wrongs that you've committed. It has more to do with developing your own mind and identity. You must take responsibility for yourself as you come to know yourself, if you wish to grow," said Sileas.

Tim scratched his beard, as he hadn't shaved since he'd returned to Fois. He concentrated better when he rubbed his face. "I've given that some thought, and I have some idea what you mean. I've thought of myself more as doing what others told me, or refusing to do what others told me. Not only Marvinian, but my brother and my folks as well."

"There you go, lad. Now you're beginning to take responsibility. You see, you can do this without tying yourself to a stake," said Sileas.

"I do want to take more charge of my own life. I hate just reacting to other people. It angers me that I do this."

"Yes, I would imagine so. Then what do you want for yourself?" Asked Sileas.

Tim looked at the floor. He rubbed his hands on his pants. Then he searched Sileas face, as if she would give him the answer. "I'm not sure I know...but I do know that I want to get over killing Marvinian. And I don't want to kill anyone else, unless I have to. And I want to find Amanda and take her home to my family. They must miss her terribly, and be ever so worried."

"Okay, you have found a beginning of a life direction. This is enough for now. There is time enough for the rest."

"Then what do I need to do for now?" Asked Tim.

"Search your soul for the answer. What do you find within?"

"I've yet to forgive Marvinian...and myself," said Tim.

"Then you have your starting place. Start there," said Sileas.

"But how do I forgive him and me?" Asked Tim.

"I believe you've already begun. Though you might ask yourself what you still want from him."

"But how could I want anything from him, he's dead," said Tim.

"That makes no difference in these matters. You're head knows he's dead, but your heart doesn't know nor care."

Tim rubbed his stubbled face again. "I'll need to give that some thought." Tim stood and said, "Thank you for helping me." Sileas smiled. Tim allowed her deep blue-gray eyes to penetrate him. He found her gaze comforting. He nodded and left.

A month later Tim sat before Sileas, as was his mid-morning habit. He began by merely sitting in her presence. There was something comforting about just being with her. Neither had to say anything, as something passed between them without the clumsy medium of words. Sometimes Tim gazed into her eyes. Other times he allowed his mind to wonder, without any conscious directing. After a spell Tim said, "I know I haven't forgiven myself and Marvinian, but I believe I've begun...I think I'll need some time to fully let us both off the hook. And I think Marvinian will be easier. Wow, it seems strange to hear myself say that. I always thought I'd never be able to forgive him."

"Yes, you've grown, Tim. I'm ever so proud of the work you've done on yourself," said Sileas.

"I am deeply grateful for your help. I couldn't have done any of this without you." Sileas smiled. Tim continued, "I find myself thinking of home. I want to go home, and I want to bring Amanda with me. But the strange thing is, I'm not sure I want to stay at home. In fact, I'm quite confident that I don't want to live there full time any more."

"Where will you live?" Asked Sileas.

"Well, I feel embarrassed to say this, but, I'd like to come back and live with you all, if you'll have me."

"Certainly we'll have you. You ask as though you expected me to say 'no'."

Tim looked away, "I hoped you'd have me, but I wasn't sure. I've been such a burden to all of you."

"You've put far more strain on yourself than you have on me. I have no reluctance to welcome you back," said Sileas. Tim smiled, and looked away as tears emerged in the corners of his eyes.

Once his tears ebbed, Tim said, "I'm ready to go find Amanda, and free her if I can. And I will need help."

"I'd be happy to help. What sort of help do you want?" Asked Sileas.

"I'm not sure exactly, but I don't see how I can free her on my own."

"Probably not. I suggest that you consult with Alec and Calum. I trust their judgment in such matters."

"Yes, I'm sure they'll know what to do. I'm off to find them," said Tim.

When Tim returned to the huts, he found that Alec and Calum were on guardian duty. While he waited for them, he offered to help out around the huts. Tim busied himself with chopping firewood. Every so often Tim glanced out at the approaching trail, hoping to see them coming. Once enough wood was cut, Tim went further away from the hut to be alone with his thoughts. He anxiously awaited Alec and Calum's return, yet used the time to meditate and ponder his future.

While Tim sat on the stump by the trail, he felt a tap on his shoulder. He looked up in surprise to see Alec's grinning face. "I'd thought we'd taught you better than that," said Alec.

"I don't know how you snuck up on me, I've been waiting for you both for hours," said Tim.

Alec and Calum sat down across from Tim. Calum said, "Now you've got me curious. Tell us what's on your mind."

Tim gathered his thoughts and said, "I'm ready to try to rescue Amanda...I feel that I must bring her home. And I need help, as I can't imagine getting her safely home on my own. Sileas suggested that you two might help me formulate a plan."

Alec and Calum looked at each other and nodded. Alec said, "Tell us everything you know about where she's being kept."

"Well, that's just it. I left that place long ago. I don't even know if she's still there."

"Let's assume that she's still in the same place. Tell us what there is to know," said Calum. Tim went on to explain everything he could remember about the place, and the guards who kept watch over them. Calum asked, "How many guards do you think they have there?"

"Damn, I don't exactly remember, but I'm guessing about twenty. Although there's never more than four or five in any given place at a time, except at night when they're sleeping."

"How many are on guard at night?" Asked Alec.

Tim thought for a moment before saying, "I don't really know, because I was locked in the bunkhouse at night, but I think only a few. There wasn't much to guard once we're all locked in."

"Then that would be the time for us to strike, once everyone's asleep," said Calum.

"For us to strike? You mean, you would come with me?"

Alec and Calum exchanged a knowing look. Calum said, "Well, you didn't think we'd let you have all the fun by yourself, did you?"

Tim jumped up and embraced each of them. He wiped away tears from his eyes as he said, "I hadn't dared to allow myself to hope that you two would help me with this mission, that's so far from your home."

"Tim, you've become like family to us. We wouldn't let you go alone. In fact, if you tried, we'd track you down again," said Alec.

Tim laughed and said, "This time you won't have to track me down. I don't think I'd stand much of a chance on my own. How many others will you bring with us?"

Calum glanced at Alec before saying, "No one. I think the three of us can do it."

"You mean the four of us," said Maggie. "You aren't leaving here without me!"

"God I'd love to have you with us, Maggie, but I can't ask you to risk your life," said Tim.

"You aren't asking. And I won't accept 'no'," said Maggie.

"Okay, but why?" Asked Tim.

"Why? You shouldn't have to ask. It's what good friends do for each other."

"Then it's settled. We will leave at first light," said Calum.

After supper with Alec and Calum, Tim and Maggie returned to the hut they had lived in since they first arrived at Fois. They packed up at their belongings, which didn't amount to much. They sat down at the kitchen table and sipped ale. Tim sighed in relief, as the relaxing ale washed down within him. Maggie played with her ale stein. Tim said, "It seems strange that we're leaving tomorrow. I feel like I'm leaving home, which seems strange, given that we've only been living here a few months."

"I'm a little sad to be leaving," said Maggie.

"Are you sure that you want to come with us?"

"I'm not reconsidering. I'm sad, but determined to go with you on your adventure," said Maggie.

"I don't know if it'll be an adventure. It's mostly a rescue mission."

"It's that too," said Maggie.

"I'm not really sad, but more nervous about what I'll find."

"What do you expect to find?" Asked Maggie.

"That's just it, I'm not sure that we will find Amanda. What if they've moved her...or worse."

"Don't think that. Let's just hope for the best, and trust that we will find her," suggested Maggie.

"Even if we do find her, I hope she's still...still in one piece."

"Don't go there, Tim. I can't imagine that will help you," said Maggie.

"No, you're right, it doesn't help me to think that way. But I can't help being nervous about the mission. I hope all goes well."

"We will trust that it will," said Maggie with a smile as she took Tim's hand. Tim found her touch reassuring, and he relaxed a bit. "Come, let's go to bed. We'll need our strength for tomorrow."

"I hope I can sleep. Tim and Maggie climbed into their respective hammocks. Tim sat staring up at the ceiling. He didn't feel near falling asleep. Hopes and dreads of possible mission outcomes kept leaping to mind. He rolled over and looked down at Maggie in the hammock beneath him. Her eyes were closed. "Maggie, are you still awake...Maggie, are you still awake," Tim said a bit louder.

She stirred and looked up at him, "I am now. What is it?" She said impatiently.

"I hate to ask you this, but do you mind if I sleep with you tonight?"

"No, you will keep me awake. Have another ale if you can't sleep," said Maggie.

"Well, okay, I suppose that might help." Tim arose and lit a candle in the kitchen. He fetched himself another ale and sat down at the table. Tim swirled the ale in front of him, taking an occasional sip. As Tim felt antsy, he stood and paced the kitchen floor. The ale relaxed him some, but not enough that he felt able to sleep. When he wearied of walking, he sat back down at the table. He finished off the ale and put his feet up on the other chair.

The next thing Tim knew, Maggie roused him. "Did you sleep here all night?" Asked Maggie.

"Did I? I guess I did, if you could call it sleep. I mostly tossed and turned all night."

"Why didn't you come back to bed?" Asked Maggie.

"I thought I might wake you, and I was too tired to walk all the way in there," said Tim with a tired smile.

Maggie set a cup of hot coffee in front of Tim and said, "Drink that down. The gray of morning is upon us."

"Yes, I want to be at Alec and Calum's by first light."

"There's no reason why we can't. I have both of our bags all packed up by the door," said Maggie.

Fourteen

Alec and Calum threw together the last of their packs as Tim and Maggie walked up to their picnic table. Alec gave Maggie and Tim each a water skin and food supplies. Calum shouldered his quiver and bow, and handed Tim the bow and arrows he had used for guard duty. Then Calum gave Maggie a longer knife, which was the length of a short sword. She already had her short knife in her belt. Alec noted Maggie's shoes, and said, "You must leave those behind."

"What's wrong with my boots. They've seen me through some tough times, I don't want to leave them. I've worn these since we left Scerlandia. Philippe gave them to me," said Maggie.

"Nay Maggie, my brother's right. Those boots will give away our position a mile off. They make the noise of school children and leave a print that a child could follow. No, we must rely on invisibility for this mission," said Calum. Maggie looked at Tim for help, who merely shrugged. Maggie sighed and sat down to replace her boots with the moccasins that Alec offered.

"Okay travelers, we're off in search of Amanda," said Alec. Alec and Calum went inside to kiss their wives and children. Their children still slept, which was probably a blessing for all. All four shouldered their packs and left.

In a short time they reached the place where the Fois had found Maggie and Tim, and lifted them into the trees and away from trouble. Maggie paused as she reached the spot. "I haven't seen these trees since you all first found us here." She affectionately patted one of the trees and she resumed her march behind Alec. Alec led the way, followed by Maggie and Tim, while Calum guarded the rear.

Tim and Maggie had to half run to keep up with Alec and Calum, who hiked like goats, and seemed to never tire nor evidenced any elevated breathing. After three or four hours Maggie begged for a break. "Can we stop now? I can't take another step until I rest and have something to eat."

Calum looked at his brother and said, "I'd hoped to reach the Green Falls before stopping, but taking a look at the two of you, I see that's not going to happen." They all shed their packs and sat. Except for Alec, who grabbed a hunk of bread and climbed into the tree the others sat underneath. "What are you doing, Alec?" Asked Tim.

Alec put his finger to his lips. Calum quietly told Tim and Maggie, "Now that we are out of Fois, we must be watchful. Alec and I will keep watch at all times. We won't allow anyone to surprise us. And keep your voices to a low level."

"Why all the secrecy?" Asked Tim.

"Our mission relies on secrecy and surprise. If we are seen, we will be expected."

"But who's going to see us out here?" Asked Maggie.

"Do not underestimate the King of Scerlandia, and his network of spies. They watch all who enter their lands," explained Calum.

A short time later Alec climbed back down and they resumed their trek. Tim and Maggie did better keeping up with the brothers, but still had to half run in spots. They sipped water as they walked.

A couple days later they hiked up a hill. Pine and Aspen dotted the forrest that contained the hill. Just before they crested the hill, Alec turned to Tim and Maggie and said in a whisper, "Leave your packs here, and don't talk above a whisper."

"What's so special about this place," asked Maggie.

"Come and see," said Alec. Maggie and Tim followed Alec up to the crest of the hill, with Calum bringing up the rear. Once they were within ten paces of the top, Alec went down into a crouch, and turned and signaled the others to do the same. On all fours they crept up to the rocks on top of the hill. They stopped behind the rocks. They peered down upon a deep valley with beautiful trees and a creek running through the middle of the valley. Beyond the valley lay a range of hills, with a narrow passage in between hill peaks. In the bottom of the valley, just beyond the creek lay a castle. "That's Teagle Castle," said Tim.

"Indeed lad, we've reached your previous home," said Calum.

"This was never my home. I always hated this place, even from the first night here," said Maggie.

"The only person here that I had even the beginning of a home with is Philippe," said Tim.

"He's the only decent man in the whole castle," said Maggie.

Turning to Tim, Alec said, "Now here's where our journey gets a bit trickier. I don't know where they have your sister. Do you know from which direction you came to the castle?"

Tim shielded his eyes as he surveyed the valley. His eyes lighted on the saddle between peaks. "Yes, I'm pretty sure that our wagons came in through that passage right there," said Tim as he pointed.

"How confident are you?" Asked Calum.

"I'm confident. Even though I was unconscious for much of the journey from the battle, I was alert when we went through that passageway. I remember thinking how beautiful it was."

"Let's go back to our packs," suggested Alec.

The others followed Alec back to where they'd left their supplies. Maggie and Tim rested with their backs against a sturdy tree. They ate some jerky and sipped some water. Alec said,

"Calum and I will go back to the crest and plot a course. You stay here. The brothers climbed back to the top and conferred quietly. Twenty minutes later they came back. "We have a plan. Let's get going. I want to be beyond eyes and ears of Teagle Castle before we stop for the night," said Alec.

"But that will be more than ten miles. Maggie and I can't make it that far before dark," said Tim.

"We'll have to do the best we can. Let's go," said Calum. The four packed up and returned to the trail. Alec led them around the North side of the castle, being careful to stay in the tree line, and away from curious eyes. Several times they stopped. Maggie and Tim had learned by now that when Alec put one fist up in the air, it meant to be silent, stop and go into a crouch. Many times Alec put his fist into the air on the way around Teagle Castle.

Four hours later the hikers approached the saddle in between hill peaks. A well-worn trail wound its way along the passageway. Alec put his fist into the air fifty yards short of the trail. They all went down on one knee. Through the trees they could see three wagons escorted by two armed horseman passing along the trail. Alec signaled them to follow him to a safer distance from the trail. "I don't believe we can safely use the trail," began Alec.

"We'll have to skirt around it in the trees. We could be easily surprised if we stayed to the trail," agreed Calum.

"Then what path will we hike?" Asked Maggie.

"We will make our own path. No established path will be safe until we are beyond this range of hills," said Alec.

"But I'm tired, and the sun will be setting within two hours," said Maggie.

"We'll have to hurry to get beyond the narrow opening between peaks," said Alec.

"How much further do we have to go?" Asked Maggie.

Alec looked at Calum, who said, "I'd say at least another hour." Calum cut himself short and put his fist in the air and dropped to the ground. The others did likewise. Down on the path a group of soldiers trotted past on their horses.

"It won't be safe for us to camp in here. We could be discovered at any time. I know you're tired, but we have to get out of this passage," said Alec.

Alec shouldered his pack and began to make a way through the trees. Maggie sighed deeply, and lifted her pack to her shoulder. She stumbled and dropped the pack. Tim caught Maggie by the arm, preventing her from falling. "Are you okay?" Asked Tim.

"I don't think I can go any further."

Tim picked up her pack, and carried their packs on a shoulder each. He handed his bow and quiver to Maggie and said, "You take my bow, and I'll carry your pack. Let's go." Tim began marching before Maggie could object.

Calum stood waiting for them, while Alec had gone ahead to scout. The others quickly caught up to Alec. He waited for them behind a boulder, peering down at the trail. As soon as he saw them he resumed his trek. Alec kept one eye on the trail below at all times.

Within thirty minutes Tim's face was red and drenched with sweat. He noticed the ache in his legs building more and more. It wouldn't be long before he wouldn't be able to go any further. But he knew he had to force himself on, for there was no stopping yet. They must get beyond the mountain pass. Tim shifted the packs on his shoulders, trying to find a more comfortable place for the straps. He looked ahead and saw that he fell behind Maggie more and more. Tim felt a hand on his back as Calum said, "How are you coming? Two packs are quite a load."

"I'm okay for now. How much further?"

"Probably another mile. Can you make it?" Asked Calum.

"Yeah, I'll be alright."

Tim soldiered on, although his legs and arms began to throb. He longed to drop the packs, but he knew it wasn't an option. The trail slopped downhill and the ground became softer. Tim's left foot gave away on loose gravel and pine straw, dropping him onto his backside. He slid down the hill twenty feet until he ran into a large pine tree. Tim came to a stop with a thud. He groaned. His back was scratched up, and he'd run into the tree with his hip, which hurt so badly that he had to bite his lip to keep himself from crying out.

The sound of galloping horses filled the air. Tim tried to gather himself up to hide behind the tree, but found that he couldn't move his hip. Suddenly three soldiers appeared before Tim, with swords drawn. "Well, look what we have here. By the looks of him, I'd say we have ourselves a runaway slave," said one soldier.

"I wonder if there be reward on his head. I suppose we ought to do him a favor and return the lost boy to his owner. They'll be worried sick," said a second one.

"Alright now, we'd better get a move on then," said the first soldier. He dismounted and pulled a coil of rope off of his saddle. In spite of Tim's efforts at resistance, the soldier sat on top of him and tied his hands together. Tim was in no condition to fight, being injured and tangled up in two packs. The soldier lifted Tim to his feet and tied the rope to his saddle horn. Tim pulled on the rope, but got the back of one of the soldier's swords for his effort.

Tim looked up into the trees above them, wondering if his friends knew he'd fallen. But he could only see shadows. The soldier remounted his horse and turned back to Tim and said, "Now you'll have a nice run. It shouldn't be more than an hour back to the castle." Just as the soldier turned to lead his horse back to the trail, he fell from his horse. An arrow stuck through his throat. The other two soldiers spurred their horses to run off, but both fell to the ground before they'd gone more than ten feet. Both had arrows piercing through their chests.

Calum and Alec ran down the hill and checked all three soldiers, yet none moved. "Are you hurt?" Asked Calum.

"I think I did something to my hip," said Tim as Alec untied his hands. Tim rubbed his wrists with his fingers.

"Can you walk? How bad is it?" Asked Maggie as she ran up to Tim and embraced him. Tim was grateful for her comfort, as he'd thought he was lost. It wouldn't take long for Tim to be identified should he be brought back to Castle Teagle.

Tim took several steps and winced. "My hip hurts, but I think I'll be okay. I think I can carry my pack, at least I can try."

"And I'll take mine from here," said Maggie. Before she picked up her pack, she rubbed Tim's hip, checking for broken bones. "I think you'll be okay." Tim smiled.

Alec searched the trail in both directions from the branches of a nearby tree. He climbed down and said, "We must be off! Those horses will return to the stable, and someone will be wondering where their riders are." Alec pulled all three arrows out of the dead men.

With that Alec resumed taking the point and hurried off, with the other three close behind. Tim limped at first. He gritted his teeth with each step. Calum noticed him struggling, and handed him a branch that made a suitable walking stick. Tim smiled in gratitude. Tim moved quicker with the walking stick, which lent support to his left leg. With each step Tim's hip loosened up.

An hour later the exhausted travelers reached the end of the passage through the hills. Below them a valley opened up, and the land sloped down gently to a river at the bottom. To their left a waterfall cascaded down to form the roaring river, which became more tranquil further away from the waterfall. The travelers made their way down to the valley floor. Here two different trails branched off in different directions. Without hesitating Alec walked beyond the fork, choosing a path in between the two paths, and led them into the forrest beyond. Once they were a good mile past the fork, Alec stopped and said, "We will camp here. We've finally found ground safe from prying eyes."

Tim and Maggie collapsed on the ground with their heads on their packs. Calum climbed a tree to survey the area, while Alec pulled together something for them to eat. He didn't light a fire, preferring to take no chances on giving away their position. By the time that the humble meal was ready, Tim and Maggie slept. Alec pulled their blankets from their packs and covered both sleepers. Then he and Calum ate.

The next morning Tim awoke to the sound of birds singing. He lay still and enjoyed the morning sounds. Then He rubbed his eyes and tried to sit up, but fell back in pain. His cry woke Maggie and Alec. Calum was already awake, as he watched the campsite from a tree. "Tim, what it is?" Asked Maggie.

"Oh my God, it's my hip, it hurts like the devil!" Maggie pulled his blanket off of him and began massaging Tim's left hip. "No, don't rub so hard. You're killing me!"

"Now hush and let me help you. I know it hurts some, but it will loosen up your hip so that you can move it," said Maggie.

Alec leaped out of his bedding, grabbed his bow and quiver and climbed a different tree than Calum. "Tim, I know you're in pain, but keep it down before you bring the king's guard upon us," Alec whispered loud enough for Tim to hear.

Tim grabbed Maggie's hands and held them tight. He grinned and said, "I appreciate what you're trying to do, but I can't stand it without crying out. Help me to stand and walk about. Maybe walking will help to relax my tight hip." Maggie put Tim's left arm around her neck and helped him to stand. Tim hopped about as he tried to find his balance. With Maggie's support Tim took a few slow steps. He grimaced, but kept quiet. Gradually he took several more steps. After several minutes his pronounced limp quieted to a barely noticeable hitch in his gait.

"Okay, I think I can walk on my own now," said Tim as he gently moved his arm off of Maggie's neck. Then he walked a number of steps on his own, and stopped to rub his hip. Maggie hurried over and took charge of the hip massage. This time Tim allowed her, as it now felt good. Tim walk about in circles until he pronounced himself able to hike.

That being settled, Calum climbed down from the tree and started a fire. He made coffee and heated up some biscuits. Moments later Calum handed two biscuits and a cup up to Alec, and then returned to the fire to eat with Tim and Maggie. The fire warmed them nicely, as the morning proved chilling.

While Alec packed away the coffee pot he asked Tim, "Does anything look familiar down here in this valley?"

Tim looked around and noted the sound of the river to their left, and then pointed off towards the right path. "I'm pretty sure we came in by that road over there. I remember we were on this side of the river."

"Then we shall shadow the right path. Let's be off," said Alec.

Alec took the lead as usual, and led the travelers to the left until they could see the river. Then he turned South to follow the river, yet remained out of sight of any who might be coming up by water. This trail also kept them off the path, and away from interested eyes. The going proved easier than yesterday, as the ground was mostly level and free of heavy brush. Both Maggie and Tim carried their own packs, and neither struggled, except at first. Tim struggled to keep up with the others for the first mile or two. Then the pain left his hip and he moved freely.

By the end of the next day they crested a rise in the ground and looked down upon a village. The village was encircled by a wooden wall, that had been blackened in many places. Little movement could be discerned within its walls. Alec wondered if the town were abandoned. "That's it! That's the fortified village that Hinters and I fought at. Along that wall I was injured with an arrow. The ride to Teagle Castle nearly killed me." Tim rubbed his left shoulder unconsciously as he spoke.

"Good, that means your memory serves, and we are on the right path," said Alec. Calum slapped Tim on the back and gave him a smile. "Let's keep moving, we've still got three hours before sunset. And I don't want to sleep within sight or sound of that village," said Calum.

"Now, from which direction did you and Hinters approach the village?" Asked Alec.

Tim pointed off towards the East immediately. "We came down from those hills over there."

The four travelers moved off towards the eastern hills, keeping beyond sight of the village, even though there appeared to be little activity within it. Tim felt a chill run down his spin when they passed the spot at which he and Hinters had camped. Tim didn't want to remember the near panic he felt anticipating sneaking into the village under siege. Tim considered passing by the spot without comment, but realized that it might help their mission. "Alec, Calum, we camped here the day before we entered the battle."

"That's great work, Tim. Perhaps we can back track from here," said Alec as he bent down to examine the old campsite. Calum joined him. "Two horses ran off in this direction," said Alec.

"And two came in from this direction," said Calum.

"Yes, this must be the way Tim arrived here," said Alec as he pointed Southeast. "Tim, does this look right?"

"I guess so. I don't have much memory of that day, except for being terrified when I looked down at the battle."

"It must be right, there are no other horse tracks except the two leading in and the two leading out," said Calum.

"Yes, I believe so. We will follow the horse tracks backwards," said Alec.

The four travelers set off to trace Tim's steps back to the prison camp. Alec led with his eyes moving between the tracks and the terrain before them. He carefully stayed off the horse tracks, in case he and Calum needed to examine them again.

Three days later Alec and Calum sensed activity up ahead. It was mid afternoon, and the sun shone at their backs. They slowed their pace down and moved away from the tracks, which seemed to be following some kind of trail. They couldn't see anyone yet, but could hear occasional shouts and the sounds of horses. They crept ahead slowly, not wanting to surprise anyone. The trees were sparse here, but Alec and Calum found a tall one to climb. From the upper branches they could see people working fields. In the nearest field men and boys of all ages lifted rocks and brush off a field. Further away women sowed young plants. Even farther away appeared to be several other plots of land. Surrounding these fields were armed guards. They wore swords at their sides, and had bow and quiver over their shoulders.

Calum and Alec conferred quietly, and then waved Tim to join them. Once Tim reached them, Alec asked, "Is this the place?"

"Yes! This is definitely the place where Amanda and I were held. Let's go get her," said Tim as he began to climb down.

Alec and Calum quickly joined Tim on the ground. Calum put a hand on Tim's shoulder and stopped him, saying, "Tim, we can't go rushing in there like untrained ruffians. That will only lead to us being killed."

"Why not? I've waited long enough to get my sister out of there."

"Think before you act! I counted at least 12 armed men guarding the fields. Those are not wise odds for us," said Alec.

"Tim, we must be patient and make a good plan. We will get your sister, but it won't be today," said Calum.

"We must wait for the cover of darkness," said Alec.

"I know nothing of warfare, but I know they're right, Tim. We have to be smart about this if it's going to work," said Maggie.

"Okay, Okay, I get it. I'll wait. I know I'm being impatient," relented Tim.

Alec pointed to a hill with a cluster of trees upon it a hundred yards away, and said, "We will camp there. It will keep us from being seen or heard." The others followed Alec to the trees and made camp. They made no fire, but restored themselves with a cold meal. Alec looked at Tim and said, "Now tell us what happens after the work day ends for the slaves."

"Not much, really. The guards give us one scoop of soup and allow us to refill our water skins. And then they march us back to the barracks. The women and girls are put in the women's barracks, and the men and boys in the other barracks. And the guard locks the door, and the prisoners remain there until the doors are unlocked at sunrise."

"How many guard the barracks after they're locked?" Asked Calum.

Tim thought for a moment before saying, "I really don't know what they do after we're locked in. The only window is fifteen feet high, and the only thing I could see out of it was the moon."

"Where do the guards go at night?" Asked Alec.

"Some stay in the house near the prisoner barracks, but most of them live at the training compound."

"Where is this training compound?" Asked Alec.

Tim pointed off to the left as he said, "It's a couple of miles away around that hillside over there."

"Okay, so how many stay at the house near the prisoner barracks?" Asked Calum.

"I'm not really sure, but I'd guess about six or eight."

"Six or eight is still too many. I think we ought to wait until most of the guards sleep," suggested Alec.

"That shouldn't be too long after dark. The guards that remain at the house eat dinner and get drunk every night. I could hear them singing and fighting from the barracks."

"So we slip in after we hear the singing and fighting turn to silence," said Calum.

Alec nodded and said, "We'll stay here until dark, and then hide near the barracks until the guards pass out."

Alec and Maggie lay down with their heads against their packs, while Calum stood guard. Tim sat on his pack, nervously checking

284

the sun every few minutes. He wouldn't rest until his sister was free. Once the last yellow of the sunset faded to gray, they slipped out of their campsite. Tim led the way, as he was the only one who knew where the barracks lie. Alec walked just behind Tim, stopping him every twenty-five yards to listen and look. Thanks to the benefit of the moon, up ahead they could see dim outlines of three buildings.

Alec put a hand on Tim's shoulder, and signaled that he would take the lead now. Alec saw a cluster of carts ahead, and headed in their direction. They stopped behind the carts, which were loaded with supplies. The carts emitted an earthy smell of farming supplies. The three buildings could now be clearly seen. The left building was aglow with lights within. Loud talking and shouts came through the windows. On the right stood two darkened buildings. Neither light nor sound could be discerned from the barracks. In front of the lightened building stood two men. They chatted while they ate their dinner. They focused on their food and drink, and seemed to pay no attention to anything else.

"Of the two darkened buildings, which is the women's?" Alec whispered to Tim. Tim pointed to the middle building. Alec and Calum nodded, and then spoke quietly. Calum waved Tim and Maggie to follow them, as they retreated from the supply carts. Alec and Calum stopped behind a clump of bushes. "This will be a good place to wait for their spirits to take effect," said Calum.

Sounds of eating and talking turned to sounds of shouting and singing before long. The guards seemed to have all the alcohol they wanted, as their volume continued to rise. Finally their sounds began to quiet, as if they all became drugged at about the same time. Alec signaled for them to follow him back for a closer look.

From behind the supply carts they spied the house. The candle light continued to shine out of the windows, but no sounds from within could be heard. Only one of the guards remained, the one that had been outside eating dinner. Now he smoked alone as he leaned against the bright building.

Tim and Maggie followed the brothers around the back way to the women's barracks. The only person they could find outside was the smoking guard. There appeared to be no other guard on duty. Alec and Calum conferred briefly, and then Alec said, "I will take position on the roof. Tim, once Calum gets you into the barracks, go in and find your sister and bring her out. You must get her to understand the absolute need for silence. Maggie, you and Calum will stand guard outside the women's barracks. Any question?" All three shook their heads. Calum examined the lock on the women's barracks, while Alec went to the far side of the barracks and climbed up on the roof. With his experience climbing, Alec managed to crouch atop the roof within a couple minutes. Once Alec signaled, Calum picked the lock. It was an old, cheaply made lock, and Calum easily bested it.

The barrack's door groaned as Calum swung it open, as if it were a haunted mansion. Calum quickly closed the door and pulled Tim and Maggie back into the shadows. The guard dropped his smoke and came around the corner of the guard house to investigate. His head swiveled as he searched for the source of the sound. Not seeing anything out of order, he picked up his smoke and resumed his lonely vigil. The guard merely did his job, as he didn't care much whether the prisoners lived, died or escaped. He just didn't want to be blamed for their escape or death.

Calum said to Maggie and Tim, "Wait here. I'll be back with something to quiet that hinge." Tim nodded. A few minutes later Calum returned with some kind of leaf in his hand. He rubbed the leave against both hinges. Then he ever so slowly opened the door an inch or two. The door made a sound, but much less than before. Calum pulled the door open far enough for Tim to slip in. This time the door's groan brought the guard back. The guard began, "Hey, what's..." and that's all he got out, as he fell to the ground in a heap. An arrow from Alec's bow stuck through his chest and into the ground beneath him.

Calum closed the door after Tim, in case the women inside made a fuss. Tim's presence likely would give them a start. It was pitch black when Calum closed the door behind Tim. Tim reached into his pocket and brought out a candle. Then he fumbled in his other pocked for his flint. He lit the candle and illuminated the front of the barracks. Several women cried out in fear. Tim quickly said, "I'm not here to hurt anyone. I'm here for my sister. Is Amanda here?"

A woman in the third row of bunks called him over. "Are you Tim?" She asked.

"Yes! Yes, I am. Do you know Amanda?"

"Yes, of course I know her. We all know every prisoner here. Well, at least all of the female prisoners."

"Tell me where she is. I don't have much time. The guards will soon know that we are here," said Tim.

"I'm sorry to tell you this, but you won't find your Amanda here. She's providing the guards with...with entertainment tonight."

"What does that mean? Are they raping her?" Asked Tim.

"Oh I don't think they go that far, at least not with the young ones. But they are making her sing and dance for them. The guards only rape those of us that are old enough to be fun for them. I wish I couldn't tell you that I speak from personal experience on that subject."

"I'm sorry for you. But are you saying that Amanda's in the guard house next door?" Asked Tim.

"That's exactly what I'm saying. And she won't be back until morning. You'll have to wait until then."

With that Tim blew out his candle and went back out the door. He opened it just enough to slip out. Tim replaced the door and the lock. In response to Calum and Maggie's looks of surprise, he waved them to follow him further away so that they could talk. They followed Tim back to the supply carts.

"What's the matter? Where is Amanda?" Asked Calum.

"Amanda is okay, I think, but she's not in the barracks. A woman told me that she's in with the guards tonight, providing them entertainment."

"I think I know that kind of entertainment. Those bastards won't live to see the light of day," said Maggie.

"If they lay a hand on her..." began Tim, but was interrupted by Calum.

"Now just wait a minute, both of you. Let's not jump to any conclusions yet. The last thing I want us to do is charge in there before we know the situation."

"We need to look around and find out exactly what your sisters' situation is. We will know soon enough. You all wait here, and I will go take a closer look about," said Alec.

Calum put his hand on Tim's neck and pulled him close, "You hang in there, lad. We'll get your sister out. We will do it before first light. I don't want the guards to find their dead brother until we're long gone." Tim put his head down and nodded.

Soon thereafter Alec returned. "All the guards that I could see inside that building are asleep. And there is a young girl laying on the rug near the fireplace. I'm not sure if she's asleep or not."

"That has to be Amanda!" Said Tim. "So how will we get her out?"

"Calum will get me inside the door, and I will carry her out," said Alec. "And you two will stand guard with Calum outside. And Tim, have an arrow on your string. And stay back far enough that any guard that awakens can't reach you before you get a shot off. Any questions?" Everyone shook their head.

Calum picked the lock in less than a minute. Fortunately, this door made little sound when it opened, as it was well tended. Alec left the door open when he entered. He stopped just inside the door and took stock of the situation. He counted seven men.

Two near the door, three in chairs and the two on the floor near Amanda. Alec soundlessly made his way to Amanda. She slept next to one of the guards, who snored like a saw.

When he reached Amanda, Alec crouched next to her. He put a hand over her mouth and turned her towards his kind face. Amanda's eyes opened wide with fear, and she struggled to pull free of him. Alec whispered in her ear, "I am here with your brother, Tim. Don't be afraid. I won't hurt you." Amanda paused, and then resumed struggling to free herself. She'd learned to trust no men at this slave camp. Alec continued, "I'm taking you to Tim." Amanda looked uncertain, yet searched the door for Tim. Not seeing Tim, she tried to pull herself out of Alec's hands, but he picked her up and held her mouth firmly.

As Alec hurried through the kitchen and towards the door, Amanda's flailing legs kicked over a metal pitcher of water, which clattered to the ground. Alec didn't stop, but heard shouts from behind him, as he bolted through the door at a run. One of the guards ran right on his heels, and grabbed onto Amanda's leg just outside the door. A moment later he dropped to the ground with one of Calum's arrows. A second guard lunged out of the doorway a second later and tackled Alec and Amanda to the ground. Alec didn't let go of Amanda, and rolled out of the guards' reach. The guard stood up and readied himself to reach for Alec, but fell to the ground with Tim's arrow in his chest.

The remaining five guards quickly emerged from the kitchen. Two of them had taken the time to arm themselves with swords. One of the armed men ran to where Tim was trying to string another arrow. But the guard was upon him before Tim could release the arrow, and knocked Tim to the ground. The guard raised his sword and began to swing it down upon Tim, yet stopped in mid swing. As Tim wondered about this, Maggie's sword appeared through his abdomen, having been run all the way through him. She kicked him off her sword and turned towards another guard.

Once Alec had Amanda clear of immediate danger, Alec pulled his own bow off his shoulder and began firing. In less than a minute Alec and Calum had dropped the remaining guards in their tracks. None remained alive.

Amanda sat on her heels in the dirt, looking bewildered. She searched each face until she found her brother. Her face lite up, "Tim, is that really you?" Said Amanda as she ran to Tim. "Oh Tim, that is you! You came back for me!" Amanda said as she leaped into his arms.

"Thank God you're okay!" Said Tim.

"When I didn't see you for so long, I began to give up hope that you'd ever come back for me," said a tearful Amanda.

"You didn't think I'd leave you here to have all the fun by yourself, did you?" Said TIm.

"So where have you been all this time?"

"I hate to break up your family reunion, but I want to get out of here before any more guards come join the party," said Alec. "We mustn't forget that there are many more a short distance away."

"Oh, right, I'll tell you all about my adventure when we're safe," said Tim.

Tim picked up Amanda, and followed the others away from the slave camp. When they'd gone a hundred yards Tim stopped. "Hey wait a minute! I can't just leave those poor souls locked up in there. I have to free them."

"I don't want to take the time, Tim. Every second we're here gives the rest of the guards a second to find us," said Alec.

Turning to Calum, Tim said, "Calum please, help me unlock those doors so those poor captives can get out!"

Calum turned to his brother and said, "You and Maggie get Amanda away from here, and Tim and I will catch up."

"But Calum," began Alec.

"I promise we won't be long. We'll be along faster than a leprechaun can wrinkle his nose," said Calum.

Alec reluctantly agreed and said, "All right, Maggie take Amanda's hand, and I'll lead us about a mile away. You will know how to find us, Calum." Calum nodded and followed Tim back to the barracks.

Tim stopped before the women's barracks first, and waited while Calum quickly picked the lock. Calum waited by the door while Tim went in and lit his candle. He stopped at the third bunk and woke the woman who had directed Tim to find Amanda in the guard house. "Ma'am, wake up."

She woke up in a start, "Yes, who's there?"

"It's Tim, ma'am, I'm Amanda's brother."

"Oh yes, is she alright?"

"Amanda'a fine, we got her out safe. I came back to free you all and the men prisoners as well. The guards in the house are dead, but there will be more by morning. You're free for now, do what you think best." The woman looked perplexed and uncertain what to do. Tim didn't wait to see.

Tim left back through the door, and hurried to the mens' barracks. Calum opened the door for him, and Tim slipped through quickly. He remembered Thaddeus' bunk and went straight to it. Tim left the candle in his pocket. He shook Thaddeus' shoulders, "Thaddeus, wake up, it's Tim! Thaddeus, it's me, Tim!" Thaddeus pushed Tim away without looking at him.

"Damn it, Thaddeus, it's Tim. Wake up!" Said Tim louder.

The man in the next bunk said, "Shut yer trap, rat. Leave us to our peace!"

Tim shook Thaddeus harder, and finally he turned towards Tim with a knife at his throat. "Thaddeus, it's Tim. Don't cut me, I'm here to free you!"

"Shut the hell up, down there," growled the man above Thaddeus.

"Tim, is that really you, lad? Where in God's name have you been?"

"Yes, it's me. There's no time to explain. The guards next door are dead, but there will be more upon us soon enough. Wake up the others and flee! I have to hurry off, as we've just freed my sister."

Thaddeus swung his feet down, and quickly pulled his boots on. "Bless you, Tim, for remembering us!"

Tim ran for the door, and Calum turned to his heels and they were off. Calum led them out of the compound towards the South. Just beyond the edge of the compound he paused to examine the ground, and Tim ran into him, knocking them both to the ground. Calum jumped back to his feet, and then he was back running with Tim on his heels.

Within a mile Calum and Tim found the others. Amanda leaped into Tim's arms, saying, "Tim, don't leave me again! You just can't scare me like that again." Tears filled Tim's eyes as he saw the pain in hers. He nodded and hugged her.

"We have to get far away from here," began Alec. There will be guards swarming the area by dawn." Calum nodded and waved Tim and Maggie to follow. Tim grabbed Amanda's hand and followed after Maggie. Two hours later they stopped. "This is far enough," said Calum. "I've stopped to erase our tracks a number of times. They won't be able to follow us."

"We'll camp here," agreed Alec.

All but Alec gratefully fell into their bedding the moment they made camp. The comfort of being safe left Amanda exhausted, as she fell asleep in her brother's arms. Tim's eyes teared softly, as he felt enormous relief that he'd finally rescued Amanda. He'd dreamt of this day for months, and it had weighed on his mind ever since he too was captured. Tim patted Amanda's hair as he tried to get his mind around the fact they she lay safely in his arms. At first he didn't want to fall asleep, fearing that someone would take her away again. Yet exhaustion finally got the best of Tim, and he succumbed to sleep.

A dark cloud enveloped the sky. As the sky continued to darken, winds freshened and drops of rain began to fall. The darkest cloud, being right over Tim, seemed to have a face in it. The features of the face became clearer. Tim thought he recognized the face, but he couldn't quite place it. Then the face said, "I'm coming for you. You can't escape me! And you can't kill me. I will have my vengeance!" The rain came harder. Tim awoke to water splashing his face. He wiped his eyes and looked up into the giggling face of Maggie.

"Time to wake up, sleepy head," said Maggie as she splashed more water on him. Suddenly Tim remembered Amanda, and his eyes darted about until he spied her lying asleep a few feet away. He turned his gaze back to Maggie, and a mischievous grin emerged on his face. By now Maggie recognized that face, and immediately turned to fly. Tim jumped up and chased Maggie down the path. She was surprisingly fast, and Tim didn't catch her until she stumbled on a tree root and lost her balance momentarily. He tackled her to the ground and pinned her. Maggie struggled to free herself, and then had another idea. She checked to see that the others couldn't see them, and then said, "Well you've got me. So what are you going to do with me?" Tim shrugged his shoulders and dipped his hand into the coffee pot that Maggie had dropped when she fell, and then he flung the water onto her. She laughed and said, "Is that all you have the courage to do to a helpless woman?"

"What do you mean?" A puzzled Tim asked.

"Well, if I have to tell you that this would be an excellent opportunity to kiss me, then you must not be the man I'd hoped you are." Tim briefly reddened, and then leaned down to kiss her.

Maggie turned her face away and said, "No, I said never mind if you can't figure it out on your own."

Tim released her hands and instead cupped her face, holding it firm. He kissed her leisurely. Within a moment Maggie ceased resisting. Then Tim pushed away and said with a smirk, "So I figured it out."

"Tim? Tim! Where did you go!" Shouted Amanda. A moment later she appeared before them. "Whatever are you doing over here? And Calum wants to know where the coffee pot is."

Before Amanda appeared Tim had rolled off of Maggie, and both of them lay on their backs in the grass. "Okay kid, we're coming," said Tim as he got up. He reached down and offered Maggie a hand. Tim looked to see if Amanda was watching, but she'd turned her back and had begun to walk back. Tim pulled Maggie into an embrace and kissed her once more. Then he turned and caught up with his sister, and walked hand-in-hand with Amanda back to camp.

Once they all held hot coffee in their hands, Tim began to think about their situation. He'd been so focused on freeing Amanda, that he hadn't thought what to do next. But it was really quite obvious. Tim said, "I'm so grateful for all of your help. I couldn't have found, not to mention freed Amanda on my own." His eyes paused at Alec, Calum and Maggie. Alec and Calum nodded, while Maggie smiled. "And I'm thankful that you stayed alive long enough for me to come back," said Tim looking at Amanda.

"What will you do now?" Asked Maggie.

"I will take Amanda home...I was hoping the three of you would help me get her there safely."

Maggie asked, "Do you expect more trouble?"

Tim paused before saying, "Not really, I can't imagine who will find us between here and home...but I can't shake this feeling of dread that something bad is going to happen."

Maggie said, "Something bad like what?"

"I can't really say. I just sense that there's something more...I don't know, maybe it was just a bad dream."

"You had a nightmare?" Asked Maggie.

Tim nodded and said, "Even though home is a short distance from here, I'm afraid to go it alone. Will you all come with me? You all can stay with us for awhile if you like."

Alec and Calum looked at each other and nodded, and then Calum said, "Of course we'll go. We've come this far, we won't be cheated out of seeing the look on your family's faces when they see Amanda."

Tim looked to Maggie, who said, "I don't know where to go now...I certainly can't go back to Teagle Castle, but I expect that they will find me if I go home to Randley. I'm really not sure what to do with myself."

"Come with us, and when this is all over I'll help you figure out what's next," said Tim as he took Maggie's hand. She smiled sheepishly and nodded.

"Then it's settled. We are off for the farm," said Tim.

There was no longer a reason to hurry, so the travelers savored their coffee and munched slowly on their morning biscuits, which were the same as the evening biscuits. After a couple hours of lying around, they hoisted their packs and resumed their trek. Amanda insisted on pulling her weight, so Tim took a few things out of his and Maggie's packs and tied them into a blanket that Tim fastened to Amanda's back.

When they came within site of Hanover, Tim noticed a pit in his stomach. "Wait, everybody, wait! I don't want to go in that town."

Calum put a hand on Tim's shoulder, and said, "What's the trouble, little brother?"

"That's the town where they took me the first night. And that's the tavern where Tim got thrown out the window by those bad people," said Amanda.

"Ah, so it's bad memories," said Calum.

"I don't expect any trouble in this sleepy little hamlet, but we can easily skirt around it," suggested Alec.

"Yes, I'd like that," said Tim.

"Do those bad men live there?" Asked Amanda.

"I don't think...actually, I don't really know," said Tim. "Maybe we could watch and see."

"Now hold on, Tim, you just said you don't want to go there," pointed out Alec.

"Maybe we can watch from a distance," said TIm. "Let's see if they're at the tavern."

The four travelers crouched in the bushes behind the tavern. The afternoon sun shone from behind them into the windows. They could discern no activity, but then again it was after dinner time and well before supper.

Tim looked at the brothers and asked, "So how do we do this?"

Alec said, "If this is the only tavern and hotel in town, then we could simply walk in and see who's there."

"No, I don't want them to see me or Amanda."

"Who is going to see you?" Asked Calum.

"The two tax collectors that took Amanda, and held us both captive," said Tim.

Alec glanced at Calum and said, "So you think two of them are going to overpower all of us? Have we not earned more trust than that by now?"

"Look Alec, I don't mean no offense..."

"This isn't about offense, little brother, this is about stepping out of fear and trusting us. You forget that security is our job with the Fois. Now we might be overmatched by some, but do we not know how to handle ourselves, lad?"

Tim thought for a moment and said, "I am being afraid, and I don't want to be. Let's go in there. How shall we do this?"

Calum said, "You, Amanda and Maggie will go in there first, appearing to merely be a traveling family. Alec and I will come in after a bit, and sit at a different table, looking like we're not together."

Leaving their packs in the bushes, the three "family members" went inside. Tim walked through the door apprehensively. He swept the tavern with his eyes. Thank God, he didn't see the tax collectors. They sat at a corner table and waited. The tavern owner washed glasses behind the bar. The only other occupant sat at the bar. He wore a hat and dark overcoat. He faced away from them. After several minutes the tavern owner approached their table, and said, "You're too early for supper, and I've already put away the dinner food. All I've got now is some bread and butter to eat."

"That will be fine," said Tim. Tim watched the man at the bar, who remained facing away from them. He sloshed his ale, and seemed to be focused on nothing but his drink. Two empty ale glasses sat next to his half full glass.

Maggie, Tim and Amanda fell to the bread and butter. They hadn't had any fresh bread since they'd left Fois. About when the bread was gone, Alec and Calum entered the tavern, looked about leisurely and took a seat at a table on the far side of the tavern. The brothers ordered bread, butter and water.

Twenty minutes later Tim, Maggie and Amanda had finished their second helping of bread. Tim paid their bill, and they got up to leave. As they walked to the door, the man at the bar stood, stretched and strode to the door. Arriving first, he held the door open for them. "Allow me, my fine fellow travelers!" He said with a grin. Several of his teeth were missing.

Tim said, "Thank you, sir." As he passed the man, Tim noticed the dagger in his belt. There was something familiar about it, but Tim didn't pay it much heed.

As Maggie and Amanda passed him, he said, "I hope the ending of your travels is everything you hope." As this comment seemed strange, Tim turned to see the man leering at them. Tim turned and began walking down the road. Amanda quickly turned towards their bags, but Maggie pulled her back and held onto her. Amanda looked up at Maggie with confusion, and Maggie said, "I don't want that man to see where we're going. We'll walk to the end of town and then double back." Amanda looked to her brother, who nodded.

When they got back to their packs, Alec and Calum were already there. As they reached the brothers, Tim said, "there's something about that man."

Calum said, "yes, I sensed it too."

"Do you recognize him?" Asked Alec.

"No, I don't think so, but there's something familiar about his dagger," said Tim.

"Many wear a dagger on the road," said Alec.

Maggie said, "I know those daggers. The king's guard wear them."

"Oh my God, you're right! That's where I've seen them," said Tim.

"We must be on our guard. I have to assume they are with the king's men, and may very likely be here for you three. You're all fugitives from the king, and they will know about the prison guards by now," said Alec.

"Did anyone see where he went?" Asked Tim.

"Yes, towards your home," said Calum.

"Tim, don't let them take me again! Please don't let them," pleaded Amanda.

"I won't, our friends will help me keep you safe," said Tim as he pulled her under his arm and held her.

"We will stay off the main road the rest of the way to your family farm," said Alec.

"And we must be off now, so that we can get a good ways from Hanover before we make camp for the night," said Calum.

The travelers stayed to the East of the road, and hiked a good four or five miles before they stopped for the night. They hadn't seen any other travelers since leaving Hanover. There was little conversation during supper, as each kept to their thoughts. All knew that they'd reach Tim and Amanda's farm the next day. Tim wondered what they'd find. Would their parents and brother be there? Would they be alive? Maybe they had been taken prisoner too. And where was the soldier from the tavern? Did he go to their farm? And if so, why?

Tim remained awake for several hours. He kept imagining what he might find at home. He figured that freeing Amanda must have tipped the soldiers off. That must be why the soldier went towards their farm.

He finally fell asleep. One of the advantages of the road is being so tired by bed time that sleep usually comes within minutes. Tim woke with a start. He'd been dreaming, but just now realized it. He'd dreamt that when they arrived at their farm, they found it burning. Tim had this horrible helpless feeling that his family was burning to death inside, but there was nothing he could do about it. Tim rubbed his face, and tried to shake off the terror of the dream. He couldn't go back to sleep right away after that, so he got up and paced about. Calum put a hand on his shoulder, "Tim, what are you doing up?"

Tim started at Calum's hand, and then said, "I had this awful dream that we found my family burned to death when we got there."

"I'm sorry for the fright you've had, little brother."

"I just don't know what I'll do if they're dead when we get there."

"Don't go there, Tim. It does you no good to give into fear. Don't do that to yourself," said Calum.

"We will find them okay, won't we?"

"Tim, we can't know what we'll find. We must take whatever adventure the great one sends us, and trust that He'll help us deal with what we find," said Calum.

"You mean you think my family is dead?"

"No, I'm saying we don't know, and can't know yet. I understand how difficult it is for you to be in suspense, and not knowing what tomorrow will bring. But I can say this, Alec and I will be with you, and will help you with whatever we find. And I know that Maggie will do the same. She loves you."

Tim said, "you think she loves me?"

"Are you so blind as that? It is as plain to me as the moon above us," said Calum.

"I've been so preoccupied with Amanda, that I haven't even thought of Maggie."

"She is a rare gem, and you would do well to value her, little brother."

"Yes...and Calum, thank you for helping me with my fear. I know that I often let my fear run away with me. I must reign it in."

Calum said, "yes, little brother, it is good that you know this about yourself. Now, go back and get what sleep you can. Whatever we find tomorrow, you will need your strength and whits about you."

Tim awoke before the others, except for Alec, who was up guarding their camp. Tim nodded at Alec and relit the fire. While Tim stood there staring into the fire, he hadn't noticed that it went out. Once he had relit the fire and had it going well, he put the full coffee pot at the edge of the fire. Tim pictured images of his family in trouble, and began to pace with his arms folded across his chest.

Calum awoke to Tim's pacing. He gathered himself and went to Tim's aid. "Little brother, it doesn't take a genius for me to see what ails ye."

"What? You mean because I'm pacing?"

"Come now, little brother, I know you better than that. You're fretting over your family again, the same as I found you late last night," said Calum.

"Oh my God, you're right. I'm doing it to myself again! When will I learn?"

"Now don't go adding more fuel to your fire. With my help you caught yourself. So admit to yourself that you're going to be a bit afraid until we find your family. Okay, let that be, but keep it on a short leash," said Calum.

Tim nodded as his eyes teared. He put a hand on Calum's shoulder and said, "thank you, big brother." Calum grinned and slapped Tim on the back. Calum folded up his bedding, figuring that Tim could use the distraction of making them breakfast.

Once Tim had breakfast ready, he woke Maggie and Amanda. Maggie understood Tim's eagerness to get home, while Amanda groaned and turned back over. Tim gave her a minute, and then picked his sister up, depositing her on a stool-sized rock near the fire. "Amanda, we'll be home today. I want to get on the trail soon. Aren't you excited to see Mama and Father?"

Amanda rubbed the sleep out of her eyes and mumbled, "yes, I want to see them, but it could have waited till I slept a little more." Tim ruffled her hair and fell to his breakfast.

The four travelers hit the trail soon thereafter, with extra energy in their step. All were excited to reach the end of their trek, and curious to see what awaited them. At first Tim held Amanda's hand, both for comfort and to keep her on pace. They walked more slowly, now that Amanda was amongst them. Her short legs didn't carry her as fast as the travel worn others.

The closer they got to the farm, the faster Tim walked. Alec slowed him down many a time, reminding Tim that his sister couldn't keep up. Each time Tim slowed himself down, yet within twenty minutes he was back in front with Alec.

"Tim, stay with you sister. She will need your steady hand once we reach our destination," said Alec.

"Yeah Tim, you're going way too fast. Slow down! I want to walk beside you. I want Mama and Father to see us both at the same time," said Amanda.

Tim silently prayed, "dear God, let us see Mama and Father at all!" And aloud he said, "okay Amanda, take my hand. We'll see them together soon."

As Tim looked over his sister, he was thankful that Maggie had been kind enough to mend her dress, which had several holes in it when they found her. Now her clothes looked well worn, but whole. Maggie had brushed Amanda's hair before they broke camp this morning. Tim glanced up. He breathed in sharply. Tim knew that from the top of the hill before them, they would be able to see their farm. Tim's legs felt heavier. His pace slowed. Even Amanda urged him to hurry. She didn't know the hill, but she knew they were close. Tim turned his eyes downward and breathed a final prayer. Then they crested the summit of the hill.

Fifteen

Below the hill lay the family farm. To Tim's eye it looked the same as it always did. Even the chimney smoked, which was common this time of year when there was a crispness to the air. He breathed a small sigh of relief; at least the farm isn't burned down. Tim scanned the property, searching for the rest of his family. He couldn't find a single person on the property, family or not. His stomach knotted. Dear God, let them be alright, Tim silently prayed.

Tim began to march down the hill when Calum put a hand on his shoulder and said, "Give Alec a moment to give the farm a gander."

Alec added, "I don't want us to walk into an ambush." Tim breathed loudly, and nodded his assent. He just wanted to be out of suspense, and find his family. But Tim trusted the Fois brothers, and resigned himself to waiting a bit longer.

Calum pulled the others back into the cover of trees, while Alec trotted down the hill. Alec went from cover to cover, rarely being out in the open more than a moment at a time. While he made his way to level ground, Alec angled his way towards the barn. He paused at the back of the barn and waited and listened. No sounds emerged from the barn, and nothing else moved nearby. Alec slipped into the barn and waited for his eyes to adjust to the dim lighting. It was just as you'd expect, several farm animals, a hand full of tools and a hay loft. But no people. The animals regarded him for a moment, and then returned to their chewing.

Alec quickly snuck out of the barn and looked towards the house. He paused behind the barn, and took stock of his surroundings. There didn't appear to be anyone in the nearby trees, nor about the house. The fields were empty. However, Alec's intuition told him that something was amiss. He sensed the presence of people, and people that didn't belong on the property.

Just as Alec began to scramble towards the house, he noticed light glint off something metal as he passed by the front window. Alec moved to the side of the house, and crouched down. He knew that glint; someone had a large metal object in the house, probably some kind of weapon. Alec waited below the kitchen window, hoping to hear any conversation inside. At first he heard nothing, yet Alec had enough experience to be patient. A few minutes later he heard muffled voices. It sounded to Alec like a man talking quietly, and then a muffled response, but he couldn't make out any words. Alec waited longer, and this time the voice sounded more distinct, but he still couldn't make out any words. Alec glanced up the hill, and was pleased that he couldn't see any of his fellow travelers.

Moving slowly, Alec raised his head until he could peak into the kitchen. There didn't appear to be anyone in the kitchen. Then he heard the voice again, and saw a man sitting in the far room with his back to Alec. He appeared to be talking with another man, but Alec couldn't see the other man. Alec risked another look. The man appeared to be holding a sword across his lap. Although when he scanned the rest of the room, Alec couldn't find anyone else. Alec knew that he and his companions were expected, but he had to know more.

Alec slowly made his way around the farmhouse, searching for another window. He didn't want to look in the front window, for the occupants would be watching the front of the house. Alec made his way around the house, and came across a window in the bedroom. He waited and listened, yet neither heard nor saw anything. Alec raised himself up, but quickly dropped to the ground. Someone was in the bedroom, and just a few feet from Alec. Damn, what do I do, thought Alec.

Then Alec had an idea. He moved around the corner of the house, and then scrambled to a nearby tree. He paused behind the trunk of the tree and looked and listened. Alec climbed the tree in a few seconds and found a sturdy branch near the top. From there he could see into the house. On the bed were three people, bound and gagged. Leaning against the window frame was a large man. He appeared to be guarding the prisoners on the bed, and glanced out the window from time to time. Alec couldn't be positive, but the man looked like the soldier from the tavern.

The door beyond the soldier opened out to the main room. Alec could see the outline of the man sitting with a sword across his lap. Alec suspected there were more soldiers in the outer room, but he could only see the one man. Alec decided to be patient. He wanted to know how many they were up against. After twenty minutes a third man appeared at the bedroom door, and said something to the soldier at the window, who nodded.

Every few minutes Tim stood and peered down at the farm. He scanned the property. The only thing he could see was Alec, now in the tree. Well, Tim couldn't actually see Alec, but he'd seen him run to the tree. Calum stood next to Tim and said, "It's best if you stay down, well out of sight."

"What is taking Alec so long?" Asked Tim.

"Come little brother, sit with me," said Calum.

Tim reluctantly sat down heavily next to Calum against the tree. Maggie and Amanda chatted quietly nearby. Tim continued, "Why isn't he back yet? Is there something wrong?"

"Give him time to do his job. You know as well as I that Alec knows what he's about." Calum's eyes darted back and forth. He too sensed that there were soldiers down at the ranch. Once he'd seen the soldier in the tavern, Calum expected to find a greeting party once they reached the farm.

Just then Calum heard a twig break. He signaled for the others to be still, while slowly crouching and stringing an arrow. Then Calum spied Alec in a tree nearby. Alec signaled to his brother and pointed. Following Alec's hand, Calum saw the two men, and dropped behind a tree. At about the same time, Alec and Calum loosed a shot. Both arrows thudded home, finding their targets in the chest. Calum and Alec ran to their victims to investigate.

Both men were dressed the same as the soldier in the tavern. After a brief inspection Calum said, "They're in Lord Teagle's guard." Alec nodded. "So how many more await us?" Asked Calum.

"At least three that I could see...we must expect there's more," said Alec.

Tim hurried up and crouched next to the brothers, and said, "These are Marvinian's guards, aren't they? I'd recognize them anywhere."

"Yes, and at least three more at the house. And they have prisoners," said Alec.

"My folks and Shane! Are they alive?"

"Yes, I think so. I saw at least one of them move," said Alec.

"Thank God! So how soon do we go down there and free them?" Asked Tim.

Calum and Alec exchanged a glance. Calum said, "You know little brother, it gladdens my heart to hear you say 'free them'."

"What else would I say?"

"You might have said 'kill them'," said Alec.

"Perhaps you learned something back in Fois," suggested Calum.

Tim pondered the distinction they made, and said, "Well, the main thing is the safety of my family. I don't care if the king's soldiers live or die."

"This is growth for you, little brother," said Calum.

"Now we must make a plan," said Alec.

Alec bent down to the ground, and the others all gathered around. He picked up a stick and began drawing in the dirt. He said, "Here is the barn, there are no men in there, at least when I was there. And here's the house. There are at least three in the house, and we would do well to expect four or five."

"Four or five? But you just killed two soldiers. Won't there be less now?" Suggested Tim.

"Yes, two are down, but we would be fools to expect an easy time freeing your family. And when these soldiers don't return, they will know that we are here. We must expect a strong force, and if it is less, all the better. Along with the four or five in the house, I expect there will be a few around the property. These will probably be hidden from plain sight. But they will come at the first signs of trouble from us. So, I expect we will be up against a force of about ten men. And not merely ten farmers, but ten trained soldiers. Maggie, I want you to remain here and guard Amanda."

"But I want to help with the fight. You know I'm quite confident with this dagger," said Maggie.

Calum responded, "Maggie, we know you can fight, and fight well. But we need you to keep Amanda safe. This will all be for naught if she's taken prisoner again." Maggie thought about that, and then slowly nodded her head.

Amanda said, "I want to stay with Tim. Tim, don't leave me again!"

Tim looked at Calum, and then said, "Amanda, I won't leave you. You must stay here safe with Maggie. I trust her, she will protect you. I must go with Alec and Calum and free Mama and Father and Shane."

Amanda ran into Tim's arms and said, "But I don't want you to go. Let Father and Shane get away by themselves. And they won't hurt Mama, cause bad men don't hurt ladies."

Maggie pulled Amanda into her arms and said, "Amanda, I need you to help me guard the camp and the food. The men will be hungry after fighting the bad men. Will you help me watch the food?"

Amanda eyed Tim for a moment, and then nodded her head and said, "Okay, I'll help you." Maggie hugged Amanda and pulled her away to make a meal. It was well past midday, and they were all hungry.

Tim watched Amanda and Maggie retreat to their gear, and begin sifting through the food packs. He felt sad, and didn't want to take his eyes off of her. "Tim, look here, I want us all of one mind when we go down that hill," said Alec.

Tim took a last glance at Amanda, and turned to Alec and nodded. Alec continued, "Okay then, here's what we'll do..."

Tim climbed up the hay loft and opened the door. He grabbed the rope with both hands, and carefully made his way up to the roof. He and Shane had been up here a thousand times, as they loved to play on top of the barn. It was the highest point on either building, and afforded a terrific view of the property.

Tim reached up to the pinnacle of the roof, and pulled himself onto the beam. He kept a low profile, and crawled across the beam on all fours. Tim paused behind the face board. At the far end of the beam was a pulley mounted on a two by three foot, sturdy piece of wood. The pulley board provided Tim with a nice blind from which to hide and watch. He pulled an arrow out of his quiver and put it on his string. Tim looked down at the house; nobody moved at the moment. Alec and Calum must be still getting into position, Tim figured.

Tim wiped his forehead, which dripped with sweat. Wow, I must be nervous, Tim thought. He wiped his eyes, not wanting anything to impair his vision. Tim's eyes swept the area near the house. This time he saw Calum slip past the side of the house.

Calum paused at the corner of the house, and looked and listened. As all seemed well, he ran to the the tree that Alec had been perched in two hours before. From the upper branches, he peered into the bedroom and saw the outlines of two people on the bed. Where is the third person, thought Calum. Didn't Alec say there were three? The guard still patrolled the bedroom window.

Calum kept an eye on the window, while he waited for Alec's signal. A second soldier walked into the bedroom and approached the tavern soldier, who stood at the window. The two soldiers conferred for a moment, and then the tavern guard left the room. The second soldier remained in the room, taking his place at the window. The tavern guard walked around to the back of the house. He stopped right next to Calum's tree. The tavern guard leaned against the trunk of the tree and lit a smoke.

Calum trained his arrow on the tavern guard, but hoped to not need to fire it. He didn't want to notify the soldiers of his position, as Alec's plan depended upon some element of surprise. The tavern guard exhaled smoke deeply. His eyes scanned from left to right, yet he appeared to relax, thanks to the chemicals in the tobacco. Calum looked up, hoping to see Alec's signal, and frowned when he didn't see it. Hurry up, Calum silently pleaded. If this guy sees me the surprise party is over.

The tavern guard finished his smoke, and dropped the remaining stub, grinding it with his boot. He took a few steps back towards the house, then paused at the corner. The guard scanned the entire area surrounding the house. He was well trained. The guard's eyes swept towards the tree, and leisurely looked up. His eyes suddenly grew large as Calum and the guard locked eyes momentarily. Calum immediately loosed his arrow. The guard cried out a second before the arrow thudded into his chest, "Enemies upon us!" Calum strung another arrow and in one motion loosed it towards the bedroom window. The soldier within ducked out of sight just before the arrow reached home.

Tim tensed as he heard the soldier cry out the alarm. Tim searched for Alec below, and spied him racing away from the house. Alec dove into a clump of bushes in front of the house, as he yelled, "now!" The front door opened and three soldiers poured out. Tim aimed and loosed his arrow towards the closest of the three, and found his target. Before Tim could string another arrow, the other two were felled by Alec's arrows.

As his eyes scanned back and forth, Tim waited for more soldiers to make themselves known. None came. Tim thought about leaving the barn roof to explore, but remembered Alec's instructions to stay at his post no matter what occurred below him. His heart rate raced. Tim's vision blurred, and he wiped his sleeve across his eyes. Tim noticed he breathed as though he were running. I've got to slow my breathing, Tim thought. It won't do if I panic up here. I can do my family no good by rushing down there and getting myself killed.

Tim searched the bushes in front of the house, but he could find no sign of Alec. Tim searched for Calum in the tree behind the house, but couldn't see the tree as the house blocked his view. Damn, what in God's name is going on down there, he wondered? Are all the soldiers dead? But if so, it seemed too easy to defeat them. His family must still be prisoner inside. Or are they unguarded?

Tim looked again for Alec, hoping for some signal. He didn't know how long to wait where he was. Then he heard a voice, "I know you're out there, rat. Come on in for a chat, little rat! I can't wait for the family reunion...Rat? I know you can hear me. Come inside and say hello to you Ma. She's just dying to see you. And you know what, she just might die saying hello to you."

He knew the voice. It was almost as familiar as his own, a voice often echoing in his mind, yet he couldn't quite place it. Then the voice rang out again, "I give you exactly five minutes to show yourself in here, and if you don't, then your Ma will enjoy the point of my sword. And rat, be sure to know that she'll die real slow-like. Come to think of it, I hope you don't show."

Marvinian! But how could it be? Marvinian was dead, killed by his own hand! It wasn't possible. Did he hear a ghost? Did he only imagine that it was Marvinian? The front door to the house opened, and his bound mother appeared in the door frame. Then Marvinian stuck his head out of the door, next to Mama's head. He said, "Now you have two and a half minutes, rat. I sure do hope you don't come, for I'll enjoy sending you Ma to the devil. And I'll bet he's eager to see her. And that's only the beginning. Next I'll take you Pa's life, and I'll save your dear brother for last."

My God, it is Marvinian! Tim sat frozen, staring at the apparition of Marvinian. Marvinian said, "Two minutes till dear Ma dies!" This startled Tim into action. He rappelled down the rope, and soon stood before Marvinian and Mama. Mama looked down at the ground, not trusting herself to look at her son. She didn't appear to recognize that Tim was before her. Her eyes were open, but she kept them averted. Her body bore the signs of exhaustion, as every cell in her body sagged towards the earth.

Alec stood next to Tim, an arrow on his string. Marvinian said, "I sure hope you'll take the shot, forest feller. I like the odds of you hitting Ma!" Alec had no intention of firing a shot now. The sliver of Marvinian's head that remained visible was just too small, especially with his moving. The chances of hitting Tim's mother were too great, even for a Fois with considerable skill.

Tim turned to Alec and said, "How is he still alive?" Alec kept his arrow trained on Marvinian.

"Now here's how this is going to work, rat. Ma and I are going to take a seat inside. And she insists on sitting on my lap. Of course, you know how your Ma is, quite the seductress. You will follow us into the room. And if any of your forest friends join us, then Ma here says goodbye."

"What do I do?" Tim asked Alec.

"I think you'd better do what he says. I don't think he's bluffing. He's got three prisoners to kill, whenever he wants. I assume he's still got at least one or two more soldiers inside with him," said Alec.

"What do I do once I'm inside?"

Alec whispered in Tim's ear, "You will stay near the window, so that I will have a shot."

Tim nodded, handed his bow and arrow to Alec, and went in. Ma sat on Marvinian's lap, as promised. Behind him stood two other guards, one held Father and one held Shane. Both were bound and helpless. Shane looked roughed up, his clothes torn and blood oozing from his head. Father had a black eye, but didn't appear to be hurt otherwise. They both might have fought, Tim thought. Ma still looked away, her eyes staring at nothing and avoiding looking at Tim. The only blessing being she appeared to be unharmed.

Turning to the window, Tim took a few steps towards it, as instructed. Marvinian didn't seem to mind. Tim said, "How are you still alive?"

Marvinian threw his head back and laughed, and then said, "You thought you'd killed me. Is that it? Like I told you at the dungeon, you ain't got it in you to kill me. A rat like you won't ever be able to kill the likes of me." Marvinian's face contorted as he said this, becoming almost unrecognizable. For a moment Tim doubted if it really was Marvinian before him. But a moment later he knew that it was he. There was no mistaking his scarred face. Tim would know it anywhere, even when distorted by rage.

Tim stuttered, "But how, how did you tend to your wounds? And how did you escape from the dungeon?"

Marvinian sneered, "Oh, it's quite an entertaining story, rat. I'd love to let you in on it. I regained consciousness just before you left the dungeon. Shortly after you left, one of the forest idiots unlocked my cell, and came in and pulled the arrows out of me. I don't know what moronic reason he had, but he bound my wounds. And then the idiot just left the cell and went outside the dungeon. As you'd expect of a forest fool, he left my cell door unlocked. I think the fool was an untrained apprentice, as he couldn't have been much older than you. Of course I immediately escaped. Given how incompetent you are with the bow, none of the arrows hit anything important. And there was never any doubt about my plans. I couldn't think of anything more enjoyable than meeting your family, and, here I am! And now I will deliver you, and your pathetic family six feet under. And then I will return to the forest fellers, and deal with them. Now tell me, rat, what could possibly make a more happy ending?"

"If that's your intent, then what do you want of me?" Asked Tim.

"What do I want? I want you to watch while I kill each of your kin, and then I will watch while life slowly fades out of your eyes, rat!"

Tim glanced out the window, trying to appear casual. "Now don't bother looking for your friend. My men will have already captured or killed him by now." Tim nervously looked out the window, but could see nothing of Alec. Tim grabbed onto the window frame, desperately searching for a sign of either brother. For he knew that without them, he was lost.

Marvinian laughed sadistically, "Can't find him, can you? Such a pity. Too bad. Now there's no one to save you. I've been waiting for this day for months, and now here we are. The whole family reunion, and it's sweeter than I'd expected."

"Why are you doing this?" Pleaded Tim.

Marvinian sneered, "Oh, I'm confident you can guess, rat. It ain't no great mystery to settle a score. And by now you ought to know, rat, that I always settle my scores."

"But what good does that do you?"

"Now look what we have here. The boy who tried to kill me wonders why I kill. Now ain't that comedy," said Marvinian.

"But that's…"

"Don't even try, rat! You and I both know that it is exactly the same."

Tim thought for moment and said quietly, "Yes, you're right, it is the same."

"Now that's the first honest thing you've said to me. I'm glad we're coming to an understanding. And now it's time for the fun part," said Marvinian. He turned Ma's blank face towards him. He eyed her briefly, and said, "you know, rat. You Ma's taking some of the fun out of killing her. She's playing possum on me."

Tim turned for a final desperate look outside. Alec, Calum, come quick! He silently pleaded. But no one came. Tim eyed Marvinian, and then Father, and Shane. Father hung his head, while Shane stared blankly at his brother. Tim searched for any signs of hope, but didn't find any. Tim considered lunging at Marvinian, but saw no possibility of success in that. He wondered if he could set Father free before the soldiers stopped him, but seriously doubted he could pull that off. Not to mention that Father might not be in any condition to help anyways. Tim searched his mind as well as the room for any strategy that might offer any hope. He neither saw nor thought of anything.

"Oh rat, it's precious to me that you're still hoping for rescue. But rat, there be none left to come to your aid. But I love the life in your eyes, which I will soon dim. You don't know how much more pleasure there is in killing those who still hope for life. Those who've given up are no fun to kill."

When Marvinian finished laughing, he slowly pulled his knife out of his belt. He dragged the blade up Mama's leg, across her belly, in between her breasts and up to her neck. He stopped at her neck. Marvinian twisted the blade around in circles, never leaving Mama's neck. Tim had the impulse to spring at Marvinian. There was nothing else to do, so he coiled and leapt at Mama.

At that moment the bedroom window crashed in and the front door burst open. Tim landed on Mama, and appeared to succeed in wrestling her away from Marvinian. Then Mama crashed to the

314

floor with Tim atop her. He pushed up, searching for Marvinian, but couldn't find him. Tim swiveled his head, looking for Father and Shane, and saw them standing where they'd been, yet with no guards. What happened to the guards? Then Calum stood at his side. Alec peered out the front window, searching for someone.

As Tim gained his bearings, he took stock of the room. The two guards that had held Father and Shane lay dead on the ground, each with an arrow in his chest. Tim scanned the room, but couldn't find Marvinian. "Where is he? Where's Marvinian?" Shouted Tim.

"Gone," said Alec from the window. "I must go to Maggie and Amanda! He might be after them," shouted Alec as he darted out the front door.

Calum crouched before Mama, loosening her bonds. "Tim, help me free your family," said Calum.

Tim came to his senses and rushed to Father, quickly untying him, and then Shane. Once he removed their gags, he asked, "Father, Shane, are you okay? Are you hurt bad?"

Father rubbed his sore jaw, working it back and forth, and said slowly, "I don't know. I think I'm basically okay, son." Tim embraced his father, grateful he still lived. Shane collapsed on the ground, once he was free of his bonds.

Tim rushed to Shane's side, "Where are you hurt? What can I do for you?" Shane merely groaned in response. "Father, what's wrong with him?"

Father fell into a chair, appearing exhausted and ten years older. Father said, "He fought back, and was badly beaten. I pleaded with your brother to not fight, but he wouldn't listen. Dear God, I hope he'll be alright. Dear God in heaven," he said with a voice devoid of energy.

Tim took off his coat, and propped Shane's head on top of it. Then he went to Mama, who sat on the ground, with her back against the chair. "Mama, are you alright?" Mama looked at Tim for the first time, and began to silently cry. "Mama, are you hurt?" She continued to cry, yet shook her head from side to side, and then reached out to embrace Tim. He kissed her forehead.

Turning towards Father, Tim said, "She doesn't look herself, but I think Mama might be okay."

Father sat in the chair and stared out the window. Mama released Tim and went to him. Mama put her arms around him. "Oh thank God," said Father. Tim breathed a sigh of relief, and returned to Shane's side. Calum kneeled next to him, mopping his head with a damp cloth. Shane's eyes fluttered, and then closed again.

Tim asked Calum, "What's wrong with him? Why won't he wake up?"

"I can't be sure, but I think he may be battle-worn. I've seen this in many a man after a fight."

"Will he be alright?" Asked Tim.

"I can't be sure, but I think he'll come to before too long. Although I'm not sure how bad his head is hurt," said Calum. "At the moment I'm more concerned about Amanda and Maggie. I hope Alec finds them in time."

"In time for what?"

"Marvinian got away. I hope he didn't find them before Alec got to them. Marvinian wouldn't hesitate to kill them instantly, now that we've freed the rest of your family."

"Oh my God, I must go to them."

"No! Stay here with me. Leave Marvinian to Alec," said Calum.

Tim sprinted to the door, stopping only long enough to pick up his quiver and bow. Tim raced up the hill, not bothering to take cover, or pause to look and listen. He crashed through the brush that gave cover to where they'd left their gear, and more importantly, Amanda and Maggie. The gear lay where they'd left it, but Amanda and Maggie were gone.

He frantically searched the surrounding area, looking for any signs of them. In spite of being tempted, Tim restrained himself from calling out to Amanda and Maggie. That would only bring Marvinian down on them immediately. Tim's only hope was that Marvinian didn't know where they were. But where were they? Alec had told them to stay put. He reiterated his instructions twice, making sure they both understood the importance of keeping their whereabouts unknown to the soldiers. Had Alec already found them, Tim wondered? But if so, then where did he take them? Did Alec take them back to the house. Tim pushed the leaves of a tree aside so that he could see the house. All was quiet. If they're not here, and they're not at the house, where could they be?

Tim remembered his training in tracking. He bent down to examine the ground, but it was too late. In his anxiety to find the women, he'd tracked back and forth so many times that there was no possibility of tracking anyone. Then Tim thought of something. He raced out of the camp site and up the hill to the right. Tim made himself slow down, as he slowly regained hold of his panic, and resumed clearer thinking. Pausing every twenty-five paces, as the Fois taught him, looking and listening before resuming his march up the hill. Tim neither heard nor saw any human signs.

At the top of the hill lay a cluster of large boulders. Tim darted in amongst them. He crawled along the top of the saddle made by two of the larger boulders. Tim peered down from his perch. To the left he saw his family house, but still discerned no activity outside it. Directly below him lie the camp site he'd just left. Through the trees he could just make out one of their packs. To the right the forest extended for many miles, with nothing to see but tree tops.

"Damn, nothing!" Tim said aloud. Where the hell are they, he wondered as he slammed his hand down on the rock. He continued searching for any signs of their whereabouts, but didn't find a thing. Now what do I do? And then Tim realized he hadn't looked behind him. He scrambled to the far side of the hill top, and peered down between two large trees. Below him and to the left was a distinct trail, that wound it's way around the hill and off to the Northeast. Tim searched along the path, and then he saw something. Several miles away Tim could just make out a group of shapes moving away along the trail to the Northeast.

"My God, that must be Marvinian! And he's got Amanda and Maggie. It must be them," Tim shouted. He quickly put his hand over his mouth, realizing how foolish he'd been. He couldn't be sure of their identities from this distance, but Tim knew in his heart it was them. Tim scampered down the hill towards the path. He kept his wits about him and kept to cover as much as possible.

Minutes later Tim merged onto the trail. He'd only taken a dozen steps when Tim felt a hand on his shoulder. Tim swiveled and strung an arrow in one motion. The hand slipped from his shoulder to the arrow, and Alec said, "it's me, little brother, it's me!"

Tim embraced Alec, and almost began crying with relief. "I feared I was alone on this part of the mission. I've found them! I mean Marvinian. And he's got Amanda and Maggie!"

"Yes, I know. I've been tracking them from the camp site. I heard you come down the hill, but couldn't see who it was. With all the racket you were making, I figured it was more soldiers, since me and Calum had taught you to make no sound. So I hid until I saw that it was you," said Alec. "But we must be off. Marvinian has them traveling at a pretty good pace."

With that Alec resumed following the tracks, Tim following close on his heels. Both men held an arrow in their hand, a bow in the other. Alec paused every so often, bent down to examine the tracks, and then resumed his trot.

Alec and Tim spent the rest of the day pursuing Marvinian's tracks. The trail left was clear, with no attempt made to disguise it. Alec figured that Marvinian didn't want to take the time to do so. By dusk Alec came to a halt. He raised his closed fist, which Tim knew meant to stop and be still. There was no sound, other than the wind rustling the tree leaves, and a few birds calling the end of their day.

"We will camp here for the night," said Alec.

"They can't much further ahead. Let's carry on and free them tonight," said Tim.

"You're thinking with your heart, and not your mind. We might find them, and we might stumble right into Marvinian's sword before we know it."

"You won't let that happen, Alec. You're too good a tracker," pleaded Tim.

"I'm too good a tracker to risk tracking at night. Be content with our progress. We have their trail, clear as the midday sun. We will catch them tomorrow."

"But Marvinian might kill them tonight. We can't risk it. If you won't go on, them I'll go on without you," said Tim as he grabbed his bow and quiver and took several steps.

Before he'd taken a dozen steps, Alec tackled him to the ground, and whispered loudly, "Damn it, Tim, you know better than this! I won't let you run off half cocked to your death. You know as well as I that Marvinian is no fool. Whatever else you think of him, he's a fine soldier and knows what he's about. You won't do you, Amanda or Maggie any good by getting yourself killed. Will you hear reason? Or must I tie you up until morning?"

Tim turned his head and looked off in the distance, and then nodded his head, "Yes, alright, I know you're right. I just can't stand the thought of Amanda being back in his power, or Maggie either!"

"Tim, if Marvinian wanted them dead, they'd already be dead. He wouldn't bother dragging them all this way just to kill them. They'll be alright until morning." Alec allowed Tim to push him off his chest.

"I suppose you're right...so how will we catch them tomorrow?"

"I've seen high ground just a few miles ahead. We will climb the hill and see if we can catch sight of them," explained Alec.

"But what if we can't?"

"Have a little faith, little brother. This isn't my first search and rescue mission. We will find them, one way or another."

"Did you bring anything to eat?"

Alec fished out of his pack two clumps of jerky, and threw one to Tim. "That will have to suffice. No fire tonight. Marvinian is likely close enough to see a fire," said Alec.

"Thank God you thought to bring one of the packs, or we'd be awful hungry."

Alec picked up his weapons and said, "I'm off to guard our camp in that tree," said Alec as he pointed to a large tree. Tim nodded and lay down with his head against Alec's pack.

The next morning Tim awoke to the smell of coffee. He sat up and rubbed his eyes. No matter how worried he might be, he still enjoyed the smell of morning coffee. Alec crouched near a small fire, and poured coffee into two metal cups. Then he stood and snuffed out the fire with his foot. Tim gratefully accepted the coffee. "Did you see anything last night?" Asked Tim.

"Quiet as a church. I expect that Marvinian's laying low. Hopefully he doesn't know that we're on his trail," said Alec.

Fifteen minutes later they'd finished their liquid breakfast, and resumed their march. An hour after that they lay in prone positions on top of the hill that Alec had pointed out at dusk yesterday. The hill was topped with tall grass and no trees. The grass gave them enough cover, as long as they stayed on their bellies. They peered ahead through the tall grass, pushing several strands out of the way to get a good view.

The trail zig-zagged away from them for many miles. Tim searched every step of the trail, but could find no signs of Amanda or Maggie. "Damn, they're gone! Where the hell did he take them so fast?" Asked Tim.

"They're about two miles ahead, and moving. Let's go," said Alec and he crawled back down behind the hill.

Tim scrambled after Alec and said, "Wait a minute! How do you know they're two miles ahead? I didn't see anything."

Alec stood and smiled at Tim, saying, "You know the basics of tracking, but these situations require a trained eye. Trust me that I know where they are. And I saw a place that we can intercept them."

"How will we do that?"

Alec shouldered his pack and marched off to the East as he replied in a whisper, "We must move quickly and quietly. We will take the trail to the East and hurry ahead, so that we're waiting for them when the trails merge."

"But where do the trails meet?"

"Lower your voice! Marvinian is only two miles ahead, and he is well-trained. Do not underestimate his abilities," said Alec in a loud whisper.

"Okay, okay, but tell me how we will get ahead of them," said Tim more quietly.

"The eastern trail winds more indirectly and is the longer path, but we can't risk following directly behind Marvinian, if were are to surprise him. He will be on the alert. We will move faster at a trot, but a silent trot at that. I'm relying on Amanda and Maggie not being motivated to run. We will be waiting for them at the juncture ten miles ahead."

"That's brilliant! I don't know how you saw all that from that hill."

"Just trust me, and keep up," said Alec as he increased his pace to a steady trot.

While Tim was in good condition, after all the traveling they'd done, he had to struggle to keep up with Alec, who seemed to be able to run all day long. Alec and Tim paused for quick sips of water, but didn't take the time to stop to eat. They chewed on jerky while on the run.

Before midday Alec slowed down to a walk, and then stopped altogether. He peered through the foliage and searched. Then he waved Tim to followed. Alec half walked and half ran until the other trail came into view before them. Alec put up his closed fist and stopped. After being satisfied that no one was nearby, Alec continued to the trail crossing.

Alec told Tim to wait, while Alec explored the other trail. He bent down and examined the dirt, looking left and right. Then he climbed a tree for further reconnaissance. Several minutes later he returned to Tim. "There's no sign of them coming yet. And the tracks on the trail are too old to be theirs. We've made it ahead of them."

"So we hike back down their trail and surprise them?" Asked Tim.

"No, little brother, that would be too risky, and unnecessary. We climb that tree and wait for them to come to us. They will walk right into our arms."

For a moment Tim thought of challenging Alec, but after a minute's reflection he realized that Alec's plan made the most sense. I keep trying to rush into harm's way. I best stop doing that. Thank God for Alec and Calum, who keep saving me from myself, thought Tim. He followed Alec back up into the tree he had just come down from. Tim climbed up almost as quickly as Alec. Tim had long outgrown his fear of heights, and now felt almost as comfortable in trees as on the ground.

"How long do you think they'll be?" Asked Tim. Alec put his finger to his lips, and shook his head. Then he put a hand on Tim's shoulder and smiled. Tim understood he was being told to be patient.

An hour later they heard a sound. Tim looked eagerly at Alec, who nodded. Finally, thought Tim. While Tim searched the trail to the South, Marvinian and his prisoners couldn't be seen yet. A minute later Amanda and Maggie appeared on the trail, walking side by side. Their hands were bound behind them. Tim could see

Marvinian's head bobbing in between the women. As they got closer, Tim saw that Marvinian held a rope that was attached to both Amanda and Maggie's hands. They had no chance to run.

Maggie walked with her head down, neither looking left nor right. Maggie's hair hung down, covering her face. Amanda stared straight ahead. Her hair was pulled back out of her face. Even from this distance Tim could see that her face was sunburned, or at least her nose. They both appeared exhausted. Tim wondered if they'd been fed or given water. Marvinian looked as he always did; smug and confident. He did look back over his shoulder. So maybe he does suspect that we're after him, thought Tim.

Tim looked anxiously at Alec, asking an unspoken question. Alec signaled for Tim to sit tight and wait. Tim kept glancing back at Alec, who merely waited and watched. Marvinian and his prisoner's progress seemed cruel in it's slowness, as if Marvinian knew they waited for him. However, Tim couldn't imagine how he'd know where he and Alec were, even if he knew they trailed him.

Finally the three approached the tree that held Tim and Alec. Again, Tim looked to Alec for guidance. Alec didn't look at Tim. He wondered what plan Alec cooked up, for he must have something in mind. Remembering his intention to stop making impulsive decisions, Tim made himself wait and trust in Alec.

Alec had pulled an arrow from his quiver once Marvinian came into view. Now he strung his arrow, yet didn't pull back on it. Tim watched Alec minutely, trying to anticipate his every move. What did he have in mind, Tim kept wondering? Amanda and Maggie passed directly in front of Tim and Alec. Once Marvinian stepped directly opposite Alec, he pulled back on his arrow and let it fly.

Marvinian cried out and fell to the ground. At first Tim didn't see where the arrow had struck him, and then when Marvinian pushed up on his knees Tim saw the arrow sticking through both of Marvinian's arms. Marvinian dropped the rope when he fell, but now had regained his wits and reached out to regain hold of the rope. "Run Maggie, run Amanda, get out of his reach," yelled Alec.

Maggie's eyes darted up into the tree and locked eyes with Tim, and then Alec, and she smiled. "Run now, Maggie, get away from Marvinian!" Yelled Alec again. This time Maggie realized their danger and looked at Marvinian. He had just grabbed onto the rope and began to pull them in.

"Come now, Amanda, run away with me!" Called Maggie. The two women took several steps until the rope went taught, and fell onto their faces, being unable to break their fall. Amanda and Maggie had succeeded in pulling the rope out of Marvinian's hand, but he quickly regained control of their rope. Marvinian reached for the knife in his belt, as he pulled on the rope with his other hand.

Tim immediately saw the danger Maggie and Amanda were in. He glanced at Alec, who was climbing down the tree. Tim looked back at Marvinian, and then pulled back on his arrow and loosed it. Tim's arrow struck Marvinian in the leg, dropping him back down to his knees. A moment later Alec kicked the knife out of his hand, and quickly knelt to retrieve it. Alec pulled Maggie and Amanda up out of the dirt, and guided them safely away from Marvinian.

Tim climbed down the tree and stood before Marvinian, arrow on string. Giving Marvinian the respect he deserved, Tim kept ten yards away. Marvinian stood before Tim, holding a second knife in his right hand. Tim saw the second knife sheath around Marvinian's ankle, as his pant leg was twisted above the sheath. Marvinian glanced from Alec to Tim, and then back at the arrow through his leg. By now he'd pulled the arrow out of his arms. Marvinian bled profusely from both arms, while the arrow seemed to keep him from bleeding much from his leg. All three of them knew he was beaten. Marvinian would bleed out soon enough, without medical attention.

Tim pulled back on his arrow and took aim. Marvinian stared at Tim expressionless, and merely waited. Tim planned to kill Marvinian, but something stayed his hand. Several times he thought to loose the arrow, but didn't. Marvinian saw Tim's hesitation, and his face drew into a sneer. "Now that I'm out from behind bars, you don't have the manhood to kill me, now do you, rat?"

Tim replied, "If you allow Alec to bind your hands behind your back, we will tend your wounds."

Marvinian laughed, and said, "You still think me an idiot. Do you really think I'll allow you to bind me? I'd rather die first, rat!"

"If I wanted to kill you, I would shoot you where you stand. You will die if you don't allow us to stop the bleeding. You'll bleed out in minutes," said Tim.

Marvinian looked at each arm, watching the blood seep out, and said, "That I might, rat. But you won't bind me, not until I'm dead."

Tim said, "I merely want to bind you so that you don't attempt to attack us again." Marvinian opened his mouth to retort, but instead slumped to the ground in a faint. Tim went straight to Marvinian, rolled him onto his stomach and bound his hands behind his back. Alec began to tend his wounds.

Once Marvinian lie safely bound, Tim turned to Amanda and Maggie. Amanda rushed into Tim's arms and held him so tight that Tim struggled to get full breaths. Amanda buried her head in Tim's chest, turning her head away from Marvinian. Her previously restrained tears now flowed freely onto Tim's shirt. "Thank God you're safe, Amanda."

Once Amanda released Tim, Maggie kissed his cheek and embraced him. Her eyes filled with tears. "Thank God you found us," Maggie said.

Tim held her and said, "I'm so grateful that you're both safe. When I saw Marvinian leading you away, I feared..."

"Don't say it. It's over now. He no longer has power to hurt any of us. In fact, he might die."

"I hope he doesn't die," said Tim.

"What? You mean you want him to live?" Asked Maggie.

"I know it doesn't make any sense, and it probably sounds crazy, but yes, I want him to live," said Tim.

"But whatever for?"

"I have something to tell him, and I can't unless he lives," said Tim.

"What could you possibly have to say to that monster?"

"That's just it, Maggie, I no longer see him as a monster."

"Have you forgotten what he did to you, and to Amanda, and to Andrew, and to me?"

"No, I have forgotten none of what he's done...but with the help of the Fois, I've come to see that I must do better for my soul," said Tim.

"But whatever does that monster have to do with your soul?" Asked Maggie.

"More than I had previously known. I've allowed myself to hate, and to hate in a way that has overtaken my mind and my soul. I will no longer allow myself to live in the fantasy of revenge. It has darkened by mind, and I will no longer tolerate such darkness."

Maggie paused to consider Tim's words, and then said, "I don't understand what you're saying...in fact it's all foolishness to me...and yet, you remind of something that Sileas told me, about caring for my own soul and mind. At first I thought you were trying to do something for Marvinian, which I couldn't understand nor tolerate...I suppose that I hate Marvinian myself."

Tim nodded and smiled at Maggie, and said, "Yes, I do something for me. And I hope you do whatever is needed for your own mind."

Maggie gazed into Tim's eyes, and then smiled and embraced him. "I'm just so happy that this nightmare is over, and that we're all safe. Wait, is the rest of your family unharmed?"

"Yes, thank God, Marvinian had them captive in our house. Father and Shane are both beat up, but I think they'll be okay. Mama seems okay. At first she was in some kind of stupor, but she came out of it. God knows what horrors they've endured in these last days."

"Marvinian might have done almost anything to them," said Maggie. Tim looked away, not wanting to think about the possibilities. He hoped Shane and Father would be okay, as they seemed far from themselves when Tim last saw them.

Alec had bandaged all of Marvinian's wounds, and had removed the arrow from his leg. Marvinian remained unconscious through Alec's ministrations. Satisfied with his work, Alec now searched Marvinian for additional weapons, and found none. Both of Marvinian's knives were safely in Alec's belt.

Tim and Maggie approached Marvinian. His eyes fluttered and then opened. Marvinian gazed at Alec, then Maggie, and came to rest on Tim. Marvinian said, "Damn you, rat." Then his eyes closed as he lost consciousness again.

Alec inspected his wounds, making sure that he no longer bled. "He's lost much blood. I'm still not sure he'll make it. We must camp here tonight. I don't think he can be moved."

Maggie looked at Tim, who said, "Then we camp here."

Tim offered to stand guard duty that night, as he knew he wouldn't sleep. Alec gratefully accepted, as he hadn't slept the last night. Tim sat against a tree trunk, and quietly talked with Maggie. Alec and Amanda slept, as did Marvinian. Once Maggie succumbed to sleep, Tim stood up. He paced back and forth across the camp site. Thoughts of his future came. He had been so focused on freeing Amanda and bringing her home, that he hadn't given much thought to what he would do afterwards. Would he return home and live with his parents again? Would he return with the Fois and live with them? Or would he seek to make a life with Maggie? He wasn't sure that she would have him, and they hadn't spoken of any kind of future together.

Tim tried to imagine returning to live at home with his family. He couldn't see himself going back to that life, not after what he'd experienced this past year. Did he want to live with the Fois? In some ways that seemed attractive. Tim felt confident that he could learn so much more from them. Yet his thoughts kept coming back to Maggie. He hadn't thought about her much since killing, or at least being under the impression that he'd killed Marvinian. Now that Tim knew Amanda to be safe, he felt ready to think about the next chapter of his life. A life with Maggie felt exciting to Tim. They could possibly create some kind of satisfying life together. Perhaps Maggie would return to her singing. But what would I do, wondered Tim?

Should I try my hand at my own farm? It is all I know of a trade...except for serving as guardian to the Fois. Although he wasn't sure how much call there was for that kind of work. I suppose I'll need some time to take in all that's happened, he thought. I suppose I don't need to know tonight. Maybe I can take some time to figure out what to do with myself. Then Tim felt a hand on his arm. He turned to see Maggie rubbing sleep out of her eyes. "What are you doing walking about?" Asked Maggie.

"I'm thinking about...uh, I'm wondering what to do with myself once I bring Amanda home safe."

"Oh, I see...and what ideas do you have?" Asked Maggie.

"Well, I thought of returning home, but...I don't think I can do that one. I also thought of returning to Fois with Alec and Calum, but I'm not sure if that's what I want...And I also thought of..."

"What?"

"I'm embarrassed to say, but...I'm thinking of a life with you," said Tim.

Maggie took in her breath sharply, smiled and said, "So are you asking me?"

Tim rubbed his face and looked away uncomfortably, and said, "Yes, I'm asking. I'd like to have a life with you, Maggie."

"Of course, I thought you'd never ask!" Tim took her in his arms and kissed her. A brief kiss evolved into a passionate, lingering expression of long pent up feeling for both of them. Finally they pulled back, and gazed into each others' eyes.

"I've had feelings for you ever since we rescued you from that dungeon," confessed Tim.

"Yes, I've known that," said Maggie.

"You did?"

"Why yes, I'm a woman. We sense such things," said Maggie.

Tim's face turned red. He said, "I feel like such a fool, that you've known all along."

"But don't feel that way! There's no shame in having feelings for a quality woman," said Maggie with a smile and a wink.

Tim laughed, and breathed a sigh of relief, and said, "Thank you for not adding to my embarrassment."

"I will add to your embarrassment, if you don't kiss me again right now." Tim readily complied.

After their moment of passion, Tim and Maggie lie in each other's embrace. Tim rubbed Maggie's back as he looked up at the trees and sky. Tim noticed Maggie's face and said, "You appear deep in thought."

"Oh, yes, I'm thinking about the future," said Maggie.

"And what comes to mind?"

"I want to find a way in our life together to return to my singing. Using my voice to move others is my passion," said Maggie

"Then you must find a way to get back to it."

"I was also just thinking about Evangeline," said Maggie.

"Who's Evangeline?"

Maggie explained the tireless energy that Evangeline put into teaching her to sing as a child.

"Perhaps you can become an Evangeline to many other children," suggested Tim.

"That would be wonderful! I would so love that!"

"Then we will find a way for you to do this, and bless many children who need such a teacher."

Maggie kissed Tim's cheek. Tim looked at her and said, "What was that for?"

"You really can be as dull as dung. It's for being willing to help me return to my singing," said Maggie.

Once the coming morning greyed the sky, Tim began a small fire and brewed enough coffee for all. While the coffee brewed, Tim check on Marvinian. He had awakened, probably by the pain of his wounds. Marvinian gazed at Tim blankly with unblinking eyes. Tim checked Marvinian's wounds, to make sure he wasn't bleeding excessively, and he wasn't.

Tim returned to the fire and poured two cups of coffee. He set the cups down next to him, and lifted Marvinian up into a sitting position against a large rock. Tim offered one cup to Marvinian, who shook his head from side to side. Tim shrugged and took a sip of his coffee.

"You know, Marvinian, I have something to tell you," began Tim.

"Save it, rat. There's nothing you have to say that I want to hear."

"You don't have to listen, but I do have something I must say...you have done great harm to my family and friends. You have killed Andrew, raped Maggie, kidnapped every member of my family, bloodied and bruised my brother and my father, and left my mother terrified, not to mention all you have done to me." Marvinian merely eyed Tim. Tim continued, "At first all I wanted was to see your dead eyes staring blankly back at me, preferably at my own hands...and yet, it brought great darkness to me."

"Is this the part where I'm supposed to feel sorry for you? Because life has dealt you a few tough breaks? Because it ain't gonna happen, rat."

"I need nothing from you," said Tim.

"Then why are you singing me all your troubles?"

"Here's what I'm getting to...I've decided to forgive you, Marvinian."

"What? Is that what this is all about?" Said Marvinian as he laughed. "And now I'm supposed to thank you for being my priest and offering me forgiveness? I guess I ought to be eternally grateful that you've saved my immortal soul from unending damnation. Is that it?"

"I want nothing from you."

"Then why bother me with all this gibberish?" Asked Marvinian.

"This isn't about you, Marvinian. This is about me. This is about me taking care of myself. This is about stepping out of the darkness I've brought on my own heart. This is about me choosing light over darkness."

"Well rat, if my hands weren't tied behind me, I'd give you a rousing applause. You know, you really ought to consider the life of a priest. They must need young, naive fools like you who can inspire other fools," said Marvinian.

"You may mock me all you like. My work here is done. Alec and I have decided to bring you back to the farm. At that point Alec, Calum and I will decide what to do with you. I forgive you, but I won't allow you to do us further harm."

"Then you'll have to kill me, rat."

"That may be what it comes to then," said Tim.

"Count on it, young rat. You either kill me, or I spend as much time as it takes to hunt you down, hunt down all you give a damn about, and then comes the good part. I end each one of them, one at a time, real slow-like, while I make you watch," said Marvinian with a gleam in his eye.

He may have imagined it, but Tim would swear he saw a dark cloud come over Marvinian's face. His eyes turned ebony, his smile lacked life, and his face appeared more dead than alive. "It saddens me that you do that to yourself," said Tim.

"To myself, you say? You misunderstand me, rat. All of this I will descend upon you!"

"I understand your intent. But I'm speaking of the enormous cost to your mind. You see, when I killed you, or thought I had, a great darkness came over me. It was such a heavy burden, even more than I could bear. I considered taking my own life...I didn't see that I could have any kind of enjoyment in life after that."

"You know, rat, the more you talk, the more I'm convinced that the church needs an idiot like you. You give sermons as good as any of them. The only problem is, you may not live long enough to become a priest," said Marvinian.

Tim turned his head back to the campfire. The others stirred and began to awaken. Tim considered saying more to Marvinian, as Tim felt full of gratitude for having escaped the hell he'd brought upon himself, but thought better of it. Whatever else Marvinian said, it was clear that all that Tim intended to communicate somehow became irreparably twisted in Marvinian's mind. What appeared to be gold in Tim's mind, was dung in Marvinian's mind. Tim saw that his job was done here. He had done well for his own mind. Marvinian must make his own path.

Alec led the trek back to the family farm. Tim walked behind Marvinian, with a knife in his hand. Tim didn't figure Marvinian much of a threat with his hands tied, both arms wounded, and one leg so painful that he walked with a limp. However, Tim had underestimated Marvinian in the past, and wouldn't make that mistake again. The trek progressed steadily, but slowly. Marvinian couldn't walk fast, nor was he motivated to.

Tim walked lighter in his step. With each step closer to home, he felt more and more energy. Finally, the mission had been accomplished! Amanda and Maggie were safe, his family was safe, and Marvinian was disabled. Tim's reveled in this realization. A smile slowly appeared on his face, and remained there much of the day. As the day wore on, Tim's thoughts turned to the future. What now? He and Maggie had spoken of making some kind of life together, but what life? And to begin when? And where?

Tim glanced at Maggie, who smiled back. He wondered about her thoughts. Did she also puzzle over her future?

The following day they arrived back at the farm house. Calum stood guard over the house, watching the roads from behind the house windows. He came outside and greeted his brother warmly, and then the rest of the travelers. Tim embraced Calum, and thanked him for keeping his family safe.

Tim took Amanda by the hand and said, "Let's go home, Amanda." She looked at her brother in wonder, apprehension and excitement. Amanda nodded, and Tim led her into the house. The first to see her was Shane, who rushed to embrace her. "Amanda, you're alive!" Said Shane. He held her at arms distance, sizing her up for damage.

Mama prepared a meal in the kitchen, but came running at Shane's shout. She stopped short and put her hands over her mouth. At first Mama appeared as though she'd seen a ghost, and then she broke into sobs and slumped to the ground. Only broken groans of fear and relief escaped her. Mama reached out for Amanda, who ran into Mama's arms and joined her in sobbing. Shane and Tim stood side by side, watching the two ladies rediscover one another. Tim brushed tears from his eyes. He'd waited far too long to bring Amanda back to his family, and to none more so than Mama. Seeing his brother's tears, Shane put his arm around Tim's shoulders, and said, "You done alright, Tim." Tim smiled at his brother through tearful eyes.

After watching Amanda and Mama for awhile, Tim turned to Shane and asked, "So where's Father?"

Shane's face darkened, he nodded towards the bedroom and said, "He hasn't left his bed since you ran off after that evil soldier. He fears he'll never see his little girl again."

"Oh, poor Father, we must show him Amanda," said Tim. He went to his sister, who still lay in Mama's arms and said, "Amanda, Father waits for you. Come with me to him. He doesn't know that you live." Amanda held on tighter to Mama. Mama pushed up to her knees and pushed Amanda to arms distance, and said, "Yes honey, go to him."

Amanda nodded at Mama, and then accepted Tim's hand. She followed Tim to the bedroom door. Tim gently opened the door. The blinds were closed and the room lay in almost complete darkness. Father's unmoving figure lie on the bed. He didn't stir when they opened the door. Tim led Amanda to the bedside. Father lay on his side, facing the wall.

Tim put his hand on Father and gently shook him, "Father, we're home. Amanda is home."

Father slowly turned, as if moving in mud. He stared at Amanda, opening his eyes wider, then narrower. His face appeared heavy, as if weighed down by a double doze of gravity. Over several seconds recognition dawned on his face, "My God, my prayers are answered. You really are home?"

"Yes Father, it's really me. I'm here," said Amanda. Father pulled Amanda into an embrace. While his eyes remained dry, his face crunched up into overwhelming emotion. He rocked himself and Amanda back and forth. Tim left the room, leaving them to their moment.

When Tim went back to the outer room, Mama took his place in the bedroom. Alec and Calum talked quietly in one corner of the room. Shane had taken over preparations for the meal in the kitchen. But where was Maggie? Did she leave? Oh God, don't leave, Tim thought. After looking around for some minutes, Tim found her pacing outside with her head down.

Maggie startled when Tim touched her arm. "Oh my, I didn't know that you were there. How is it going inside?"

"Mama and Father struggle to allow themselves to believe she's actually home, safe and sound...it's really quite beautiful to watch."

"I can imagine," said Maggie.

"So what's on your mind?" Asked Tim.

Maggie gave Tim a strange look, and said, "What do you mean?"

"Come on Maggie, you're out here pacing with your head down. You must be working on something."

Maggie uttered a short laugh, "Oh that, yes, it's that plain?" Tim nodded. "Oh well, I'm just wondering what to do with myself now."

"I'm not sure I follow."

"Well, the mission is over. We've freed Amanda again...and I'm aware that we talked about a life together..."

Tim looked off in the distance while he gathered his thoughts. He breathed a sigh and said, "Yes, we did mention that."

"But I'm not holding you to anything. If you've decided against it I would, I mean I know that, I know you have a family and, of course you'll want to..."

Tim interrupted her by putting his hand on her mouth. When Maggie stopped talking, he took her head in his hands and kissed her passionately. After several minutes Tim pulled back and said, "Does that clarify things for you?"

Maggie hit him on the arm and said, "Yes, and you know, you could have saved me from making a fool of myself a bit sooner."

"I could have, but it wouldn't have been quite as much fun to watch you," said TIm.

"You're an ass," said Maggie with a sly grin.

"Did you really fear that I'd change my mind?"

"Yes, I was afraid. I feared that you said what you said in a passionate moment, just after rescuing me and Amanda, so I didn't know if you really meant that," said Maggie.

"No, that wasn't just the heat of the moment. I want a life with you…in fact, when I didn't see you in the house, I had a nervous moment…I thought you might have left."

Maggie smiled nervously and said, "Thank God…then what's next?"

"I'm not sure… I want to help my family settle back in. I'm worried about Father. He doesn't seem himself. I'm hoping that Amanda's return will bring him back."

"What's wrong with him? " Asked Maggie.

Tim rubbed his hands across his face and then said, "I'm not exactly sure… he was in bed while we were away, and Shane said he hadn't been up since Marvinian took Amanda again. And he looked…he looked just awful."

"It must have shaken him pretty good, her being gone so long. He couldn't have known if he'd ever see her again," said Maggie. "Let's go check on him."

Tim nodded and followed Maggie into the house. Just before they got to the front door Maggie stopped and turned around. "Tim, there's something else. Wherever we go, I really want to return to my singing. It is the only work that I truly love."

"Yes, I remember this. We shall find a way to do it," said Tim.

"I don't know how though."

"I will help you find a way," said Tim. Maggie hugged him and kissed his cheek. Then they both walked into the house.

Shane put food on the table for all. Tim asked his brother, "Is Father still…" Shane nodded. Tim turned right into the bedroom, with Maggie behind him. Mama and Amanda leaned against Father on the bed. Father sat up with his back against the wall. His face looked less burdened by gravity, yet still pale. He had an arm around each of them. Tim glanced from face to face. Mama and

Amanda looked like themselves, while Father appeared better, but not quite himself. Father looked Tim in the eye and said, "thank you for bringing her back."

"And for bringing her back unhurt," Mama added.

Father continued, "But I must say, I'm disappointed that you took your sweet time in getting the job done. I had expected that…"

Mama interrupted her husband, "Father, that is hardly fair of you. We have no idea what Tim's been through to bring both of them home safely."

"But he must have some idea what he's put us through in making us wait so long," countered Father.

"Perhaps we owe Tim the curtesy of hearing his story, before we pass judgment. I for one, would like to hear your story," said Mama.

"Yes, I'd like to tell my story, but first let's eat. And I don't see how I can tell my story without an ale or two," said Tim.

Sixteen

The next morning Tim awoke early. Lying next to him, Maggie still snored. Tim stared out the window, wondering what the day would bring. He watched the sun slowly brighten the bedroom window. Tim knew he had to face Marvinian today. He couldn't just keep him tied up forever, as much as he might like to. He didn't want to get out of bed, for then there would be no avoiding the issue. After some minutes, Tim groaned and rolled out of bed. Maggie stirred, but remained asleep.

Out in the main room, Calum watched over the prisoner, while Alec slept on the couch. Calum nodded and smiled, while Marvinian stared right through Tim. My God, what do I do with him, thought Tim? Can't he just disappear? Tim rubbed the sleep out of his eyes and went into the kitchen to make coffee. He came back with a cup for both him and Calum.

With coffee cups in hand, Tim waved Calum outside. They stood side by side watching the sun come up over the horizon. Calum stood so that he could watch Marvinian through the window. Without turning his head, Tim said, "So what do we do with Marvinian?"

"I don't know what you'll do with him, little brother," said Calum.

"What do you mean, me? I thought you and Alec would help me do something with him."

"Come now, you must make your peace with Marvinian. Neither Alec nor I can do this for you. We will help you, but at the end of the day you must decide for yourself."

After thinking for a moment, Tim said, "I suppose deep down inside I knew that. It isn't fair for me to put that on you and Alec, although I wish I could."

"It isn't about fairness, little brother, it's about you making your own peace. You must decide if you will take your revenge or forgive him," said Calum.

"Can't I just let him go?"

"You know as well as I that won't work," said Calum.

Tim sighed deeply, "Yes, I know that he will never stop hunting me down...so I have to kill him?"

"Are those the only two options?" Asked Calum.

"What else is there? If I don't kill him, he will forever hunt me and my family down. I can't live my life looking over my shoulder."

"Alec and I can see that Marvinian never hunts you again. But, the greater concern is whether you will forever hunt Marvinian," explained Calum.

"What are you talking about? I won't go looking for him."

"You know little brother, there's hunting, and then there's hunting. They have little to do with one another in outward appearance. Are you with me?"

"I'm not sure that I am," said Tim. "What other hunting is there besides tracking a man until he's dead?"

"Have you learned nothing from my people? There's hunting with your body, and then there's hunting with your mind."

Tim looked away as he rubbed the side of his face. "Ah yes, how can I have been so dull. You Fois have taught me of releasing...I must let him go in my mind, or I suppose I might be his prisoner for life."

"Yes! Now you have it, little brother."

"Something in me doesn't want to fully forgive him. Something in me still wants the satisfaction of seeing the life fade from his eyes."

"Yes, I know this part of my own mind, only too well," said Calum.

"You do?"

"Of course! Did you think that you are the only person to wrestle with the desire to kill?" Asked Calum.

"You just seem so mature, and at peace, that I didn't imagine that…"

"I haven't always been this way. There was a time when I struggled as you, maybe worse," said Calum.

"Then how did you get past it?"

"I'm not sure that I am past it. I have to continually choose to forgive. At times it is still not easy for me," said Calum.

"I don't know if I can do that for the rest of my life…I don't even know that I can do it for now," said Tim.

"You can and you must."

Tim thought for a moment before saying, "So how can you and Alec keep Marvinian from hunting down me and my family?"

"We will take him back to Fois for rehabilitation," explained Calum.

"What does rehabilitation involve?"

"There's a short answer and a long answer. I think I'll give you the short one. It means we won't let him leave us until he no longer wants to hunt you, or anyone else," said Calum.

"But Marvinian will never stop wanting to hunt us down!"

"Then so be it! He will never leave," said Calum.

"But how will you know if he truly, I mean, what if he tricks you?"

"We are not easily tricked, especially Sileas. A rehabilitation guest is not released until the whole council agrees unanimously. There are many he will have to trick," said Calum.

Alec brought Marvinian outside, and tied him to a sturdy tree, and then joined Calum and Tim.

"I am ready," said Tim. "I've decided I mustn't kill Marvinian. I can't do that to myself, again."

"I'm glad for you, Tim," said Alec.

"You and Calum have helped me to realize some of the cost to myself, and that it is a cost that is not necessary. I simply won't live this way."

"You have grown so much in the time we have known you," said Calum.

"I had my doubts about you. My brother has prodded me to keep faith in you these many months," said Alec as he pat Calum's back.

"I'm grateful to both of you. You have been like fathers to me. I don't know how to properly thank you."

"You have just done so," said Alec.

"There is no greater thanks than to see you find peace," said Calum.

"Now wait a minute, I have another question. How do you know you can keep Marvinian safe in Fois? I mean, he did escape once," said Tim.

Calum looked to Alec, who said, "He could only have escaped if the Fois thought him dead. The only way he could be here before you is if someone didn't carefully check to see that he'd truly died. In fact, this is what happened. An apprentice safety cell worker was on duty the day you thought you killed Marvinian. The apprentice failed to go through the proper procedure to pronounce him dead."

"Okay, but how often does that happen? What if he does it again?" Asked Tim.

"This is the only time in my lifetime that someone has escaped the safety cells," said Alec. Calum nodded his agreement.

"But you can't guarantee it then," said Tim.

"Guarantee it, no. But do you imagine that anyone will be easily fooled by Marvinian now?" Said Calum.

Maggie came out of the house, holding a plate of food. She walked up to Tim with a sly smile, kissed his lips and moved on to the prisoner at the tree. Marvinian's hands were bound in front of him, and he was made fast to the tree. Maggie set the plate down in the dirt and began to walk away. "And how do you suppose that I'll be able to eat off of that," said Marvinian.

"I don't give a damn if you eat it or not. And I'm not about to hand feed you," said Maggie. And she turned and started to walk away.

"If you'd slide it a bit closer then I could feed myself. I don't need to be fed like no baby."

Maggie stopped in her tracks and sighed loudly, turned around and bent down to the plate. As she pushed the plate across the dirt, Marvinian suddenly reached out and grabbed her wrist. He yanked her into his lap, and threw his bound wrists over her head and began choking her neck. Maggie cried out for a moment before the rope closed on her neck.

Alec broke into a sprint the moment he heard Maggie's cry. Tim cried out, "Noooo!" Alec pulled his knife as he ran and drove it into Marvinain's left arm as he landed on him. Alec yanked up on the rope and pulled Maggie out of Marvinian's arms. Alec hit Marvinian in the face with the knife handle, and then carried Maggie a safe distance away.

Tim hit Marvinian in the face a half dozen times before Calum pulled him off. Tim suddenly remembered Maggie, and sprang to her side. Alec was bent over her. "Is she okay? Is she still alive?" Yelled Tim.

"Yes, she's breathing, but her breath is shallow," said Alec.

"Oh my God, look at the marks on her neck!" Shouted Tim.

"Yes, they are bad. However, there's a chance that she might yet live," said Alec.

"Let's get her to bed," said Tim.

"No little brother, she can't be moved. Maggie's situation is critical. There's a risk of closing off her breathing while we carry her. We must allow her to return to normal breathing, and regain consciousness before we move her," said Calum.

Tim leaned down to Maggie and put his ear to her mouth. He could hear her breath, but barely. "Are you sure she will live?"

"No, I can't be sure, but I think her chances be fair," said Alec.

"Wait, you mean she might die?"

"Now Tim, don't get ahead of yourself. Let's just wait and see and hope for the best," soothed Calum. Tim knelt down next to Maggie and began to pray silently. Dear God, I shouldn't have allowed her to approach Marvinian. By now I ought to know what he's capable of. But don't let Maggie die; not now after all we've been through. Please let her live!

Tim opened his eyes and stared at Maggie's face, but she seemed the same. Tim looked at Alec and said, "Does she need her head supported better?"

Alec regarded Maggie and said, "No, I don't believe so. My coat under her head keeps her airway open. That's the critical thing, keeping her airway unobstructed."

Marvinian snorted as he regained consciousness. He spat blood out of his mouth. Once he'd seen Maggie on the dirt he said, "Oh dear, is the young lass dying? I pray for her swift recovery." Tim stared penetrating eyes at Marvinian, and had the impulse to lunge at him and finish him off. Tim forced himself to look back at Maggie, and told himself to stay with Maggie, that Marvinian no longer mattered.

However, Marvinian had noticed Tim's glaring stare, and said, "Now rat, the invitation still stands. I'd give my right testicle to have you come at me and give me your best shot. Now that I'm conscious, I don't think you'd have a chance, even with my hands bound. Tim glanced at Marvinian briefly, but redirected his attention to Maggie. He knew no good would come of allowing himself to be goaded into a fight with Marvinian. Tim determined to stick to his decision to let the man go. Yet Marvinian's invitation was tempting.

Marvinian continued, "I know you can hear me, rat. And I know you're dying to give me another go. And you must know that you have a sliver of a chance with me wounded and bound. But I still like my chances. Maybe you're waiting until the lass dies before you come at me. I hope she dies, if that's what it takes to get you to take a pass at me."

Tim wanted to shout, "Shut the hell up!" It took all the determination that Tim could muster to keep himself from responding to Marvinian's invitation. Tim knew it would hurt him more than Marvinian if he allowed himself to be pulled into another fight, even if he succeeded in killing him.

Tim's thoughts were interrupted by a gasping sound. Tim's eyes darted at Maggie's face. She sputtered and gasped as she sucked in air. Maggie reached for her throat and rubbed at it. "Oh thank God you're alive!" Shouted Tim. He pulled her into his arms and held her tight while she wept. "I was so afraid that he'd finally succeeded in killing one of us," said Tim as he rocked her back and forth. Maggie attempted to speak, but no sound came out of her mouth except a loud breathing noise.

"Maggie, can you talk?" Asked Tim with alarm. Maggie attempted to talk again, and barely a sound came out, but it was unintelligible. Then Maggie shook her head from side to side. Tim looked at Calum and said, "She can't talk! Will her speech return?"

Calum said, "I don't know, little brother. I sure hope so, but I've seen cases like this where victims never regain their ability to talk."

"Really? No, but she must regain her speech. I mean we've just begun to, I mean, we're starting to talk about, but if she can't..."

Calum interrupted Tim with a hand on his shoulder and said, "Be at peace. All we can do is wait and hope for the best. Help me to get her to bed. And she should drink a little water to soothe her throat. Actually, tea would be better for her throat."

"Oh dear, the poor little lass can't talk. Now isn't that a shame. I suppose the great spirit in the sky doesn't listen to the prayers of the likes of me," said Marvinian with a chuckle.

Tim forced himself to not look at Marvinian. Tim didn't know what he'd do if he even glanced at him. He and Calum gently lifted Maggie and slowly carried her into the bed in the front bedroom. Tim ran to the kitchen and came back with a cup of water. Calum lifted her head gently while Tim held the cup to her lips. She drank some, dribbled some down herself, and sputtered the rest out. Maggie made a face. Tim said, "I know it must hurt to swallow right now. Don't drink anymore until you want it." She smiled weakly and closed her eyes.

Calum said, "I think one of us ought to watch over her, in case she has trouble breathing."

"I'll stay with her," said Tim as he took a seat on the only wooden chair in the room.

Maggie appeared to go to sleep right away. Tim got up and checked on her breathing, by putting his hand in front of her mouth. Yep, she was still breathing all right. Tim relaxed some and returned to his watch on the chair.

A strange sound woke Tim with a start. At first he was disoriented. The window was dark, and no wind rustled the curtains. What am I doing sleeping on this chair? As he swept his eyes across the room he saw Maggie. The memory came flooding back to him as he realized Maggie tried to signal him. Tim leapt to her side. "What is it, Maggie?"

She tried to speak, but only a rasping sound emerged. Tim cringed at the pain on her face. He followed her hand and realized what she pointed at. "Oh, you want more water," said Tim as he lifted her head and put the cup to her lips. This time Maggie drank more successfully, as most of the water made it into her mouth.

Maggie put her hand to her throat as her face scrunched up. She tried to say something, but still couldn't talk.

"Don't try to talk yet. You need more rest. You'll be fine after you're rested," said Tim, although he didn't believe the words himself. He had no idea if she'd ever talk again. And what if she didn't? Well, he didn't want to go there yet. That thought only brought fear and anxiety.

Maggie touched Tim's arm, trying to get his attention. When he looked at her she pulled him towards her. At first he wasn't sure what she wanted, "Do you want more to drink?" She shook her head from side to side, and then scooted over and pointed next to her. "Oh, I get it now, you want me to lie down with you." Maggie smiled and nodded her head.

Tim took off his boots and gently lie next to her, being careful not to bump her. Once next to her, she pulled his arm up and around her. When she looked at him, he smiled and said, "Sure Maggie, anything you want." Satisfied, she placed her head on his chest and entered peaceful sleep.

The next morning Tim woke to the sensation of being wet. Tim looked down and saw that Maggie cried on his chest. He soothed her hair and said, "Hey Maggie, what is it? Do you need something?"

Maggie could whisper, yet in such a low voice that Tim could only understand her if his ear was right in front of her mouth. She rasped, "Dear God, I still can't talk!"

"Oh Maggie, I'm so sorry. You'll get your voice back. We have to just be patient."

Maggie became quickly frustrated trying to talk, yet with Tim's patience she settled in to pulling his ear close when she had something to say. She told herself she could tolerate this arrangement, as long as it only lasted a short time.

After Maggie's experience with Marvinian, it was decided that only Calum and Alec would have any dealings with him for now.

Marvinian remained tied to the tree in front of the house, and was only fed by the Fois brothers. Marvinian mostly kept quiet, as he soon learned that neither Alec nor Calum would respond to his taunting. It's not much fun to taunt and provoke if no one responds.

Maggie spent her days sitting in the front room, mostly reading the few books that the family had to offer her. She rarely spoke, and only into Tim's ear, and only then when she needed something. Her spirit grew heavy, as her speech wasn't improving much. Her whisper became a bit louder, but still required a close ear to be heard. Tim often sat with her, but she seemed to take small comfort in his presence.

Maggie kept telling herself that her speech would return the next day, and then the next day. However, each new day her speech was not much improved. With each day that her condition didn't improve, her spirit became less hopeful. She wondered what kind of future she'd have if she couldn't speak more than a whisper. She thought of singing, her great love. Would she ever sing again? Maggie couldn't imagine singing anytime soon, if ever. And would Tim still want her? She doubted he'd want a mute wife. When he drew near, she gazed at him with sad eyes.

By the end of a week, Maggie could still only whisper, yet she could make herself understood if she were within a couple of feet of the listener. No longer did she need Tim's ear directly in front of her mouth, unless there was background noise. While it was somewhat satisfying for Maggie to be able to speak better, it hurt her throat each time she talked. Maggie kept her words to a minimal few, and sipped lemon water and tea throughout the day, which provided her throat with some comfort.

Tim sat down with his family and told them his story, as did Amanda. When Tim and Amanda finished, Father immediately stood and went to the kitchen. He picked out the largest knife and started for the tree outside the front door. Once Tim realized what Father had in mind, Tim went after him. "Father, don't do this! Don't lower yourself to this."

"Lower myself? I will lower that animal to beneath the ground! After what he's done to you, well to all of us, I won't have him live another day!"

"I understand your anger, really I do. And I've wanted to kill him myself, and even attempted to do so. But my friends helped me to see that it wouldn't help. Even more than that, that killing him would do me harm," explained Tim.

"You're talking nonsense, son. It may not do me good, but I'll sure feel a whole lot better once he's dead. And you won't talk me out of it." Just then the Fois brothers arrived at Marvinian. They stood before him, blocking Father's path to Marvinian.

"What's this? You're now protecting that animal? After all that he's done to my family, you believe he deserves to live?" Asked Father.

Alec glanced at Calum, who said, "We do not judge who has the right to live, that is for the Creator to decide. But we won't let you do this to either of you. It is the same as with Tim, when we prevented him from killing Marvinian."

"I have every right to kill any man who comes onto my own property with ill intent, not to mention a man who takes us captive, and mistreats myself, my wife and my son. And that's nothing to say of what he's done to Tim and Amanda!"

"Now you just untie me and let that pathetic excuse for a man..." began Marvinian. But Alec gagged him before he could say more and make the situation worse than it already had become.

"I know Marvinian's crimes are great," began Calum, "very great, and yet the crime you intend to do to him, you will do to yourself. This will cause you more harm than you know."

"I know what I'm about..." began Father.

Calum cut him off by saying, "Now hear me out! You expect great satisfaction and relief from killing Marvinian. But this will not be so. For whatever you do to him you do to yourself. I know

348

this sounds crazy, but you must trust me on this. For sadly, I know from personal experience."

Alec said, "Calum, we must take him from here, for the temptation is too great for them. And Marvinian keeps inviting them to kill him. It's no small wonder that he yet lives. We must take him back to Fois, where he can receive what he needs."

Calum looked away sadly, and said, "Yes, I fear that you're right. I had hoped that they would let Marvinian go. And I think that Tim is well on his way, but perhaps not quite there. We will leave first thing in the morning."

Alec nodded in satisfaction and said, "I will make preparations for food and water."

Maggie stood by the window in the front bedroom and watched Tim and Father walk back into the house. She slipped out the front door and approached Calum. She whispered, "Can I have a word?" Calum nodded and took Maggie by the arm and walked her away from Marvinian's earshot.

Maggie kept her eyes on her feet as she gathered her thoughts. "I want to come with you, you and Alec. I want you to take me back to Fois with you."

Calum opened his eyes wide with surprise, and he said, "But what about Tim? You want to go with us without Tim? I thought you and Tim..."

Maggie cried and averted her eyes. She said, "He doesn't want me now that I can't talk."

"He said that? Tim told you he doesn't want you anymore?"

"He didn't exactly say that in words, but..." began Maggie.

At that moment Tim put a hand on Maggie's shoulder. Calum smiled and turned and walked away. Tim said, "I heard what you said. So you've decided for me. You were making plans to leave without me?"

Maggie wiped her face and said through shining eyes, "Oh Tim, I won't try to hold you to our plans. I know you won't want me now that..."

"Now that you can only whisper? You thought I'd give up on you because of your voice?"

"Well, yes, I mean, I can no longer have a conversation. I can't ask you to sign up for that kind of a life," said Maggie.

"You must not think much of me as a person. You must not think much of me as a man."

"How can you still want to?"

"Yes! I absolutely still want a life with you! You're voice doesn't change that," said Tim.

Maggie ran into his arms as she broke into sobs. Tim held her tight, rocking her from left to right. He whispered into her ear, "Don't think just because you now have a sexy bedroom voice, that gets you out of being with me." Maggie pulled away and hit Tim in the shoulder. And then she stepped back into embracing him with all her might.

Alec and Calum took turns guarding Marvinian from Father all night. How strange to go from protecting the family from Marvinian, to protecting Marvinian from the family. Before first light broke the morning Alec went into the kitchen to make coffee. Tim already had coffee made and handed a cup to Alec. He went outside and gave the second cup to Calum. Tim said, "Maggie and I are coming with you, if you'll have us."

"Of course we'll have you. I'd hoped you'd come home with us. What made you decide?"

"I no longer have a life here with my family. I cannot go back to farming as a child on my parent's farm...not after what I've been through...though I must admit that I feel bad leaving them. I wonder how much harder it will be to keep the farm running without my pair of hands."

Calum responded, "I understand you thinking of them. But Tim, you must free yourself to make you own way."

"But I might also be hurting them by leaving."

"It would be no gift to stay with them, and then resent them for it," furthered Calum.

"I'm afraid that Father won't understand my leaving."

"What if he doesn't? I don't see what that has to do with you," said Calum.

"Yes, I know you're right. I must make my own way now. Staying here would feel like going backwards. And I want a life with Maggie, and we've agreed that the best life we can imagine is with you and the rest of the Fois."

"I'm so pleased to hear this."

"I still have much to learn, and you Fois seem well equipped to teach me."

"Perhaps we can learn from each other," said Calum. "Now, get packed, we're leaving at first light."

Tim went into the first bedroom and found Maggie putting the last items into her pack. Tim's pack already leaned against the door, ready to go. "All set?" Tim asked.

Maggie nodded and hoisted her pack to her shoulders. She whispered, "Let's go!" Tim shouldered his pack and opened the other bedroom door. The room was empty. Surprised, he turned and walked out into the main room. There stood his family. Father shook his hand and said, "I hate to see you leave us again, and I'm not sure I understand...in fact, I don't understand."

"It's time I make my own life, father."

"But you have a life, a good life here with us."

"Yes, you have made a nice life for all of us. I make no complaint, it's just...it's just that it's time I make my own way," said Tim.

Father looked at mother, who cried and remained silent. Father shook his head and shrugged his shoulders, but didn't say any more. He turned and went back into the bedroom, and shut the door.

Mother said, "Tim, you must understand how hard this is for Father. He thinks you're..."

Tim cut her off, "Mother don't. You don't need to make excuses for him. Just wish me well." Mother nodded with tears in her eyes.

Tim smiled and turned to Shane, who said, "You take care of that lovely lady of yours. And write to us when you get where you're going."

Tim said, "Sure, Shane." And turning to Amanda he said, "I'm sad to leave you, after we've only recently been reunited. Now you stay safe." Amanda leapt into Tim's arms and wept wordlessly.

Tim released her and turned to Mama. Her eyes shone, yet she appeared surprisingly poised. She hugged Tim and handed him baked goods all wrapped up. "You promise me that you'll visit sometime."

"Sure Mama, we'll come back when we can," said Tim. "Well, I'm off." With that Tim picked up his pack and headed out the door. Maggie and the Fois brothers awaited him there. Marvinian was bound with hands behind his back and a rope around his neck. This was to discourage him from attempting to flee.

As they reached the edge of the property, Tim turned around and gazed at the house. Mama stood on the porch and waved. Tim waved back, and then followed after Maggie. Tim so appreciated Mama's sturdiness in being willing to release Tim to leave, even though everything in her heart wanted him to stay.

They reached Fois within a week, and were relieved to have no incidents on the way back. Marvinian was uniquely quiet, and had given up attempting to taunt Tim into a conflict. Perhaps Tim had convinced him that he no longer desired a fight. The few occasions that Marvinian did go after Tim verbally, Tim merely shook his head and looked away without saying a word.

Calum and Alec took Marvinian to the underground safety cells first thing upon reaching Fois. Tim had never seen these cells before, and asked the brothers about them.

Alec explained, "These are for our longterm guests. The ones that we have little hope for. Down here they are more safe, as the cells are stronger and doubly locked. The upstairs cells are for those we are actively working with."

Once he was safely secured, the four travelers paid a visit to Sileas. Alec and Calum updated her on the events since leaving Fois. She said, "Marvinian will remain in the safety cells alone for a week, only being visited to feed and water him. After that he will be offered the opportunity to restore himself. He will remain in protective custody until he restores himself fully."

"May I ask a question?" Said Tim. Sileas nodded her assent. "But what if he never restores himself? Did you consider that he might not?"

"I fully expect that he will not. And if so, then he will remain in our protective custody for the rest of his days. However, it is my intent to offer every embattled soul the opportunity to release themselves from suffering. Whether Marvinian does or does not will be entirely up to him." Turning to Alec and Calum she said, "I thank you for your good service to these two beautiful souls."

Alec and Calum nodded their understanding, bowed and left. Then Sileas turned her attention to Tim and Maggie. "What brings you back to our lands?"

Tim glanced at Maggie and then answered, "We would live amongst you, if you will allow it. We have known great love and wisdom from you Fois, so much so that we desire to live alongside you, at least for a good while." Maggie leaned over and whispered something to Tim. Tim continued, "Maggie reminds me that we still feel that we have more maturing awaiting us. We believe that you and your people can help us with this."

Sileas smiled and said, "You are most welcome to remain amongst us as long as you like. It gladdens my heart to hear you desire this. You have returned to your true home."

"Our true home? We have never lived here before this year. Although I must say that I find a strange familiarity in Fois," said Tim.

Sileas smiled and said, "You return to a home that you have no memory of, yet do recognize."

"But how can this be? How could I have no memory of having lived here. I surely would have remembered this place. And I was born in Scerlandia."

"If you search you mind perhaps you will find a recollection, like a long lost friend you haven't seen in ages," said Sileas.

Tim looked at Maggie, who shrugged her shoulders. Tim looked back at Sileas and said, "I don't know what to say. I want this to be true, but I don't see how it's possible."

"Your home has been maintained for you in your absence, not only these past weeks, but for a lifetime. Go to it and live there as long as you desire. Go in peace."

Seventeen

"And that is the end of my tale," said the old woman.

The boy paused, hoping there would be more, as he shifted his weight on the log. He didn't want the story to end so soon. And then something occurred to him. "Wait a minute, you have a whispering voice. That means, could that mean, does that mean that you are Maggie!"

"Well done, young lad! I hoped you would be bright," said Maggie as she turned her full face towards the boy for the first time.

"You're the woman in the painting over the fire place! The painting next to grandfather! Although you look younger in the painting."

"That's right, my boy. You've guessed well again," said Maggie.

The boy looked away and thought for a moment, and then said, "So why is your painting next to grandfather's painting?"

"Have you not yet guessed it? Do you not know who your grandfather is?" Asked Maggie.

"Why yes, I know my grandfather. I played in the wood with him when I was wee high to his knee."

"I'm sure you did. Yet do you not know his name?" Asked Maggie.

"His name is grandfather. Who else would he be?"

"He was once known by another name. I knew him simply as Tim," said Maggie.

The boy's eyes grew wide as he said, "You mean my grandfather was the Tim in your story?"

"And there you have it, my boy. I knew you would put the pieces together once they were all on the table," said Maggie.

"So if grandfather is Tim, and you are Maggie...then you were grandfather Tim's wife?"

"Why yes," said Maggie.

"Then that means...that means that you are my grandmother!"

"Indeed I am," said Maggie.

The boy averted his eyes as he stared off at the forest. Then he looked back at his house. He slowly turned his gaze back to Maggie, and felt an impulse to embrace her, but thought better of it. The boy asked, "Then if you are my grandmother, how is it that I have never met you before?"

"Oh my boy, now that is another story, perhaps for another time," said Maggie with a sigh.

"No, I want to know now. My parents told me that you were dead, but here you are alive right before my own eyes." The boy rubbed his eyes and looked again, just to make sure.

Maggie sighed more deeply, and then made a decision. "I suppose you have a right to know more. In a sense your parents are right. I am dead to them."

The boy stared and Maggie and said, "How can you be dead to them, but alive right here to me."

"I am alive to you, and I am alive to me, but I am dead in your parents' minds. Of course my body still lives, as does my spirit. Yet to your parents, sadly, I no longer exist. I am merely an embarrassing member of the family tree to them," explained Maggie.

"But why did they make you dead?"

"Oh my boy, this will be difficult to explain. And I don't know that it's my place to do so."

"You're right! It's not your place to explain anything to our son! You have no rights to him. You have been banished, so be gone with you!" The boy turned to see his parents standing behind them. The loud voice was Mother's. The boy looked at Father, who appeared to have seen a ghost, and stood speechless.

The boy turned quickly to Maggie and said, "No Grandmother Maggie, I don't want you to leave." Then turning to his parents he said, "She's not leaving until you tell me why she's dead!"

"Do not call her Grandmother Maggie, for she is no relation to you! And I thought you were up to no good out here, Marvin. When I couldn't find you I expected something evil to be about. Your father and I should have seen you from the window," said Mother as she eyed her husband.

"How is it possible that Grandmother Maggie is dead to you?" The boy asked Mother.

"Do not call this woman by that name! She does not deserve to be called your grandmother," said Mother. She looked to Father for help, but Father remained still like a statue. Mother turned back to her boy and said, "Marvin, this woman is of no concern to you. It would be best if she were on her way, and we spoke no more about her kind. She has nothing for you."

"No Mother, I'm now fifteen years of age, and almost a man. It's past time for me to know about my grandmother."

"This woman has been no grandmother to you!" Said Mother.

"You're right, because you have kept her from me! Tell me why she's dead to you!" Said the boy.

Mother again looked to Father, who motioned for Mother to speak. She relented and said, "Marvin, we have disowned this woman, because she is of ill repute, and an embarrassment to the family."

"What has she done to embarrass our family?"

"She is a woman of the night," said Mother in a low voice. Mother glanced at Maggie, who merely held her gaze without speaking.

The boy looked at Father and said, "You mean that she's a whore?" Father shrugged his shoulders as he stared at his feet.

Mother said, "Yes she is! And you know it too, husband. We will have no such woman in this family! And I will never understand why Grandfather Tim tolerated her as his wife!"

Father finally opened his mouth to quietly say, "Now dear, we don't know for sure..."

Mother said, "You may not know that, but I do! You have always been too trusting, too naive with people. I've always had to be the strong one to stand up for this family's good name. And she is YOUR mother. You of anyone ought to know who she is! How is it that I have to explain your own mother to you?"

Father had been averting his eyes, but at this he looked at Mother and said, "Maybe you worry too much about our good name. Or is it your own good name? Perhaps we have kept Marvin's grandmother too long from him."

"I can't believe you said that to me! And we have been over this more times than I'd care to remember. That woman is evil, and I won't have her corrupting our only child...She must go!"

Marvin turned to Maggie and said, "You must tell me the truth, for I will believe you. There is something about you that smells fair to me, though your voice is strange. Are you a whore, as Mother claims?"

Maggie looked at Mother, and then Father. Her eyes saddened as she gazed upon her son. She turned back to Marvin and said, "To you mother I am a whore. To me and to Grandfather Tim I am not."

"How dare you pretend to speak for that great man! I know he knew you to be a whore. What is beyond me is how he brought himself to forgive you, and to stay with you all those years."

"Stop interrupting, Mother! I want to hear it from her own mouth," said Marvin. Mother stared bewildered at Marvin, being stunned that he had spoken to her so.

"Why would they think you're a whore? How can they think that if it's not so?" Asked Marvin.

Maggie thought for a moment before saying, "I won't try to speak for them. You must ask them why they see me so."

"I will tell you," began Father.

"No husband, do not…"

"I will say my peace, wife. I have kept quiet too long about my own mother. I should have spoken up long ago," said Father raising his voice.

"But how can you…"

"Be still! I will speak plainly for myself, and I won't be quieted this time." Turning to Marvin, Father said, "Grandmother Maggie has long been considered a whore because of her voice. In this land only women who seduce men use such a whispering voice, and most assume that her own voice condemns her rightly."

"I see…I must know what you believe, Father," said Marvin.

Mother put a hand on Father's arm, but he brushed it away before saying, "I must confess that I have never been sure. Most people about, including your mother, have no doubts. However, I have never known Grandmother Maggie to be unfaithful to Grandfather Tim. And I don't believe that my father would have stayed with an unfaithful wife. And to my everlasting shame I must confess to having been weak, at least when it comes to my wife here. But I am done with that," said Father as his voice grew in strength.

"No husband, you have always…"

Father cut her off by saying, "No, I will finish what I have to say. I will be weak and passive no longer!" Turning to Marvin, Father said, "I believe Grandmother Maggie deserves the benefit of our doubt. We do not know for sure if she deserves her reputation, and the only one who knows is no longer with us." Father turned to Grandmother Maggie and said, "Dear mother, please forgive me. I have kept you away too long. Can you ever overlook my foolish weakness as a man?"

With tears in her eyes, Maggie embraced her son. Mother said, "I won't stand another moment of this," and went back into the house.

Maggie said, "Oh my dear son, of course I forgive you. I have done so years ago."

"Why have I given away my strength to my wife?" Bemoaned Father.

"Perhaps your error has been to trust her too much, not trusting yourself enough," said Maggie.

"Oh my God...I love my wife, but I cannot give myself away to anyone," said Father.

"And you won't again," said Maggie.

"But how can you get past the way my wife has seen you? And the many things she's said about you?"

"It's already done. What happens in her mind is no business of mine. I'm to be the master of my own mind," said Maggie.

"Oh dear God, if only I'd been the master of my own mind long ago."

"So you shall be now," said Maggie.

"But Grandmother Maggie, why have you waited till now to come to see me?" Asked Marvin.

Maggie sighed deeply before saying, "I believe my time draws near. I wanted to know you before I pass into the next life."

"You're dying?" Cried Marvin and Father at once.

"Yes, but I don't think of it that way. I will live on, yet I will give up the use of this now frail body."

"But what is wrong with you?" Asked Marvin.

"I don't have an illness, if that's what you mean. I merely feel that my time here is near."

"But I'm not ready for you to leave," said Marvin. "I don't want you to die, now that I'm just meeting you."

Maggie pat his head and said with a smile, "Well, perhaps I'll linger a bit longer then. So, I think I'll be heading home. I want to be home before dark."

"Wait, I have one more question," began Marvin. "My name, Marvin, am I named after the Marvinian of your story?"

"I would think that a better question of your father," said Maggie.

Marvin and Maggie looked to Father. He shuffled his feet uncomfortably before answering, "I hate to admit it, but yes. You are named after Marvinian."

"But why, Father? Why would you name me after a man who tried to kill Grandfather Tim and Grandmother Maggie?"

"I uh, well, to my everlasting shame, I allowed Mother to name you. Mother considered Marvinian a hero, for saving the king's life on two occasions."

"But did Mother know what Marvinian did to Grandfather Tim and Grandmother Maggie?"

Father averted his eyes as he said, "Yes, she has heard the stories, but...but she refuses to believe them. Mother can't believe a hero of the kingdom would commit such crimes."

Marvin's face turned crimson as he said, "I will go inside and ask her about this right now!"

Father put his hand on Marvin's shoulder to stop him, "Marvin, you must know that Mother will not take kindly to such a line of questioning. You must be ready for a fight."

"Then a fight she will get. If she does not answer my questions to my satisfaction, I will change my name!" Said Marvin. "Father, are you upset that I will question Mother?"

Now Father smiled, "Oh far from it, my son, I deeply respect you for your strength. I am greatly relieved that you don't follow in my footsteps with her." Marvin smiled briefly, and then stormed into the house.